A Return of Spark

SHELBY A. SETTY

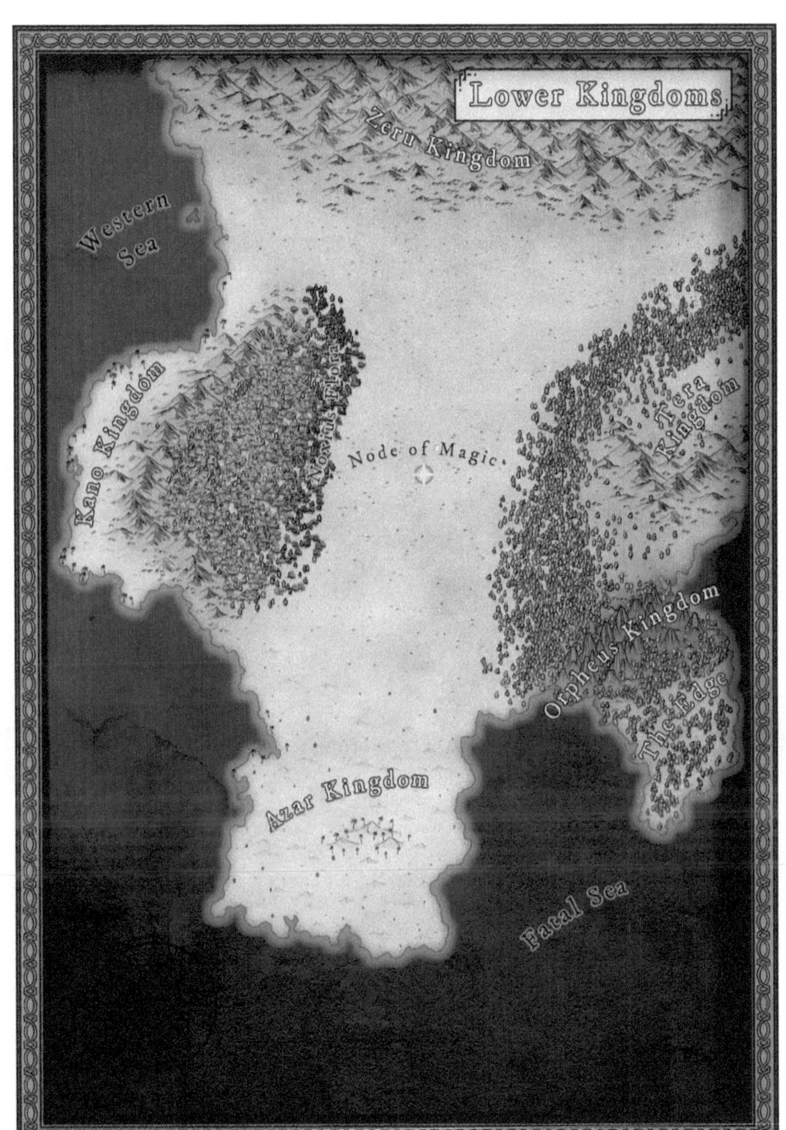

Lower Kingdoms
Zeru Kingdom
Western Sea
Kano Kingdom
Novus Flora
Node of Magic
Tera Kingdom
Orpheus Kingdom
The Edge
Azar Kingdom
Fatal Sea

CHAPTER 1

The Return

It was a cold night in Ridgewood Hollow. The trees were bare, and the frigid air was crisp. Snow blanketed the creek, and the familiar neighborhood I strolled toward was strung and lit with Christmas lights.

Exiting the passageway left me dry as it had the first time I went through its enchanted water. Thankfully, the portal liquid had warmed me, allowing the cold of the snow I trudged through to be slightly more bearable.

I stopped in my tracks at the park across from my childhood home. A Christmas tree shined majestically in the frosted window beside the front door. The star I knew so well sat atop the lit tree, twinkling its lights.

I pushed through the cold in the outfit I had last worn in this small town; it was my poor attempt to look as familiar as possible and perhaps to feel like a part of me still belonged here on Earth with the Chambers.

My denim jacket and yoga pants couldn't handle the cold much longer. But now that I stood in front of the familiar red door once more, I hesitated before knocking.

Why hesitation still ran through my bones after my enlightening journey through the portals was beyond me. I suppose it was my nerves taking over.

Would the Chambers be upset with me for leaving without a goodbye, as James had done? Did James tell them the truth of where I had been, or had he come up with some fictional story that would be easier to digest?

How long has it been since I last saw my family?

I swallowed my nerves. *Knock-knock.*

My chest filled with sparks of excitement that faded the longer I stood in anticipation. I knocked a second time, and after waiting another few minutes, I lifted an icy, trembling finger to press the doorbell. Except it was frosted and unmoving. So I turned, wondering if I should come back later.

But the waldworfs were clear; I had only one earthly hour before the passageway closed for an entire lunar cycle.

The frigid air made it difficult to think clearly. I whirled back to face the door and knocked a third time. With no answer, I turned to leave, wondering if I would ever see the Chambers again.

I had begun to walk down the steps toward the street when—

Click.

With a glance over my shoulder, I was greeted with a growing smile, and my heart nearly leaped out of my chest with elation. I almost forgot just how tall he was, standing at six-foot-two.

"Atti?" Surprise fell over James's expression as he pulled me in for a bear-crushing hug. I hugged him just as tight before he brought me inside to the nostalgic view of Mama's famous holiday wonderland decor.

I wasn't sure how close it was to Christmas, so I asked, "What day is it?"

"It's Christmas Eve." He pulled me by the warm fireplace in the living room, where the scent of fresh pine wafted from the gleaming tree.

After scanning the room, I peeked around the wall to the kitchen. "Where is everyone?"

"Asleep. It's two in the morning."

Sadness instantly fell over me. I came back to see my family, and they were deep in slumber, unaware that I was just one floor below.

"What are you doing up?" I asked, wondering if it was my pestering knock that woke him.

"Ever since leaving Elloriya, I've had trouble sleeping. That realm required less sleep than this one. I guess my body still hasn't adjusted back, even after a year."

My eyes widened. "It's been a year?"

"Yeah. On Earth at least."

After trying to make sense of how long I'd been gone, I asked, "What did you tell Mama and Dad after I left?"

"The truth." His head lowered, and he suddenly seemed to have difficulty making eye contact.

"Seriously?"

His eyes finally met with mine again. "Yeah. Of course, they didn't believe me. But I couldn't lie to them. Dad lost his trust in me and has hardly spoken three words to me since I told him everything."

"Then I'll tell him!" I stood up, prepared to run upstairs and wake Dad.

"No, Attica!" James pulled me back from my leap toward the stairs. "Something weird happened when I returned." He paused and stared heavily at me before saying, "Actually, I think it happened when you left."

With a deep swallow, his brown eyes settled uncomfortably above the fireplace at a family portrait. Standing before Mama and Dad was ten-year-old James. Beside James were the twins—little Jasmine and Jada—with wild curls of hair I always admired. But where I once stood on the other side of James was an empty space. My mouth fell open at the void where I belonged—where I used to belong.

James released a sigh. "Since you returned to Elloriya, it's as though all memories of you have been erased, and not just from the pictures, but—" He cut himself off, dropping his head low. I feared what he hesitated to say. He couldn't seem to conjure up the words, so I did it for him.

"My family doesn't remember me?" I asked in a cracked voice.

"They want to have me evaluated, Atti. They think I've gone crazy. And the more I talk about you, the crazier they think I am. Well, not Jasmine. She's the only one that believes me."

It felt as though the human world had crushed my heart before shredding the remnants in a triple-bladed blender. Tears suddenly rolled down my face at a rate I couldn't slow.

"Can't I just wake them up and remind them?" I inched closer to the wooden stairs.

James grabbed my hand, gently pulling me back. "I don't think that's going to work—"

Creak.

Our heads swiveled to the top of the stairs, where the mother that raised me stood wide-eyed in her fleece plaid Christmas pajamas.

"Mama?" I uttered.

Just seconds ago, I had felt like I was being torn from my family for all eternity, ripped from their minds. But now, my incredible mother was within my grasp, just feet away. And I was real to her, alive—not just a stolen memory.

She stepped hesitantly down the stairs, narrowing her eyes on me. Then, as she moved even closer with a curious expression, she gasped and mumbled, "Violet eyes." She strolled farther down the steps, her shaking hand over her mouth.

When she reached the bottom, she halted with her gaze still on me before finally crossing the hall to the living room where James and I stood. There she scrambled for a family album on the coffee table, immediately turning to a page with a picture of young Jada floating, her arms and legs wrapped around absolutely nothing. There were only trees and people in a frozen walk behind Jada. But I knew exactly where it had been taken and what the photo should have looked like.

"The zoo," I said, more so to myself, but Mama surely heard.

I remembered that day perfectly. I was about eight years old and gave Jada a piggyback ride, hoping we could get her as tall as the giraffe we had just seen. We weren't even close.

Mama sat on the couch, hands trembling as she analyzed the picture. Finally, she peered up at me, and her words were slow and shaky when she asked, "Were you in this picture?"

"Yes," I managed to say over the nerves sparking through my chest.

A tear rolled down Mama's face. "Why can't I remember you?"

James sat next to her. "Do you believe me now, Mama?"

She didn't respond but swept her eyes from me to the picture in her hand, to the empty space in the family portrait above the fireplace, and back to me.

I moved to sit beside her. "When I was a child, you told me if I quiet my mind and listen to my heart, I'd know the truth."

Her eyes widened and swelled with more tears, and to my surprise, she pulled me in for a hug. While holding me in a tight embrace, she whispered, "My nana used to tell me that."

I took her hug as a sign that she believed James. And that was enough for me, at least for now.

James and I spent the next half hour reminding Mama of all our favorite childhood memories: the cinnamon rolls she made on Sunday mornings, carving pumpkins with Dad on Halloween, decorating gingerbread houses with the twins, watching silent movies together—James and I would always add playful dialogue to make Mama smile.

Mama cried and laughed and cried again before a familiar falcon perched on a snowy branch outside the window screeched— an indication the passageway was preparing to close.

I was hesitant, fighting myself from having to say the words that would break my freshly mended heart. "Mama, I have to go now."

Her brows furrowed. "Can't you stay for Christmas morning?"

"I'm sorry. I wish I could." With a regretful sigh, I set the mug of hot chocolate Mama made me on a peppermint coaster before getting up from the couch.

"Before you go . . ." She hurried to a Christmas box in the room's corner and pulled something out. "I want you to have this so you never forget you will always be a part of this family, no matter what."

She handed me a scarlet Christmas stocking with *Attica* embroidered on the top. It had me wondering if whatever power removed me from this world wasn't strong enough to eliminate all traces of me.

"When I found this, I knew James was telling the truth."

I looked over to find her handsome son with a slight grin.

After taking the red-knitted stocking in hand, I wrapped my arms around Mama so tight; to let go was more of a challenge than I was prepared for. As she squeezed her arms around me, I glanced again at James, who was smiling with glossy eyes.

James moved toward us and joined in on our hug.

Seconds later, a soft voice broke our embrace. "Do we have a visitor?"

Tracking the voice to the stairs, I turned to find Jasmine. She looked inquisitively at Mama and James before turning back to me. She saw the stocking in my hand and instantly beamed, prancing to me with open arms.

"You must be Attica!" She gently took my face in her dainty hands. "James was right. You have the most incredible eyes!"

My eyes dampened at the sight of my childhood best friend and sister. She was always the brightest light in my life, and here she was, embracing me even though her memories of me had gone.

With a glance at the clock, I knew my hour was almost up. If I waited any longer, the passageway would likely deny my entrance back to Elloriya.

"Are you staying for Christmas morning?" Jasmine asked.

"No. I actually—" I began, but James cut me off.

"She has to return to Elloriya now. I was just about to walk her back to the passageway."

"Oh. Can I come?" Jasmine begged with a pleading grin.

James looked at me before responding, "If it's okay with Mama."

"In this cold?" Mama must have noticed the longing in Jasmine's eyes as she said, "You best put on layers." Then she turned to me. "Attica dear, take my scarf and mittens." Mama opened the hall closet, handed me warm knitted mittens with a trembling hand, and then wrapped a green scarf around my neck.

James and Jasmine layered up, and I gave Mama one last hug before stepping outside with my brother and sister.

To part from Mama was a struggle I was not entirely prepared for. I looked wistfully over my shoulder to find Mama smiling at me with a hand over her golden heart. A heavy tear rolled down my face as I took a mental picture of her beauty, hoping this would not be the last time I set eyes on her.

Jasmine's arm linked with mine as we started back toward the passageway. The snow had already covered my tracks from when I had first arrived nearly an hour ago.

"Tell me everything," James said.

So I did. I told him about the chakra portals, my encounters with the Orpheus and Shakar, Queen Eloise Adaire and the coliseum, and even my underwhelming wielding ability. James listened with wide eyes and a mouth dropping farther with every word. Jasmine was completely and obliviously enthralled, as if I were merely telling a fictional fantasy.

When we finally arrived at the passageway, my heart sank at the sight of ice layered over the creek water, blocking my only way back to Elloriya. A light shone below the ice, so I knew the passageway was still open. But how I would get to it now was beyond me.

James searched around and picked up a rock, easily as big as a football, if not bigger. He threw it onto the frozen passageway, and the sheet of ice broke.

"This is the way back to your world?" Jasmine questioned.

"Yes," I replied, realizing how absurd it appeared.

She stood there shivering with a chattering smile as she gazed at the golden light resting at the bottom of the pond.

A layer of ice was quickly forming over the water again. At long last, though I didn't want to, it was time to say goodbye.

I turned to Jasmine. "I don't think I ever told you this, but you added so much magic to my childhood." Forcing a smile through my sadness, I added, "Say hi to Jada and Dad for me. Even if they don't remember me, they'll always be my family."

Jasmine wrapped her arms around me with a squeezing hug. "Maybe I can visit one day," she said.

Knowing how unlikely that was, I simply replied, "Maybe."

Then I turned to James. His eyes were moist, and with a flared nose and clenched jaw, his lower lids held his tears tightly.

"I'm happy you returned, Atti. Even if it was for just a short hour."

He peered at the onyx necklace he had given me, resting on my chest with a moonstone attached to it now. His face turned inquisitive.

"Oh, the white stone is from Darian. He gave it to me when we were just kids, before I came to Earth. But I left it behind, and he kept it for me until—"

James chuckled, cutting me off. "I don't care, Atti. As long as you're happy and never forget me."

"Forget you? I could never!" I said truthfully, heeding his soulful eyes.

He lifted me off the ground, squeezing his sturdy arms around me like he would never see me again. My lungs painfully deflated at the dreadful thought that this might be the last hug I ever received from my big brother.

"Tell everyone I say hi," he said, setting me back down. "Oh, and" —his face turned even sadder— "give Zella a hug for me."

"I will."

I took off Mama's mittens and scarf and handed them to James while still holding my Christmas stocking tight in hand. He took them with a grain of hesitation, as if he knew Mama would have preferred me to keep them.

The longer I stood beside my brother and sister—bones chilled in the snowy creek—the harder it was to part. And though I wasn't ready to jump in, time was greedy. I took a deep breath and—

"Atti?"

I turned back to James.

"I'm happy to see you're no longer hiding," he said with a familiar wink.

I hadn't even realized my hair was tucked behind my ears during my entire visit until he said those words.

With a proud smile, I winked back and then jumped in.

CHAPTER 2

Training

The cold of my icy skin broke as the passageway water warmed the chill away. A hum of blissful music moved through the crystal-blue water as I swam toward the light, maneuvering around the heavy rock James had thrown in as it lingered between the two worlds. The closer I was to the golden gleam, the warmer the water became.

Before reaching the world I belonged to, I turned over my shoulder to find the sizable rock was nowhere in sight, as if it had suddenly vanished. As I tuned out the enchanting music the water hummed, sweeping my view every which way for the rock that was certainly no longer floating about in the passageway, all I could think was: *Such strange water.*

When I finally broke through the surface to Elloriya, I first glimpsed sun rays nestled over finger-length strands of aqua-blue hair. Calder was there, ready to pull me out.

"An entire hour on Earth was a blink of an eye here," he said with a grin. "Did you see James?"

11

"Yeah." I didn't want to tell Calder how my family had forgotten me, mostly because I didn't understand why, so instead, I asked, "Where'd the waldworfs go?"

"I think they were annoyed having to wait for a new lunar to begin for the passageway to open back up, so they left when you jumped in. But they rarely stick around after granting passage," he said as we headed toward the manor.

"So any human from Earth that may have found the passageway could have come to Elloriya without the waldworfs knowing?"

He chuckled. "Not without their permission and an Elloriyan guiding them. They'd likely get lost in the passageway and drown before finding the surface again."

The bleak thought reminded me of the time I jumped in the passageway to return to Earth when I had first arrived—or rather, first returned after seventeen years. Perhaps it was because the waldworfs didn't grant me permission, but the passageway was dark and silent when I tried to escape this world. And to find the surface in a dead passageway seemed impossible. If it weren't for Darian pulling me out, I fear I would have never returned to either world that day.

As the sun's rays followed my effortless steps through the furlike grass, Calder raised his brow at my hand. "What's that?"

Quickly realizing he was talking about my stocking, I began explaining the magic of Christmas and how, if you're nice all year, "Santa" puts goodies in your stocking while you sleep. He looked at me like I had gone bonkers crazy. Clearly, they didn't have such a holiday in this realm.

Just as we reached the manor's ivy-covered entrance, Calder asked, "You ready to practice?"

I sighed. "I practiced with Ignatius for an entire starlight this morning."

Calder put his hand on the ivy, which parted, granting us passage to the manor. "Yes, and he said you did terribly."

I turned to him with a deadpan stare. "Maybe because I can't wield fire."

As we strolled toward the manor's high copper doors, Calder said with a sideways glance, "Maybe it's time we find out how well you can wield water."

"Or if I can wield water at all," I corrected him. But then I suddenly remembered that I had wielded droplets in the sunroom before. However, it was far from impressive.

When we reached the manor's front entrance, Calder ran two fingers along Esmond's slithery-scaled spine. The sapphire eyes of the gilded snake gleamed at his touch.

"Messssage for you," he said, slithering his tongue at me. His jeweled eyes grew brighter when he added, *"You are requesssted in the garden."*

Calder smirked, though I didn't understand why. "Perfect. Thanks, Esmond!" he said, swishing his head to the east side of the manor as he strolled toward the garden trees.

Esmond hissed in response before becoming still again.

When we turned the corner, catching a full view of the colorful garden, with trees surrounding a spectacular copper fountain filled and flowing with glistening water, a fireball of pink flames headed straight toward us. Calder immediately threw up a shield of water, putting the fire out.

An exceptionally tall and brawny man with dark skin and shoulder-length dreadlocks bellowed, "Aghh!" Ignatius had revealed himself from behind a tree and spat before a heavy accent rolled off his tongue. "One of these days, I will get you!"

Calder laughed. "How many zeniths have passed since you first said that?"

"What are zeniths?" I asked.

"Remember how I told you that years are different here?" Calder asked.

I nodded.

"Well, think of the years as seasons since there's one season per year in Elloriya, and think of zeniths as years. So every four years is one zenith. A new zenith begins the first day of spring and ends the last day of winter."

"Oh," I uttered, wondering why time had to be so complicated in this realm.

I was sure Calder noticed the confusion on my face since he added, "Don't overthink it. Many people here refer to time as years rather than zeniths, anyway."

"Look out!" Razz's voice sounded in my mind.

I wasn't sure why until I noticed Ignatius's hands behind his back and Razz's curly blond hair peeking out from the nearby hammock made entirely of vines.

Ignatius switched his gaze onto me, and I knew what was about to head my way. A ball of pink fire came hurtling toward my head. Instead of attempting to wield anything, I ducked, turning to find a patch of flaming pink bark on a tree behind me before it finally faded into the balmy air.

Without Razz's warning, I wondered if my skin would have turned rosy at the touch of Ignatius's flames. But I knew that sort of fire wouldn't burn me. Otherwise, Ignatius wouldn't use them against us, even as a joke. At least, I hoped he wouldn't.

Thanks for the warning, I sent my thoughts to Razz, unsure if my telepathic message was strong enough to be heard. But when I switched my gaze back to him, his eyes were still on me with a charming smile that seemed to say, "Hey, no problem."

"Perhaps we should play a game, Attica," Ignatius said. He grabbed familiar metal armbands from the tree with four gold flowers on one branch and four silver flowers on another. It was the same tree that had kept score during the wielding game I had played only once before. But I had a feeling we weren't going to play that sort of game.

I held up my Christmas stocking. "I'm not playing any games until this is safe in my room."

"Attica," Ignatius began, "you have two small feet and one big sock. It is no good. Just throw it out."

Calder held out his hand. "May I?"

I hesitantly handed the stocking to him, and within the blink of an eye, he created a whirl of water before him and stepped inside. Then, a moment later, he stepped back out empty-handed.

"Done!" he said proudly.

Ignatius threw me a gold band. I had only ever used the silver one, but I was curious how or if they differed besides their metals and ornate designs.

As I placed it around my forearm, Ignatius locked the other gold band on himself. It was only a moment before I felt the blood in my veins boil as the cuffs synced. It was undoubtedly a sensation Ignatius was used to.

"Shouldn't we tap them?" I asked from across the garden.

"The couplings sync our energy without needing to. If we want to strengthen our connection, then we tap them. But not for this game," Ignatius said.

The connection I had with Ignatius through the couplings was nothing like when I had used the cuffs with Razz. With Razz, I saw life through his eyes. Everything appeared more vivid, and the energy connected to nearly any living thing was so vital. I felt and saw life differently when I was attuned to Razz's energy, almost as if I had taken a mind-altering substance.

But with Ignatius, my surroundings looked the same, and mostly felt the same too. The only difference was a slight increase in passion and much warmer skin.

"Okay, Attica, we are now connected. Let us play a simple game of catch." Ignatius threw a white fireball in my direction. My instinct was to duck once again.

"That is not how we play catch. Try again."

"You got this, Attica," Calder said, sitting on the garden bench nearby.

Ignatius threw a second hurl in my direction. Knowing full well that the white flames were cool to the touch, I opened my hands, but instead of catching them, my fingers broke through the bleached fire.

Wielding ivy vines, flower petals, or something I could physically hold in my hand wasn't very difficult. At least if I was close enough to them. But wielding elements like fire, water, or air . . . they always slipped through my fingers.

Calder held a hand up to Ignatius, signaling him to stop, and then moved close to me. "You don't give your mind enough credit. You rely solely on the energy that lies dormant in your palms. But your mind is where the true power lies. So use the power of your breath and focus your mind."

Turning my back to Ignatius and Razz, I took a few deep breaths. As I did, Calder continued to guide me. "Imagine a light anchoring you to the land. Grounding yourself will help you focus."

I imagined a light pouring through the top of my head and running down my body, through my feet, and deep into the soil below. And to my surprise, my palms buzzed stronger. As I cleared my mind with each breath, I became slightly more connected to the surrounding energy. Then, with a final grounding inhale, I turned back to Ignatius with a nod.

He didn't hesitate to throw a ball of white fire a second later. I launched my buzzing hands up, and to my surprise, I caught it.

"Good! Now throw it back!" Ignatius shouted from across the garden.

So I did, and it turns out my aim sucks. It went straight past Ignatius, toward the hammock Razz was lounging on. Though it appeared Razz had just begun taking a nap, without even opening his resting eyes, he jumped out of the hammock just in time to not get hit. He had a knack for seeing things right before they happened.

My eyes were settled on Razz when a fireball was thrown in my direction. Even though I felt it heading toward me, I wasn't fast enough to stop it.

Smack!

The white-flamed ball hit me hard, smack-dab in the middle of my chest. Though it wasn't as warm as actual flames were, annoyance had woken within me.

Smack!

Another fireball hit me in the stomach.

Smack!

A third fireball of cold flames slammed into my shoulder. He was throwing them too fast, not allowing me enough time to focus on catching them. My irritation was growing with each hit.

In the corner of my eye, I saw Ignatius preparing to throw another damn fireball my way. The rage rising within me caused my hands to buzz stronger than I was used to. And before another flame was thrown, I swept my buzzing hands toward the copper fountain, swishing the water out and sending a wave crashing onto Ignatius. My mouth dropped at my own doing.

"That's my girl!" Calder shouted, jumping off the garden bench.

Ignatius strolled toward me with fountain water dripping from his dreadlocks. I couldn't read his bland expression. Was he upset?

It wasn't until he towered over me a short foot away that he said, "What took you so long?" And then he grinned. "There is power in you, Attica. You must learn your power and how to summon it on command. Good work, for now." He turned and headed toward the side door entrance to the manor.

"What happened to you?" A smooth voice I hardly recognized addressed Ignatius.

I turned to find a tall man with sandy surfer hair and a blue tattoo branching up his shoulder, who I had officially met yesterday, now standing in the garden. It was Keane. At the gala, Keane had asked to touch the white flames on the draping sleeves of my dress, and then he had spent the rest of the night flirting with Cece.

Ignatius and Razz clearly didn't like his presence based on their glowers and clenched jaws. Instead of Ignatius giving Keane a response, he simply heated his skin and dried the dripping water off within seconds.

Cece stepped out of the manor to the garden and grabbed Keane's hand. "I was looking for you." She addressed the rest of us. "We have a meeting at nineteenth starlight."

There was a sorrow in Razz's eyes as he watched Cece walk off hand in hand with Keane and a perky flip of her dusty pink hair. I couldn't help but wonder what had happened between them. Was Cece now officially with this new guy?

While everyone dispersed in their own directions, I unlatched the metal band from my arm and headed toward the library in the West Wing. When I arrived, it was dark, but flames ignited as I passed each lantern, shedding light onto the thousands of books neatly shelved in the sky-high library.

As my eyes scanned the stacked shelves, they landed on a maroon leather-bound book high up labeled *The Nine Realms.* I was much too short of reaching it. So I focused my gaze on the book. As I did, my palm buzzed. I aimed my pulsing hand high in its direction.

Come to me. Come to me. I repeated the thought over and over in my mind. Finally, after the fifth time, the book shook. But to get it off the shelf was a struggle.

I tried again and again, making little to no progress. But I didn't give up. I knew I had the power in me. I wielded parts of a velociraptor-type creature, for damn sake. Of course, my life was at stake then, so summoning that power seemed easier. Though a part of me wondered if the crystal tower in the South Wing gave me the ability to wield with such force that day. But if I could wield such a creature at all, then I indeed had the power to wield a measly book off the shelf.

If I convinced my mind that it was a life-threatening situation, I would undoubtedly attain the book. So I tried again, telling myself I needed this book for survival. And to my surprise, the book flew off the shelf. But instead of it flying into my hands, it soared far over my head and into the hands of whoever had just stepped into the library.

CHAPTER 3

Unanswered

It had been twelve suppers with his empty chair and thirteen days since I had last seen his quiet, cryptic, beautiful face. Had he purposely avoided me since the coliseum? Had he used this massive manor to his advantage, escaping my presence behind the many corridors and rooms? Or had he shut out the world behind the black walls of his fireside bedroom?

The last time I saw Darian's tantalizing eyes was after the soul star portal. And now, with his gaze on anything but me, he was walking down the library stairs with the book I was desperately trying to wield in hand. He held a brown leather book in his other hand that read *Kingdoms of Elloriya*.

My breathing lost its rhythm as he moved toward me. He stayed quiet, keeping his gaze on the bookshelf as he handed me *The Nine Realms*. He returned his book to the shelf and grabbed a new book titled *Transferable Powers*.

Without so much as a glance in my direction, he continued back up the steps, quietly and mysteriously, as always.

I don't know what came over me, but the words anxiously sitting on my tongue—the same words that swirled through my thoughts each time he appeared in my mind—couldn't refrain from finally firing out. "Will you ever let your walls down?"

He stopped in the middle of the stairs, keeping the sharp muscles of his back facing me. He didn't even turn a slight tilt of his head. Instead, he just stood there, likely digesting the words I abruptly shot at him.

To get a response, I continued speaking with only a view of his dark hair and the three small braids trailing just below his messy bun. "I don't know what to consider you. Are you my friend? Are you an acquaintance? Or are you just someone I share a living space with?" When he still didn't answer, I added, "Sometimes I wonder if you don't even like me."

His head lowered. I was sure he'd walk down those steps and press his forehead against mine, reassuring me he cared and that, of course, we were friends, but instead, he continued up the stairs and closed the library door behind him.

It felt as though my heart turned to glass before falling to the floor, shattering.

Darian kept me at a distance by choice. He kept his walls high up, not seeming to care about leaving me in the cold. He left me with a twisted puzzle of absolute bewilderment as I thought back to the coliseum when he risked his life for me and shed tears over my death. But now that I was alive and well, it seemed he couldn't care less about me.

It was the eighteenth starlight—one starlight away from the manor's meeting. I went across the hall to the West Wing bathing room and took off my denim jacket, white tee, and yoga pants, wondering when Calder would fix the bathtub knob in my bathing room as promised.

The crystal tub quickly filled with pear-scented soap and warm water. Hoping the bath would wash away the icy feeling left behind by Darian, I stepped in, wondering if he would ever be like that young Zayd he once was—the kid who played and talked with me and reassured me of our friendship.

The memory of our friendship from so many years ago was something I was afraid I would never have with him again. Of course, those years were long gone, not that I truly remembered them to begin with. But whatever Darian—whatever Zayd—and I shared as children was nothing more than an ancient memory, a bond that had withered away with the years.

Perhaps it was for the best. Maybe Darian keeping me at a distance would allow me to get over my strange feelings for him. But no matter how hard I tried, I couldn't understand what I felt for him.

What I did know was this: I had never been more attracted to anybody in my life than I was to Darian. Something about his sun-kissed skin, square jaw, heart-shaped lips, and enchanting blue eyes drew me in like a magnet. But it wasn't just his good looks that had a hold on me. There was something else—something deep beneath the surface of my soul that I couldn't quite reach. My heart seemed to know a forbidden secret; it responded to his presence whenever he was near. Just a glance at him altered my breathing and made my stomach dance.

I splashed the bathwater. It was my poor attempt to get Darian off my mind yet again.

And then there was my family in Ridgewood Hollow. Were my childhood memories forever lost in both worlds, from my mind in Elloriya and the Chambers' minds on Earth? Would Dad and Jada finally believe James when he spoke of me now that Mama and Jasmine had seen me in the flesh? Or had my second return to Elloriya wiped their memory of me again?

As I lay in the warm, bubble-filled water—head and pruney fingers resting over the tub's rim—my mind traveled to my parents from this realm. I attempted to uncover any memory of my birth parents.

Did I look like my mother, or perhaps my father? Did either of them have violet eyes like me? Did they miss me? Did they know I was in Elloriya again? Did they know I ever left? How long had it been since my mother held me in her arms and my father kissed my forehead goodnight? Did they ever do those things? What were they like? How could I find them? Would I ever find them? How would they respond to my return? Would they welcome me with open arms? Did they even want me to return?

The funny thing was that even if someone had these answers, I wasn't sure I was ready to hear them. A part of me wanted to wait to meet my parents to find out for myself. But, for some absurd reason, the thought of asking anyone about my Elloriyan family and home was unsettling, and I wondered if it had to do with my family back in Ridgewood Hollow—the family I apparently hadn't entirely let go of.

Grasping the sides of the tub with water dripping from the tips of my fingers, I pulled myself up to grab a soft blue towel a mere foot away with the thought of leaving this manor behind to search for my parents, somewhere near or far in Elloriya, regardless of being trapped on the edge. I would find a way past the Fatal Sea or the barrier. There had to be a way!

If I were to go alone, would I find my way to them? Likely not. But I couldn't possibly ask someone who knew this world better to come with me, could I? And if so, who?

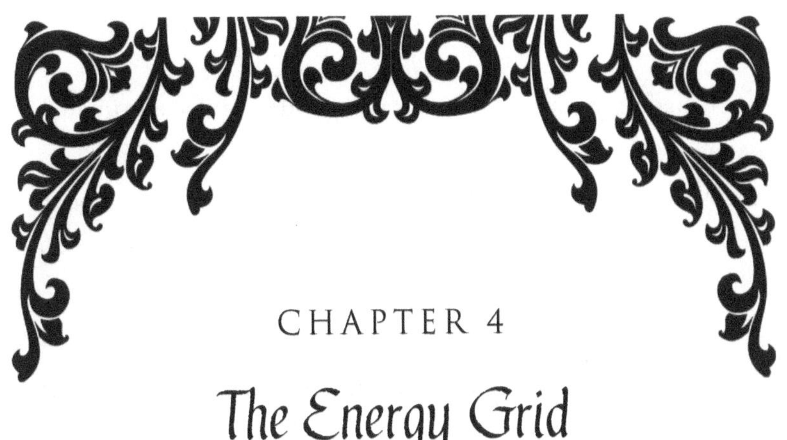

CHAPTER 4

The Energy Grid

The nineteenth starlight had struck, and the sun had lowered, scattering a wave of pink, orange, and purple throughout the dusk sky. As I had soaked in the tub, I had nearly forgotten about the manor's meeting, for which I would surely be late.

After dressing in a comfortable set of dark blue joggers and a fitted tunic from the emporium, I was just about to hurry to the first floor when I heard shouting from downstairs.

"We do not know you!" Ignatius shouted. "You are not welcome at this meeting!"

Keane strutted toward the front doors of the manor. There was no glimpse of anger or resentment on his face, just calmness.

Cece ran after Keane. "You don't have to go! Ignatius just doesn't trust easily."

"It's fine," he said before kissing her cheek. She muffled a goodbye, returning to the dining room with red ears. And before Keane closed the door behind him, he glanced up, catching my prying eyes as I stood peering over the second-floor railing. I responded with an awkward smile as he left.

I made my way down the stairs wondering if I was invited to the manor's meeting since I had never been to one before.

As I stood somewhat hidden in the main room of the manor, I heard several voices travel from the dining room in the East Wing. I stepped closer to the entrance and then stopped, concealing myself behind the wall as I overheard my name.

Calder's voice said, "It has to be Attica that goes. The portals chose her for a reason."

"But there's no way past the barrier," Cece chimed in. "And even if there was, she doesn't know the lands."

"She doesn't have to go alone," Calder responded.

"Have you all tried going through the energy grid?" Razz asked.

"Yes," Ignatius muttered.

"I have," Calder said.

"Me too. I think we've all determined the energy grid is closed past the barrier," Cece added.

Calder's voice shook as he said, "We have to do something. We can't just stay trapped on the edge forever. We must return to our kingdoms. The tether to my kingdom has weakened so much over the last few zeniths. I fear what may happen if it withers to nothing."

"I know," Cece said, wobbly. "I feel it too, with my home. It's as if the kingdoms are dying."

As I stood out of sight behind the wall of the dining room entrance, I glimpsed Gemma with her lengthy strawberry hair and striking green eyes, strolling down the arched stairs with a lazy hand grazing the wall and her fingers leaving a trail of green moss and blooming flowers along the way.

Before Gemma saw me, I entered the dining room where Calder, Cece, Ignatius, and Razz sat in gold-trimmed thronelike chairs with blue velvet seats. They surrounded the marble table that emanated a soft glow.

While I sat in James's old chair, noticing Darian's and Zella's absence, Gemma walked in with an already bored expression on her face and sat in the empty chair beside Cece.

Ignatius turned to Gemma. "Have you tried going through the energy grid, past the barrier?"

Gemma replied in her usual sign language with a voice sounding from her hands. "You know I'm not comfortable using the energy grid. So, obviously not."

"What are we talking about?" I asked casually, acting as though I hadn't overheard a thing before stepping into the room.

Calder responded, "We are trying to find a way past the barrier."

Only moments ago, I was in the bath, desperate to leave this manor and find a way past the barrier myself so I could finally return home, wherever that was.

Footsteps sounded near the entrance of the dining room. My chair was faced away from the sound, but I knew who had stepped in from the glitch in my chest.

An arm reached over me and placed a piece of rolled parchment on the table. My heart pounded as the skin of his veiny arm grazed my honeyed hair. The empty chair beside me was pulled out, and Darian sat down.

What the hell was it about Darian that gave him the reins to my heart?

He unrolled the parchment, revealing a map I once saw on the desk in his room. Except now, there were far more details. Words and impressive pictures of fields, mountains, and kingdoms covered the map. The Zeru Kingdom was in the north, the Tera Kingdom in the east, the Azar Kingdom in the south, and the Kano Kingdom in the west. I was most impressed that I could read his minuscule writing so well.

Calder turned to Gemma. "Would you be willing to go through the energy grid? You're the only one with access to the grid that hasn't tried passing the barrier."

All I knew about the energy grid was that it was used to travel between places, like some invisible door that took you from one place to another. I traveled through the grid twice: once with Ignatius when he wrapped us in violet flames, turning up at the gala moments later, and then after the coliseum when Calder created a swirling loop of water for Darian to carry me through to the manor.

Gemma's eyes swept the table, expression unchanged when she signed with scarlet pollen light trailing her palms, "Fine, I'll try."

Ignatius pushed his chair out and stood up. "Good! Let us go outside then."

Everyone made their way toward the glass doors connected to the garden . . . everyone except Darian and me. Darian placed his hand on mine for a brief second before retracting his fingers, getting up, and exiting the room. My heartbeat fell and then rose before returning to its average speed.

What the hell did that mean? Why did his hand touch mine? Was it an accident? No, it had to have been intentional. Or perhaps I was overthinking his short touch. It was an accident . . . end of story.

I pushed myself out of the chair and followed the others to the garden, under the slowly darkening sky.

Calder narrowed his attention on Gemma, Ignatius, and Cece when he said, "Maybe we should all try going through the energy grid again. If we reach the lower kingdoms simultaneously, perhaps we can break through whatever barrier is blocking the grid."

"Okay!" Ignatius pounded his chest with his fist.

Calder shifted his attention. "Cece?"

"Yes, okay," she responded confidently.

"Gemma?" Calder looked at her with raised brows.

"I already agreed," she signed somewhat irritably.

Darian's eyes momentarily shifted in my direction as I stepped beside his brother, Razz.

I was trying to understand how the grid worked when I turned to Razz and asked, "How come you're not trying to go through the energy grid?"

"Only those from the lower kingdoms have that skill," he said.

"And you're not from the lower kingdoms?"

Razz turned to me, baffled. "No. I'm from the higher kingdoms, like you."

My stomach turned at his words. I had always avoided asking where exactly I was from in this world, likely because I wasn't quite ready to release my life in Ridgewood Hollow. Not entirely, at least. But now that I understood Elloriya was where I truly belonged, perhaps I was ready to ask more about my origins.

It was difficult to get the words out, but I ignored my nerves and asked, "Do you know how to get to the higher kingdoms?"

"If I could get past the barrier, then yes, I think so. But it's not a light journey."

The pounding of my heart sounded in my ears. Razz could lead me back home.

My thoughts of returning home broke as a rush of air hit me. I was now watching a gust of wind swirl around Cece, purple flames engulfing Ignatius, water whirling around Calder, and mossy branches circling Gemma. Then, within the blink of an eye, they were gone, and so were their elements.

One, two, three, four, five, six seconds went by.

Razz, Darian, and I stood silently as the last starlight struck, wondering if it had worked as the garden slowly filled with a glow under the now dark sky. If it had worked, then what would come next?

Seven, eight, nine, ten, eleven, twelve—

Whoosh! Slam! Bonk!

Calder, Gemma, and Cece flew back through the water, branches, and wind. Had Ignatius gotten through?

Thud!

Nope. He came crashing back through weak flames.

"And that's why I loathe traveling through the grid," Gemma signed fiercely.

"That only happens if we try to leave the edge," Calder said as he brushed himself off the ground.

With the newfound knowledge of where I had come from still echoing in my mind, I asked, "Has anyone tried going through to the higher kingdoms?"

"That's a great idea, Attica," Cece responded. "Except, the energy grid would normally only allow us to return to our own territory, unless cordially invited by another kingdom."

I was determined to find a solution, so I asked, "Is there any way I can try?"

Calder stepped closer to me. "We know you can wield. But unless you can produce some element of your own power, you won't be able to create enough energy to get through any grid."

"Darian." His name blurted from my mouth before I had a moment to think much through. His blue eyes turned and fell on me, finally. "Can you still produce lightning?"

For a moment, he just stared at me, unreadable as always. Of course, no words escaped his mouth. He kept his hands by his sides as subtle bolts of yellow lightning spread over his fingers, sweeping a smile over Ignatius's and Calder's faces.

Ignatius walked over to Darian and gave him a pat on the back. "I will teach you how to go through the grid."

"No!" Razz barked. "It's too dangerous for someone who is not familiar enough with the grid."

"No one seemed to mind when I went through, and I'm not that familiar with the grid," Gemma signed with an unsettling calm voice coming from her hands.

"It's different with you. Your kingdom is closest to the edge, making it far less dangerous. The higher kingdoms are at least ten times farther." Razz turned to his brother. "No, Darian. Please."

Darian strolled to his brother and lifted an arm to him. Razz met Darian's forearm with his own. They silently looked at each other. When their arms broke apart, Razz pulled something out of his pocket. It was a dark green teardrop crystal suspended from a six-inch brass chain.

"Will Darian get through the energy grid to the other side of the barrier?" Razz asked, seeming to address the dangling crystal. It began to swing back and forth. For a moment, Razz just stared at the swinging crystal with a look of despair. But then he finally said, "Fine."

Ignatius took Darian beside the copper fountain in the garden's center. As Ignatius enthusiastically explained the whole energy grid thing to him, I couldn't help but notice how the fountain's luminescent water reflected perfectly on Darian's face.

When I finally broke my gaze off him, I noticed his brother had caught my stare. Razz looked from me to Darian and then back to me again. I could tell he was about to speak when I cut him off.

"Where's Zella?" I asked Razz in a poor attempt to brush off any speculation he may have had about my feelings toward his brother.

"She's in the chakra portals. And knowing her, she'll attempt to go through them all in a single day. It'll never happen."

"Oh, that's great that she's trying, though." I smiled lamely and looked in any direction but Darian's.

Razz only sighed, looking back at his brother, undoubtedly still concerned about him going through the grid.

"Okay, ready?" Ignatius bellowed enthusiastically.

Darian looked around, not at the people surrounding him, but as if he were searching for something. Darian gave Ignatius a nod when his eyes finally settled on the massive balcony overlooking the garden.

Electric currents spread over Darian's skin. The yellow lightning branches multiplied within seconds, spreading fast until the electric web swallowed him whole. Then—*poof*—he was gone.

Ignatius grinned at the balcony where Darian now stood. Though it was a short distance, he successfully went through the grid. Within seconds, lightning blanketed him again, and he appeared beside Ignatius once more.

Ignatius gave him a pat on the back. "You are ready. Remember the plan," is all he said before Darian spread lightning once more over his lightly tanned skin.

Darian turned and laid eyes on me—not his brother, not anyone else, just me. My heart stopped as our gaze locked from a distance between the shield of lightning encompassing his body when finally, it spread over his eyes, and—he was gone.

Suddenly, I felt the heavy pressure of my feet as we all stood in dead silence. The seconds piled up, quickly turning into minutes.

Razz began to pace, taking deep breaths.

How long would it be till he returned? Would he return? The more time that passed, the heavier my feet became.

Razz walked over to the spot Darian vanished into, looking around as if he could find some loophole to his brother.

"What now?" Cece asked.

No one responded, but instead, Calder asked Ignatius across the garden, "Did you tell him the plan?"

Ignatius walked toward us with his hand over the crook of his neck. "I told him to return if he gets through so he can bring us."

Half a starlight had passed before Gemma was the first to give up, heading back to her room. Cece was quiet as a tear fell down her face. She was next to resign for the night. Ignatius began blaming himself. He grew furious before his anger settled, turning to an unbearable silence as he slumped on a nearby bench.

I was quietly blaming myself. If it weren't for my stupid suggestion, he would have still been here with his high walls strongly in place.

An entire starlight had passed when Calder finally turned to Razz and me with the gut-wrenching words, "I don't think he's returning."

Razz's heavily glossed eyes had a faraway gaze when he said in a strained voice, "I fucking knew it."

CHAPTER 5

The Reading

While the others went to sleep, Calder, Razz, and I stayed awake, waiting for a knock at the door. Not for a second had I believed that Gemma, Cece, or Ignatius had made their peace with Darian's disappearance. On the contrary, I was nearly certain they convinced themselves he had made it to the higher kingdoms. So I suppose they went to sleep with hope. And there was nothing wrong with that.

Zella still hadn't returned from the chakra portals. And as for Calder, Razz, and me . . . well, we had an unsettling feeling. It was a feeling none of us could shake.

Knock-knock.

Esmond had already opened the door for our guest. But she was clearly more than just a guest in this manor as I had never seen the golden snake show so much respect to anyone as he bowed his slithery head to her with the utmost regard.

The sight of her kind hazel eyes and ramlike horns gave me enough ease to finally take a decent breath of air.

Calder was the first to greet her. "Etiwa! Thank you for coming during the dark starlight." She responded with a nod before turning to Razz.

"Razzertaine, I sensed the urgency in your call," she said in a solemn voice.

Razzertaine? Was that his proper name? Come to think of it, I've heard that name before. And in what way had Razz called her? Through telepathy? Or maybe with a courier.

We led her to the dining room, where we sat dispersed around the marble table embedded with a warm glow. The swirling vined chandelier glittered a soft light throughout the room.

Calder began explaining what had happened.

"And you knew the dangers of this?" Etiwa questioned.

"Yes," Razz answered. "I begged him not to, but he suggested I ask my pendulum and leave it up to spirit."

"What specifically did you ask your pendulum?"

"Will Darian get through the energy grid to the other side of the barrier?" Razz recalled perfectly.

"You know you must always be as precise as possible when using such divination tools. Not to mention that unreliable sources can interfere, giving false hope." When Razz dropped his head, unresponsive, she added, "Did you envision a protective light around you or address a reliable higher source directly when you asked?"

He slammed his head into his hand. "Shit! I forgot."

She didn't make Razz feel any worse than he already did. Instead, she asked the three of us, "Do you have something of his I can hold?"

"Should I grab something from his room?" Calder asked Razz.

I suppose running it past the brother would be less of an intrusion.

Razz shook his head. "He started locking his door since the day of the coliseum."

"I may have something," I added while taking the silver-chained necklace off my neck. The chain held two stones. The triangular onyx stone was from James, and the slightly larger white crystal held below the black stone was from Darian.

I handed her the necklace. "He held on to the moonstone for years—I mean, Earth years."

Etiwa clutched the necklace tightly under her hooved fingers and closed her eyes as she quietly said, "Zaydarian Bader."

Bader? I didn't know his last name until now.

Calder, Razz, and I watched intently.

Her voice bellowed louder this time. "Zaydarian Bader, it is Etiwa. Show me where you are." She paused as her eyes fluttered below her eyelids. "Show me! Show me! Zaydarian Bader, show me where you are!" Her lids swiveled in every direction for some time. Then her eyes sprang open.

"Did you see him?" Razz asked eagerly.

"Yes," she simply replied.

I couldn't read the strange expression on her face as she handed me back the necklace.

Razz pushed for more of an answer. "So then he made it to the higher kingdoms?"

"No," she said, matter-of-factly.

"Then where is he?" Calder asked hesitantly.

She took a moment before responding, "He is trapped in the grid."

Calder pushed his chair out and stood up. "Then I'll find him!"

Etiwa remained calm. "It is not that simple. You know full well how complicated the grid is. For all we know, the grid has a mind of its own."

Calder paced before sitting back down.

Razz looked as though he had lost himself in a far-off daze before he said, "How can we get him out?"

She stood up and moved to an open area in the room, where she drew a strange symbol on the floor with white chalk. She closed her eyes with a heavy breath before lifting her hands to twirl them, repeating words I couldn't understand. The air grew heavy, and the chandelier flickered and swayed. For a moment, I could have sworn there was a quick flash of blue above her symbolled drawing.

She tried opening the grid in a way I hadn't seen before, but after several unsuccessful minutes, she sat back down. "Though we still have magic on Elloriya's edge, there seem to be some restrictions on how it can be used. There is no way for me to get him out with magic. He must find his own way out."

"And if he can't?" Razz asked.

She shook her head as fear swelled in her eyes.

"There has to be another way!" Razz pleaded.

She reached into her velvet indigo bag and pulled out a tarot deck. A moment later, her deck began shuffling itself from a simple swish and sway of her finger.

She whispered, "Show me the way to Zaydarian's escape from the energy grid."

One card flew out while the deck continued to shuffle in midair. The card placed itself on the table, facedown. Seconds later, another card jumped out, placing itself neatly next to the first card.

Then two more slid out from the carousel of cards, settling themselves beside the others, all facedown. Then the flying cards came to a stop and stacked itself neatly into a pile on the table.

Etiwa's gaze over the spread narrowed on the first card that came out. At Etiwa's nod of approval, the card turned itself over.

It read: *Ace of pentacles.*

A gold coin centered the card. Vibrant flowers and ivy rapidly grew and bloomed around the gilded coin until a spectacular floral arrangement covered the entire card. It was strange how a flowery scent suddenly filled the room.

Etiwa blinked in thought before sliding her gaze to the next card. Another slight nod and the card flipped over.

It read: *Ace of cups.*

A silver chalice embellished in intricate designs centered the card. Then suddenly, five streams of water poured out of the chalice, causing the water to rise in the card until the chalice became submerged in aqua liquid.

Etiwa lowered her brows before turning to the third card with a nod. Without a moment's hesitation, the card flipped.

It read: *Ace of wands.*

A wooden rod centered the card. It was rather dull compared to the other cards. At least until it suddenly ignited in flames. Perhaps it was in my head, but I could have sworn I felt heat emanate from that card.

Etiwa's eyes had widened. With a twinge of hesitation, she turned to the last card—the fourth card—and nodded. It lifted off the table at her command and turned itself.

It read: *Ace of swords.*

A cloud filled the card for several seconds before a blade cut through from beneath, breaking the cloud into a thin fog now encircling the resting sword.

"What do they mean?" Calder asked.

"Their meanings are different individually. But all of them together have something to do with the lower kingdoms." She analyzed the cards. "And the result? Will it be favorable?" she asked, addressing the cards directly.

The deck lifted off the table and began circling and reshuffling midair. Four more cards came out one by one before the deck settled on the table once more. And just when I thought it was done, the top card on the sitting deck flew before Etiwa, isolating itself at the very top of the reading.

Etiwa scanned the four facedown cards, each lying beneath a faceup card. With a nod, all four of the new cards flipped over.

The first one read: *Six of pentacles.*

A vintage scale held six gold coins on one side, weighing it down, with nothing on the other. A man in a scarlet robe walked into the image and grabbed the coins, leaving the now empty scale balanced. The scale faded and was replaced with an image of a homeless woman. The robed man handed her the coins.

"Be open to receiving help if one offers," Etiwa said, glancing up at me.

I had no idea what she was talking about and why she was only addressing me.

The second card read: *Three of cups.*

In a field of fruits and flowers, three witches happily join with hand-held cauldrons raised in the air. The image showed them dancing and laughing in a circle. The strangest part was the celebratory music playing softly from the card.

"Join them in celebration." Again, Etiwa spoke aloud, but not to the cards. It was as though she was giving us advice that made no sense.

Razz opened his mouth, surely to ask who she was talking about. But then he closed his lips as he watched Etiwa scan the next card.

It read: *Five of wands.*

Five knights on heavily armored horses held jousting sticks against each other as each tried to knock the others off their horse. It caused Etiwa to look up at Razz as she said, "Stay strong and cunning in conflict."

And then she turned to me. "You too."

Razz appeared just as confused as me, likely wanting this reading to be over as much as I did. But I sat patiently as I looked at the next card.

It read: *Ten of swords.*

It was by far the bleakest card on the table. One glance at the image had my stomach turned to knots.

The card revealed a blackened sky with a white dragon lying dead in the dirt, with ten long swords pinned into its back. Not much was moving in this card except some gray clouds floating by.

The only remaining card sat facedown atop all the cards. Etiwa showed hesitance before finally nodding. It flipped. And to my relief, Etiwa smiled.

It read: *The sun.*

An imposing sun shone brightly over a baby unicorn trotting in the picture. And the big bright sun taking up nearly half the card suddenly had a face on it. Was it there before? As I examined the sun's face, I could have sworn it looked right back at me with a quick smirk.

Etiwa stayed silent for a moment, searching her mind until she finally said, "If magic returns to the lower kingdoms, the grid will release Zaydarian on the other side of the barrier."

Calder perked up. "How can magic be returned? Shakar robbed every kingdom of their magic."

Etiwa turned to me. "Do you still have the relics?"

"Yes."

"You must find a way past the barrier and take the relics to their proper kingdom—to all four lower kingdoms—"

"I knew it!" Calder said, cutting her off. Etiwa looked at him with a raised brow. "Sorry. I just mentioned something similar in our meeting earlier. I knew the portals must have picked her—" When Etiwa's raised brow didn't waver, he said, "Never mind. You were saying?"

She turned back to me. "The relics should tell you in some way where in the kingdoms they belong. If it works, magic will return to the lower lands of Elloriya, the grid will unlock, and Zaydarian will be freed."

"And if it doesn't work?" I questioned, hesitant to hear the answer.

Her green-brown eyes turned bleak. "If it does not work, he will likely be lost in the grid for eternity."

My stomach dropped, and my heart felt as though it had burst. My stupid, ignorant, amateur suggestion got Darian in this mess. It was my fault. It was all my fault!

Razz was in a daze with glossy eyes before stumbling across the room to the glass door. He opened the door to the garden and vomited on the grass. I wouldn't blame him if he hated me. I hated myself! I hated that I spoke up when I should have stayed silent.

When Razz returned to his seat much paler than before, he studied me, indeed reading my thoughts as he said, "It's not your fault, Attica. We will get him out."

My shaky voice snapped, "How?"

"First, we need to find a way past the barrier," Calder said sharply.

"Not you," Etiwa barked to Calder.

"I'm going!" Calder countered.

"No. You must stay. Only Razzertaine and Attica must go," she said with such certainty, whatever was left of my sickened stomach twisted.

I silenced my nerves and scanned the map Darian had left on the table, finding only two ways across. One way was through the barrier, if that was even possible. And the other way was crossing the Fatal Sea. It was a small sea separating the edge of Elloriya from the land closest to the Azar Kingdom.

"Why don't we just cross the mountains and take a boat across the sea?" I asked.

Calder looked me dead in the eye. "I'm a water wielder, but the sea surrounding the edge cannot be wielded. I don't know if Shakar cursed it or something, but the Fatal Sea has some sort of gravitational force. All we know is if any boat touches this sea" —he pointed to the waters surrounding the edge— "it sinks. And if anybody attempts to swim across, they drown. Even birds that fly over end up falling into the water. It has all been tried by others. And each one of them is rotting at the bottom of—"

"Enough!" Razz stood up, slamming his hand on the map. "She gets it."

Razz pulled something out of his pocket and placed it on the table. It looked familiar, and it took a moment before I finally recognized it. It was that strange circular-shaped key he had taken from the Orpheus when they had once captured him; a key that would surely get us past the barrier Shakar had put in place, keeping us far from the rest of Elloriya.

Razz glanced at me gravely. "We'll leave at first light."

"And if you get caught?" Calder questioned.

Razz looked down with an inward gaze and then up at us. "I've been working on something." He closed his eyes, and within seconds, a new layer of skin formed over him. It was gray and scaled. The tips of his fingers turned sharp, like claws. And when he opened the eyes of his now gray-scaled face, they were yellow and centered with black slits for pupils. He looked just like an Orpheus, causing me to step back.

"How?" I questioned.

A smile grew wide on Calder's face. "You're the best damn mind-bender I know!"

"I'm the only mind-bender you know," Razz said with a half-smile.

Calder glanced at me curiously before turning back to Razz. "What about Attica? Can you conceal her?"

Razz breathed in at the sight of me before closing his eyes. For a moment, a layer of gray-scaled skin spread over me. But in the same breath, it vanished.

Etiwa observed Razz and then me. "Your connection must be strengthened." She turned to Calder. "Do you have the couplings?"

Calder went out the glass doors to the garden, carefully avoiding Razz's vomit, and a moment later, he returned with a set of gold bands in one hand and a set of silver bands in his other.

Etiwa scrunched her forehead. "You keep the couplings outside?"

Calder hesitated before awkwardly responding, "Yes."

Etiwa's face read unsatisfied as she handed the gilded bands to Razz and me.

"Put them on," she instructed.

Razz obeyed and put one band on his arm while I clasped the other over my forearm with an already spinning head. My dizzy mind caught sight of my skin changing once more, but it was fragmented. It was like a puzzle spread over me with many missing pieces. I could hardly take the spinning, so I unclasped the band and dropped it to the floor, wondering why it wasn't that intense when I had worn the gold couplings with Ignatius.

Etiwa handed the silver bands to Razz and me. I hesitated before taking mine in hand, clasping it around my arm. The moment it latched, dizziness took hold, but I could handle it. And then a bond locked between Razz and me. His energy was strong and fluid as it synced with mine. To my dismay, I suddenly felt his sadness and bewilderment over his lost brother.

"Try again," Etiwa instructed.

Razz closed his eyes, and almost instantly, my fingers elongated to sharp claws, and my skin turned gray and scaled. Etiwa and Calder glanced back and forth between Razz and me. Razz looked like an Orpheus. And apparently, so did I.

After we came up with a decent plan, I was ready to go to bed with a grain of hope. But before I exited the dining room, Etiwa said one last thing to me.

"This journey is not to be taken lightly, as magic tends to have a mind of its own."

I swallowed, ignored the sickening feeling in my chest, and headed to my room, replaying her warning in my head.

CHAPTER 6

Departure

My sleep was rocky and broken throughout the short night. When I had finally fallen into a decent slumber, a voice spoke somewhere deep in my mind: "Wake up! Time to go."

It was undoubtedly Razz. No other person had ever communicated with me in this form of telepathy. It wasn't until I felt the cold metal of the coupling still latched to my arm that I realized why his telepathic message slipped so easily into my normally chaotic head.

While forcing my drowsy body out of bed, I glanced out the wide arched window. The light of the sun had barely pierced the night sky.

I dressed in a gray snakeskin jumpsuit with sharp shoulders—my newest outfit from the emporium. It was a bit pricey, but I earned seven gilds after helping Gemma with some floral arrangements for a wedding in a nearby village. Ignatius paid me three more for simply shining some jewelry he made from annealing metal with a lot of red fire.

I packed a crossbody sling bag with the bare necessities: the relics, extra clothes, toiletries, and my beloved Christmas stocking Mama had given me, in case I was never to return to the manor.

While securing the strap of my stuffed bag over my chest, there was a soft knock on my bedroom door. I opened it, finding a tall man with golden curls and a single braid behind the black metal cuff masking his left ear.

"Ready?"

In that one word Razz spoke, I detected a tone of worry crept alongside pain.

My voice cracked as I replied, "Yes. Is anyone else coming?"

"No! It's risky enough with the two of us," he said, sharper than I think he intended. He softened when he added, "You heard Etiwa last night. It has to be you and me, no one else."

As we silently moved down the corridor, he turned to me with scanning eyes. "Is that an Orpheus-themed outfit?"

I hadn't even noticed the resemblance my outfit shared with their gray-scaled skin before now. I responded with a shrug.

Razz took us through the side doors in the East Wing to the garden and filled his bag with enough food to last us a few days if we ate sparingly. I did the same, adding a canteen of water and as much food as I could to my already stuffed bag.

As we headed toward the camouflaged gate, I turned back to take one last look at the ivy-covered brownstone manor, unsure if I would ever return. The thought of not returning made me want to run inside and hug everyone goodbye. Though I was sure I'd see them again, something was still tugging me back.

"Hang on," I said to Razz just before he opened the gate. I turned and ran to the front doors. For a moment, I hesitated—

perhaps afraid to hear what the slithery voice had to say, if anything. But I pushed past my hesitance and stroked my fingers over the gilded snake's spine, nested in the center of the giant mandala embossed on the copper doors.

His dull blue eyes filled with sapphire light upon my touch. Esmond stretched his scales and slithered up into the air until he was at eye level with me.

"I—um—" My throat dried.

"*Yessss?*" Esmond hissed. His sapphire eyes gleamed brighter than the rising sun.

Finally, I managed to lift my chin. "I haven't known you for long, but I just wanted to say bye in case I don't return."

His head moved closer toward me, closer than he had ever been before. "*Goodbye, Attica Ssspark. You will be missssed.*" He retracted his head and curled himself back into the center of the door before becoming still again. The light in his eyes went out, but I stayed staring at him for just a moment, admiring his glinting scales before heading back to Razz.

As we made our way through the waking woods, I turned to him and stupidly asked, "How did you make a call to Etiwa?"

"Last night?"

I nodded.

"Telepathically, obviously."

"Are there other ways to communicate from afar with others?"

He looked at me strangely. But it seemed to suddenly dawn on him that I had lost my memories of this world I once lived in as a young child. How was I to know all the ways people communicated in this realm? Even though I had already been here for a little over a year, it was still an entirely different world. But to be fair, a year in Elloriya was not nearly as long as a year on Earth. A year here was just a very long season.

He kept his eyes on the rising sun. "Using a courier is the most common manner of communicating from afar."

An image of that turquoise seahorse creature thing with dragonfly wings and a swirled shell on its back popped into my mind. James had sent me a courier once with a message before he left Elloriya. But I already knew about couriers.

"Any other ways to communicate here?" I asked, just in case a courier didn't show up when or if I ever needed one.

"Is there someone you'd like to reach out to?"

There was. Maybe. But then again, maybe not. Of course, I thought about reaching out to my birth parents, sending them a message of some sort. I wouldn't even know what to say.

But it wasn't them I was thinking of sending a message to while I walked through the woods with Razz as dawn continued to crack. It was Darian. Could he even receive a message while lost in the grid?

I didn't even have to ask aloud. Razz looked at the ground and kicked a pinecone as he said, "I already tried. It didn't work."

At first, I didn't know how he knew what I was thinking until I noticed again that the couplings were still latched around both our arms from the night before.

"Just because I'm wearing this thing," I said, lifting my arm lazily, "doesn't give you the right to read my mind whenever you please."

He cocked his head. After a moment, his tight jaw loosened. "You're right. I'm sorry. Sometimes I can't help what thoughts I hear or feel, especially through the couplings. But you are right."

I muttered a word of thanks while taking in the honey-filled sunlight spreading past the wavy bark of the woodland trees.

The farther we walked, the more my nerves unraveled at the unknown journey ahead. But several calming breaths convinced me that the momentary look Darian had given me right before he disappeared into the grid was not the last time I'd see him.

I would do whatever it took to get Darian back, even if it meant the end of my life. After all, he was stuck in the grid because of my ignorant suggestion.

It took what felt like two hours, maybe even three, to get through the woods and over a barricade of mountains when, finally, Razz held his arm out before me. We came to an abrupt stop as a wave of smoke drifted toward us.

Razz sighed. "We're nearly there."

The scent was thick of burning charcoal as we continued tiptoeing through the smoke dispersed heavily around us. The early sun rays barely traveled through the smoke drifting over our feet.

It wasn't long before we saw a massive mountain of stacked black tourmaline, rough and raw in the distance. It was not only one of the strangest mountains I had ever seen, but it spread far in both directions.

"Welcome to the Orpheus Kingdom," Razz said in a low voice.

My mouth fell open. "This is the Orpheus Kingdom?" It hadn't met a single expectation of what a castle of any kingdom should look like. There were no windows, no architectural design, not anything that made it look livable. Instead, it was mountains of black, stacked, rectangular boulders. "I thought we were going to the barrier?"

The morning light shone over his navy-blue eyes as he turned to me, completely understanding that I didn't know any better. "The Orpheus Kingdom *is* the barrier separating Elloriya's edge from the rest of the realm."

I knew he was planning to bend our appearance in case an Orpheus saw us. But I didn't realize he was disguising us as Orpheus so we could sneak through their damn dwelling.

Nausea hit me hard. But I bit my nerves as I thought of Darian and doing whatever the hell it took to get him back.

Razz took his coupling off and asked me to do the same. I did as he commanded. "Now switch," he said, handing his coupling to me and taking mine from my hand.

"Why?"

"Your energy in this coupling will strengthen my connection to you, making it easier to bend your appearance while bending my own," he explained, placing the coupling that had been on my arm onto his.

The moment I latched his coupling around my forearm, he tapped them together, and our connection synced stronger than ever before. My body broke into goosebumps as the energy between us tightened.

Razz closed his eyes with intent focus. His skin turned gray and scaled. His fingernails grew sharp as a lizard's. And when he opened his eyes, they were yellow with black-slit pupils.

He turned to me and asked, "How do I look?" revealing a glimpse of his now razor-sharp teeth. I nearly stumbled back.

He still managed to look handsome as ever in Orpheus form. Although to be fair, the Orpheus had flattering humanlike facial features, so Razz didn't look all that different from his usual good-looking self.

"Well?" He waited with raised brows.

"Good. You look good!" I said honestly.

He closed his eyes again, and a single breath later, my skin turned gray-scaled, my nails grew pointed, and I imagined my eyes appeared different too.

Razz must have noticed my tongue sliding over the bridge of my teeth as he said, "They look like Orpheus teeth, but they won't feel like it. I'm just bending our appearance. I can't actually change our form."

I then ran my scaly fingers over my lizardlike nails. Razz was right. They looked sharp, but felt like my standard, short, rounded nails. His mind-bending was so realistic, it was hard to fathom that what I saw differed from what I felt.

"Stay close," he said in a commanding voice. "The farther you go, the weaker our connection through the couplings will be. I can only keep your appearance up if you're in my sight. Otherwise, you're on your own."

My stomach turned.

"Ready?"

"What about our clothes? Shouldn't you change those too?" I asked, eyeing his all-black outfit. I wasn't sure if he had ever worn any other color.

He scanned my gray snakeskin jumpsuit with an arched brow. "Hmm. I practically know what an Orpheus looks like nude."

I playfully slapped his chest with the back of my hand.

He chuckled lazily before his face turned sullen, as if suddenly remembering we were moments away from risking our lives. "Only those we've seen outside their kingdom wear armor. The ones inside dress in variations of casual clothing. We'll be fine."

For a moment, I wondered how he knew of their inner world. But then I remembered how he was held captive by the Orpheus, getting the rare opportunity to see their dwelling. His captivity was entirely his choice—his sneaky way of snatching something we needed now more than ever.

He pressed his hand over his pocket, surely checking for the strange key we relied on to pass through the barrier—to pass through their kingdom.

"Follow my lead," he said, jolting the loose curls on his head as he moved forward. "And do not speak a word inside."

No guards were standing outside the dreary, mountainlike castle. There couldn't be, I don't think. No one had ever seen an Orpheus in the daylight. They only came out at night, and there must have been a good reason for that.

As we cautiously continued forward, I hardly felt like myself with this strange layer of scaly skin. The only thing that felt familiar was my dark golden blonde hair, left untouched by Razz's mind-bending.

The ground we trudged over was hot and charred, releasing smoke through its cracks. As we stepped through the rising smoke, the smell of charcoal thickened.

An enormous red bird was singing its morning song as it soared over the barrier. My eyes widened at the sight of the bird hitting some invisible electric wall above the tourmaline mountain. Before I could comprehend what had just happened, scarlet feathers rained down as the bird spiraled to the charred ground.

I swallowed with sorrow at the sight of its nearly lifeless body twinging in pain. Reptilian Razz bent down and snapped its neck, quickly putting it out of its misery. He gently petted the damned bird before continuing forward through the heavy smoke.

It wasn't until we were nearing fifty feet away from the wretched barrier that I took sight of decaying bodies pinned along the black mountains—a malicious form of decor. None of the pinned bodies were Orpheus. Some of the dead had decayed so much, I could nearly see every bone of the dangling skeletons.

I gasped, quickly switching my sight to anything but those who surely failed to pass the barrier. Razz whipped his head back to me with a silencing finger brushing over his gray lips.

If I had never gone through the chakra portals, I would have certainly had an anxiety attack by now. But I had freed my anxiety in the solar plexus portal. And now, I was left with nothing but unsettling nerves. And though my fear was kept under control with each step closer to the stone door, my stomach quickly turned to knots.

We passed the front entrance. Instead, Razz led us to a side entrance, where the strange-shaped key he pulled out of his pocket—circular with many ridges—fit perfectly in the tarnished lock. He turned the key, and with a click, the rocky-black door opened.

CHAPTER 7

The Barrier

My heart pounded as I followed Razz inside the blistering hot barrier. The smell and heat were surprisingly more bearable inside. It was the only sense of relief, since danger undoubtedly loomed in every corner.

All we had to do was make it through the barrier—through the Orpheus Kingdom—without getting caught.

The size of this strange place was far bigger than my mind could wrap around.

There were stone stairs leading up and down in nearly every direction without an Orpheus in sight. And though soft sunlight peered between small pockets of the black tourmaline walls and towering ceiling, it was still dark and dusty in every corner.

We walked in bone-chilling silence through the dust and darkness, searching for an exit to the other side. My chest tightened at the eerie sound of nothing but our graveled steps.

We tiptoed down the shadowed hall before descending a set of stairs, taking us below ground level, where it was sweltering. When we reached the bottom of the steps, my breathing came to a sudden halt.

We stood in a massive room with women and children Orpheus, all sleeping in nestlike hammocks. As I scanned the room, hoping to find some hidden door to the other side, I took a step back at the sight of a child looking at Razz and me.

My heart suddenly raced as I stilled on his yellow-slit eyes. We looked like Orpheus, or at least similar enough not to cause alarm. Razz put a finger up to his mouth and gently smiled at the little boy.

Razz grabbed my hand and turned back up the steps. I followed close behind, turning over my shoulder to find the child still watching us.

My chest tightened as we continued farther down the dark hall to another underground staircase leading straight into a giant den of at least a couple hundred Orpheus warriors sleeping, each in their own nestlike hammock; some nests lay on the floor, while others were higher up, hanging off the walls or ceiling. There were plenty of rope ladders and bridges in every direction.

In the center of the den was the largest nest with three female Orpheus wrapped around Shakar. His nest was the highest and most extensive, hung from the ceiling.

My stomach turned when Razz continued farther down the stairs, passing some of the most imposing warriors I had ever seen. Razz seemed to know where to go as he was determined to sneak past the army. My chest tightened more with every step.

At one point, I wanted to punch Razz in the back when he attempted to take one of the warrior's black saber swords. It appeared they all slept with their swords still belted on them. But the one Razz had reached for was not attached to the slumbering warrior we were passing. Just as his fingers nearly touched the handle, I grabbed his hand and shook my head with a warning look. Thankfully, he continued forward without pushing his luck any further.

When we passed all the sleeping reptilians, I was finally relieved enough to take a deep, dust-filled breath. At least until I realized we had entered a hallway that felt more like a black stone maze. When I turned a corner, I quickly realized Razz was nowhere in sight.

Razz? My telepathic attempt to call out to him was pathetic. I sent out another telepathic message. *Where are you?* I moved through the mazelike hallway, desperately scanning every direction for him.

It had been several minutes since I lost him, and now—*Shit!* My lizardlike appearance was fading. My hands and arms appeared human again.

Considering all the Orpheus were sleeping, I tried not to worry about my human appearance. At least until I turned another corner and ran right into a set of yellow slit eyes. And it certainly was not Razz.

He was a young Orpheus. Perhaps a teenager. He wasn't dressed in black metal armor like the warriors we had just snuck past. Instead, he was wearing a brown tunic and cuffed trousers.

He scanned me. "Who are you?"

"I'm—I'm—" I tripped over my tongue and swallowed. I took a breath and finally said, "I'm trying to find the exit." What else was I supposed to say? He saw I was not an Orpheus. I was already doomed.

Footsteps came from around the hall.

Please be Razz, please be Razz! I silently prayed.

The young Orpheus pushed me behind the stone wall, concealing me to whoever had just turned the corner.

"Ekon, who were you talking to?" a sharp voice asked.

"No one," the teen lied.

But why would he lie for me?

"You were talking. I heard you and a female," the man pushed. He slowed his words. "Who were you talking to?"

Footsteps moved closer in my direction. My heart pounded so loud, I was certain I'd be found if he only turned the next corner. I moved farther down the stone pathway in the opposite direction, running directly into another set of yellow slit eyes. Whoever it was snatched my body to the side and covered my mouth.

I couldn't move. I couldn't scream. While gripped from behind, my body began to fade entirely. Then, as I looked up at the man who had snatched me, I was relieved to see the yellow slit eyes had changed to navy-blue. Razz turned back to human form for a split second before disappearing into thin air. And even stranger, I disappeared with him.

A vicious-looking Orpheus turned the corner, peering directly at Razz and me. Nerves sparked throughout my chest until I realized he couldn't see us. Razz was surely bending our appearance, making us invisible. Though they could not see us, I was certain the Orpheus could feel us if he got close enough.

He sniffed the air and moved in our direction. My heart pounded harder with every heavy step he took, inching closer and closer, tightening the four feet between us. To calm the pounding of my heart, I focused on the feeling of being safe, tucked tightly in Razz's arms. His protection soothed my nerves as best they could.

The teen Orpheus—Ekon—followed the man. "Fine, I'll tell you who I was talking to," he began.

Shit! Would this place be turned upside-down with Orpheus warriors searching for me?

The man turned to the teen with sharp eyes, unaware that the tips of his long red hair brushed over my nose.

Ekon continued, "I was practicing asking Shakar if I can join the fighters on the next outing. I've been training for three seasons now."

"I heard another voice—a female voice. Explain!" the Orpheus man demanded.

"That was my voice too. Puberty," he added.

The reptilian man scanned Ekon from head to toe. "Aren't you a little too old to go through puberty?"

"No. I mean, yes." Ekon shrugged. "Late bloomer, I guess."

The red-haired Orpheus laughed before walking off. Ekon smirked as he looked around the mazelike halls, probably searching for where I had gone to.

Razz grabbed my hand, keeping us invisible as he led me through the stone halls, holding another key I hadn't recognized, which would explain where he had snuck off to.

My entire perspective of these beings had suddenly changed. Perhaps they were more like humans than I previously thought. Some were good, and others were wretched. Or maybe Ekon was the only good one. Either way, I didn't want to judge them all based on the few wicked Orpheus I had become familiar with.

When we finally neared the end of the hall, we saw the exit. Sun was gleaming thinly around the stone door. The only problem was another Orpheus sat asleep on a chair a foot away from the tarnished lock. His deeply scarred face and slashed arm lay over the brim of the chair as he breathed heavily through his snores.

Razz kept us invisible as he held my hand, guiding us to the door.

The guard started sniffing in his sleep. I was sure he had smelled us. Razz dared to move beside him and tried to open the door, but it was locked. He pulled out the key he had just swiped and silently placed it in the lock, turning it. Then—

Clank.

The slumbering Orpheus beside us opened his eyes from the sound of keys hitting the stone floor. He didn't see Razz or me, but he saw the key on the floor and picked it up. He sniffed the air, surely picking up on our scent as his menacing eyes scanned the room. Razz's hand squeezed mine, pushing us quietly against the door.

Ekon turned the corner. "Than!" he said, calling out to the guard.

"What?" the scarred Orpheus snapped.

"Your daughter was asking for you," Ekon said.

The man grunted with another scan of his surroundings. Then he dragged his tattered boots as he walked off with a twinge of irritation.

The teen moved closer, also seeming to pick up on my scent, or perhaps Razz's.

"Go, now!" he whispered toward us.

Razz opened the black tourmaline door, and we finally stepped through to the other side of the barrier.

CHAPTER 8

Connection

My chest loosened as we walked up the outdoor steps and back to ground level. We made our way into the moss blanketed woods with birds twittering and the scent of bittersweet cedar kissing my senses.

We had only traveled a quarter mile before I turned to a pale-faced Razz, who suddenly looked like he hadn't slept in days.

"You okay?" I asked.

He leaned against a tree, lightly panting before releasing his bag to the ground, keeping me silently waiting with anticipation. He dropped lazily down on a mossy cloud, resting his back against the rippled bark, when he suddenly broke into a brief beaming laugh.

"What's so funny?"

He glanced up at the vivid blue sky, unfazed by the golden rays sprinkling him, then dragged his eyes over the sun-soaked trees. While fully bathing in the moment, winded with a huff and puff, he finally said, "My intuition always told me I would one day make it to this side of the barrier, but I was beginning to believe otherwise. For some reason, I always imagined it happening during the night."

Any hint of a smile had vanished when he added, "Except, I envisioned it being with my brother."

I wanted to say something of comfort—anything to make him feel better. But my gut told me to steer away from speaking of Darian. So instead, to dissolve the awkwardness of this moment, I glanced past layers of trees at the distant tourmaline mountain and asked, "Why did that Orpheus help us?"

After a few recharging breaths, he answered, "They're not all evil. Shakar started his army before you were born, so the ones we know as heartless warriors were trained to be that way."

"Oh," I muttered. "Why didn't you make us invisible to begin with?"

He gulped from his canteen, then wiped his dripping chin with his black tunic before answering, "It requires a lot more energy to remove every aspect of our bodies altogether than to simply change the surface of our appearance. That little disappearing trick really did me in."

It wasn't until he snacked on a purple bristled fruit that color finally returned to his pretty face. He offered me a bite, but I kindly declined.

In Elloriya, instead of eating for the delight of pleasing my taste buds, I only ate when I was hungry. Strangely, the food here kept me full a lot longer than any food from Earth ever had.

As I studied Razz through his every bite, I couldn't help how parts of him reminded me of Darian, like their almond-shaped, blue eyes—though their eyes were like two entirely different worlds. Razz held a midnight blue with whispers of stars captivating his onlookers. Darian had a celestial world of electric blue, always closed to the public, except for the rare fleeting moments when he dropped the velvet rope just long enough for me to glimpse the real him.

Razz switched his gaze from his food to me, surely catching my stare.

"So, what now?" I blurted, brushing over my lingering attention on him.

He reached into his scuffed pocket, pulling out a brass compass. "Where to?" he asked. But he wasn't speaking to me.

I cocked my head when the face of the compass illuminated in response. The arrow spun wildly until it finally pointed east, and then the light faded. It seemed to have a mind of its own.

"Where did you get that?" I asked, my eyes still fixated on the enchanted compass.

He surveyed it fondly. "My father gave it to me when I was a child." With an exasperated chuckle, he added, "I asked the compass how to get past the barrier every season since my entrapment on the edge. And every time, it led me straight to the Orpheus Kingdom. There was no other way."

Before I could respond, a sudden shriek bellowed around us. I winced as the inside of my ears shook in rippling pain.

Turning to Razz as he packed his food away, I asked loudly, "What the hell was that?"

He looked up, focusing on a spot of the woods about ten trees away. "A faun," he said with annoyance. "It wants us to leave." Razz got up and strapped his bag across his chest.

I saw nothing as I peered between the surrounding trees at the same spot Razz had looked. At least until I heard the shriek again. A gray creature with small horns and white goatlike legs peeked at us from behind a mossy tree. A part of me felt bad for it, as its silvery-white eyes kept glimpsing to see if we had gone. Was it afraid of us?

The faun shrieked again. It was as painful as the torturing sound of nails on a chalkboard.

"Settle your damn horns! We're leaving!" Razz bellowed at the faun still cowering behind the tree.

It was the first time I had ever heard Razz use such a sharp tone with anyone. He always appeared so mellow. But I shrugged it off and headed east with Razz by my side.

As we continued through the woods, I glanced inside my bag under my cloak, reassuring myself that the relics were secure.

"How far east are we traveling?" I asked, returning the leather strap of my bag across my chest.

"Not too far. We should arrive at the Tera Kingdom in about six days."

"Six days?" I snapped. *Not too far, my ass!* I irritably released a heavy breath, preparing my body for the journey ahead.

I wanted to understand this strange world, so I continued pressing Razz with questions. "For the lower kingdoms, there is one in the north, one in the south, one in the east, and one in the west, right?"

"Correct," was all he said.

"And the higher kingdoms?"

He swished a fly away from his face. "That's a little more complicated to explain."

"So? I can handle complicated."

He glanced at me with a curious eye, seeming to weigh if I would understand the complexities of the higher kingdoms.

When he turned his attention back on the woodland path, he said, "The higher kingdoms are a great distance north, far past the mountain range, and somewhere in the ether."

"You mean, like, in the sky?"

He looked at me with a sly grin and shrugged. "Sort of."

I didn't push any further on the matter. Instead, I began thinking of Darian. Zaydarian. Zayd. Whatever, or whoever, he was to me, I still didn't know. When I called him Zayd as a child, we were good friends. He cared for me. But as Darian—as a fully grown man—he distanced himself. He had a wall up, seemingly made of steel. Anytime I thought of his birth name, "Zaydarian," it felt like I was another step closer to the real him. But then again, anytime I thought of him with his true name, it felt like a lie, like I had no right to call him anything but "Darian."

As I stepped over a bed of white flowers, for a split second, I wondered if I would ever see him again. Or would he stay lost in the grid for eternity? Ugh! The thought of it made me sick. The more I let my worries consume me, the sicker I felt.

I took a painful, unworthy breath as I grabbed the necklace I was given by one man I had already lost in my everyday life, wondering if I would forever lose the other as my fingers slid from the onyx to the moonstone.

"Thinking about him?" Razz asked, interrupting my thoughts.

"About who?"

"You know who. My brother."

"What makes you think that?" I said defensively.

He stopped in his tracks and turned to me in a manner that was far more serious than I would have liked. "Not to pry, Attica, but I can feel your thoughts as if they were my own. Not always.

But if the emotion is strong enough, I can't help but pick up on it. Especially when we're both wearing the couplings." He moved even closer to me, and in an uncomfortably firm tone, he said, "Believe me, I would cut the cord of our connection if I could." He broke his harsh gaze on me and continued forward.

Perhaps it was because I was so thrown off by his jarring tone, but I took off my coupling and threw it in my bag. "There! Now you don't have to worry about my thoughts, and I can keep them private as God intended!"

He didn't respond. Instead, he pulled on a low-hanging branch of a tree he passed by—a branch that hit me in the face a second later.

Was he mad? Had I done something wrong? Did he blame me for Darian's shitty predicament? Did he blame me for us having to take this stupid journey to get Darian back? It didn't matter. No matter what he thought, I knew this was all my fault.

My tone was just as serious as his was when I said, "And what connection do we have, Razz?"

He chuckled in an almost patronizing tone. "You know damn well what connection I'm referring to."

At first, I wanted to deny it. But I did know what he was referring to. I hadn't thought about the connection we had shared since the night of the gala. And if I did, I immediately pushed it out of my mind.

He had once appeared in my sacral portal, one of the several portals that allow only one soul to enter at a time—or so I've been told. And somehow, both Razz and Darian had entered the portals that were only meant for me.

For Razz, it was a dream he had dreamed, but for me, it had been real. There was even a strong connection we shared through the couplings that I hadn't felt from anyone else I wore the couplings with.

When I wore the couplings with Razz, it felt comfortable, like our energies enjoyed each other's company. Well, usually.

This thought led me to wonder how it would feel to wear the couplings with Darian. Would it be as tight of a bond as Razz and I shared, or would it feel as ordinary and somewhat uncomfortable as it had with Gemma and Ignatius?

The chirps of woodland birds grew louder as I wondered what Razz truly meant when he said, "I would cut the cord of our connection if I could."

CHAPTER 9

Silence

We continued through the woods on what felt like a never-ending trail, Razz walking a few feet ahead of me at nearly all times. I did my best to keep up with his pace, but his strides were much longer than mine. Not a word was spoken from either of us for nearly four starlights. It was probably the longest hours of my life.

When it finally reached nightfall, we stopped by a cluster of close-knit trees.

"We'll sleep here for the night," Razz said, not bothering to even glance in my general direction.

Was he intentionally trying to make things awkward between us? If so, he was succeeding. Not even one day had passed, and it was already tense and miserable.

Perhaps it was my chaotic mind that made it impossible to sleep. Or maybe it was my stirring emotions of guilt, sadness, and wanting to kick Razz in the shin for acting like such a prick. Or because I was on a damn blanket in the middle of the woods. But I slept like garbage, and a tiny part of me wondered if I deserved it.

Another day went by without more than three words spoken between us. I didn't bother to communicate. If he wanted to be an ass, then fine. I had bigger things to worry about, like getting Darian back.

It wasn't until we were both falling asleep the second night in the woods that I realized how much more difficult this journey must be for Razz. Regardless of how deeply I felt about Darian, Razz was his brother for damn sake. They shared blood!

The second night I slept like shit, again. Though our surroundings were beautiful, I was tired of seeing nothing but endless trees in every direction.

I spent a portion of the sleepless night ensuring that I finally understood time in this realm. Since there are twenty starlights in one day, and the first eight are dark, the ninth through the twelfth starlights would be morning. That would make the thirteenth starlight midday, right? And the fourteenth to the eighteenth starlights would be afternoon, and the nineteenth and twentieth starlights are evening. *Yes! That sounds about right.*

By late afternoon on the third day, we reached a creek in the woods with a decent-size pool of water.

"Do you mind if I quickly wash up?" I asked somewhat awkwardly, finally breaking the silence between us.

Razz glanced at me and then at the pool. "Oh." It must have dawned on him that I would have to undress because he turned with pink cheeks. "Yeah. I'll just be over here," he said, walking toward a boulder at the other end of the water.

I quickly undressed behind a tree and jumped in. Razz kept his eyes averted, looking anywhere but at the pool where I washed buck naked. He even pulled out Darian's map and stared blankly at it until he heard me get out of the water.

"Let me know when you're dressed," he called out, still averting his eyes.

"Okay," I responded.

He must have assumed that I meant I was already fully dressed, rather than just a response to him, because he turned around and saw my wet hair dripping down my bare stomach. My bottom half was fully clothed, but my top half had only a bra still.

Even from a distance, I saw him swallow deeply. It seemed difficult for him to pull his eyes off me as I put my shirt on.

He brushed his fingers through his hair when he said, "I think I'll take a rinse off too."

"Go ahead," I said as I pulled out a small hairbrush from my bag, running the wooden bristles through my wet hair.

Razz didn't ask me to look away when it was his turn. He just kept his back to me the entire time as he undressed. Though his shoulders weren't as broad as Darian's, he still had muscles that painted his back beautifully. It wasn't until he took off his pants and I saw his bare ass that I turned away.

By the time he was done, I had already long finished brushing my hair. He stepped out of the water, covering only his cock while he walked to his clothes, lying disheveled on the nearby boulder. He flipped his wet hair, and a splash of water jumped off his golden curls. And to my complete humiliation, he caught me watching as he got dressed.

A feeling of heat rushed over my ears. He had every right to be upset with me for curiously eyeing him. Instead, he half-smiled and said, "Let's go."

We spent the rest of the afternoon continuing our marathon of silence as I followed close behind him. Though I did catch him glance at me quite a few times. Whenever I looked back, he would turn away.

I spent most of the third night thinking about Darian. If I were honest with myself, he was always somewhere in my mind.

We passed a lonely village on our fourth day traveling east, perfectly set in a grassy field with mountains a short distance away. It was a village with about a hundred people and fifty or so cottages.

When Razz helped an older woman we were passing reach some fruit from her orchard tree, she insisted on making us food. It was nearing dinnertime, so we graciously accepted.

It wasn't so much a meal, but a plate of bread and fruit. Regardless, we were both grateful. She even gave us a cup of cider that caused me to feel a bit tipsy. Razz had two cups and certainly felt tipsy too, considering how clumsy he suddenly became.

The older woman must have felt lonely, as she insisted we stay overnight. She had a spare bedroom with only one bed, though it was big enough to fit both of us.

Razz was a complete gentleman and insisted on sleeping on the floor. I told him how ridiculous that was, considering we both could easily fit in the bed. So he agreed to sleep beside me.

Though summer had just begun, it was an exceptionally warm night. We both kept fully clothed, which only made it warmer. But he was too tipsy to care.

His back was facing me when I asked, "Did all these people come from one of the nine realms?"

"Obviously," he said with a brief grin. "Most villagers in Elloriya, like these people, are known as The Ordinaries. They rarely possess powers from their realm. Some villagers have supernatural abilities but still broke ties from their kingdom by creating their own village on free land."

"But what if some of The Ordinaries are from this realm? I mean, how do you know for sure that there were no people here when everyone first arrived in Elloriya?"

"Because it was a small realm that was void of life. The more people and animals that came here, the bigger the realm became," he said, ending with a sigh.

"How did the realm grow?"

The bed shook as Razz turned to face me and propped himself up on his elbow. He scanned me before he said with eyes half-closed, "You ask a lot of questions."

I kept my head resting on a pillow as I looked back at him. "Oh, sorry."

"Magic."

"What?"

He yawned as he said, "You asked how this realm can grow. The answer is by magic."

"How can magic be so . . . powerful?"

He dropped his propped elbow and allowed his head to fall onto a pillow a few inches away from me.

"How did you come to be born?" he asked, eyes still half-closed.

"Um. The same way you came to be born," I responded rather awkwardly.

"Which is?"

"Well, two people came together, and had—" I paused, feeling more awkward.

"Sex," he said, shyly smirking.

"Yes. Then a sperm found an egg, and I grew in my mother's belly until she was ready to give birth," I said quickly.

He softened his voice when he said, "Some people might just call *that* magic. Just as your mother's belly grew over time to make room for you, Elloriya too grew bigger to make room for all those who came here."

"Oh. Okay. I guess that makes sense. Sort of."

"Never waste your time trying to make sense of magic," he said with heavy eyelids. "Magic can be anything it wants to be and do anything it wants to do. Those who harbor magic think they're in control when it's really their magic that makes the final decision."

A yawn later, his eyes closed, and so did mine.

CHAPTER 10

The Blue Light

The next day, Razz was far more pleasant to be around. After our kind host insisted we take some fruit from her orchard, we continued east. Razz walked beside me the entire day instead of always being several feet ahead, as I had quickly gotten used to.

"When's your birthday?" I randomly asked, attempting to get to know him better since I would spend every day with him for the next—however long this journey would take to fulfill our mission of getting Darian back.

"My birthday is the sixteenth of the fifth lunar in autumn."

My face twisted in confusion. "What?"

With a look of sudden realization, he explained, "Your age goes up once every four years, depending on the day, the lunar, and the season you were born. For example, your birthday is the eleventh of the first lunar in winter."

"You remember my birthday?"

"Most people in Elloriya remember your birthday. You were the first life born in this realm. So it's kind of a big deal."

I always wanted to know when my birthday was. And now that I knew, I didn't know what to make of it. I couldn't even understand it, let alone wrap my head around it being a big deal.

"So, in Elloriya, everyone grows a year older once every four years? That doesn't make sense."

For whatever reason, he looked admiringly at my stupidity as he broke into a beam before responding a little slower. "There are six lunars in each year, or rather, each season. Each lunar consists of twenty-two days. So each year here is one hundred thirty-two days. And there are four years—one for each season—in one zenith. So your age goes up once every zenith, which is five hundred twenty-eight days. Understand?"

"Yes," I said, half truthfully.

A slight grin hid on his face. "Liar," he teased.

The conversation was so good between us; the day went by rather quickly.

It was already well into the night when we had settled ourselves at the top of a mountain, allowing a perfect view of the stars. We set up a blanket and stared at the night sky in silence. When I glanced over at Razz, he was looking despairingly at the stars, and it broke my heart a little.

Perhaps it was out of pity, or maybe an act of comfort, but I scooched closer to him and grabbed his hand. He broke his gaze off the night sky and looked at my hand before his eyes settled on mine. I looked back at him with a friendly smile before removing my hand from his.

The mountain grass was thick below the blanket, adding comfort as I readied myself for sleep. "Good night, Razz," was all I said as I turned my back to him and fell into slumber.

The sixth day had finally arrived. If Razz was correct, today would be the day we reached the eastern kingdom. We had long passed the woods and were now continuing through the grassy mountains.

With much effort, I attempted to make conversation with Razz, but today he chose silence over talking to me. He wasn't rude about it. He just shut me out.

I watched from behind as Razz repeatedly pulled seeds from his pocket. He would chew on a few at a time for a while before spitting them to the ground. Then he would return his hand to his pocket to pull out a few more.

I tried to ignore the irritating sound of Razz's teeth grinding those damn seeds as I held the moonstone on my chest. *Can you hear me, Darian? Can you hear me?*

My thoughts repeated over and over, desperate to make some sort of connection with Darian. Hoping he had the gift of telepathy—shit—hoping I had the gift of telepathy, I kept trying, unsure of how to properly speak to another's mind. I had sort of used telepathy before, with Darian in his charzdaine form and with Razz a couple of times. So, with a thread of hope, I kept trying.

Where are you, Darian? Can you hear me? It's Attica. Darian, where are—

Suddenly I turned dizzy. My body went numb as my surroundings folded. I lost my balance and surely fell to the ground, though I didn't feel it. Once the dizziness stopped, a gleaming blue light encompassed me. It was perhaps the bluest light I had ever seen.

"Attica." The blue light faded as someone called out my name. "Attica." My name was called louder. "Attica, wake up!"

My eyes shot open to the rays of the sun lacing through the golden curls atop Razz's head. The short braid behind his left cuffed ear was nearly touching my face as I realized I was lying on a bed of rotting grass in the middle of the valley.

Razz grabbed my weak arm and gently sat me up. As he did, the sun gleamed brightly on his black ear cuff, revealing dark stones embedded inside the metal. I had never noticed the stones until now.

"You okay?" he asked as he ran his hand over the back of my head, perhaps checking for blood from my sudden fall.

My voice cracked when I asked, "What happened?"

"You took a plunge to the ground without giving me any warning to catch you." He pulled out his canteen, placing it in my hand. "Hydrate," he instructed.

So I drank, and as the lukewarm water poured down my throat, I thought of the blue light I had seen.

He went through his bag and pulled out a white apple. "Perhaps you should have eaten earlier." He handed me the fruit as I sat by a stream of water running down the center of the valley.

As I sunk my teeth into the sweet, crisp apple, Razz moved his hand toward my face. "You have dirt on your cheek," he said softly, wiping it off with his thumb. His voice remained gentle when he asked, "Are you okay, Attica?"

"Yes, I'm fine!" I responded, somewhat defensively. And I was fine.

After pushing myself off the ground, I brushed my clothes and gave Razz a fake smile. I took small bites of the fruit as we continued our stroll under the baking sun.

My fainting didn't change the silence between us, but Razz had now walked beside me instead of a few feet ahead. He glanced over every other minute, likely making sure I wouldn't faint again. After the fifth time of him glancing at me, I made a stupid face that cracked his solemn lips into a grin.

It was finally comfortable walking beside him again, even with silence filling the space between us. With Razz, I felt like I could be myself, for the most part. Unlike his brother, he never made me feel unsure of our friendship. Well, at least not before this journey we began six days ago.

With Razz's brutal honesty of wanting to "cut the cord of our connection," I still fell back into ease with him, even when he wasn't talking to me.

"How much longer?" I asked, nibbling the half-eaten apple.

"I take it you don't travel by foot very often." His response was hardly an answer.

My voice was flat and somewhat irritated with how sore my feet were when I responded, "No. Not long distances."

He chuckled. "Unless you figure out how to travel through the grid, get used to it." His chuckle quickly faded into silence as he lowered his brows in discontent. I knew he instantly regretted his choice of words as he was surely thinking of his brother lost in the grid.

He had never really answered my question. I had no clue how much longer our journey east would be.

We had passed seventy-nine bushes in the last starlight alone. That's how bored I was; counting bushes along the valley was my only source of entertainment that kept me from thinking about my aching feet.

Razz pulled out the compass, still pointing east. He put his arm up in front of me at the sound of rustling leaves nearby. We were no longer alone. Was it another faun?

I prepared to cover my ears from the dreadful shriek when, finally, the source of the sound revealed itself from behind a bush. It was a white rabbit with red eyes and small antlers on its forehead like a deer. I had never seen a rabbit with antlers before now. It cautiously hopped toward us and began sniffing our feet.

Razz looked curiously from the compass to the antlered rabbit. He put a hand in his pocket and bent down, speaking to the little animal as if it could understand him. "We have come with a gift for the Tera Kingdom." I assumed he meant the relic. "We are friends of Gemma's. Can you lead the way?"

He pulled his hand out of his pocket and opened his fingers. The white-furred animal eyed his palm, then sniffled its little nose over the handful of seeds. After the creature finished eating, it looked back at Razz and turned, hopping away from us.

"Follow the jackalope," Razz said.

"Why?"

"Because it will lead us to where we need to go."

I thought it was strange, but nevertheless, we followed the hopping jackalope to a hidden part of the valley surrounded by bushes of bramble. The jackalope went through the bramble to the center. It wasn't until we made our way through the tangled branches that we realized the jackalope had vanished down a tunnel below the ground.

Razz looked again at the illuminated compass before pocketing it. He turned to me at the entrance with his hand held out. I reluctantly took his hand, and we descended into the underground tunnel of intertwined branches.

He kept a tight grip on my fingers as we followed the jackalope. It was dark, and I knew we must have been deep underground from the earthy smell.

A bouncing vibration shook under my feet with every hop the jackalope took.

As we silently made our way through the dim tunnel, I continued eating the apple, wondering why Razz had such a tight grip on my hand. Perhaps it was his way of ensuring he would catch me in case I fainted again.

Each crunch of the apple was so loud, I overheard Razz say to himself, "Oh sweet heaven, she is still eating that damn thing." His soft breath brushed my ear when he whispered, "I could have eaten an entire cauldron of those by now."

I responded with a weak chuckle.

Just as I wondered how long the tunnel continued, I finally caught sight of light peering at the end of the tunnel. The farther we moved forward, the brighter it became. When it was bright enough to see the intricate details of the woven branches encircling us, Razz released my hand.

When we had finally reached the tunnel's exit, the jackalope hopped up branch-braided steps. With a curious peek outside the tunnel, my sight was greeted with sunlight spreading its shimmering rays over a wonderland of nature.

CHAPTER 11

The Way In

Razz held out his hand to me as I exited the tunnel. Instead of placing my hand in his—as if I needed help climbing the last two steps—I simply smiled and said, "Thank you," as I placed the remains of the apple I took "so damn long" to eat in his hand. Passing him, I looked over my shoulder, catching a smirk on his dapper face.

A path lined with towering ancient-looking stones lay just ahead, and it wasn't long before at least thirty jackalopes surrounded Razz and me. Some had large antlers, others small. Some were snowy white. Others were varying shades of brown, gray, and black. A brown jackalope with green eyes seemed especially fond of me as it stayed by my feet while the others hopped toward Razz.

Razz knelt and handed the apple core I gave him to the jackalopes and whatever remaining seeds he had. They swarmed to the fruit and seeds, devouring what was left of them.

Razz pulled out the brass compass. "Where to?" he asked. The tarnished arrow spun fast until it suddenly stopped, pointing at the path between the stones.

It certainly seemed like the obvious path, except it led to nothing but mountains that were undoubtedly too steep to climb—another dead end.

With a heavy sigh, previously thinking we had arrived at our destination, I turned to Razz with lowered brows. "Where do we go now?"

All the jackalopes passed us with a spring in each hop along the path toward the mountains ahead.

Razz shrugged with a stupidly endearing half-smile. "Follow the jackalopes."

There was hardly enough room for my feet as I struggled along the narrow path between the touching mountains. Turning my gaze over my shoulder, I found Razz chuckling, obnoxiously finding humor in my struggle as he effortlessly followed my stumbling steps.

Past the mountains was a forest. A beige boulder with three small flowers growing from it caught my attention at the forest's edge. But how could flowers grow out of a giant rock?

As I questioned what my eyes were seeing, the boulder moved and grew taller until I realized it was no boulder at all.

Looking back at us was a shirtless man with beige skin—the same skin I was sure was a giant rock a moment ago when the man was kneeling.

When we were finally close enough, I was quick to notice his hair, brows, and lashes were made of thin green grass. He even had sparse grass in place of hair on his chest. The closer we got, the more I noticed an occasional flower on parts of his body, which grew from his skin, as some flower buds had yet to bloom on his shoulder. As I fully took in the strange sight of him, I couldn't help but admire the raw beauty of his uniqueness.

He picked up a basket of berries and looked inquisitively at us before wandering off. We followed in his direction and found ourselves in a canopied forest engulfed by moss, ferns, and the fresh scent of cedar. Though it provided an abundance of shade with every step, the sparkling sun dusted the assorted leaves.

It wasn't too long before we reached a gardenesque village spread with people and the sight of the Tera Kingdom in the distance.

The jackalopes scattered, and we seemed to have lost the one we were initially following. We were now on our own.

I took in the beautiful appearance of a dark-skinned woman with thick dreadlocks of moss and intertwined flowers flowing well past her shoulders. There were many around her with similar dreadlocks. A shirtless man with pale freckled skin, thin copper dreads, and a patch of vivid green moss on his muscled chest kept his eyes on me with a questionable smile until I was out of sight.

As I passed under a floral archway filling the air with a pleasant aroma, I caught an even stranger sight: a posh-looking woman with fluttering monarch wings on the outer edges of her bright honeyed eyes. She was talking to a man with black fluttering wings cornering his hazel eyes. I couldn't tell if the eye-wings were a fashion choice or genetics.

Some people in the village appeared far more ordinary, allowing Razz and me to blend in. Except most of them had pointed ears like Gemma.

We were strolling in the direction of a beige stone castle engulfed in vines, branches, and decaying roses—surely the Tera Kingdom. We nearly reached a tall garden maze filled with the sweet scent of blooming roses when my breathing halted at the sudden appearance of a dreary-looking courier in my path. The much-too-pale turquoise seahorse thing had a noticeably bent wing as it wrestled with gravity. The swirled moon shell on its back, weighing it down, surely didn't help.

Razz was talking with a villager to get information on how to enter the Tera Kingdom when the courier appeared in its struggle before me. A ribbon of orange light barely escaped its shell, carrying the whisper of Etiwa's voice. "Remember, each kingdom has a place for its relic. You will know when you find it. But you must tell no one of your plan." Just when I thought that was the entirety of her message, her voice continued. "Zaydarian's life depends on your success." And just when I expected the courier to vanish, its wings gave out, and it spiraled to the ground, where it suddenly twitched.

Razz must have seen the color leave my face as he broke his conversation with the villager and returned to me. I knelt to the ground and held the nearly lifeless courier in my hands as its already pathetic coloring dwindled.

"Why is it dying?"

Razz knelt beside me. "It shouldn't have been able to make it past the barrier. What a champion." He looked from the courier in my hands to my saddened eyes. "Who was the message from?"

"Etiwa said not to tell anyone of our plan to return the relics." I didn't bother mentioning the last part that made my stomach turn.

"She must have used a shit-load of her magic to get the courier past the barrier. It was a risky move on her part."

"So then, why didn't she just tell you telepathically? Was the message really worth robbing the courier of its life?"

The courier turned gray and still.

He shrugged and guessed, "Etiwa must have read something in her cards—a message telling her how important it was that you hear it from her."

Razz dug a small hole in the soil with his bare hand, took the dead courier from me, and buried it before plucking nearby flowers to place on top. Then he grabbed my hand and stood, gently pulling me up with him.

"Why do you think she wants us to keep it secret?" I asked, still staring at the courier's fresh grave beside the nearby bush.

He pondered for a moment before responding, "Well, if Shakar found out about our plan to return magic to the lower kingdoms, he would have every Orpheus after our heads. Not to mention," — his face turned sour— "I'd likely never see Darian again."

The beat of my heart stopped at the dreadful thought of Razz never seeing his brother again—and of me never seeing his brother again. And it would all be my fault.

Fear, worry, and doubt bled through my already tangled thoughts. And just like that, everything I had learned about being balanced and detached from my ego withered from my mind.

Razz moved before me and gripped my shoulders, but I stayed staring at the pebbled path we stood upon with shrinking hope. I finally looked up at his calming eyes as he said, "We will get my brother back. We will succeed at this!"

"We don't even have a suitable plan!" I snapped.

He released his grip from my shoulders. "So we'll improvise. These people are not our enemies." He quickly silenced himself and smiled at a passerby with sporadic markings of tree bark and heart-shaped leaves on his otherwise humanlike skin. "We can make friends with them. We just have to keep one part of our plan secret."

He grabbed my hand and strutted forward through the garden maze, smiling at everything and everyone around us. I couldn't help but be impressed by his carefree essence and biting confidence while also wondering where the hell this Razz was for the last five days. Though I was sure a part of him was putting on a brave face for the both of us, I was quickly feeling more certain that the plan could work. Razz gave me that sense of hope we both needed.

As the tightness in my chest loosened, the vibrance of the floral maze popped. It was so enchanting and vivid; it was like a dream. But the farther we strolled, the drier and more rotten the green leaves and pastel roses became.

After being denied entry to the castle through several well-thought-out excuses to why we needed to enter, we stayed in a shabby abandoned shack in the nearby village for three days trying to come up with a plan. The guards hadn't once opened the doors of the court in those passing days, so to sneak in with Razz's ability to turn us invisible was not even an option. Razz didn't know what anyone looked like inside the castle, so he couldn't bend our appearance to look like someone who belonged.

On the fourth day, when he changed his appearance to a short man with dark hair, brown eyes, and a rough beard—looking like one of the guards—that same guard came out of the village to rotate shifts.

As we strolled through the maze on the fifth day of our arrival, trying to see who had finally stepped out of the castle, we heard the cries and swearing of a child—a boy with curly red hair, bright green eyes, and small pointed ears. He had to have been no older than ten. He was wrestling with a thorn bush tightly gripping his leg, using threatening words as if it could understand him.

Razz knelt beside the boy and whispered, "Run your finger between the thorns, gently."

The boy stopped cursing and ran his nimble finger between the thorns as instructed. The branch almost immediately released its tight grip on the boy's leg and slowly retracted as if it were a snake returning to its den. The boy jumped up and spat on the bush, angrily mumbling, "Never playing with you again," before turning to Razz, unfazed by his scratched and pricked leg.

"Who are you?" the child asked sharply.

Razz calmly responded, "I'm a friend of Gemma's. Do you know her?"

"Do I know my own sister?" he questioned grumpily, looking around in a moment of panic as he lowered his voice. "No! Never met her."

He headed toward the castle doors. As the boy continued forward with a tantrumlike stomp in each step, he turned over his shoulder and barked, "Aren't you coming?"

Razz turned to me with a grin. "Looks like we found our way in."

CHAPTER 12

The Tera Kingdom

We caught up with the boy—Gemma's little brother—who had yet to acknowledge me. He asked Razz, "How do you know my sister?" The boy spoke sharply, as if every question was an interrogation.

"Well, we sort of lived together for some time on the other side of the barrier."

We followed the boy down a path lined with towering standing stones toward steps that led up to the front doors of the vine-covered castle. Peach roses rotted on the high beige stone walls.

The front door's gilded antler handles were just a short distance away when the boy asked, "Have you come for the equinox festival?"

"Equinox? I thought that had to do with the sun and Earth," I said, looking to Razz instead of the boy for clarification.

The boy lowered his brows. "Earth? I have a book about that place. It says it's a planet that looks like Elloriya." He looked up at me for the first time. "Is that true?"

"Yeah, I guess," I answered.

The boy gasped. "You've been?"

"Yes," I replied. "And so has your sister."

His green eyes sparkled.

The boy led us up the steps and straight to the castle doors, where two knights dressed in gold armor guarded the entrance. The boy grabbed a dead rose off the wall, crumbling it to the ground as we stood waiting. Then he looked at the knights and shouted, "Well, what are you waiting for? I'm not going to stand here all day!"

One of the knights turned to the boy. "Bartlett, sir, these are not people of the court. You know the rules."

The boy moved in front of the knight with narrowed eyes, squinting up at a man several feet taller. "They are friends of my sister's. Now open the doors, or I'll tell my mother that you tried to touch my—"

"Okay, okay." The knight obeyed and opened the doors for us with a shade of terror in his eyes.

I couldn't help but wonder if Bartlett was a master manipulator or if what he was about to say was true.

Before us now was the inside of a beige stone castle engulfed in greenery—though much of the greenery had withered. The high ceilings, the archways, and nearly everything in between the plants and potted trees had stunning accents of gold.

Many of the aisle ceilings were draped with pale blue wisteria flowers. Though they were dried and nearly lifeless, they still released a pleasant aroma. Even with all the dreary plants, every sight was a delight to my foreign eyes.

Gilded pillars had hundreds of vibrantly colored crystals wrapped around them, each in an elegant, swirled design. There were windows and openings in every direction, including the ceiling, allowing the sun's light to shed over the courtyard.

People were working around us, polishing the gold, shining the crystals, cleaning the little statue gnomes spread throughout the courtyard garden, and tending to the dead plants. And each one gave young Bartlett a nervous bow of their head as he passed. For such a small boy, he seemed to have a large presence in this kingdom.

"So," the boy said, looking up at us, "why are you here?"

"Well," Razz began, and I had no idea what fabricated lie would roll off his tongue.

But before he had a chance to deceive Gemma's little brother, we turned a corner and ran into someone else—a teenager with reddish-blond hair, green-blue eyes, a freckled nose, and pointed ears. He glared at Bartlett before eyeing Razz and me.

"Bartlett, you brought strangers into our home?" he asked calmly.

"Not strangers, Wystan! They're friends of Gemma's!"

"Is this true?" The teen turned to Razz for an answer, again overlooking me.

"Yes," Razz replied.

"See!" Bartlett barked. "Now move, Wystan!"

A high-pitched scream nearby stole our attention. We all turned to find a small monkey attacking a woman tending to the indoor garden.

"Get your animal under control," Wystan said in a calm but authoritative tone to Bartlett.

Bartlett ran toward his pet, yelling, "Branch! Get your monkey butt on my shoulder!"

Razz laughed, adding to the irritation of the teenager standing before us now.

"Follow me," Wystan said with a deadpan stare.

Razz gave me a look of uncertainty as we followed Wystan, who kept silent while we trailed behind him down many halls.

We passed one tree I was especially fond of, filled with the most curiously shaped leaves, and though the edges and veins of the leaves were blackening, the remaining green was vivid like dazzling emeralds.

The castle was a golden wilderness that seemed endless as we passed countless crystal-embellished pillars and indoor gardens. Before turning a corner, I admired a sizable scarlet crystal fountain filled with rotting flowers.

We came to a sudden stop where a knight guarded an ornate gilded door.

Wystan whispered to the knight, just loud enough for me to hear, "Can you watch these two a moment?"

The knight responded with a nod before opening the door for him.

"That has to be heavy," Razz said to the knight, eyeing his gold metal armor. The knight didn't so much as look at Razz.

As we stood in awkward silence waiting, an attractive twenty-something-year-old girl with brown hair and matching eyes wearing a scuffed white dress with a beige apron strolled down the neighboring hall. She carried a stick of burning sage, gracefully sweeping it through the air.

Burning sage was something Gemma did nearly every day in the manor, so I had quickly learned of its cleansing energy.

The beautiful girl glanced at me before landing her eyes on Razz. Her cheeks swiftly surfaced a rosy hue as she bashfully looked away. Razz's stare followed the girl as she smoothly made her way in our direction. The closer she got, the more she eyed Razz. And the more she eyed Razz, the more he straightened.

The taste in my mouth turned sour as she glided her burning sage mere inches away from Razz's cock with a playful grin. It certainly caught any of his residual attention that wasn't already on her. It even caught the damn knight's attention.

As she happily lured Razz and the knight's interest, I stepped a short distance down the hall to a wall of draping purple plants. The smell of fresh lavender and eucalyptus grew stronger the closer I got.

My fingers were curious about the smooth texture of the leaves, as they indeed were neither lavender nor eucalyptus. As I dared to reach for a purple vine, I was startled.

"What are you doing?" a not-so-friendly voice spoke over my shoulder.

I turned to find none other than Wystan.

"Oh, I was just—" My tongue froze, and my thoughts tangled. I had done nothing wrong to my knowledge. But his tight lips and apparent distrust had me wondering otherwise.

"Attica, are you admiring the plants again?" Razz said, smoothly stepping in.

"Oh—yes!" I responded with a phony smile. "This one is especially my favorite," I stupidly said, lifting a wilted purple leaf, identical to the others.

Wystan clenched his jaw until I finally released the vine.

As his cold gaze pierced mine, he sharply said, "Come with me."

He led Razz and me through the golden door and into a massive room with soft pink wisteria flowers draping from the high ceilings and a colossal floral hill at the far end of the room.

On each side of the hill were twisted branches forming stairs to the top. A queen sat regally on her carved wooden throne, garnished with dazzling crystals. The empty throne beside her was engraved with a circled five-pointed star, also bedecked with impressive crystals.

The queen's head was delicately wrapped in a crown of gilded antlers, with jewels hanging elegantly between each point. She wore an embellished and embroidered ruby-red dress perfectly matching her red hair.

Wystan straightened. "Mother, these are the people Bartlett brought into our home."

Her rich green eyes bore into me. "What are you doing in my kingdom?" she asked coldly.

My tongue tied. I didn't have a decent answer. Etiwa had made herself clear when she warned me not to tell anyone of our plan to return the relics.

Razz stepped forward, bowing his head. "Your majesty. We are friends of Gemma's and—"

The queen stood up from her throne, and before Razz could speak another word, she said, "You know my daughter?"

"Yes," Razz replied as the queen made her way down the stairs.

"Where is Gemma?" The icy tone of her words rattled my bones.

Razz was hesitant to respond. "She's outside the barrier."

"That doesn't explain what you're doing here in my home."

"I have a way with energy, ma'am. I believe I can find an opening in the grid to help bring your daughter home to you." Razz was far more convincing than I could have been.

"She hasn't responded to any of my couriers since the Orpheus took her from me thirteen zeniths ago." Her eyes glossed over. "I thought she was dead. We had prepared to go to war with the Orpheus again to get her back, but it was too late. Shakar said he had her sent to another world and then threatened to take my next child if we tried to get revenge." She touched her belly. "I was pregnant with Wystan at the time."

Razz stepped closer to her. "I'm sorry to hear that. Unfortunately, Shakar did send Gemma to another world—to Earth. But a friend of ours, Etiwa, and the waldworfs helped us get her back to Elloriya."

She let out a relieving gasp with a hand over her chest. "Then I'll send her a courier now."

Razz took another gentle step forward. "You can try. But we believe couriers don't make it past the barrier anymore unless powerful magic is used, and even then, it is still dangerous. I've tried sending my parents couriers when I was trapped on the edge. They stopped replying twelve zeniths ago. And I know Gemma tried sending you couriers when she returned to Elloriya. I saw for myself. But I think Shakar started tracking our messages initially when he forced the rest of us on the edge. After a year, I believe he created some magical wall that refused couriers to pass between the barrier."

At first, she said nothing. But then, the queen looked from me to Razz. "Are you two an item?"

Razz quickly responded, "No, ma'am."

She moved close to Razz and unlatched his vest. "Good. You may stay in the guest quarters until first light tomorrow."

Gemma's brother clenched his jaw at this.

The queen's emerald eyes narrowed deep into Razz. "I expect you to come through on your word and bring my daughter home."

"Of course, your majesty," he said with that damn charming smile as he gently bowed the tip of his head, keeping his steady eyes on the queen.

The queen moved her rosy lips to Razz's ear and whispered something, leaving her older son and me in awkward silence. Finally, she released her hand from Razz's chest and turned to her son. "Wystan, show them to the garnet room." She looked at me when she said, "It has two beds."

"Thank you, Queen . . . ?" Razz gave a tilt of his head.

"Blair," she responded, eyes heavy on Razz.

"Thank you, Queen Blair," he said with a bow before we crossed the throne room to the exit.

Before we stepped out, the queen casually added, "Oh, and if you do not fulfill your promise, or I find you have come here with other intentions, you will be beheaded."

I practically choked on my nerves as we stepped out the door.

CHAPTER 13

The Tree Cottage

We walked in silence to the guest quarters, passing more withered ferns, gilded accent walls, crystal-embellished vases, and hanging lanterns along the way. This had to have been the wealthiest kingdom ever in existence, with the amount of gold in nearly every direction.

When we finally arrived at the garnet room, Razz turned to Wystan with a delightful smile. "Thank you, Wystan. You have been most kind," he said in an overly friendly tone, layered in sarcasm.

Wystan squinted his green-blue eyes as the freckles on his nose crinkled and then whipped his strawberry blond head around, striding back toward the busy part of the castle.

We stepped into a room with dead plants in every corner, accents of red stone, and two beds adjacent to each other. It was a dreary-looking room.

Razz sat on the farthest bed with a grin on his face.

I raised a brow. "What's with the smile?"

"We have officially made it into the Tera Kingdom. That's not an easy task!" He tossed his bag on the bed and threw his head on the pillow.

"We got lucky. But if we're caught returning the relic or cannot bring Gemma back by tomorrow morning, our necks will be met with a blade," I reminded him.

"So, we won't get caught," he said with relentless confidence.

I sat on the other bed and looked back at Razz. "What did the queen whisper to you?"

His grin turned cocky. "She wants me to visit her chamber when the king is out later."

For some reason, this made my stomach irk.

"What about Cece? Weren't you two a thing?" I was looking for any excuse to find out what happened between them.

His cheerful grin turned sour. "We were hardly a thing. Plus, she has a man now. So she made her choice."

"But—"

"Can we not talk about Cece?" he said, his tone rough as rocks.

"Yeah, sorry. But you're not actually going to visit the queen's chamber, are you?"

"No," he said, getting up and heading toward the door.

"Where are you going?"

He didn't even bother to look at me when he replied, "To get some fresh air."

And then he left, leaving me alone in the room, regretting that I brought up Cece at all.

An entire starlight passed, and Razz still hadn't returned to the garnet room. I spent the whole time trying to silence my mind, hoping for some guidance or feeling to arise, telling me what to do next. But I received no internal advice or response of any kind. Instead, thoughts of Darian were like weeds in my mind, relentlessly growing.

It was nothing new. My thoughts always circled back to him. *Where is he now? Is he still stuck in the grid? Probably. Is he safe? Does he blame me?*

I couldn't help but blame myself, even though Razz told me it wasn't my fault. Maybe that was true, but it was my suggestion that put Darian's life in danger after all.

My chest tightened every time I replayed the moment he stepped into the grid with unreadable eyes on me before he vanished. I could hardly breathe at the thought of never seeing him again.

It was nearing lunch, and all I had eaten was an apple. But the thought of eating anything didn't appeal to me. All I wanted was to get Darian back. And to do that, I had to leave the garnet room and find where the relic belonged in this vast kingdom, whichever relic that was.

Maybe I was being paranoid, but I hid my bag under the bed before getting ready to leave the room. Just as I prepared to exit, there was a gentle knock on the door.

"Is anybody there?" a male's voice said.

I opened the door to find a young man with brown hair and hazel eyes dressed in casual, yet tattered, clothing. He was ordinary in looks, but something about his energy was inviting and pleasant. I smiled as a means of greeting.

"I was told we had guests staying here. I brought fresh towels for the bathing room. May I?" he asked, tilting toward entering the room.

"Oh, yes, of course."

I stepped aside, and he made his way to the attached bathing room. He set the towels down on the bathroom counter before turning back to me. "Is there anything I can do for you?"

I didn't hesitate to ask, "Would you be so kind as to show me around?"

With a genuine smile, he said, "I'd love to. I'm Lance, by the way." He bowed his head, opening the door for me.

"I'm Attica," I replied, stepping into the hall.

If it wasn't beige walls garnished in gold meeting my sight, it was rotting trees, plants, flowers, or jaw-dropping crystals—some of which were larger than me.

"We hardly ever have guests the queen approves of staying overnight. You and your friend must have important matters here." He looked at me with an arched brow, likely waiting for an explanation of our visit. Instead, I changed the subject.

"So, I hear there's a festival tonight. Are you going?"

"If my sister and I finish our duties around the court, then yes," he said, polishing a towering amethyst crystal on our path.

Just then, the heavy smell of burning sage surrounded us, and a familiar girl strolled up the hall.

"I was just speaking of you," Lance said to the girl with matching brown hair and rich brown eyes. "Attica, this is my sister, Camille."

She smiled, glancing past the smoke of burning sage. "Hello, Attica. Where did your friend go?"

It seemed all the females here were interested in Razz. They couldn't care less about my being here, which might actually work in my favor if I was going to secretly find where the relic belonged.

"Your guess is as good as mine," I replied, glancing at the sage stick she so comfortably caught Razz's attention with earlier. She sauntered off without so much as a goodbye to her brother or me.

"I need to pick up some tea leaves for the festival. Would you like to join me?" Lance asked.

To find where the relic belonged, I needed to see more of the Tera Kingdom, more of their land, more of their people. So I responded, "As long as I'm not intruding."

There was a kindness in his grin. "Not at all. As I said, we rarely have guests, and some company would be nice."

He headed toward the castle's exit, and I followed beside him. Lance turned to the guard blocking the door. Why there needed to be guards on both sides of the castle entrance was beyond me.

After an awkward moment of waiting at the door, Lance finally said, "Queen Blair has sent me off for essentials."

The guard didn't move.

"It's for tonight's festival, and the queen's guest will be joining me on this errand."

The guard looked at him, then me, then back at him, and with slight annoyance, he finally stepped aside and opened the door.

We walked outside under a blue sky, overlooking a green land of exotic people selling their goods.

Before entering the maze of pastel roses, Lance looked over his shoulder at the guard before turning to me. "Sorry about that. He doesn't like me very much."

"Why?" I asked, noticing a mint green rose in the garden maze that I could have sworn moved as I passed by it.

"I don't know. It might have something to do with me kicking his ass in the last thorngore tournament."

"What's thorngore?"

"It's a game with a labyrinth for a board, a rolling stone of numbers, and a pawn for each player. If you have time, we should play."

"Yeah, maybe," I responded, knowing full well that I couldn't spare any time to play a board game.

When we exited the garden maze, an older woman with disheveled moss dreadlocks and bushy moss brows stepped before me with an outstretched arm filled with hanging flower crowns.

"For the festival, miss? Only one gild a piece." She smiled kindly, preparing to place a floral crown on my head.

My eyes fell longingly on the purple one, but I replied, "I don't have any gilds. Thank you anyway."

Her smile vanished as she walked off, searching for her next buyer.

It surprised me how the purple crown would have been my first choice since there were yellow flowered crowns to choose from, and yellow was always my favorite color. Even after going through the chakra portals, I was still discovering hidden parts of myself I had no idea existed.

We strolled through the marketplace, passing many exotic, earthy people selling goods for the festival. I was tempted to stop at each station to see what things I'd find. But Lance walked past each one without the curiosity I held.

While passing the decorations, showcasing a sparkling, towering image of the sun, my eyes swept around for Razz. But of course, he was nowhere to be seen, leaving me to wonder where he was and what he was doing.

"So how does equinox work here? I don't know much about astronomy," I admitted.

"Well, tonight is the night of equinox, which means the sun will be in perfect alignment with the nine realms," Lance explained. Though I didn't understand how the sun could align with other realms, I at least knew more than I did before.

It wasn't long before we reached the enchanting, canopied forest where we walked up a long bridge made of vines and branches. The bridge arched upward, taking us at least fifty feet off the ground before it finally leveled flat in the air.

The bridge had an archway made from braided branches and ventured off in many directions, creating paths to hundreds of trees. Children ran past us, laughing and playing.

Each tree we passed had a cottage home high off the ground. The tree cottages were a delightful sight. Each one was strung with twinkling fairy lights, adorned with flowers, and had doors and roofs made from wood and branches.

We finally arrived at a tree cottage with an exceptionally large door. The cottage did not appear as cheery as the others. It may have been the only one not decorated with flowers or fairy lights.

On the wooden door was a circle of small stones and a braided *X* made of laced twigs and vines centering the ring of rocks. Lance knocked, then turned back to me with a comfortable smile. His hazel eyes blended effortlessly with the surrounding brown bark of the trees and their cascading green leaves.

I was quick to bring my attention back to the door. He must have noticed my interest in the strange symbol as he whispered in my ear, "It's for protection."

From what? I wondered.

When the door finally opened, my lips parted in surprise. A sizable man with gray stonelike skin answered the door. He scanned me, appearing uneasy in my presence.

"Augur, this is Attica. Attica" —he held up a hand toward the stonelike man— "Augur."

The man grunted.

"She's a guest at the court," Lance clarified.

The man raised a stony brow at me before cautiously stepping aside, allowing us entrance to his home.

Sun peered through the branched walls and ceiling. The ceiling was lush with an array of vines and flowers draping low. The sun's rays spread between the hanging plants onto the wooden furniture where Lance and I seated ourselves. I found it strange that none of the plants or flowers were dried or wilted like in the castle. Instead, each was lush with life.

Under a cauldron of water, Augur prepared a small fire nested with stones. He handed Lance and me each an empty wooden cup before sweeping his gaze over the plants hanging from his ceiling. His gray eyes stilled on a plant with yellow leaves. He grabbed a few leaves and crushed them in his stonelike hand before releasing them into the wooden cups we held.

It was silent for some time before Lance spoke up. "The queen requested violet shrune tea leaves for the festival."

Augur looked puzzled. "You mean green shrune?" His voice was like heavy rolling gravel.

"No," Lance replied surely. "She was adamant about having violet shrune tea at the equinox celebration."

With a wooden spoon, Augur poured hot water into both our cups. The steaming water mixed and swirled with the yellow leaves, releasing a smooth, buttery aroma.

Augur grabbed five lush vines of purple leaves and placed them in a burlap bag before turning back to Lance.

His voice was deep and gravelly when he said, "I hope your queen knows what she requested." He handed Lance the bag of shrune leaves. But before he released his grip from the bag, he warned, "I suggest no more than one cup per guest."

Augur was busy putting out the fire under the cauldron, so I stood to leave, but Lance grabbed my arm and whispered, "It is insulting if we leave before we finish our tea."

I quickly sat back down.

Lance had nearly finished his tea, but I had yet to take a single sip. As I began drinking from the wooden cup, sending the buttery sweet liquid down my throat, I wondered if Augur or Lance knew anything about the relics.

As I attempted to conjure up some not-so-obvious questions, I finished my tea, leaving nothing but soaked, crushed leaves at the bottom of the cup. Augur held out a wooden tray, relieving Lance and me of the teacups.

Just as a perfectly meticulous question about relics and the kingdom's lack of magic prepared to escape my tongue, Augur looked curiously at my emptied cup, breaking the silence before my prying question had a chance to be heard.

Augur's gaze wandered further into my teacup, and I was certain he was speaking to me when he said, "There are two paths destined for you. One is filled with danger, the other with greatness. Without one, the other cannot be fulfilled."

Lance glanced at me in confusion while reaching into his pocket, pulling out five gold coins—not gilds, not clusters of gold, but actual coins—and setting them onto the wooden table. It was the first time I had seen coins in this realm.

"Thank you, Augur," Lance said.

"The queen is very generous. Relay my thanks," Augur said, placing the coins into a nearby bowl. Then his gaze fell onto me, expressionless. His gray eyes were so heavy on me, I nearly forgot my manners.

"Um, thank you for the tea. It was lovely."

His response was a simple grunt.

Just as Lance and I stepped out of his tree cottage, Augur reached a heavy fist out the door before me. He opened his stone-plastered hand, revealing a small red mushroom.

"When the sun goes down, you may eat it." He placed it on my palm then closed his front door.

Lance looked just as confused as I did.

"Whatever he saw in that cup of yours must have been compelling," Lance said, leaving me to wonder what exactly it was Augur saw in my tea leaves.

CHAPTER 14

Vindication

By the time Lance and I returned to the castle after eating a late lunch together, it was mid-afternoon. During lunch, I thought or hoped, he might help me uncover details, valuable knowledge—something, anything—about the relics and where the one for this kingdom belonged, but he seemed utterly oblivious to any such thing. The only thing I learned was the king's name: King Cashel.

Of course, I didn't ask Lance directly about the relics, at least not with Etiwa's warning of keeping it hushed. I was careful not to raise suspicion with my curious questions. He was hardly helpful with information about the kingdom's history, magic, or relic. But he was kind, and for that, I was grateful.

Back at the castle, Lance welcomed me to accompany him as he checked off his chore list, continuing the preparation for the equinox festival. I glanced in every room we passed, hoping I'd discover on my own where the kingdom's relic belonged. But nothing stood out except maybe Bartlett, who was running up and down the court halls chasing his wild monkey.

113

It was nearing time for the festival, and I had yet to bathe and ready myself. Lance kindly walked me back to the garnet room, where Razz opened the door. He didn't so much as look at me. Instead, his sight fell heavily on Lance.

"You are?" Razz asked coldly, eyes sharpening on him.

"Lance. You must be our other guest," he said kindly, holding out his hand.

Razz's eyes rocked between Lance's unwavering smile and his cordial hand. I had never seen Razz so stern before.

After an uncomfortably long moment, Razz shook Lance's hand before returning to the bedroom. He sat on the bed watching as I thanked Lance for allowing me to tag along for the day. Lance thanked me for my company before turning to leave the guest quarters.

The moment I closed the door, I turned to find Razz kicked back on the bed, still staring at me, face unreadable, as if he were his brother. Though, for some reason, I felt like a child in trouble.

"So . . ." A heavy weight of silence filled the tense space between us before he finally asked, "How was your day?"

I broke our awkward gaze and rummaged through my bag I hid under the bed before casually replying, "Um. It was okay, I guess. What did you do?" I couldn't help but wonder if he went off to find Lance's sister, who had clearly taken a quick liking to him.

"It seems I was the only one who spent the day looking for where the relic belongs because, believe it or not, we are here to restore whatever magic those damn relics hold so my brother doesn't lose his life to some soul-sucking garbage grid!" His words were sharp as blades. He had never spoken to me with that sort of intensity. And I had never dared to speak to him like that, until now.

My head whipped around. "Excuse me? You were the one who left me high and dry without the decency to tell me where you went off to! I waited for you, but you never returned. So I was left to figure out the puzzle of this kingdom on my own. At least until Lance showed up to take your place! Do you really think I forgot why we're here? I did everything I could think of to find where the relic belongs. Thanks for having little faith in my intentions!"

Before giving him a moment to respond, I grabbed my bag and headed straight to the attached bathing room, slamming the door behind me. I turned the bathwater on as loud as I could, stripped down furiously, and nearly threw myself in the gilded tub.

As I watched the water pour out from the faucet, I didn't expect so many tears to roll down my face. It had nothing to do with Razz and the way he spoke to me or how he assumed I wasn't trying everything I could to do my part with the damn relics. No! It had everything to do with Darian.

I missed every part of him. Even the wall he kept so high to shut others out. I would take that torturous distance any day over the relentless pain of not knowing if I'd ever see him again. And it was all my fault. No matter what anyone said, I was the one who had made the stupid, ignorant, psychotic suggestion that got him stuck in some fucking energy grid. I'm to blame!

The water rose higher and higher in the tub, nearly pouring over its brim. I had no choice but to turn it off, which meant I had to stop sobbing unless I wanted Razz to hear—which I didn't.

The moment I turned the water off, Razz's voice traveled through the other side of the door. "Attica, I'm sorry. When I was searching for you, I saw you walk off with Lance toward the forest, and I assumed you forgot why we came here. Or maybe I assumed your priorities changed. But I should have known better. And I'm—well, I'm sorry."

The tone of his voice held a high note of sincerity. I didn't know how to respond. I opened my mouth to try, but no words of forgiveness came out. But I did forgive him.

I prepared myself for the festival in the bathing room. Of course, I couldn't care less about the equinox celebration. But my gut told me to go. And my gut knew why I was here. So, I abided.

As I opened my bag and pulled out a long-skirted jumpsuit Gemma had given me with a rayon fabric coated with maroon leaves, my eye caught sight of something odd about the empty glass relics. All were empty except for one. They usually only filled when I touched them. But the cube-shaped relic was bare of my touch, yet there it sat, filled with dirt.

I quickly dressed, pinned my hair back, and grabbed my bag before opening the door to find Razz studying Darian's hand-drawn map on the bed.

"Thank you for your apology," I blurted, as my attention focused solely on the relic.

His jaw nearly dropped as he eyed my outfit, and in a partially tamed voice, he said, "You're going to the festival?" He failed his attempt at grasping the judgmental tone fraying off his tongue.

"I don't know why, but I feel like I need to go. It's somehow tied to the relic." I dumped the relics onto the bed. All but one was empty still.

Razz picked up the glass cube filled with dirt. "Well, we know which relic belongs to this kingdom."

After returning the rest of the relics to my bag, Razz handed me back the cube one. I placed it securely inside the small leather pouch purse strapped over my torso. I held the red mushroom Augur had given between my fingers as I turned back to Razz. "Are you coming?"

"I think it may be better if I continue to search here, inside the castle." Razz's brows lowered as his attention moved to my hand. "What's that?" He pointed at the mushroom.

"Oh, someone gave it to me." I quickly added it to the pouch resting on my hip, unsure if I would actually eat it.

Just as I prepared to exit the room, Razz grabbed my arm. He latched one coupling onto me and placed the other on himself.

"It's probably best if we have some sort of communication." He tapped his silver band with mine. My mind went numb, my body spread with chills, and a breath later, an energetic tie locked between us.

I couldn't help but ask, "What would happen if you didn't tap the couplings? Would it still work at a distance?" The feeling was rather unpleasant each time he clinked them. If I could avoid the dizzying sensation, I would, even if it weakened our connection.

"It would still work if we were near each other. But to be connected from a distance, we would need to tap the couplings for our energies to stay tied."

"Oh," I uttered, dissatisfied.

Razz opened the door for me, and we exited the guest quarters. We strolled through the castle together, passing an abundance of trees, including my favorite emerald tree of asymmetrical heart-shaped leaves with wilting edges. A maid was tidying the ground of dried leaves that had fallen off the dying branches in the courtyard, while another knelt to wipe dirt off a grumpy-looking statue gnome.

A deep voice echoed down a neighboring hall. When the man turned the corner, I knew it was Gemma's father, King Cashel, from his extravagant appearance. The king had dark blond hair, a heavy beard, an embellished fur cape, a much-too-big gold coin necklace, and a gilded antler crown like his wife's, but even bigger and without jewels hanging between each point. Wystan was walking beside him.

"The smartest kings are always prepared for war," King Cashel said to his son as we discreetly passed by. "But the greatest kings seek peace ahead of bloodshed. Don't tell your mother I said that. War is expensive, though sometimes necessary. But the wealth of our kingdom must always come first." His deep voice traveled effortlessly down the hall.

The king didn't look twice at Razz or me on our crossed path. Wystan, on the other hand, turned back with squinted eyes and a clenched jaw.

Razz broke his glance from Wystan with a slight shake of his head. "The kid doesn't trust easily, does he?"

When we finally reached the castle's front doors, the guards opened them, releasing a perfect view of the setting sun resting its remaining rays on scattered clouds.

My ears were greeted with a rhythmic mixture of steel and tribal drums. Fairy lights strung along the festival grounds, over the extensive garden maze, all the way to the forest in the distance.

Razz leaned close as he whispered, "Be careful, Attica."

I don't know what possessed me, but I leaned even closer to Razz and kissed him on the cheek at the sight of Lance's flirtatious sister walking up the steps of the castle in our direction.

What the hell was that? Why did I kiss his cheek? It was surely because I saw Camille, who I expected would do all she could to seduce Razz. The thought of it sickened me. I pushed the stupid kiss out of my mind and focused on my mission.

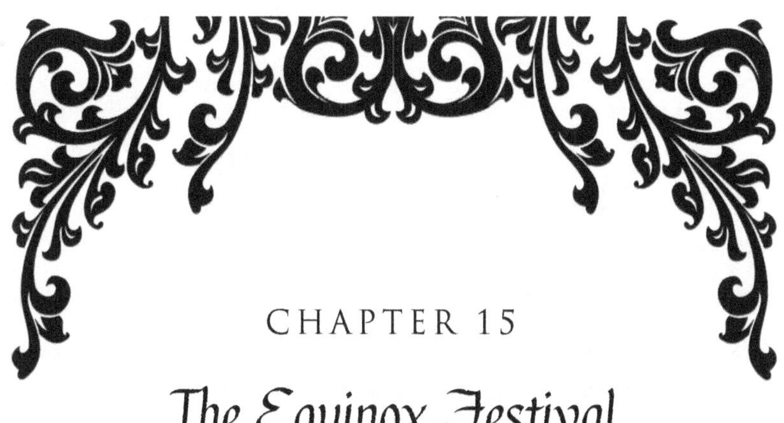

CHAPTER 15

The Equinox Festival

As I walked along the garden's pebbled path, a subtle light slowly brightened beneath the petals of the flowers and plants. The land was waking with illumination as the sky grew darker.

Moments later, I was snacking on the free food surrounded by several hundred extraordinarily exotic people. Some had pointed ears, some had moss dreadlocks, some had actual butterfly wings fluttering in the corners of their eyes, and others had hair and skin freckled with flowers or grass. There was even a group of people with patches of tree bark and sporadic leaves on their skin. I couldn't tell if one of them was flirting with another when she plucked a leaf off his arm with a playful smile.

People danced to the singing chants of the drummers, unfazed as children darted past, waving long ribbons of red, purple, yellow, and orange light. It took me a moment to realize they weren't ribbons at all, but vines of luminescent flowers weaving through the crowds.

A part of me wanted to forget my worries of Darian, of returning Gemma to her kingdom, of the sickening thought of the queen's order to cut off our heads if we failed her. But those worries reminded me of the importance of my being here.

So instead of losing myself to the festivities of the equinox celebration, I took a deep breath in the center of the joyful chaos and asked my gut what the hell I was doing here. To my dismay, no inkling came to mind.

Another deep breath filled my lungs, and this time, I closed my eyes. Surely, I was attracting stares from strangers, wondering what I was doing standing in the middle of a festival with my eyes closed, but I didn't care. As I focused on the soothing sound of my breath, the drumming, the chanting, the laughter, and the chaos became quiet.

What am I doing here? How will my being here help Darian? Where does the relic belong?

My inner questions received no response. My gut and intuition kept silent. My spirit guides kept quiet. So I made my inner voice even louder.

What am I doing here? How will my being here help Darian? Where does the relic belong?

My gut began gnawing. It was trying to tell me something. But what?

"Tea?"

A gentle voice jolted my eyes open. A plump woman with a kind smile was holding a tray with several wooden cups of glistening purple tea—undoubtedly violet shrune tea. I was prepared to kindly decline, but I couldn't ignore the intuitive feeling telling me to take a cup and drink. So, with a little hesitance, I took a cup, thanked her, and poured the warm liquid down my throat.

By the time I finished the cup of tea that tasted of sweet plums, it was officially the first dark starlight as all the plants, flowers, and trees were fully glowing their enchanting luminescent light. Even the earthy elements of people glowed where the beauty of nature grew from them. And to my surprise, the blue-inked tattoos on those dancing in the center of the drum circle were gleaming too.

It wasn't long before I realized the tea had an alcoholic effect on me. It was as if the tea itself grabbed me by the hand and pulled me to the drum circle. I didn't put up any sort of fight, but instead, I went along toward the rhythm of the drumming.

The purifying sounds of the steel drums swept through me, soothing some part of my soul as I moved with the dancers to the beat of the pounding drums intertwined with the harmony of steel.

With closed eyes, the drumming intensified. My soul searched for guidance as I danced and danced to every pound and sound of the varying drums.

Perhaps it was the hallucinogenic drink, but my soul found a light, blue in the distance. My body stayed dancing as my mind moved toward the light, and as I did, the drumming fell silent. I couldn't open my eyes, and no part of me fought it.

Physically, I was still dancing in the drum circle at the equinox festival. But mentally, I drifted to a place surrounded by nothing but sapphire light. In this place, I could see my hands and feet. My body was fully present in this endless blue void I knew I wasn't physically standing in. But it felt just as real as if I were there.

I mentally shouted, "Hello?"

Footsteps sounded from the empty distance. A man was walking through the blue light. Instantly, I recognized him as my spirit guide and the voice from the manor's golden room of stars: Astrophel.

His familiar, deep voice was a caress to my soul. "Hello, Attica. I see you have found a new form of communication."

"Yeah, I guess. But I don't know what I'm doing here."

He showed no doubt when he responded, "Yes, you do. You are looking for the relic's home."

"Is it here?" I stupidly asked.

He laughed and looked around at the blue void. "Where? There is nothing here but a grid of energy. However, I believe what is in your pouch will show you the way." He didn't even allow me to ask questions before he said, "Goodbye, Attica Spark. And best of luck on your journey." He turned and walked into an invisible exit.

"Wait!" I shouted after him, but he was gone.

In the blink of an eye, I was back in the center of the drum circle, heart pounding at the thought of what Astrophel revealed to me. He said we were in a grid of energy. Could that mean I was in the energy grid? I think I had somehow gone to the place Darian was lost in.

I replayed Astrophel's words in my mind: *I believe what is in your pouch will show you the way.* So I opened it, finding the cube relic and the red mushroom.

I took out the mushroom and dizzily stared at it as it lay harmlessly on my palm. The festival sounds and lights twirled in my head, faster than I could keep up.

As I wobbly stood, stilling my gaze on the mushroom, Augur's words filled my mind: *When the sun goes down, you may eat it.*

The sun had gone down nearly half a starlight ago, so I did what any desperate person would do in my shoes. I threw the mushroom into my mouth and swallowed it.

At first, nothing happened. But it wasn't long before my vision sharpened and my swaying mind calmed. The damn thing sobered me up! My irritation grew as I now stood in the festival, utterly sober, with no inkling of where I needed to go to return the relic.

I was closer to finding answers when I was drunk on shrune tea. So I spun around, searching for the kind woman carrying the tray of tea. I was ready to throw an entire cup down my throat again. Maybe I'd return to the blue light—to the energy grid—and find Darian myself.

I was quick to spot the woman holding the tray across the lawn near a man selling flower wands. After marching right up to her, I grabbed a cup of violet shrune tea. Just as I lifted it to my mouth, a stupid, sloppy drunk bumped into me, knocking my tea to the ground.

Irritation grew wildly within me, and just as I went for a third cup, I saw a red light galloping on the tray. It took me a moment to realize it was a small red horse about the size of my hand, jumping over the teacups.

"Are you all right, dear?" the kind woman asked, not showing any interest in the miniature horse trotting on her tray.

"What kind of magic is that?" I asked, mesmerized by the horse.

"What kind of magic is what, dear?"

"The horse," I clarified, not understanding why she didn't know what I was referring to. I couldn't believe she had yet to look at the bright red galloping horse running around the very tray she held.

She analyzed me as if I had gone mad. "Are you feeling all right?"

The horse jumped off her tray and suddenly became life-size. Even though it was somewhat transparent, no one took notice of the now sizable, gleaming red horse on the festival grounds. It seemed only I saw it.

My heart nearly stopped when the horse turned back and looked directly at me. Then, the moment it broke our locked gaze, it headed toward the castle.

It not only walked past nearly a hundred people who still didn't take notice, but it even walked through an entire group of women wearing different colored floral dresses matching the beautiful arrangement of flowers in their hair.

Of course, I couldn't help but follow the horse. I stayed close as it walked into the garden, through the maze, past the towering standing stones, and up the castle steps. It turned back to me once more before walking through the closed castle doors.

I turned to one of the guards and asked, "Can you please let me in?"

The guard looked me up and down. "And who might you be?"

Annoyance sprang from my tongue. "You know who I am! I'm a guest here, staying in the garnet room."

He didn't respond.

I turned to the other guard. "You recognize me, right?"

He didn't respond, either.

"Well, I drank too much tea, and I'm feeling pretty sick. I'm happy to hurl right here if I have to!"

The guards glanced at each other, then at me, surely questioning my bluff. But I made some retching noises believable enough to surface a look of revulsion on their faces.

"Okay, okay!" the guard on the right said, opening the door in a hurry.

The guard on the left grunted. "What'd you do that for?"

"I just shined my armor this morning!" the other responded.

"Power-hungry pricks," I muttered under my breath as I passed them.

I hurried through the castle, looking in every direction for the horse. Finally, I spotted it standing in front of the throne room. The knight at the throne room door didn't seem to notice anything out of the ordinary.

I walked right up to him, beside the gleaming horse, and asked, "Am I late? The queen summoned me here."

"The queen just left for the festival," he responded.

I hadn't expected that. I was stumped. But I squashed my nerves and pivoted slightly. "I know. She told me to wait in her throne room. I don't want to upset her. Do you?"

He hesitated before unlocking the door, letting me and the horse only I could see in the room.

"I will find the queen and let her know you are waiting." It was more of a warning than a courtesy.

There I stood in an empty throne room with gleaming pastel pink wisteria flowers draped from the high ceilings.

I turned to the red horse. "Why are we here?"

The horse walked to the right side of the light-filled floral hill below the thrones and pressed its forehead against a bed of yellow flowers. Then, it turned back to me and walked right through the hill like a ghost.

I stood, bewildered. What was I to do here?

There were brittle roses and other flowers I recognized from Earth among the many florals that were far too exotic for the human world. My sight fell on where the horse stood moments ago—before yellow draping flowers growing from the right side of the hill, farther hidden under a blanket of ivy. Something was gleaming behind the yellow flowers. I brushed the petals aside.

Hidden under was a golden flower so small, it could have easily gone unnoticed. The tips of my fingers tingled as I inched closer and touched its gilded petals.

Upon my touch, the petals closed. At the same time, the sound of muffled talking behind the door had me whipping my head around.

The queen's voice on the other side of the door struck panic in me. I jerked my head back to the golden flower, and to my surprise, a well-hidden hatch engulfed with moss and leaves was ajar. I pushed it open, ducked down, and stepped inside. The queen stormed into the room just as I closed the hidden entrance behind me.

It took me a moment to realize the hill was hollow and much darker than I would have liked. Had I stepped into a cave or tunnel?

An earthy smell lingered through the blackened space. My only light source was that of the gleaming red horse peering back at me. I heard tiny whispers but saw no one.

"We are not alone," said a small voice. "It is a girl."

I swiveled my head in every direction, but darkness gripped my sight.

"What does the girl want?" another little voice said.

At first, I thought someone had grabbed my leather pouch as it suddenly shook. But instead, it was as though the relic was trying to escape. So I opened my pouch and pulled the trembling relic out.

Before I could make sense of why it was shaking, wings darted past the horse and circled me too quickly to catch sight of what it was.

"A relic. She carries a relic!" a voice whispered.

More wings fluttered. The fluttering wings were too soft to be birds, but too hard to be mere insects. Whispers continued to fill the darkness.

Another voice said, "The animal guide knows the way."

My nerves unraveled from the hidden voices, pulling me closer to the horse. Whoever—whatever—was down here with me could also see the horse no one else had noticed at the festival.

The relic in my hand trembled more furiously with each step forward.

It wasn't long before the horse halted. The subtle red glow allowed enough light to see a tall ancient-looking stone beside it.

The relic trembled so hard; it nearly ripped my clasped fingers open. It was using all its might to tug me toward the towering stone. The horse stood lamely as I wrestled to contain the relic.

With little hesitance, I swept my free hand over the cold surface of the rock and felt a divot. At the same moment, the horse vanished, and the relic broke free from my hand.

As if it had a mind of its own, it shot straight into the divot. And to no surprise, it was a perfect fit.

Boom!

The ground shook furiously, and the force of the relic knocked me hard off my feet. Then darkness gripped my senses, throwing me into the abyss.

CHAPTER 16

Execution

"Attica, where are you?" a voice said.

My heart nearly skipped a beat as I lay lifeless, clinging to his voice. It was Darian's voice that woke my unconscious mind.

"Attica? Are you okay? Say something! Attica?"

As my consciousness slowly returned, I realized I was mistaken.

"Attica! I'm coming to find you!"

It wasn't Darian's voice at all. It was Razz using the couplings to communicate, or perhaps using his telepathy. Or both.

I opened my eyes to find something hovering over me. As my vision sharpened with each blink, the flying something scattered.

I sat up, taking sight of those who whispered in the darkness, as each one now had a subtle glow. Though I couldn't fully make out what the hell they were, I could see they were each about the size of my palm. One of them flew closer to me, almost as curious about me as I was about them.

They were tiny people with pointed, elegant wings and ears. Except their skin and hair were moss green. I didn't know what they were, but the closest thing I could relate them to was fairies.

"Thank you," a fairy said to me.

"For what?" I asked, brushing dirt off my elbows.

"For returning our magic." She bowed her tiny head, and the rest fluttered closer to me and did the same.

"Are you okay?" another fairy asked. "You have slept through all the dark starlights."

"I have?" I asked, jumping to my feet. Eyes widened and heart sunken, I ran back to the secret hatch door, passing all the fairies without so much as a goodbye.

Chest pounding, I opened the hatch to the view of the queen and her guard gripping Razz by his throat.

The queen's cold, empty eyes buried so deeply into Razz, she hadn't even noticed I had stepped out from under the hill beneath her throne.

"Your time is up! Where is my daughter?" she asked so sharply, I nearly felt her words pierce my skin, even though she was addressing Razz.

Razz released a sigh. "I don't know, your majesty. All I know is she was never comfortable traveling through the grid."

For a moment, the queen appeared lost. Then a tear fell down her face, a tear that seemed to pull her out of her daze.

"Guards!"

Two more guards strolled in with a gold-bladed axe and an execution block.

It wasn't until Queen Blair parted from Razz and her guard that she finally noticed my presence beside the hill.

"You!" she said, her fierce eyes pinning me. "Where the hell did you go to?"

Razz looked at me with relief.

The queen headed toward the exit as she said to the guards with a twinge of hesitance, "Kill the girl first."

"Wait!" Razz shouted.

By her expression, when she turned around, it was clear no one ever dared raise their voice at her.

"Your entire court is talking about the return of magic in your kingdom. You've seen it yourself!" he said, pointing toward the throne room door. Then he switched his pointed finger to me. "Attica brought back your kingdom's magic." He dropped his finger and took a pleading step toward Queen Blair. "For that, don't you think you can spare us our lives?"

She straightened. "Don't act like you did us any favors. You made us a target for war!" she said, her emerald eyes filled with fury.

She nodded to the guard. The guard grabbed me so fast, Razz hadn't even noticed until my forced head was already on the execution block. The queen continued toward the exit with no concern for my life as the guard held the heavy blade over my head.

"No!" Razz yelled.

The queen stopped but did not turn.

"I beg your pardon, but if you are going to have my friend executed, the least you can do is look her in the eyes before her last breath."

The queen stayed standing but still did not turn.

"Or are you too weak to demand the life of someone you're too cowardly to look at as they take their last breath?"

I had never heard Razz speak to anyone with such disrespect, never mind a queen in her own court. I was quickly seeing all the colors and sides of Razz I had never known existed before this journey began.

His words must have struck a chord in her, as she finally turned to look at me.

I was ready for her to yell loud enough for the entire kingdom to hear, but instead, her mouth fell open, and she trembled as she walked toward me. Her mouth was still gaping when she stood mere inches away. I couldn't help but flinch when she lifted her hand to my cheek.

"Gemma?" she whispered. Confusion took hold of me briefly until I noticed long red hair draping from my head. She swept her hands over my hair, or what appeared to be Gemma's hair. The moment her hands reached my ears, her gaping mouth shut, and my heart sank.

A pit of fear grew in my stomach. She knew I wasn't her daughter. She knew she had been deceived!

Razz must have made me look identical to Gemma. But he had forgotten one minor detail: the queen didn't feel Gemma's pointed ears, but rather, my round cartilage.

The queen held back no hesitance this time. "Kill her!" she demanded.

The guard lifted his axe once more. I looked at Razz, whose eyes had swollen with tears.

Utter shock took hold of him as failure gripped me. I felt everything Razz felt through the couplings we still wore, and neither of us cared about failing the queen. It was failing Darian that would haunt us both for the remaining seconds of our lives.

Time slowed for just a moment as pink wisteria petals suddenly drifted down, down, down from the lush ceiling high above. I wanted so badly to take in the beauty of raining petals. But in the corner of my eye, I caught sight of the guard who had already lifted the axe that was sure to decapitate my head any second now.

My body shook fiercely as my heart raced faster than it ever had before. The sound of my heart beating through my chest filled my ears. I shut my eyes tight and thought of one thing only: Darian.

It was the longest second of my life. Time had slowed too much. I should have felt a blade cut through my throat by now. I should have died several seconds ago.

Except, I was connected to Razz through the couplings. We were still tied, and I felt his mind fighting with everything he had against the guard holding the axe mere inches over my neck. He had a tight hold on the guard's mind. If Razz let go for even a second, my life would end.

"Mother?" a voice said from across the room.

Razz unintentionally released his mind-bending off the guard. I winced as the guard dropped the gold axe beside me.

My eyes sprang open. I looked up at the guard who was certain to end my life moments ago, but his mouth had dropped as he stared at the throne room entrance. I turned to find Gemma standing at the door, right before the queen.

The queen cocked her head at the sight of me, then back at Gemma. It seemed she knew it was her daughter, as she pulled Gemma into her arms without checking the point of her ears.

Razz ran toward me and helped me off the execution block, warning the guard with a glare. He grabbed my hand as I stood shaking, trying to calm my nerves by reminding myself that I was still breathing.

After a while of Gemma hugging her mother, she walked over toward us. She eyed my clothing. "That outfit never looked quite right on me. But it suits you," she signed with green light and a voice trailing her hands.

"Thanks," I said, trying very hard to fathom the fact that I was still alive.

"Calder told me your plan after you already left the manor," she signed. She looked back and forth between Razz and me. "It sounds crazy and . . . dangerous. Would you like me to come with you and help?"

Razz responded, "No. You should be with your family."

"You know where to find me if you change your mind." She looked at her mother, standing across the room with an expression of bewilderment. "I suppose it's time to explain my new way of communication to her. Although, a part of me enjoys the look of confusion on my mother's face." Her crystal ring had lit up and then faded as she finished signing.

At this moment, I realized for the first time that the gold band blue crystal ring on Gemma's hand lit up only when she signed. The pollen light she signed with always seemed to steal the show of her sign language. But now, I finally understood how a voice spoke from her hands. Her ring somehow acted as a translator, surely with the help of magic.

I kept the realization to myself as we shared a laugh before she joined her mother once more.

King Cashel and his two sons stepped into the room. "It's true! My daughter has returned!" he shouted gleefully. He took Gemma in for a crushing hug before holding his hands victoriously in the air. "My daughter and my kingdom's magic are back. We are throwing a feast tonight to celebrate!"

Wystan and Bartlett stood silently to the side, both seeming unsure of how to react, considering neither of them had ever met their sister.

We stood watching Gemma meet her brothers for the first time. For siblings who had never met before, they were more alike than they knew.

Commotion filled the hall outside the throne room now. Perhaps it was Gemma's sudden return, or maybe it was the unexpected return of magic to the kingdom. But the energy was lively and joyful.

Razz turned to me. "Are you ready?"

"For what?" I asked, eyes glued to the joy of Gemma and her family reuniting.

"To continue our mission."

I broke my stare from the happy family's reunion and responded, "As ready as I'll ever be."

We exited the now crowded room to gather our belongings before taking off. We had nearly reached the garnet room door when we heard a voice down the hall.

"Wait!" We turned to find Queen Blair striding toward us with damp eyes. It wasn't until she reached us that she said, "I'm grateful to you both. I'm unsure how I feel about the return of our magic. If it gets back to the Orpheus—"

Razz cut her off. "Then we will return and do what we can to assure peace in your kingdom."

A wavering smile swept her face as she held out a red velvet pouch. "I want you both to have this." She placed the heavy pouch in my hand. "And please know, you are always welcome here."

She was about to walk off when she twisted back around. "You are Attica Spark, correct?"

Taken by surprise at the sound of my last name, I hesitated before responding, "Yes."

Her face softened with a smile. "I remember the day you were born. Our kingdom raised a toast in your honor. And we'll be doing the same tonight." She looked at ease for the first time since we had arrived before she strolled off.

Razz turned with a grin. "What's in the pouch?" he asked with glittering eyes, as if he were a child opening a gift on Christmas morning.

I opened it to find a large sum of gold coins.

"That's a lot of pentacles," Razz said, eyes widened.

"Pentacles?" I questioned.

He pulled out a coin, identical to the ones Augur received for the shrune tea. "Just one of these is worth about five gilds."

"I don't know if we can accept this. We didn't do it for payment," I said, feeling the heavy weight of the pouch.

Razz gave a hearty laugh. "This entire castle is covered in gold. I think she's happy to spare it."

After grabbing our belongings and heading toward the castle's exit, I took in the majestic sight of the many trees, plants, and flowers—

each one now filled with lush life and vibrant colors. Not one dead leaf or wilted plant was left.

The hundreds of elegantly swirled and vibrantly colored crystals wrapped around the many gold pillars were now brightly lit. Some beaming lights within the crystals were rhythmically flickering up and down the pillars.

As we passed the courtyard—the most lavish garden in the castle—I gasped at the sight of the short statue gnomes. They were no longer still and lifeless, but instead, they were moving about the yard, growing mushrooms with just a touch of their little hands over the soil before ripping them from the ground, and flinging them at the buttocks of passersby. Naturally, Razz got a kick out of them and their cheekiness.

It wasn't until we were nearing my favorite emerald tree of strangely shaped leaves that my jaw dropped. The blackened edges and veins of the vivid leaves were not wilted at all. Instead, the tree was filled with hundreds of green butterflies that were no longer closed and still. Now, they were all delicately moving their wings, revealing their elegant black design. As we passed the tree, they fluttered their wings hard until they all took off in the air, flying peacefully throughout the court. It left me wondering if it was a tree of magic butterflies or if the butterflies just happened to be sleeping every time I passed them before.

Every inch of nature in this castle was not only lively in color, but as we walked by them, they moved on their own with no wind or breeze. Somehow, they were more alive than I ever thought they could be. So much so, that I could have sworn a tree waved bye to me before I exited the castle.

It was early morning when we left the Tera Kingdom, not yet realizing the wild journey that still lay ahead. And we were without a doubt unprepared.

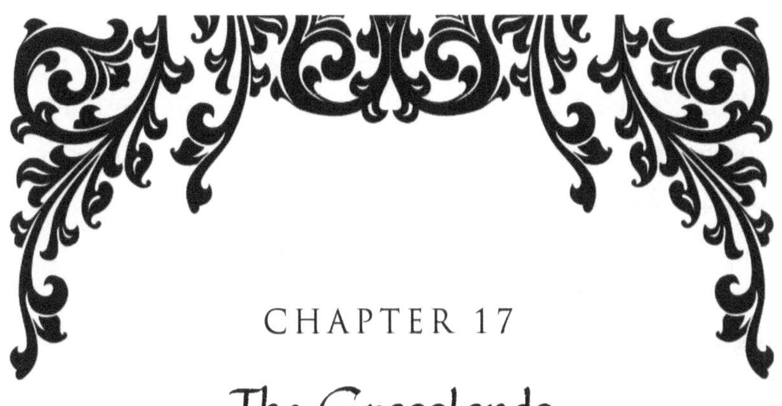

CHAPTER 17

The Grasslands

We continued our journey through a valley a mile away from the Tera Kingdom. Razz held the compass in one hand and Darian's map of Elloriya in his other. With a glance at the compass, he halted, studying the map in confusion.

He reached into a pocket on his black leather vest and pulled out that familiar green stone suspended from a brass chain. He asked the pendulum, "Where to?"

"Doesn't the compass tell us which direction to go?" I asked.

"Yes. But it's telling us to go west when it would make more sense for us to go north."

As he held the chain over the map, the teardrop crystal began to swing toward the west.

"How does it work?" I asked, with narrowed eyes on the pendulum.

"I ask a question and it acts as a guide. It's how I communicate with my higher self and spirit guides when my intuition is clouded."

"Why is your intuition clouded?"

He responded so softly, I hardly heard him say, "From worrying about my brother." He rolled the map up and tucked it in his bag. "We have a long journey. We better get going."

"So, we are going west, then?" I clarified.

"Both the compass and pendulum pointed west. So, yes." He began strolling toward the west.

I followed with slight irritation. "But wouldn't it make more sense for us to go north or even south? You even said so yourself. The northern kingdom is much closer. And if we need to go that direction anyway, shouldn't we go now?"

"No. We need to go west," he said, unwavering, not bothering to even look at me.

"But why? You're adding wasted time to our trip because a stupid compass and pendulum pointed in the same direction?"

"Yes, Attica," he replied calmly.

"Don't I get a say?"

He finally turned to face me. "Always. You know I value your opinion. But both the compass and pendulum are adamant that we go west, so we're going west."

"But it makes no sense!" I pushed. "What is worth adding more time to this journey when you know how time-sensitive it is?"

He clenched his jaw and didn't bother answering. So that was that—end of discussion.

The tension between us faded as the days passed. We journeyed through the same woods we spent days in a couple of weeks ago, only now heading west instead of east.

We saw a familiar-looking faun, gray with short horns and white furry goatlike legs, standing upright, matching Razz's six-foot-one height. Instead of shrieking at us again, it ran behind a tree, cowering until we passed.

As we continued through the balmy woods the next day, something was hanging in a distant tree. I was far more curious than Razz, especially when I realized it wasn't just something hanging in a tree at all, but someone.

A young man with dark skin, bleached hair, and pale green eyes was dangling upside-down from a rope tied around his ankle. The sun beamed behind him, creating a halo around his head.

There was no struggle or discontent as he hung with a crossed leg behind his suspended knee and hands resting behind his waist. He had what I hoped wasn't blood, but rather red paint spilled on his pants and splatters of blue on his beige belted tunic. I wondered if he was an artist, like Darian.

"Are you all right, man?" Razz asked him.

His voice was so calm it was almost unsettling. "I am not me as you are not you. I am more soul than I am a man. If I am all right, then you are all wrong. So, are you all wrong, or are you all right?"

Razz gave me a sideways glance before looking back at the hanged man. "Whatever. Do you need help?"

"Do I need help, or do you need help, for I have surrendered, and you have not?"

Razz rolled his eyes and said, "I don't have time for this," and continued past him.

"Perhaps if you look at things from a different perspective, you will come to see that time is all you have, though it is an illusion created by man." That was the last we heard from him.

I had lost track of the days when we had finally reached the grasslands. We walked through the tall grass under a vivid blue sky as the beaming sun painted my shoulders red.

The small distance between Razz and me felt like miles. Only the sound of chirping birds filled the silence.

Was he mad at me? Did he think I was mad at him? We hardly talked at all in the last few days.

The grass filled the open air with its fresh scent as we continued for several starlights through the scorching plains. With each passing starlight, the sun grew sinisterly heavier with its rays grilling my sticky skin. The smell of fresh grass grew stronger the farther into the grasslands we walked, serving as a slight distraction from the summer heat.

The surrounding grass spread for miles in all directions. Some villages were in the far distance in the north and the south. Other than that, there was nothing but tall green grass brushing past my knees and the occasional pestering fly.

Eventually, we passed a village of familiar-looking people with ramlike horns and hoovelike hands. Thinking back to the memory Darian showed me of our last moments in Elloriya as children, I wondered if any of them were there when Etiwa sent me to Earth. Perhaps they were all there that night.

I scanned them until my sight fell on a woman with only one horn. The moment I saw her familiar protruding eyes, I knew she was the one who had defied Shakar when he asked her to kill young Darian, Gemma, and me. And she paid her price for refusing.

Nearly all the horned villagers cautiously watched us as we passed by a short distance away.

It had been days since we had a conversation of any sort. I couldn't take the unbearable silence any longer. So, to finally break the silence between Razz and me, I turned to him and asked, "How did Gemma know the grid to her kingdom was open?"

To my surprise, he quickly answered, though he didn't look at me when responding, "Etiwa is still at the manor and will probably stay there until everyone returns home. She's the only one I can reach telepathically from this distance. I assume she told Gemma after I informed her of the returning magic. Though I wouldn't be surprised if Gemma felt a tug from the tie to her kingdom. She's connected to the same magic, after all."

"Oh." We both fell quiet. To break the silence again, I asked, "How does your magic work?"

He raised a brow and responded defensively, "I don't have magic."

I picked up my pace to keep up with him. "Some would argue that what you do is magic."

He turned to me with a sideways glance. "What do you mean?"

"How you can change our appearance and bend minds. . . . Where I come from—I mean, on Earth—what you can do would be seen as magic."

"Well, we're not on Earth. This is Elloriya. And what I do here is nothing more than an ability."

Sometimes, he was pleasant to be around, but other times, he was clearly not in the mood to talk. This was one of those times. So I didn't bother responding.

Instead, I did my best to ignore the growing pain in my feet as we walked endlessly.

I ripped a handful of tall grass out from the ground, mostly out of boredom. When I felt as if a spider's web had stuck to my fingers, I nearly panicked, hoping there was no spider attached to it. But when I looked down at my hand as I continued forth, my mouth dropped. Several blades of arm-length grass were trailing my fingers. I was wielding without even trying.

It had me wondering how much potential I had, still hidden and untouched.

CHAPTER 18

The Node of Magic

As we continued through the grasslands—Razz walking several feet ahead—I held my hands out, feeling an energetic bond between my fingers and the grass blades. It was strange how I felt such a strong connection, and it seemed the grass felt it too, as the blades moved with my outstretched hands, clinging to the subtle energy from my fingers.

While the starlights passed as we endlessly walked under a sun slowly painting my bare skin a shade darker, I kept wondering when Razz would turn around and say something—anything. But he never did.

It took two more days before we reached a four-pointed star embedded in the grass, easily as large as a dance floor. Its gilded surface shimmered, and it was labeled like a compass with silver writing at each of the four points.

Razz walked in slow circles atop the intrusive gold flooring when he finally broke the silence. "This is known as the Node of Magic. It once held the crystals that powered the lower kingdoms with their magic."

Confused, I asked, "If crystals powered the lower kingdoms from out here, then why can't we just bring all the relics here to power them again?"

"Will any of the relics fit?"

I moved to the point of the star closest to me, bent down, running my fingers over the empty divot before doing the same with the other three points. Each divot had an identical oval shape.

"No," I responded.

He walked past the star and continued west. "There were no relics before. I read of them, but I had never seen any until that day in the library. From what I've read, the relics can hold more power than any crystal in existence."

At those words, I wondered why I was chosen to harbor the relics in the first place, all the while feeling grateful that the sun's rays had finally softened as it crept slowly into early evening.

"So the magic in the kingdoms were not powered by relics, but by crystals out in the open grasslands?"

"Yes," he responded, still looking straight ahead.

"No wonder it was so easy for Shakar to gain power over the kingdoms," I said, wondering whose brilliant idea it was to place the crystals out in the open to begin with.

But then, Razz explained, "The four crystals had to be close together and connected to work at their fullest potential. It's like the crystals fed off each other's energy and then worked together to power the lower kingdoms. At least that's what I read."

"So the chakra portals created the relics?" I asked, while taking in the beauty of soft golden rays spread richly over the miles of vacant grasslands.

He chuckled, and I was grateful the energy between us had lightened. "I love how you ask me all these questions, as if I have all the answers."

"Well, you know more than I do."

"Can't argue with that," he said with a cheeky grin. "I don't know if the portals created the relics or if it was Etiwa herself. But since the portals were created after the wars, I think Etiwa may have used a spell to reveal the relics to whoever the portals chose. If it weren't for her, I don't think the relics would even exist. Her magic is beyond comprehension."

"No shit! She once told me it was her magic that created the chakra portals. But, what if Shakar and the Orpheus take the magic all over again?" I asked, shielding the lowering sun from my eyes.

Razz watched a flock of birds flying by when he said, "It'll be far more difficult. After Shakar stole their magic, the kings and queens worked with the alchemist to create a hidden place in their kingdom for something else to generate their magic. The alchemist reached out to Etiwa for help. I think Etiwa knew about the power of the relics and somehow brought them to life through the chakra portals. She thought her attempt had failed until you went through the portals."

"How do you know all of this?"

"Etiwa told me the night she came to the manor." He dropped his head when he added, "The night Darian went into the grid."

I didn't remember any such conversation that night. So I asked, "Where was I?"

"You had gone up to bed at that point. I stayed up with her so she could prepare me as much as possible."

"So the alchemist is the one who created the place in each kingdom for the relics?" I clarified.

"That's what I was told."

"And who is the alchemist? Why aren't they on this journey with us?"

"The alchemist—Magus—has a way with the elements and ethereal world. He's so good at whatever he does, some people call him The Sorcerer."

I lengthened my strides to keep up with Razz. "But if Magus worked with the royals to create a hidden place in their kingdom to generate magic, then why can't we just tell them we have the relics and ask them to show us where theirs belong?"

Razz stopped and faced me as he pulled his canteen out of his bag. "Apparently, there was a lot of fear regarding the relics and bringing magic back to the kingdoms. I think Etiwa told you to keep our plan of returning magic to the kingdoms secret because otherwise, it might create too much fear that the Orpheus would find out. If they did, they'd likely respond by hurting or even killing the heirs—our friends—still on the edge, and we would risk the royals banning us from their lands, making it even more difficult to fulfill our mission. And it's already complicated enough. So whatever we do, we must follow Etiwa's orders." He took a swig of water and closed away his canteen before continuing forward.

I opened my mouth, hoping to develop a logical rebuttal that would somehow make this mission easier. But I couldn't think of anything. So, that was the end of that conversation.

We had walked nearly the entire day without a rest. The bottom of my feet ached, my shoulders were crisp from the relentless sun, and fatigue quickly took over my body.

After I argued about how time-sensitive our mission was a week ago, I was embarrassed to bite my pride and finally ask, "Razz, I'm in as much of a hurry as you, but can we sit for just a moment?"

"Sure," he said as he tossed his bag to the ground and lay down on the tall grass. I did the same beside him.

Perhaps it was just my exhaustion, but as I lay on the ground, I could have sworn I heard music playing in the grass.

I turned to look at Razz between the blades. The black metal cuff over his left ear shined brightly under the low evening sun, revealing the many embedded black crystals. The curls of his blond hair shined nearly as brightly in contrast to his sun-kissed skin.

He must have felt my gaze on him as his navy-blue eyes suddenly turned in my direction, landing on me. There was only a foot of towering grass separating us. But it didn't stop us from silently gazing at one another.

Strangely, it wasn't nearly as awkward as the silence we shared earlier. It didn't feel uncomfortable at all. Whatever connection I had with him felt natural.

I was the first to break our gaze before we hydrated and ate some food we had filled our bags with on our way out of the Tera Kingdom; my favorite being what looked like a purple tomato, but it was much sweeter until I reached its sour center, which was still delicious.

It was officially night by the time we finished eating. The grass had filled with a soft green light.

I lay back down and closed my eyes, breathing in the fresh-scented grass as the night breeze spread over me. It wasn't long before I felt Razz's hand on mine.

There was nothing more than friendship between us. It was just a bond that ran deep. And I was sure he felt it too as I fell asleep beside him.

CHAPTER 19

Noxius Flora

The morning sun kissed my eyes awake. Razz's hand was no longer on mine, but he was still lying there, staring at me through the foot of tall grass between us.

"Hey," he whispered.

"Actually," I whispered back as I spread my fingers through the soft green blades, "hay is much drier. This is just grass."

I wasn't sure if he picked up on my stupid joke until he let out a roaring laugh. He pushed himself off the ground, brushed himself off, and stood over me with a helping hand and that charming smile of his. I grabbed his hand, and he pulled me up with surprising ease.

We continued toward what appeared to be a forest of blue trees in the distance. We still hadn't said a word to each other since my lame joke, but this time as we walked in silence, he joked back with a sly kick on my butt, pretending it wasn't him every time I looked over. He even gave me a ridiculous face anytime we looked in each other's direction at the same time.

By around lunchtime the next day, we had finally reached the end of the grasslands—thank the heavens above. But what was now before us made me feel as small as an ant.

From a distance, it looked like we were heading toward the woods or a forest, except the trees had blue leaves rather than green. But as we got much closer, I quickly realized the trees were not trees at all.

We stood before a seemingly endless wall of thirty-foot-high blue flowers, each facing downward from their heavy stem. They reminded me of bluebells, except their trunks and petals were so massive, few sun rays passed through to the ground.

The sight was devastatingly beautiful. At least until I realized the yellow anthers in the center of the flowers were not only moving but were making sounds—hissing sounds. It was unsettling and quickly tested my absent anxiety. But there was no way around them, as they seemed to stretch as far as the grasslands in both directions.

Razz's voice shook when he asked, "Did you bring your cloak?"

"Yeah. Why?"

His eyes narrowed on the hissing anthers when he said, "You'll need it."

My bag became significantly lighter after removing my gray cloak. Razz watched as I put it on.

"The hood too," he demanded.

"Why?" I asked, already abiding by his demand.

"You do not want the anthers to touch you. They sting, and if I'm not mistaken, they're venomous," he warned.

My stomach turned. "Don't you have a cloak?"

"No," he responded. "I don't think they can see us, but I'm pretty sure they can feel footsteps if we don't tread lightly." And with a bit of hesitance, he cautiously moved into the flower forest. I swallowed my jitters and followed close behind.

We moved slowly and as lightly as possible with every step forward. I even tried to slow my breathing out of fear that one of the many trunklike stems might feel my exhale.

As we continued sneaking under the canopy of monstrous flowers, the tail of my cloak accidentally brushed a stem. It seemed not to have noticed, and I was grateful. At least until I realized the sound of hissing grew suddenly louder.

I looked up, and when I did, my nerves shook. The anthers had begun to slither slowly down in our direction. The hissing grew louder as the flowers descended lower and lower above our heads.

Razz stopped before me and whispered, "They already know we're here. We need to move faster. Can you run?"

"Yeah," I whispered back.

And without delay, he said, "Run!"

The hissing multiplied in all directions as if they were communicating across the menacing flower forest. The anthers continued to creep lower and lower.

Anthers snapped at the hood of my cloak, pulling it off my head and sending me tumbling to the ground. Razz turned around to pull me up, but I was already jumping back on my feet.

There was light at the end of the tunnel. Though I couldn't see where the end of the tunnel was taking us, the hissing floral forest was shortening with every stride. We were sure to make it. We were only a short distance away from collapsing when we finally reached safety.

The rays of the sun pierced through the lush green trees before us now. Though they were all green, they were not all the same kind of tree. Each tree had different shaped leaves of varying sizes. Beneath the trees were vivid plants full of yellow, orange, pink, purple, and blue sprinkled throughout the tropical rainforest.

The sound of hissing anthers behind us withered away as the whistling of birds filled my ears.

I threw myself on the ground and gasped for fresh air. "We made it through hell's garden!" I said, feeling victorious. Razz was still catching his breath with his bag on the ground beside him. "What were those, anyway?"

"Noxius flora," he said, gripping the side of his neck.

"What's with your neck?"

He didn't answer.

"Were you stung?"

"Go in my bag and pull out the jar of salve root," he demanded.

I immediately rummaged through his bag and found two jars. One was filled with dried purple petals, which I had seen him chew every morning since we left the manor several weeks ago. The other was a mush of green herbs.

"Which one?" I asked in a panic.

He grinded his teeth. "The green one!"

I opened the jar, and he removed his hand from his neck, revealing a small black puncture covered in yellow pollen. He dug a couple of fingers in the jar, and just as he was about to spread the green herbs over his wound, I said, "Wait!"

I blew the pollen off his neck. He jerked his head at me, surprised, or perhaps even confused. It was a strange look he had never given me before. It came and went too fast as he spread the mushy herbs over his neck.

"You can close it," he said, glancing at the jar in my hand.

I put the cork back on and returned the jar to his bag.

"Now what?" I asked hesitantly, unsure if I was ready or strong enough to hear the answer.

"I hope for the best." He secured his bag's strap over his torso and said, "Let's go."

I stayed glued to the spot. "Are you really okay to keep going?"

His tongue sharpened. "We have to keep moving!"

"I know. But maybe you should sit for a moment," I said gently.

He whipped his head to me, and with fury in his dark blue eyes, he bellowed, "We don't have a moment! We have no time to spare!" The anger vanished from his heavy gaze. He dropped his head, took a breath, and said hopelessly, "My brother is stuck in some piece of shit grid that will suck his soul to death if we don't get these relics to where they need to go before our time is out—before *his* time is out. And we don't even know when that is. For all I know, he's already—" He cut himself off.

"Okay. Let's keep going." My voice didn't sound as hopeless as his, but there was no doubt I shared his fear. The thought of losing Darian—never seeing him again—turned my stomach to knots, quickly making me feel nauseated.

We strolled through the rainforest beside a creek for nearly an entire starlight before Razz swayed.

With hesitance, I said, "Razz, I know we're short on time, but you need to sit."

"No, we need to—" He lost his breath and leaned against a tree as the venom seemed to suddenly kick in. "Help me up here." He pointed a short distance away, up a short hill beside a flowing stream.

I wrapped his arm around my shoulders, bearing as much of his weight as I could. The moment we reached the stream, he collapsed.

"Razz? Razz?" His eyes rolled back. I slapped his cheek enough times for them to turn red. I even splashed water on him. Still no response. "You need to stay awake!" My voice shook in desperation. "How can I help?" He was unresponsive, his eyelids fluttering.

I cleansed the dried herbs off his neck and froze at the sight of the sting. Black veins had spread over his neck like a cobweb.

Shit, shit, shit!

I didn't know how to help him or what to do.

I pushed my panic aside and took three deep breaths. By the third breath, I was calm enough to think clearly. And what came to mind was a medicinal flower petal.

Etiwa had given me a red petal to eat when I had passed out and again when I was healing after the coliseum.

I was desperate and could think of nothing else. And we were in a rainforest surrounded by plants and flowers. Except—where in this enormous rainforest would that petal be? What did the flower it came from even look like?

All I could think over and over was, *Please help me!* I didn't know who or what I was addressing, but I was desperate.

Razz was only getting worse. His forehead was heating quickly. I was running out of time. He was running out of time! And for the first moment since the solar plexus portal, I felt anxiety grasping at me.

No! I wouldn't allow anxiety to reach me. I had already set mine free. *Don't come back!* I begged. *Not now!*

I took more deep breaths. *Astrophel, are you there?* I was hoping to hear my guide's reassuring voice somewhere in my mind or suddenly see him walking toward me. But nothing happened. *Kamali, please help!* I begged my other guide. I was so overwhelmed, I hardly felt tears roll down my face. *Where can I find that damn petal or anything that can help Razz? Please help!*

Still no response. But after a moment, there was a sudden screech on the tree branch above. It was a bird with brown feathers and gleaming yellow eyes. And it was not just any bird; it was a falcon. And I was certain it wasn't just any falcon. It was my spirit animal.

He pushed his talons off the tree and flew through the rainforest. I ran after him.

It wasn't long before he landed on a thin branch, peering at the ground below. A yellow plant with long, succulent leaves and pink flowers with wavy petals took up more than its fair portion of the ground. But I did not see any red petals.

When I looked back up at the falcon, he was gone. My stomach dropped. What was I to do here? How could any of this help Razz?

I closed my eyes and calmed my mind and body so I could think clearly. When I opened my eyes, I was drawn to the yellow succulent leaves. As I reached out at it, my hand tingled, causing me to wonder if it was confirmation.

I followed my gut, plucked as much as I could, and ran back to Razz.

It wasn't just his forehead that had heated, but now the rest of his body was quickly warming. I splashed water from the nearby stream on his neck, and then, as if it were instinct, I broke open the succulent. It was filled with a sparkling, gooey liquid.

For a moment, I didn't know whether I should put it over the blackened wound on his neck or in his mouth for him to consume. But, since I didn't think he could get any worse, I did both.

I opened his mouth and poured the goo down his throat.

"Razz, you need to wake up!" I begged, but he was still unresponsive.

The succulent goo was not thin enough for him to swallow while unconscious. I tipped his head to the side so he wouldn't choke before I grabbed a wooden bowl from Razz's bag and broke open another succulent. Sparkling goo poured out and into the bowl. I added a splash of water from my canteen and mixed them. The goo thinned to a liquid.

Razz was heavy as I lifted him onto my lap, drizzling the liquid in his mouth. It took a while, but the entire bowl eventually seeped down his throat.

I cleaned his neck and put a fresh layer of the succulent goo and green mushy salve root over his wound. As he lay on my lap, I did what Etiwa had once done for me and prayed. As I did, an idea suddenly popped into my mind.

I went through our bags and pulled out the couplings, placing one on his arm and one on my own. I tapped my cuff with his, and both cuffs suddenly tightened, spreading a buzzing chill over my body.

He moaned as our energies synced. My mind began to spin, so I grabbed his hand and lay beside him, hoping I could somehow give him strength through the bond.

After a couple of minutes, he uttered, "Attica."

I squeezed his hand. "I'm here!"

"Do you—" he uttered, but said nothing more.

"Do I what?"

"See it?" he managed to say.

"See what?"

No response.

I closed my eyes and breathed into the space between him and me. His mind was suddenly tugging on mine. The more my mind merged with his, the brighter a blue light shined—the same blue light I had seen before when I had fainted and at the Tera Kingdom when I had seen Astrophel while dancing in the drum circle at the equinox festival.

The blue became even brighter until I was finally standing in the light beside Razz, who looked perfectly healthy as he stood strongly beside me.

"Hello?" he shouted into the void. But silence was all there was. "Hello?" he shouted even louder. This time, footsteps moved toward us.

"Hello," said a voice behind us.

And when we turned to see who it was, Razz woke up, pulling me awake with him.

CHAPTER 20

The Rainforest

There we were in the rainforest beside the babbling stream, awoken from what we had seen in the blue light. Razz turned to me wide-eyed, and I returned the same astonished stare.

"Did you see him?" he asked.

My lips broke into a smile. "Yes!"

Razz sat up, looking far better than he had looked earlier.

"Do you think it was a dream, or could it have been real?"

"It wasn't a dream!" I said surely.

"How could you know for sure?"

"Because that was the third time I saw that light. We were in the energy grid." I sat up. "Well, at least our consciousness was."

"So then, my brother is still alive?" Hope filled his voice.

"Yes, Razz. I believe he is," I said happily, thinking back to the sight of Darian's soulful eyes, looking right back at Razz and me.

Razz was silent for a moment. Then he looked around, scanning the broken apart succulent and the emptied wooden bowl beside it, before landing his eyes on me again. "What happened?"

"You passed out. I think the venom sent your body into shock. I didn't know if you were dying, so I—"

He grabbed the succulent as he cut me off. "Analeptic bevel? Brilliant. How did you know this would work?" But before I could answer, he added, "You saved my life, Attica."

"Well, I would have been beheaded if it weren't for you, so now we're even."

He laughed. "Thank you," he said, gratitude in his voice. He noticed both of us wearing the couplings. "So that's how you tapped into my mind." He removed the coupling from his arm, and I followed suit.

Then we both took swigs of water from our canteens, packed everything away, and continued under the heavy sun. Thankfully, an abundance of trees generously provided us with shade along our path.

Razz looked like a brand-new person as he strolled through the rainforest, grabbing fruits from the trees and tossing some my way that I added to my bag. When I pulled a fruit from a tree and broke it apart, nearly ready to sink my teeth in, he knocked it out of my hand.

"The fruits with red seeds are not safe to eat," he said.

So I ate a fruit he handed me instead.

At times, we walked in silence, undoubtedly thinking of Darian. I did so while collecting pollen from my favorite colored flowers. At first it was out of boredom from endlessly walking, but then I thought it might be good to have on hand in case I needed pollen light during this journey. So I put some in a little empty pouch in my bag that previously carried berries from the manor's garden. If I wasn't thinking of Darian or collecting pollen on our trail, then I was pestering Razz with questions.

There was one question I had wanted to ask long ago. But I never did. And I never really understood why, other than feeling as though I'd be cheating on my family in Ridgewood Hollow if I had asked earlier. But I was finally ready to ask, "So, where on the map am I from?"

He stopped and turned to me. "You don't know where you're from?"

I felt foolish when I shook my head.

Perhaps someone told me where I was from already, but I couldn't remember if so. When I first returned to Elloriya, there was too much going on and so much to digest. It was all so overwhelming. I knew I was from the higher kingdoms, but that's all I knew.

"I feel honored to show you," he said. He took out the map and pointed near the mid-left to where we were. "We're traveling west, between the lands of the lower kingdoms. These kingdoms are the foundation of ours. And therefore, they are extremely treasured by the nobles." He then moved his finger past the kingdom in the north to the top of the page where the map was unfinished. "These are the higher kingdoms. Darian and I are from the Luminar Kingdom in the lunar node." He didn't move his finger very far when he stopped and said, "And you're from the Syrus Kingdom in the solar node. You'll love it there."

He rolled up the map and continued walking as I tried to wrap my head around what he had just said.

He didn't even look at me when he said with a smirk, "Go ahead, Attica. I know you have questions stirring in that mind of yours."

"How am I from the Syrus Kingdom?"

I don't know why it was such a shock when he said more casually than he should have, "Your mother is Queen of the Syrus Kingdom and the solar node."

I came to a sudden stop. This entire time, I thought Shakar banned me from this realm because my grandfather was the noble that killed his brother. Perhaps that played a significant role, but I certainly didn't expect to come from a line of royalty. It suddenly seemed to take a great deal of effort to draw breath.

"Attica, are you okay?"

I pulled myself out of shock to find Razz a few inches from me with a face of concern.

"How come no one told me?"

"I didn't—I don't know. I'm sorry. I guess I thought you knew. You spent a lot of time with Calder, and I thought he would have told you. But maybe he wanted to give you enough time to adjust to this world first." His voice wasn't as gentle when he added, "No one was stopping you from asking."

I didn't know if I was upset with him or myself. I didn't even know why I was upset at all. But, for whatever reason, I couldn't move.

"You and Darian . . . are your parents—"

But before I could finish my thought, Razz clarified, "King and Queen of the Luminar Kingdom."

I mindlessly nodded.

When I stood frozen in a daze, Razz grabbed my hand and said, "Come on. Let's continue."

After traveling in silence for half a starlight while I attempted to digest what I had now known, I finally summoned the courage to ask, "What's it like in the higher kingdoms?"

He took a deep breath before he responded. "That I will not answer for two reasons. I don't know how much it's changed over time. I haven't been there since I was a child. Shit, I don't even know if my parents would recognize me."

"And the second reason?"

He looked inward with a half-smile when he said, "My memory of it is nostalgic." Any trace of a smile was gone when he looked at me. "I don't want to disappoint you with high expectations. But if it's anything like I remember, I wouldn't want to ruin the surprise."

The rainforest was unfathomably large. We spent seven nights sleeping on a bed of leaves from whatever nearby tree had the biggest selection. It was surprisingly more comfortable than I expected, except for when I'd wake up with a bug crawling on me or the sound of some wild animal screeching.

The animals were exotic, beautiful, and often quite annoying. Some resembled animals I was familiar with, but none of them looked exactly like the ones I had seen or learned of in the human world, except maybe the wild monkeys. But even they appeared slightly different with their shades of green and blue fur, allowing them to blend easily with the trees and sky.

There were shimmering yellow birds with fanlike tails as impressive as a peacock's. Their tails were long and condensed when they soared between the trees. But the moment they would land, out came their extravagant tail feathers, mimicking the brightness of the sun.

There were other birds—some gray, others white—each as tall as me, with beaks as big as my head. Several walked by us chewing fruit from the trees. One piece of fruit was a single bite for them.

We even caught sight of some insects that looked like twigs and leaves. My heart ached whenever I accidentally stepped on one of the camouflaged bugs. Razz, on the other hand, thought it was funny, which was strange since he avoided stepping on them himself. Or perhaps it was my sincere apologies to the dead critters that made him laugh. We both had a decent amount of bug bites by the eighth day.

Thankfully, we didn't have to worry about bathing, considering how much it rained each day. If we were lucky, we'd find a giant leaf to hold over our heads, keeping us mostly dry. By the time the rain would stop, my arms would undoubtedly be heavy and sore from holding up my self-made umbrella. It was certainly not the same type of magically drying water that I had become familiar with from the passageway.

On the ninth night, it rained so much, Razz and I huddled close under a canopy we had made of giant leaves and vines. As I watched the rain pour over the canopy above us, shivering, I whispered, "Are you awake?"

"No," he responded. When I said nothing, he added, "I was kidding. What's on your mind?"

"Warmth. Fire. The sun," I said as my teeth chattered.

It was so chilly; we had to hold each other the entire night for warmth. It was the first time I had ever fallen asleep in someone else's arms. It didn't help that we were both soaked in rain halfway through the night.

The following day, I was miserably cold with damp clothes, trying to make sense of the nonsensical summer weather. Razz was just as cold and wet, but somehow found our predicament to be hilarious. He kept trying to make me smile as we continued through the rainforest that seemed never to end. Anytime I questioned if we were lost, Razz would pull out his trusty compass and reassure me we were on the right path.

By early evening on the eleventh day in the rainforest, the sound of pouring water in the distance piqued our interest. We followed the sound on a rocky trail until we finally reached the most spectacular waterfall I had ever laid eyes on, easily a hundred feet high.

Razz turned to me with a raised brow. "Up for a swim?" he asked, standing before a sizable pool of turquoise water.

"Not really," I answered honestly.

"I guess I'll go to the Kano Kingdom by myself then," he said as he removed his shoes, adding them to the bag on his back.

I scanned my surroundings. Tree-covered mountains went on for miles on each side of the towering waterfall. But there was absolutely no kingdom in sight.

"Where exactly is this kingdom?" I questioned.

He was putting away the compass when he said, "Follow me, and you'll see." And with his stupid, charming smile, he jumped into the water.

CHAPTER 21

The Kiss

With some irritation, I removed my shoes and put them in my bag before stepping into the water myself, careful not to get my bag wet from the splashing of the waterfall. I somehow managed to keep most of my things dry in my bag and would not let this last part of the rainforest rob me of that.

Thankfully, the pool wasn't too deep, so I was able to tiptoe through the cooling water while holding my bag over my head as I followed Razz toward the skyscraping waterfall.

Then he suddenly disappeared behind it. The closer I moved toward it, the deeper the pool became. So I threw my bag to the wide rocky ledge at the corner of the waterfall and swam the rest of the way.

When I reached the end of the pool, I finally saw Razz standing behind the pouring water with a smirk on his face. "What took so long?" he asked before moving farther behind the waterfall and out of sight again.

I picked up my bag with a glance at the dusk sky and followed along the bend of the ledge, quickly finding myself in a sizable cave.

171

And to no surprise, it was filled with water. The water was only a couple of feet high, so we were able to walk through it, but somewhat uncomfortably as my bare feet felt the curves of every rock.

The cave went on for at least a mile, perhaps even longer. After a miserable amount of time traveling through the cave—my feet sore as hell—the water we walked through suddenly filled with light, a silent indication of the last starlight.

Razz was a few feet ahead when he looked back at me with a finger pointing up. I had been so captivated by the enchanting light of the glowing water that I hadn't even noticed the high cave ceiling had scattered blue light as well. I wasn't sure if they were drops of water splattered on the top, but it looked like the night sky was above us, glittering blissful blue stars.

The cave seemed to be never-ending as we walked for another starlight before finally reaching a sizable ledge for us to rest. We sat on the crusted shelf against the rocky cave wall as our clothes dried.

"How much farther?" I asked, attempting to find any comfort on the gravelly ledge, in drenched clothes, nonetheless.

"Not much, but we should probably rest for the night," he responded with heavy eyes, placing his bag beneath his head as if it were a pillow. I pulled out my soft, suedelike cloak from my bag, rolled it up, and set it beneath my head.

Razz was lying on his side with his back to me when he said, "I'm sorry."

"For what?"

"Since we started this trip, I haven't been myself. I've been short-tempered with you, and for that, I'm sorry. I know there's no excuse for my behavior, but I've allowed my worries about my brother to get the best of me. And I've been taking it out on you since you're the only one around. I hope you can forgive me."

I truly meant it when I said, "Razz, of course I forgive you. You have every right to be worried, and I wasn't expecting you to be chipper for this trip. We're on a stressful mission, and it's bound to get the best of both of us at times." I didn't know what else to say, other than, "You're a good brother."

"Thank you. But I also want to be a good friend."

"You are. Stop being so hard on yourself."

We fell into silence. Both of us tossed and turned in our wet clothes on the hard ledge we lay on. The physical discomfort of it was nearly unbearable. Half a starlight later, I rolled over to find Razz facing me with eyes closed. I wondered how in the hell he fell asleep in such discomfort. At least until he said, "Still awake?"

"Yep."

He opened his eyes. They were as beautiful and as navy-blue as the night sky.

"Are we going to talk about it?" he asked. I had no idea what he was referring to. He must have seen the confusion on my face since he added, "So, do you kiss all your friends on the cheek or just your favorites?"

Immediately, I felt embarrassment fill my ears with heat. I had not a clue what to say since I wasn't even sure why I kissed his cheek to begin with. Maybe it had something to do with the sight of Lance's flirtatious sister and her lusting eyes fixed on Razz. But I wasn't going to tell him that. I didn't want him to think I was jealous because I wasn't, I don't think.

Razz propped his chin in the palm of his hand, looking handsome as hell as his curls fell loosely over his forehead. He leaned on a single elbow when he inched closer to me until, finally, his lips met my cheek with a kiss. He retracted himself, though slowly.

"There. Now we're even," he said, lying back down with his back to me.

I awkwardly said nothing back. Maybe I didn't have to. It wasn't long after that before we both drifted to sleep.

As I slept rather uncomfortably, a chill crept through the cave overnight, sending Razz closer to me. I wanted to scooch nearer to him too, if it meant warming up, but I didn't. We were growing so close during this journey, and it scared me if I were being completely honest with myself.

The only guy I had ever been this close with was James. And that was a different kind of closeness, a brotherly kind. Razz was just a friend, after all. And I certainly didn't want him to think of me as anything more than that.

When I finally woke the next morning, the light of the water had gone, which meant dawn had broken. Razz was still asleep beside me, so I whispered, "Wake up." He didn't budge. So I nudged his arm. His natural impulse was to roll over to the other side and continue to sleep.

He left me no choice. I freshened up as much as possible with what little I had and jumped back in the water with my bag secured over my shoulder. Before continuing forward, I splashed water on Razz's face.

He shot up. "What the hell?"

"Oh, I'm sorry. Did I wake you?" I said innocently.

"No," he said coldly. "The water you splashed on my face did."

With a shrug, I said, "Nothing else worked." I smiled to ease the tension. "You coming?"

He chuckled as he pulled a glass jar with purple petals out of his bag. He took one out and began chewing on it. "Want one?" he asked.

"Sure," I said, purely out of curiosity.

He handed me one before returning the jar to his bag and throwing his bag over his shoulder. Then, he jumped in the water, purposefully splashing a fair amount onto my face.

"We're even!" I said, wiping the water off my face before throwing the dried purple petal in my mouth as Razz had done. Every crunch of the petal between my teeth released a robust minty taste. Moments later, the rest of the chewed petal dissolved on my tongue. It was rather refreshing.

It took nearly an entire starlight until we finally saw the light of the sun break through an opening high above the cave wall. We followed the light to the end of the cave.

My stomach turned at the sight of our only exit. The only way out would be to climb up to the opening and hope we fit through.

So, without hesitation, I handed my bag to Razz and began to climb, strategically stepping on the nits and grits of the cave wall. Razz watched as I fell into the water once, then twice, then three more times.

"You done?" he asked, unimpressed.

I grunted. "Do you have a better idea?"

He handed my bag back to me before rummaging through his own. A moment later, he pulled out a rope with a grappling hook, effortlessly throwing it up the cave wall and through the opening above.

My mouth dropped with irritation. "So, my many failed attempts to climb the wall were just for your entertainment?"

"Well, I mean" —he turned to me with that stupid alluring smile— "it was cute to see you try."

I ignored him with an eye roll.

He tugged on the rope. "Ladies first," he said smugly.

"Well then, what are you waiting for?" I replied, matching his smugness.

"Actually, I take that as a compliment," he said as he began to confidently climb up the rope with ease. "Women can do many things men can't, like grow life inside them, get turned on without detection, and even fake an org—oh shit."

Just as Razz was nearing the opening, the cave wall cracked. Razz released the rope and jumped off, pushing me out of the way just as the wall crumbled down in the spot I had stood seconds before.

"You okay?" he asked as he handed me my soaked bag that had floated feet away from me.

I didn't know if I wanted to hug him for saving me from being crushed or hit him for knocking my bag in the water when I had been so careful not to get it wet before now.

Instead of doing either, I grabbed my bag from his hand and gave him my thanks through gritted teeth before walking over the crumbled wall and out of the cave to the fresh morning air.

What stood majestically in the far-off distance was a white stone palace surrounded by miles and miles of crystal-blue water. The sunny, white sand beach was beckoning my cold, damp feet.

CHAPTER 22

The Nixies

"Razz?" I looked around me, but he seemed to have vanished. "Razz?" My heart pounded as I stood alone in this foreign place. I scanned the palm trees and sand, and even the beach in the distance. Where the hell had he gone to? "Razz?" I shouted.

A moment later, he strolled toward me from around the corner of the cave, adjusting his pants. "Sorry, I was taking a leak."

I responded with a look of irritation despite my relief at his sudden reappearance.

We walked a short distance toward the palace before we came to a stop behind a few tropical trees.

The distant palace was wrapped in an abundance of white stone pillars and buildings, topped by several dome structures. It wasn't just a pearly palace on water. It was an entire city on the sea, perhaps more than one.

"The Kano Kingdom!" Razz said in awe.

"I suppose this is Calder's kingdom?" I questioned as I returned my shoes to my feet.

"You suppose right," Razz said as he pulled out the couplings, handing one to me.

While he latched a coupling on his arm, I asked, "Why do we need these?"

"We'll need them. Believe me," he said as his hair suddenly changed to seafoam green. And his arms now had glimmering patches of green scales matching his new hair. It wasn't until I looked up from his arms that I realized he had shiny, minty hues of scales around his eyes. The utter beauty of it took me by surprise.

The moment I put the other coupling on my forearm and tapped it with his, my hair turned pastel yellow, and I suddenly had patches of glimmering yellow scales on my skin.

As I ran my fingers over the patches on my arm, Razz said, "It's not real. I'm just bending our appearance, so we blend in."

We walked on sand toward a white stone pathway that led to the city's entrance.

"But why do we need to blend in? Calder doesn't have scales."

"As far as Calder goes, he did have scales. He also told me what to expect here, so just trust me. It'll be our only chance to get past the nixies."

Since when did Calder have scales?

"Wait—past the what?"

He didn't answer as he continued toward the glistening pathway.

Calder looked so human, without a trace of scales. I didn't understand how or why he didn't have them anymore. I had so many questions for Razz but now was apparently not the time as he kept hushing me while we stepped foot on the pathway toward the pearly white city.

I glimpsed my reflection in the vast crystal-blue water surrounding the pathway. The yellow scales Razz had obscured me with were not around my eyes like his, but rather freckled on my cheekbones.

Razz strolled confidently toward the city while I walked the narrow path with uncertainty. I had no idea what we were walking into.

Just as I took in the blissful beauty of the perfectly blue water, I saw something swimming toward us. My stomach turned when I saw another figure and then another. I quickly realized eight things were swimming toward us on one side of the pathway and another eight on the other side.

My chest tightened as faces surfaced from the water. Sixteen sets of massive, entirely gray eyes followed our every step down the path. We nearly made it to the entrance before one of what I assumed to be a nixie flew out of the water and moved in on us with a sharp hiss, revealing dagger teeth.

Her wings were unlike any I had ever seen. Each one was like a shimmering white flowy cape. She had a mermaidlike gray tail coated in spikes, with fins at the ends like razor-sharp scythes. Her long hair matched the gray of her tail and eyes, each strand sparkling under the sun.

Her bulging gray eyes were mere inches away, bobbing between the two of us. "And who might you be?" she said in a chilling whisper.

My nerves kept my voice locked. But Razz remained calm when he said, "We have been stuck on Elloriya's edge. We found a way past the barrier and want to return home."

Another nixie moved farther above the surface of the water. "He speaks truth," she said in a breathy voice to the one blocking the entrance of the city. Her gaze was so heavy on us, I was sure she was silently searching our minds.

"He may speak truth, but the home he speaks of is not here," she said to the nixie in the water before turning back to Razz. "Have you come here with ill intent?"

"No, not at all. We are good friends of Calder—the next heir to the Kano Kingdom."

She darted closer to Razz when she said, "I know who Calder is!" She lowered her hairless brows and squinted her eyes. "Because you have not lied, I will let you pass. But if I were you, I would keep up with your false appearance for as long as you can."

"Yes, ma'am," Razz said.

"Do not call me 'ma'am'!" she hissed before darting back into the water. She and all the nixies kept their heads above the surface, their eyes following our every step.

Finally, we passed the white archway and were now in the most beautiful city I had ever seen.

Fanciful restaurants, stores, and decorative pools lined the outdoor path we walked along, all made of glistening white stone.

The people here were the only source of color with freckles and patches of shimmering scales matching their pastel hair—the most popular colors being soft shades of blue, green, and yellow. Razz and I quickly blended in with the locals. At least in the false appearance Razz had camouflaged us with.

Though most of the locals appeared very human, besides their scale markings, a few appeared more fishlike, with fins on their heads and arms and gills in place of ears. These rare people were wholly submerged in rough scales. Although I had only seen a few of them, they appeared unfriendly with a scowl and withering stares.

As Razz and I strolled through the city, many passersby eyed our clothing. The only people who didn't seem to mind our outfits were the children we passed. Razz wore his usual black leathered clothing, and I wore my plum purple skirted jumpsuit Cece had gotten me at the emporium. Everyone else mainly wore white or beige.

"It seems you failed in dressing us appropriately," I joked.

Razz suddenly grabbed my waist and pulled me behind a towering dried fountain in a well-hidden corner beside a restaurant.

He leaned over me with a forearm resting on the fountain behind my back and whispered, "I can dress us however I'd like, whenever I'd like." He scanned my body, and in the blink of an eye, I wore the same beige wrap-around outfit as a passerby. He smirked, and a second later, I wore the obnoxious purple gown Queen Eloise Adaire had worn at her gala. Another blink and I wore my beloved gray cloak with nothing but a bra and panties underneath.

Razz didn't dare look at my unclothed body, but stayed inches from me, staring smugly into my eyes as I attempted to grasp at the cloak to cover my bare stomach and legs, even though no one could see in our hidden corner. But as my fingers clutched at the cloak, it caught nothing but air. It looked so real, I had forgotten for a moment that it was just a mind-bending trick.

The way Razz could bend my mind and sight as easily as taking a breath was impressive as hell. But instead of giving him the satisfaction of knowing this, I slipped my arms behind my back and unlatched the coupling. Our tied energy severed, and I was instantly back in my skirted jumpsuit with my dark blonde hair and all. The smugness on his face dropped.

"Better luck next time!" I said with a chuckle as I sneakily latched my coupling once more, followed by a gentle push on Razz's chest away from me.

Razz must have felt the sudden reconnection as he looked at my arm with a snicker. "Cheater!"

I prepared to walk off with my head held high when he threw his arm in front of me, keeping me pinned to the corner. My heart raced as he leaned in.

He gently laced his free hand over my fingers as he stayed staring into my eyes. He didn't bother to break our gaze when he tapped our couplings together. The energy tightened between us.

He had yet to release my hand, and I didn't know why until my hair turned pastel yellow again, matching the reappearance of scaly patches on my arms and any other part of my bare skin on display. Then, he released his hand from mine and dropped his arm, waiting for me to walk on in the same outfits we arrived in.

"So, I guess you're not going to mind-bend our clothes or whatever?"

"No. It takes more energy than I care to use. So I was thinking"—he grabbed my hand and pulled me into a nearby clothing store—"we'll go shopping instead."

The store didn't have a wide variety of options. Most of the clothes were the same, except in different sizes. Although the majority were white or beige, there were pricier options in silver.

"Oh, hello!" a gorgeous seller said, with a twirl of her aqua hair, speaking primarily to Razz. Her turquoise eyes and scales freckled over her dark skin only added to her beauty.

Razz sent a handsome smirk her way, and as he did, I could have sworn the scales on her cheeks glowed.

"What do you think?" Razz asked, holding up a stunning silver outfit in my size.

"Well, if you were to ask me" —the seller circled Razz with her striking blue eyes climbing every inch of him— "anything in my store would make you look absolutely delicious."

His brows raised, and he smacked on that damn alluring smile, per usual. "Thank you, love. But I was asking my friend here." He gave the seller a subtle but smooth wink before turning back to me.

I didn't hesitate when I said, "I think it looks expensive."

Razz moved in close, out of the seller's earshot. "And I think we have a heavy pouch of pentacles."

"Just because we have some gold coins doesn't mean we should spend them carelessly," I said firmly.

"I don't think you realize how much one pentacle is worth. I just want to make sure we properly use it. And just because we made it into the city, doesn't mean we'll make it into the palace. So proper attire is a must." He slowed his words down when he held up the silver outfit once more and asked, "So, do you like it?"

"Well, yes, it's beautiful. But I had something else in mind."

I grabbed an outfit that caught my eye the moment I stepped into the store and went to the dressing room behind gray silk curtains. I slipped on a white-iridescent fish scale fabric with a high neck collar and a sharp upturned shoulder blade on the left side. It was elegant, and surely worthy enough for the palace. At least, I hoped.

While adjusting the new outfit, my gag reflex tugged my throat as I overheard aggressive flirtation between Razz and the salesgirl.

All the while, my yellow hair and freckled scales had faded. Perhaps Razz wasn't good at multitasking while a beautiful woman stroked his ego.

When I stepped foot outside the dressing room, Razz didn't even realize my aquatic disguise was gone until I cleared my throat, gesturing toward my hair and skin.

The seller kept her eyes on Razz as he realized his poor effort at bending my appearance. I wondered what would happen if she saw me. Would she even care?

My hair turned yellow, and the patches reappeared once more as Razz eyed my outfit and said, "It's perfect!"

He grabbed a handsome white tunic with even nicer pants. Then, he went to the dressing room and lazily closed the curtain halfway, allowing the seller and me a glimpse of his perfectly sculpted body. I rolled my eyes, as I was nearly certain he did that on purpose.

He stepped out, looking far more handsome than usual, which I didn't think was possible. White was a good color on him.

He grabbed a silver cape and threw it over his shoulders, latching it with a fancy clasp below his Adam's apple. The cape covered nearly all his white attire. Though he looked handsome as hell, it was strange seeing him in a color that wasn't his usual black clothing.

The seller sucked on her lower lip as she hungrily took in the sight of Razz.

He removed three pentacles from the red velvet pouch and placed them on the counter. "Keep the change, love," he said smoothly.

She appeared pleased. I just wasn't sure if it had to do with the high payment or Razz's enticing charm.

After we stepped out of the store, I turned to Razz and finally asked, "Why doesn't Calder have any scales?"

He hesitated, took a breath, and then said, "After traveling so many times through the passageway, it took them. He thought maybe his scales would return, like Darian's voice had when he came back to Elloriya, but they never did."

My mouth went dry. I didn't know what to say or even think. My heart ached for Calder. A part of him was stolen when he traveled between worlds, just like my memories of Elloriya were stolen from me. I swallowed at the thought of it.

We continued in the direction of the palace with smiles and admiration of our clothing from passersby.

The dome at the far end of the city was our guide. It was easy to follow, considering it was the only silver dome and towered over all the others.

The court was so far on the other side of the city, it took nearly four starlights to get there. When we finally reached the pearly white palace capped with silver, we were surprised and a little unsettled. There were no guards, or anyone, for that matter.

The number of steps we had to climb to get to the palace doors was enough to have us panting at the top. Razz tried pulling open the doors, but they were locked.

"Cover me," he said as he pulled out some small tools from his bag and began picking the lock. I obeyed and kept him hidden behind me, even though there was no one to hide from.

It wasn't long before I heard a *click*.

Razz uttered, "Child's play," as he put his tools away. Then he grabbed my hand and pulled me inside the palace.

CHAPTER 23

The Kano Kingdom

The pearly white palace had expansive, arched, glassless windows in nearly every direction, welcoming the sea breeze to roll in. There were enough windows to allow a perfect view of the vast, bright blue sea.

A sizable pool of crisp water with several fish was centered under the massive palace dome. And in the middle of the pool was a monumental silver chalice twice my height.

The sun gleamed through the vast columned halls, all of which were empty of people.

Only a few steps into the empty palace, and a sound—soft and distant—captivated my every sense. Though it was quiet—nearly undetectable—it felt as though it had come to life, taking me by the hand and leading me to the most elegantly enchanted music I had ever heard.

Perhaps I was in some sort of trance, but I had been swept away by musical waves, though delicate they were. I hadn't even turned to Razz to tell him where I was off to as my mind and body surrendered to the music.

As I slowly and quietly followed the sound down a few halls, it grew louder—still soft, but more powerful. Finally, when I reached a significant door moments later, I stood, captivated by the most breathtaking orchestra I had ever seen, centered in a circular theater and an audience of hundreds.

Each poised musician had clothing of pure silver, dressed as if they were attending a royal ball.

There were violins, cellos, harps, and even a piano. They may have held slightly different shapes than those from Earth, but they played the same sounds. I couldn't believe my eyes when colors rolled and splashed with the music, then flowed from the instruments.

The violins made waves of soft blue. The cellos released a playful orange swimming with every glide of the bow and seafoam green with every strum. The harps rained violet. And the piano splashed yellow for the high notes, red for the low notes, and pink in between. When the colors lingered through and past the circled audience, finally reaching me, they tended to my every sense and desire.

The soft blue caressed my skin, carrying the heavenly scent of the sea. The playful orange was slightly ticklish, especially when it swam over my shoulders. The seafoam green was like kisses wherever it could reach me. The drops of violet felt like rain and smelled like it too. And the colors from the piano, to my complete bewilderment, didn't feel or smell like anything. Instead, they had flavor.

The yellow was tangy but perfectly subtle. The pink was sweet and fruity. And the red was delightfully sour. Yet, each one was delicious as they magically poured over my tongue from the floating colors simply touching my skin.

Encircling the silver-dressed musicians and colorful music was a pool of water. Inside the water were six synchronized swimmers, wearing iridescent orange from head to toe. The swimmers climbed up pearly silk ropes that had just dropped to the water, held by the high theater ceiling.

They were suddenly acrobats as they wrapped themselves and glided in their ribboned rope high over the circled audience, elegantly moving with the music.

Everyone in the audience had colored hair like those outside the palace and gleaming scales around their eyes, cheeks, chins, or foreheads, matching the scales scattered in other areas around their bodies.

I had seen no one with silver scales until my sight landed on Calder's parents in the first row, sitting in the only thronelike seats. The king had the darkest blue hair in all the audience, with silver scales on his forehead and chin. And the queen, holding the king's hand, had beautiful aqua-blue hair with silver highlights matching the scales around her eyes.

My attention turned back to the show. I could have stood there forever, watching, feeling, tasting every perfect musical note. But then a hand grabbed my shoulder and pulled me away. When my trance broke, I turned to find Razz.

He said, "Now would be our best chance at finding where their relic belongs."

I only nodded, struggling to part from the majestic performance.

With another glance inside the theater, Razz said, "Smuggled magic at its finest."

When we were finally far enough from the theater, Razz pulled out his pendulum, silently asking it questions as we swept through the empty palace, looking down every hall, in every gigantic room, finding no sign of where to return their magic. But then, an idea poured into my mind. I don't know how I hadn't thought of it sooner.

"Do you think the compass will show us where the relic belongs?" I asked, trying to contain my excitement at the thought of it working.

His eyes sparkled at the idea as he pulled the compass out. "Where does the relic belong in the Kano Kingdom?" he asked.

My heart stopped for just a moment as I waited eagerly for the compass to light up and move its arrow. But my heartbeat continued disheartened as the compass did not light up, and the arrow did not budge. It seemed we were on our own.

"Don't you have some superpowered third eye or something? Can't you use your intuition to help us find it faster?" I asked, desperate for a glimpse of hope.

"*Not* superpowered," he corrected me, then lowered his brows with an inward gaze. "Well, maybe superpowered," he said with a grin of smugness. "Anyway, I've tried that. But bending our appearance is taking all my energy. Whenever I mind-bend, my intuition shuts down. Not to mention the stress of our situation." His face went suddenly solemn. "Of my brother's situation."

"How have you bent our appearance for this long, anyway?" I questioned, just before seeing a guard strolling up the hall. We stayed hidden and quiet until the guard had passed.

Razz was inspecting a white fountain enveloped in sunlight when he said, "It's tiring, but it's also far easier to change our hair color and add some scales than changing every detail of our appearance to Orpheus. Plus, I think seeing my brother in the grid, or whatever that was, has given me more strength." Then, with a moment's hesitation, he said, "But to be honest, I'm not sure how much longer I can keep this up."

I tried not to give in to the hopeless feeling flooding my chest.

But then, one room caught my attention that we hadn't checked yet. It had double doors adorned with silver designs. The only problem was that the doors were sealed shut by nothing other than six long silver tentacles. The center of it was bumpy and about the size of a large hand. But there was certainly no head attached.

Razz ran his hand over a tentacle, just as he would have to wake Esmond at the front doors of the manor. Nothing happened. He then tried to move the tentacles by force. They didn't budge.

So, I gave it a try. I took in the sight of the strange silver-tentacled thing, and instead of going for its arms, I ran my fingers over the bumpy center, where all the tentacles met. And to my surprise, the bumps opened. Suddenly, six bright blue eyes were staring back at me. Until a moment later when the eyes closed. And still, the tentacles stayed glued to their spot.

Razz pushed me aside without warning, and in a single blink, his eyes turned brown, his nose grew rounder, his stomach grew larger, his hair straightened and shifted to dark blue, and he suddenly had silver scales lining his forehead and chin. He had completely transformed into looking like Calder's father. If I didn't know any better, I would have thought him to be the king of this palace.

He ran his fingers over the center, and the six eyes opened for a few moments before closing once more. Except this time, the tentacles peeled off, and the silver creature moved over to a single door, allowing us passage. Razz pushed the free door open, but something stopped us just before we stepped in. Or rather, someone.

Razz still appeared as the king when a young man with aqua-blue hair and matching freckled scales said, "Uncle Malik? I thought you were watching the show."

With a deep voice, Razz said, "I was, but I wanted to um, sit—on my throne."

With lowered brows, swaying his brown eyes between Razz and me, he asked, "What's with your voice? And who's this?"

Razz's impersonated face drained of color as he peered past the young man. I turned to look in the same direction and immediately felt sick to my stomach.

The actual king was walking toward us.

CHAPTER 24

The Water Reader

Razz quickly changed back to himself, but with seafoam green hair and freckled scales around his eyes. He silently closed the door, and the tentacled creature moved over the center, sealing the doors once more.

The young man before us looked puzzled for just a moment before losing his balance.

"Hey, man, are you okay?" Razz asked him.

"Kai!" the king yelled from down the hall. "Just the man I was looking for!"

Kai? I thought back to the first time I met Calder in Ridgewood Hollow when he introduced himself with that name.

Kai's bewilderment nearly pushed him in a stumble to the floor. Razz held him up.

A baffled expression poured over the king as he stepped beside his nephew. "Kai, what's the matter with you?"

Razz bowed his head. "Your majesty, he somehow thought I was you. He seems to be hallucinating. I think he needs to lie down."

"Very well!" the king said as he moved in front of the double doors and petted the silver creature in a way someone might lovingly pet their cat. As it moved to allow entrance, the king said, "Bring him in. Lay him down over there." He pointed to a clam-shaped, gray-cushioned bench in the corner of the throne room. "And then tell me who you are and why you're not watching the show."

Blissful energy filled every corner of the room. A long pool of water flowed under a silver bridge that led to two impressive thrones, not surprisingly, made of silver.

The top of each throne appeared as a decorative tidal wave hovering over where the king's and queen's heads would be, but still allowing enough room to display their impressive crowns.

"We are friends of Kai's. He mentioned earlier that he was feeling dizzy, so we came to check on him," Razz said convincingly. Kai was out of earshot, rubbing his temples across the room.

While Razz effortlessly spewed lies, I scanned the throne room, hoping to find where their relic belonged. After all, the Tera Kingdom's throne room led me to where their relic needed to be to return their magic. Perhaps it was the same here.

The king flung his head in surprise, absentmindedly stroking the silver scales on his chin. "Really? I didn't know Kai had friends. He always keeps to himself. Anyway, will you be joining us for tonight's feast?"

"I wouldn't dream of missing it, your majesty. Where will we dine?"

"In the kelp forest, as usual. It begins at the nineteenth starlight. See you there!" He walked off with a cheerful hum and left us in the throne room with his nephew.

Razz walked up to Kai, who was still lying in the corner of the room, holding his head. "Hey, man! You might be coming down with something. You'll want to rest in bed during the feast. You'll feel much better in the morning. I'll take you to your room."

Kai nodded.

Razz held Kai up, and Kai pointed toward his room down each hallway. We had a view of the sea through the columned arches nearly the entire way there. When we turned down a hall with nothing but a dead-end, we were sure we took a wrong turn. At least until Kai weakly pressed a silver starfish on the turquoise crystal wall at the end of the hall.

The crystals on the wall parted, revealing a hidden set of stairs. We walked Kai down the wavelike steps, and when we got to the bottom, we were suddenly in an underwater corridor entirely made of glass.

As we passed a few arched doors, a school of orange fish swam over our heads—each with flowy fins as long as my waist-length hair. I even glimpsed a four-eyed shark.

The moment Kai entered his bedroom and closed the door, I turned to Razz, who suddenly looked like his usual self. "What did you do to Kai?"

"What I had to do. Getting my brother back alive is my priority. And unfortunately, he got in the way, so I just made him feel a little dizzy and tired. I honestly didn't know I could do that since I've never exercised bending someone's mind in that way. But I'm sure he'll fall asleep, and it'll wear off."

As we moved back toward the stairs, Razz suddenly lost his balance. He leaned his hand against the glass separating us from the sea.

"Karma's a bitch, isn't it?" I joked as I pulled him to the floor to sit.

"I've been bending our appearance for too long. I just need a moment."

It wasn't until I sat beside Razz and saw my reflection on the glass walls that I realized he had stopped bending my appearance too. He released his bag from his shoulder and pulled out food he had collected from the rainforest. He handed me a fruit with a soft orange peel and vibrant blue flesh sprinkled with tiny green seeds before devouring one himself.

We sat in silence, watching the sea creatures swim by. Most of them looked like those on Earth. There were dolphins and jellyfish, except the dolphins were more silver than gray, and the jellyfish were the size of Ignatius. The fish looked as ordinary as tropical ones on Earth, except it seemed they communicated through flickering lights on their scales, as did the jellyfish with their tentacles.

After a few minutes of mindlessly watching the sea creatures swim by, I broke the silence. "I know Etiwa said not to tell anyone about the relics. But why didn't you just tell the king that we're friends of Calder's? Wouldn't it be easier to pull this off without so many lies?"

"No!" Razz said sternly. He withdrew for a minute before he continued. "There was a moment at the Tera Kingdom where I thought I had let Gemma's mother down. I don't want to feel that way again, and I don't want to get anyone's hopes up. Not even my own."

"Okay. So, what's the plan?"

He let out a chuckle. "I'm flattered you think I have one."

"We're attending a royal feast this evening with no plan whatsoever?"

"Yep," he said before taking another bite of his fruit without a care in the world. Or so it seemed.

Click.

Swish.

The sound of slow footsteps coming down the stairs caused Razz to immediately bend our appearance yet again. It was an elderly woman with soft white hair and shimmering white scales around the sides of her eyes and spread elegantly over her brows.

As she moved slowly in our direction with a blue crystal cane carved into a thin ocean wave, Razz immediately pushed himself off the floor and gave her a short bow of his head. I followed his lead and did the same. She stopped before me and stared into my eyes without so much as a hello or smile.

Razz interrupted her silent stare with a clearing of his throat. "Hello, ma'am. We are friends of Kai's." Her silent gaze fell on him now. "We just helped him to his room. Poor guy is not feeling well. But he mentioned something about a guest room for my friend and me. I don't suppose you know where that is, do you?"

The woman lifted her wrinkled hand and gestured for us to follow. She took us down the glass corridor and to the very last room. She pointed at the tentaclelike handle. Razz opened the door to reveal a guest room with one large circular bed, a small rock pond in the corner, a bathing room, and glass walls, allowing us a view of the underwater life, just like in the corridor. Except the glass wall separating the bathing room from the bedroom appeared frosted, permitting privacy.

"Thank you, ma'am!" Razz said as we stepped inside. But just as Razz began to close the door, the woman stopped him with her cane and walked inside too.

She moved toward the rock pond—home to at least a dozen miniature fish. She pulled a dazzling shell out of her pocket and held it out toward Razz. Razz looked just as confused as me, but he took the opalescent shell anyway. She then pointed to the water.

"Would you like me to toss it in?" he asked.

The woman nodded, so Razz obliged.

Plop.

Hmm, that's odd. As the shell met the water, it didn't create a single ripple, but instead sunk quickly to the bottom.

The woman crossed to the pond and stayed staring at where the shell had sunk. Then, suddenly, her eyes widened at the clear, still water. Was she seeing something we didn't?

She looked up at us, and to our surprise, she spoke. Her voice was delicate but strong when her eyes pierced Razz, and she said, "You can drop the illusion."

My heart pounded, and I was sure I felt Razz's nerves through the couplings too. But he kept his calm and replied, "I'm not sure what you're talking about."

She moved slowly toward Razz, and when she was as close as she could get, she looked up at him with squinted eyes. "Do I look like a fool to you?"

His eyes widened. "No, ma'am!"

She began to walk away, but then she turned back to Razz and lifted her blue crystal cane, tapping it against his chest when she said, "Just like you, young man, I too have a third eye, and I know how to use it better than any other in this kingdom." Her delicate voice strengthened. "You may have fooled my son, but he is still king of these waters, and he can have you drowned for your lies alone." She slowly paced back and forth with her cane marching beside her. When she looked back at Razz and me, she said with a twinge of irritation, "Go ahead. Let's see what you really look like."

I was sure Razz wouldn't budge. He was a charming liar who effortlessly talked his way out of any situation. But then, my stomach turned when the scattered scales on us faded, and our hair turned back to their normal shades.

"Good!" she said with a sharp nod. "Now that we are being honest, I can care less that you're not who you say you are. You're obviously not friends of Kai's because he doesn't have any. But if I read the water correctly, I believe you know my other grandson. Am I correct?"

"Yes, ma'am," he said respectfully.

She continued to pace. "And if you succeed in whatever plan you have, it can bring him back to the Kano Kingdom?"

Razz swallowed, clearly impressed. He looked at me, then back at her with a nod.

"Well then, you better get to it! If you need my help, ask for Madam Mira!" she said as she headed toward the door. Before she opened it, she turned back to Razz. "In all my years, I have never met a mind-bender." She studied him for a moment before she ended with, "You have not disappointed."

His cheeks filled with color as his lips broke into a proud smirk.

The moment she closed the door, I unlatched the coupling from my arm and threw it on the bed, desperate to feel nothing but my own energy.

Razz did the same before unlatching his new cape, taking his fancy tunic off, and neatly tossing them beside the bed. After glimpsing his lean, modest muscles, I turned away, unsure how much more he was planning to strip off.

"What ya doin there, Razz?" I asked as casually as possible.

He threw himself on the bed half naked, then replied, "Taking a nap."

"Shouldn't we spend this time searching for where the relic belongs?"

"Perhaps you should, but if I'm going to make it through tonight's feast bending our appearance, then I need to recharge." He gripped the pillow and buried his head in it.

"You know very well that I can't go looking around the palace without you changing my appearance. And how is attending the feast going to help us?"

His eyes were closed when he said, "I don't know yet. But it will. I can feel it."

CHAPTER 25

Blue Opal

The sun poured into the sea, spreading its rays throughout the underwater bathing room. As I lay in the tub, I closed my eyes and saw only one thing in my mind: Darian.

I had spent my time bathing, thinking back to every action between him and me before he went into the grid. The way he walked past me in the library without a single glance. The way he held my hand for a fraction of a second at the dining table. The way he looked at me before stepping into that damn grid!

My heart ached to see him again, even with him being as cold and distant as he was to me. I didn't care. I just wanted to see his dazzling eyes looking back at mine—if not for just a moment. I wanted to feel his body in the flesh, even if it was just a brush against my skin.

Does he have any idea how I feel about him? Does he ever feel my thoughts consuming him? Could he feel my thoughts now?

As if time had stilled, my oxygen suddenly deflated mid-breath as I was pulled into an impossible world illogically close and far. It wasn't a dream my imagination conjured up. It was bright, endless, and I could have sworn it was real; it was a blue light that abruptly flashed, consuming my sight beneath my closed lids. I gripped the rim of the tub, and my eyes sprang open.

What in the hell was that? Was that Darian somehow communicating?

With a heavy breath, I cleared my mind. The only distraction was the thunderous pounding of my heart. Three more deep breaths, and I was ready.

While making sure the voice in my head was loud, I thought the words, *Darian, are you there?*

No blue light. No response whatsoever.

I tried at least ten more times before finally giving up. I didn't know for sure where my mind traveled to or what exactly traveled to me, but deep down, I truly believed it was some knowing part of him—of Darian—reaching out to me.

It was still a few starlights away from the feast, and Razz was in a deep sleep. I couldn't just sit around the room twiddling my thumbs. I was far too anxious.

So instead, I jumped out of the tub, dried myself, dressed appropriately for the feast, pulled out my pouch of yellow pollen from my bag, mixed it with a dab of water, and began painting scales—not on my cheeks where Razz had placed them, but more discreetly, around the sides of my eyes.

My long sleeve outfit and hooded cloak allowed me to cover most of my skin so as not to be detected by my lack of scales. I pulled the hood of my cloak low over my eyes and grabbed the glass icosahedron relic—a faceted ball with twenty faces, each face in triangle form—that magically filled with water since stepping into this palace. And then I left the room with the relic secured in my pocket.

As I walked down the glass corridor, catching sight of a translucent stingray swimming above me, I nearly turned back to grab the coupling. But instead, I clutched the fused onyx and moonstone hanging from the silver chain around my neck, swallowed any concerns, and continued up the wavelike stairs to the corridor's exit.

The show had ended starlights ago, and now people were moving about throughout the palace. Some were dressed elegantly, chatting in small groups here and there. Others were maids, attendants, and kitchen staff hurrying up one hallway and down another.

I was careful to keep my much-too-ordinary hair tucked out of sight under the hood of my cloak. My face was hidden just enough for others to see scales around my eyes, but not well enough to see they were painted on.

I scurried through the halls, sweeping my sight in every direction, hoping to find some inkling to where the relic belonged. After searching the inside of the palace with no luck, I made my way outside.

The moment my gaze fell onto the expansive blue sea with the softening sun resting its reflection comfortably over the water, my mind and soul had simultaneously suspended into pure bliss. I stood there in captivation for so long, I had nearly forgotten what I was doing outside to begin with.

The sea just about surrounded the entire palace, and went on for miles beyond sight, and still, there were pools of water surrounding the outdoor pathways as if the sea was not enough.

A sizable dome gazebo was across the water, with something silver sitting on a narrow platform in its center. It was another chalice. But it wasn't a monumental statue, like the one inside the palace. It was, however, slightly bigger than an ordinary drinking vessel. And I wondered if it was the home for the Kano Kingdom's relic.

With only the thought of being another step closer to getting Darian out of the grid, I jumped in the decorative pool without hesitation and ran toward the silver cup.

The bottom four inches of my cloak and pants had soaked. But I didn't care. All I wanted to do was throw the relic in the chalice and move on to the next kingdom. Except, when I placed the relic inside, nothing happened.

I didn't understand why, but it tied me to the idea of the relic belonging to a chalice. Perhaps it was this idea that now had me running toward the monumental chalice under the massive palace dome.

Water dripped from the bottom of my cloak with every step in the palace. I turned a few heads with the squeak of my shoes, but I couldn't care less as I now stood before the thirty-foot silver statue cup.

I walked in circles around the fish-filled pool displaying the statue, waiting for the relic to tremble in my hand. There was no tremble of any sort, and no sign of this towering chalice being the place the relic belonged.

Just as I was about to step foot inside the water to get even closer to the towering cup—to be sure I wasn't missing something—a hand on my shoulder jolted me. I turned around to find a displeased man carefully scanning me.

"Who are you? And what is your business here?" he asked with a tilt of his head, attempting to see under my hood.

My heart pounded at the thought of him glimpsing the poorly painted scales around my eyes. I was sure he caught sight of the phony scales cornering my lower lashes. And I was even more certain that I was about to be thrown out of the palace before I could come up with a suitable response.

"Deniz, there you are," a vaguely familiar voice said.

I looked up, just barely to catch a peek at Calder's grandmother.

"I believe I overheard my son asking for your whereabouts," she added.

"Madam Mira, I was just—" He gestured toward me, but before he could finish, the king's mother interrupted.

"Oh, I see you met my guest. It is certainly nice to have her back in the palace." She grabbed me by the arm and looked again at the man. "Thank you, Deniz, for kindly greeting her." He looked bewildered. "Hurry on now."

She said nothing to me as she led me through many hallways until we finally reached a sizable room, luxurious enough for a queen. Instant peace washed over me the moment I stepped foot inside.

The room walls mimicked the sea, appearing as a light blue marble. There were even splashes of green mixed in. But the most mesmerizing element was how it seemed to contain light, as the blue-green walls glistened all around.

She must have noticed my fixation on her bedroom walls as she said, "It is blue opal."

"It's beautiful," were the only words I could conjure up while entrapped in its beauty.

I was so fixated on the blue opal walls, I hadn't even noticed her magnificent bed. It was a giant pearly clam, with the bottom shell holding her mattress and the top shell acting as a canopy. The magnificence of it certainly matched that of her bedroom walls.

She sat on her bed, looking down at the water dripping onto the marble floor around my feet. She lifted a hand toward me, and suddenly water drifted out of the soggy bottom of my cloak, pants, and shoes. She directed the water to a stream encircling her bed as her feet stretched out, resting over a compact bridge between her bed and me.

I watched the colorful fish swimming in the stream around her bed until she finally spoke. "Now, tell me why you were so foolish walking around the palace with the mockery of my people's markings painted on your face."

I broke my gaze off the fish, forcing myself to look her in the eyes. "I, um—" I cleared my throat, remembering Etiwa's warning. "I was searching for a way to bring Calder back," I said honestly.

"And did you find it?"

"Well, no. Not yet."

I don't know why it surprised me when she asked, "How can I help?"

I didn't hesitate to respond. "Is there a hidden place—somewhere in the palace that would be the source of magic for this kingdom?"

Her eyes glossed over, and I stood waiting in silence for an uncomfortable amount of time. "Your friend is good with telepathy. He has a gift beyond any I have ever met."

Her response threw me off as I tried to make sense of how Razz was in any way related to my question. It made a lot more sense moments later when a loud knock sounded on the door, and then Razz appeared tight-lipped on the other side.

He stepped into the room and closed the door behind him. "What the hell were you thinking?" he said, not bothering to contain his anger.

I was careful with my wording, considering we weren't alone. "You were the one that suggested I continue our mission while you 'recharged'!"

His eyes widened. "You didn't actually think I was serious? You, of all people, can read sarcasm as well as you speak it. So don't play stupid with me! You should have waited till I woke to leave the room." He moved even closer to me. And this time with a lowered voice. "You could have jeopardized everything." I stayed silent as he gripped the back of his neck. He let out a sigh before asking, "Did you at least make progress?"

I glanced at Mira sitting on her bed, comfortably watching us argue.

"Um . . ." I tried to conjure up some silver lining to my stupidity before I finally responded with, "No."

He clenched his jaw and lowered his voice. "Did anyone see you?"

With the corner of my eye, I peeked at Mira who gave me a subtle, but encouraging shake of her head. I looked back at Razz with my chin held high. "No!" I said confidently.

Razz looked from me to Mira and back at me again. "You're a terrible liar." He then ripped off a small part of his pricey tunic hidden under his silver cape. He turned to Mira. "Are you by chance a water wielder, like Calder?" he asked, holding out the torn cloth.

She chuckled. "Who do you think taught him?" she said with a hand opened toward Razz. A handful of water escaped her palm and glided effortlessly onto Razz's cloth. She dropped her hand beside her with a weary breath. "Since my kingdom's magic was robbed many zeniths ago, it takes a hundred times more energy to wield such a pathetic amount," she said with an overwhelming amount of sadness in her voice.

For a moment, I wondered why it was so easy for Calder to wield water. But then I remembered that there was still magic in the elements on the edge of Elloriya. For some reason, Shakar never cared to steal it as he did with the kingdoms. Or perhaps he just didn't know how.

Razz gave Madam Mira a thankful bow before turning back to me with the now wet cloth. He moved even closer to me until he was a few inches away. He gently grabbed my jaw with a firm hand and lifted the wet cloth to my face. I took in the dark blue of his eyes as he cleaned off the painted scales. When his sight moved from my temples to my violet eyes, I instantly broke our locked gaze.

Mira used her cane to pull herself up from her bed. "If you two are done with whatever this is, it is time for the feast."

For the first time since Razz stepped into Mira's room, he glanced around at the gleaming blue opal walls, her enormous clam shell bed, the fish-filled stream circling the bed, and the narrow bridge over the stream. After taking it all in, he said, "This room is wicked cool."

"I know," she said surely, leading us out of her bedroom.

"Eh-um," Razz said, clearing his throat before we exited the room. I turned to him with a raised brow. "Are you forgetting something?" he asked testily.

I felt the relic securely in my pocket while glancing back in Mira's room to assure I had left nothing behind. I turned back to Razz with a vacant face. He grabbed my arm and latched a silver band around it with an exasperated eye roll. I instantly felt his frustration through the couplings after he tapped them together.

Within a matter of seconds, Razz had bent both of our appearances. We then stepped foot into the vast columned hall and headed to the dining room.

Kelp Forest Dining

In a magnificent underwater glass-walled dining room, a white marble table with decorative silver trim around the edges sat centered in the middle of a lush kelp forest. Twenty matching silver-trimmed chairs were on each side of the table, with two thronelike seats at the ends. Soft sun rays spread between the many yellow kelp vines, reflecting scattered light throughout the room.

Many of the seats were already filled with talkative, elegantly dressed guests. My nicest and most expensive outfit couldn't compare to a single person here, other than Razz, perhaps. Still, our attire fit in well enough.

Just as expected, everyone wore either white or silver. Thankfully, I was also wearing an all-white iridescent outfit that could easily be seen under my gray cloak—though my cloak certainly did not belong in this room. And Razz wore a long silver cape latched over his right shoulder, covering most of his newly purchased attire.

The moment we walked into the room, I felt Razz's nerves through the coupling bond. It was amazing how I could feel it through my own nerves. It took me by surprise since Razz had always been so fearless—or so it seemed in the last year I'd known him. It was almost as though he sensed something was wrong.

Razz sat beside Mira, and I sat beside him. I listened in on the conversations as more guests shuffled in, many glancing curiously at Razz and me. But we were not interesting enough, or perhaps worthy enough, to be looked at for longer than a few seconds.

"Gali, dear, your scales are shimmering," said a plump woman with large yellow scales over her cheekbones, wearing a sparkling tentacle headpiece atop her lemon hair.

"Thank you. I had them polished last lunar. I'm nearly due for another," replied a woman with dainty, shimmering green scales around the corners of her eyes. The mint green of her braided crownlike hair and scales contrasted beautifully with her hazel eyes.

As I sat in silence while Razz and Mira discussed the ways of communicating telepathically, a young man easily as handsome as Razz, with deep tan skin, turquoise hair, and matching scales on his forehead and chin sauntered down a wavelike slope into the room. He scanned the table and available seats so thoroughly, it took me by surprise when he sauntered across the room and settled himself in the chair beside me.

"Hello, I'm Aalto." His voice was much deeper than expected, yet soothing, like a flowing stream.

"Hi. I'm Attica."

Razz looked over at Aalto with sharp eyes that seemed to say, "I'll be listening," before turning back to Mira.

Aalto put an elbow on the table and rested a cheek on his propped hand. "I've never seen you here before."

"That's because it's my first time." My thoughtless words sent Razz's heel into my shin under the table. "Ouch—I mean, since I was much younger."

"Oh, I'm glad you returned. Who is your host?"

"My host?"

"You had to have been invited by someone of proper stature."

I quickly straightened, putting on what I hoped was a believable face when I said, "Oh, yes. Kai invited me."

His brows lowered. "Kai, as in the king's nephew?"

"Yes!"

"Hmm. He doesn't seem like the type who would host anyone. I don't know him well, but he's always seemed like a locked book, unwilling to open for even the kindest or most beautiful person," he said, giving me the sort of smile an old friend might give after having shared some inside joke. He then shrugged. "Good to know he has friends."

I responded with a simple smile, wondering why the hell I didn't just say Mira was my host. It would have made a lot more sense, especially considering she offered to help, and we were sitting beside her.

His attention shifted to my arm rest. He peered at the metal band strapped over my arm—at the coupling. "Nice bracelet," he said, still analyzing it.

My heart rate rose. Did he know what it truly was? Did he sense whatever magic it contained? Or was I simply being paranoid?

"Thanks," I uttered, just before three men walked down the slope carrying trays full of stainless-steel goblets. They went around the table, placing a goblet in front of each guest.

Then all three men lined themselves by the entrance, and each held up a glass goblet filled with water. As they ran their fingers along the rim of their glass, the most delightful sounds echoed around the room. It was a musical signal for all guests to stand.

A gray-haired, gray-scaled man that stood by the entrance said, "Welcome, Queen Cordelia!"

Calder's mother walked gracefully into the dining room. Silver highlights sparkled among the soft aqua-blue of her hair. And the scales around her eyes shined brighter than all the silver in the palace. She sat on the thronelike chair at the end of the table closest to the entrance.

The music played from the glass rims shifted to a deeper tune. Down the wavelike steps came Calder's father.

The same gray-scaled man beside the entrance now said, "Welcome, King Malik!"

The guests bowed their heads. Razz and I did the same.

"Sit, sit, sit!" the king said with a jubilant smile as he sat on the thronelike chair at the other end of the table. "What did everyone think of today's show?"

Seaweed salads were passed around the table as the dinner guests chattered about the impressive performance. My taste buds shied away as I eyed the emerald noodlelike dish. With a bit of hesitance, I took a small bite. As the seaweed swirled through my mouth, its seasoning spread over my tongue like melted butter. I was, without a doubt, the first to finish the salad.

Aalto chuckled with a glance at my emptied plate before leaning close to my ear and whispering, "Glad to see how much you enjoy the food here."

I blushed.

Just as the staff carried more food down the dining steps, the room emptied of sunlight as the last starlight arrived, filling the ocean and kelp forest with an enchanting glow. The bliss of blue and yellow radiating from the sea and kelp swallowed the dining room. My mouth nearly dropped at the beauty of it.

Plates of steamed clams and cooked fish were passed around the table. As I kept busy filling my stomach, I nearly forgot why we attended the feast to begin with. At least until Kai came trudging into the room with unforgiving eyes locked on Razz and me.

My heart dropped into my stomach and relentlessly turned.

Kai's hair was disheveled, and his eyes were half closed. He appeared utterly hungover.

The glowing light of the surrounding ocean poured over Kai as words tripped off his tongue. "You t-two." He shuffled closer in my direction with a hand held up, pointing lazily at Razz and me. "N-not friends." He fell to the floor.

Razz jumped out of his seat and ran toward Kai, who appeared to be having a seizure beside the queen's chair. Razz opened Kai's eyelids and patted his cheek.

As I scanned the room, my stomach turned further in discomfort, as everyone had gaping mouths and heavy stares directed at Razz and me. Aalto had stepped away from me in what looked to be fear.

It wasn't until my eyes settled back on Razz that I realized he was no longer bending our appearance.

The king stood up. "Guards!"

Two guards rushed down the dining room steps.

"Take them to the well!" the king demanded.

As the guards grabbed Razz and me, I turned to Mira. She was looking from Kai to Razz in disbelief.

Razz must have intuitively sensed Mira's disappointment in him for what he had done to Kai. And through the couplings, I felt her every ounce of it.

Queen Cordelia told the man that had announced her entrance to gather all the healers, and then she got on her knees and held Kai in her arms.

That was the last I saw of the dining room.

CHAPTER 27

The Glass Well

Two guards roughly escorted Razz and me outside to the view of three moons in the night sky dazzling over the illuminated sea. It wasn't until we reached a lonely corner on the outskirts of the palace that I realized we were about to be tossed down a glass well in the sea.

The well's entrance was at least a foot higher than the ocean's surface, which seemed to prevent the now calm seawater from entering its hundred-foot plunge.

One of the guards unwheeled a chain clasped to a fan-shaped shell big enough to sit on and still have space.

"Get on!" the guard demanded.

"No!"

"It's that or," —he grabbed another nearby chain clasped to a heavy stone block— "I'll throw you in the water with this locked around your feet." He kept an unsettling straight face while threatening my life.

All the while, Razz appeared to be lost in some inward gaze. He seemed so far gone; I wasn't even sure he knew what predicament we were in.

The other guard took advantage of Razz's state and pushed him on the massive shell. Razz didn't seem to care as he fell in, still locked in a daze. The guard unwheeled the chain, descending Razz to the bottom of the well and dumping him like garbage.

When the shell returned to the surface, the guard assigned to me said, "Your turn."

"I'd like to speak to Madam Mira!" I demanded.

His voice sharpened. "You will speak to nobody. Now get on!"

"No!" I said, with my feet settled firmly into the pearly stone ground.

"Okay," was his only response before dragging the heavy chained block toward my feet.

"Fine!" With a clenched jaw, I stepped on the damn shell, and in a single breath, I was descending to the bottom of the glass well.

Clink.

I stumbled off upon a rough landing, and the massive shell was immediately pulled back up. Now sitting hopelessly beside Razz, I wondered if we were fated to starve at the bottom of a stupid well. At least we had one hell of an ocean view, as the illuminated sea poured its enchanting glow through the glass and into the spacious well.

Razz cocooned himself with his arms and knees. I sat in silence beside him, resting my eyes on fish swimming between a nearby coral reef.

With a numb mind, I didn't expect tears to roll down my face. At least until I realized why I was even crying.

We would never get Darian out of the grid. That alone haunted me beyond despair. As if that wasn't enough, another cruel thought snuck out from the back of my mind; I would never return home.

I wanted to scream at the top of my lungs to release an ounce of the torturing pain devouring my emotions. But instead, I wiped the tears off my cheeks and turned to Razz.

"I'm so sorry. If it weren't for me making a suggestion on a topic I had no right to, Darian would have never stepped into the grid, and we wouldn't be here."

It took me by surprise when Razz grabbed my hand. "Stop blaming yourself," he said weakly. He removed his hand before it settled itself. Just when I thought he was falling back into a silent trance, he shook his head. "I shouldn't have used my abilities on Kai. At least not to the extent that I did. It was my first time intentionally bending another's mind into what I thought was a simple headache. I never thought it would—" He cut himself off. "Do you think . . . I killed him?"

"No! He just needs a little healing. After that, he'll be fine!" I said confidently. But I wondered if Razz sensed my uncertainty through the couplings binding our energies.

He still appeared lost in a faraway gaze when he said, "I can never forgive myself, even if he lives." His midnight-blue eyes glossed over. "And if he dies . . ." Razz's face went so pale, he didn't even finish his sentence. Several minutes had passed before he finally spoke again. "Calder won't be able to look at me after he hears what happened."

Conjuring up the right words of comfort seemed impossible. I tried, but my voice only sunk deeper into silence. So instead, I rested my head on his shoulder. And eventually, I managed to say, "He'll be fine. Everything will be fine." Though I knew everything wouldn't be fine. And I was sure Razz knew it too.

It wasn't long before we both fell asleep, leaning against each other. I don't know how much time had passed or how long we slept before—

Boom!

My eyes sprung open as the well violently shook.

"What the fuck!" Razz shouted, jumping to his feet.

I turned to find a shark with blue eyes and heavy black lines trailing its silver back. It was circling the well with ferocious eyes glued to Razz and me. Just when I thought the shark had given up as it swam away, it turned around, and without hesitation, it darted toward us.

Boom!

The glass shook even harder, throwing us to the other side of the well. My heart pounded so hard, my body trembled. At least that's what I thought until I realized only one part of my body was trembling.

I opened my pocket to find the relic shaking. My heart jumped from shock to confusion to hope.

I scanned the gleaming sea in every direction, searching for where the relic belonged. There was nothing but the lunatic shark, some fish in the distance, a nearby coral reef, and a corner of the palace.

Boom!

The shark struck again. And this time, the glass cracked, inviting water to seep through.

I turned to Razz in a panic. "Is this the same fatal sea that surrounds the edge of Elloriya?"

His eyes were darting in every direction, likely trying to come up with a plan of escape, when he said, "No. The Fatal Sea has no life or light."

The water pouring through the cracks had long soaked our feet.

"Can you bend minds underwater?" I asked, eyeing the shark still circling the well with nothing but fractured glass separating us from our death.

"I don't know," Razz said, his voice shaking. "Why?"

I didn't answer. Instead, I secured the trembling relic in my pocket and waved my arms at the shark.

Razz whipped his head to me, wide-eyed. "What the hell are you doing?"

"Getting us the hell out of here!" The colossal shark began to charge again. "Take a deep breath and prepare to mind-bend the fuck out of that thing!"

"I don't even know if I can bend a shark's mind!" he retorted. But it was too late.

Boom!

The monstrous shark rammed into the already broken well with such force, the glass shattered, and shards spread through the water.

Precious time didn't allow me to glance at Razz or the shark. All I could do was pray that all went according to my poorly established plan. But as I cautiously swam through the explosion of glass, I was suddenly pulled back.

I turned to find my cloak stuck on a jagged part of what little remained of the well. I tried to tug, but it wouldn't budge, and my lungs were quickly deflating of air.

There was no time to play tug-of-war, so I unlatched my beloved cloak and swam freely in the direction the relic responded to. The closer I swam toward the palace, the harder it shook.

When I finally reached a barrier of kelp beside the palace wall, it took all that I had to keep myself from passing out as my lungs grasped at any remaining oxygen they desperately held.

I opened my pocket and pulled out the relic—it nearly jumped out of my hand as it trembled more fiercely than my dwindling consciousness could handle. I spread the kelp apart, revealing a sterling chalice built into the palace wall under the sea.

"What are you doing?" a hissing voice said.

I turned to find a nixie with menacing gray eyes and sharp teeth fiercely swimming toward me.

With an outstretched hand, I ignored the approaching nixie and dropped the trembling relic inside the chalice. In a bright flash, water suddenly swirled around it.

The force of the water consumed me as my lungs were officially depleted of oxygen. My eyes closed, my thoughts fell silent, and all went dark as I surrendered myself to the sea.

CHAPTER 28

Water Key

I had been in this place before—my consciousness lost in oblivion. Time ceased to exist in this dark place of nothingness. Perhaps minutes had gone by, or even hours. But finally, I awoke as water hurled itself out of my mouth.

When I opened my eyes, the glistening stars of the night sky took hold of my sight, embracing me with its dark magic. My gaze moved to Razz sitting beside me and the nixie I had seen just before all went dark, with her head bobbing above the nearby sea.

Razz's bicep was wrapped in seaweed with a stream of dried blood down his lower arm.

"What—" I couldn't seem to get any more words out until I took a deep and painful breath. "What happened?"

Razz moved wet strands of hair off my face when he said, "You drowned, but" —he pointed with a bloody thumb at the nixie— "she saved you."

The nixie said nothing as she flapped her blanketlike wings above the sea.

I turned to the nixie and weakly said, "Thank you."

Razz propped me against the palace wall with his bloodless arm, water dripping from the loose curls of his hair. More air painfully filled my lungs, and I finally had enough energy to ask Razz, "I meant, what happened to your arm?"

He let out a lazy laugh. "This happened when you practically served me to the shark as her next meal."

"Shit. I'm sorry! Are you okay?"

"I'll be fine." He pulled more wet strands of hair off my face. "Are you okay?"

"I'm alive."

While Razz moved a few feet toward the sea to clean the dried blood off his arm, the nixie glided over to me.

"You have returned magic to the Kano Kingdom," she said in a breathy voice. "In return, I will warn you with what is to come." She moved to my ear and whispered, "When the moons align, the realm will open its doors, and invaders will reign death. The choices you make, Attica Spark, will determine the fate of Elloriya."

My stomach turned, and my gag reflex tugged at any digested food. As I fought the nauseous grasp, I turned to the nixie and asked, "I don't understand. How do you know this?"

"The waters whisper the moons' secrets."

My thoughts froze. I was dumbstruck. I couldn't find logic in what she had said.

Instead of asking for any clarification that would surely make no sense anyway, I asked, "What choices should I make?"

"You must decipher that for yourself." And with that, she jumped back into the sea.

Razz turned to me with a helping hand. The moons glowed brightly over his head as he grabbed me and pulled me up.

"Let's get our stuff and get out of here. For our sake, let's hope everyone's still asleep," he said, adding to my nerves. I almost suggested we just leave without our stuff, but I quickly remembered the rest of the relics were in my bag, still sitting in the guest room.

I glanced at my cloak at the bottom of the illuminated sea as we walked along the edge of the palace. When we turned the corner, passing a fanciful outdoor pool, I couldn't believe my eyes.

Light-filled water swept my sight. Streams of luminescent liquid arched over the dark pathways. Vines of flowers made entirely of water wrapped around the many white-stone pillars. And many small fairylike creatures, also made entirely of water, flew above the pools.

"What are those?" I asked Razz.

He looked over at the tiny fluttering water people and said with a shrug, "Water sprites, I think."

I took one last glance at the enchanted forms before we stepped inside the sleeping palace.

The monumental chalice under the palace dome was the only source of light as illuminated water now poured over its rim and into the fanciful pool below.

We walked silently through the empty halls until we finally reached the guest quarters. Razz pressed the silver starfish on the wall, and when the turquoise stones parted, we walked down the wavelike steps into the underwater corridor.

When we finally reached the room holding our belongings, relief fell over me, until I pulled the handle. It was locked.

Razz turned and headed back toward the stairs.

While following his steps, I asked, "Where are you going?"

"To wake Mira," he said without looking back. He climbed the stairs and pressed the starfish to exit. And when the wall parted—

Click.

A door opened behind me. With hesitance, I looked over my shoulder. My nerves had unleashed as I was now facing Kai.

Shock struck my senses as Razz pushed past me and hugged him. By the befuddled look on Kai's face, it seemed shock struck him harder.

When Razz released Kai, he said, "I'm so sorry, man! I was only trying to—" He stopped himself for a moment before saying, "I was trying to bring Calder back home."

At first, Kai was speechless, likely still digesting Razz's bear hug. "Why should I believe you?" Kai asked, his words ice cold.

Razz appeared speechless. So I stepped forward and said, "Razz has lived on the edge of Elloriya with Calder since they were both taken from their home years ago."

"Zeniths ago," Razz corrected me.

"Whatever," I uttered.

"And you?" Kai asked.

"I was born in Elloriya but grew up on Earth. Calder came to Earth to find me and brought me back." I smiled. "When I first met him, he said his name was Kai."

"Why would he use my name?" Again, he spoke in an icy tone.

"Because I missed my cousin," said a familiar voice at the top of the stairs. "Well, that and Etiwa suggested I use a different name. She never told me why, but I never dare question her."

The sight of Calder spread a wave of joy over me so strongly, I wanted to jump him with a hug. Just the sight of him made me feel like everything would be all right.

Calder turned to Razz and me. "Thank you for bringing me home," he said with a proud gaze.

Before either of us responded, Kai moved toward Calder and asked, "Where are your scales?"

Calder's smile vanished as quickly as his face went pale. He shrugged. "I went through the passageway in and out of this realm too many times. I guess it wanted something in return."

He looked at his cousin with a quivering grin, but I saw right through it.

Razz put a hand on Calder's shoulder. "I'm sorry, man. I should have been the one to get my brother from the human world."

"It's okay. You and Etiwa did plenty by locating where on Earth our friends had gone with that brilliant third eye of yours," Calder said with a genuine smile now.

Razz grinned, then asked, "Any way you can help us unlock that door?" He pointed down the corridor.

On Calder's way to the guest room, he cupped the side of Kai's neck and said, "Good to see you, cousin."

Kai didn't respond with anything but a grin, an expression I hadn't seen on him before.

Calder's gaze swept the surrounding sea as Razz and I followed him to the end of the glass corridor. "It's good to be home," he said as he swished a hand through the air.

His palm released just enough water to form a key. The key-shaped water entered the lock with ease, and when Calder turned his hand, *click,* the door unlocked.

We grabbed our stuff as quickly as we could.

The nighttime glow of the sea slowly faded as sun rays spread over the water. The morning starlight woke the people of the palace, and it wasn't long before commotion filled the halls.

Razz changed our appearance to a palace maid and a footman as we hurried past a hall filled with befuddled people—some celebrating, others concerned.

"How has our magic suddenly returned?" asked Queen Cordelia to one of the wary guards, as Kai guided Razz and me toward a hidden exit.

Just before turning down an empty hall, I took one last glance over my shoulder at the sight of Calder's grandmother, Mira, embracing Calder in her arms. As Calder caught sight of his parents for the first time since his return, Mira looked directly at me with a respectful bow of her head. Did she recognize me, even disguised as a palace maid?

"You coming?" Razz asked, several feet ahead.

When we finally made it through the hidden exit safely, we thanked Kai and continued on our way.

The Kano city looked different. The pools turned to spout fountains as the water shot high in the air in nearly every direction. Vibrant turquoise liquid climbed up several white-stone walls in the shape of vines and flowers, like at the palace. There were even some water sprites flying through the city from fountain to fountain. But somehow, the most incredible sight was a giant tree made entirely of water.

As I passed under the water tree, a liquid leaf fell off. I opened my palm and caught it before it hit the ground. After about three seconds, the leaf morphed back into ordinary water.

The energy in the city shifted. It felt hopeful and strong. But the strangest part was the sudden connection I felt to the water. I felt both its calmness and its strength.

Before we left the city, four starlights after leaving the palace, we refilled our canteens and purchased enough food to last us several days.

As we exited along the white-stone pathway, grateful for our lives and freedom, all sixteen nixies fluttered above the turquoise sea and gave us a gentle bow.

CHAPTER 29

The Chariot

The day passed by much too quickly as we walked south along the sea for six starlights, following the guidance of the compass. The white sand beneath our feet didn't make the journey any easier. But the breathtaking view of the lowering sun sparkling over the sea made it worth the trouble.

Every thought I had analyzed the nixie's warning. No matter how many times I played it over and over in my head, I still couldn't make sense of what she meant when she said: "The choices you make, Attica Spark, will determine the fate of Elloriya." The thought of her warning made me feel sick.

"So what did the nixie say?" Razz asked, as if he could hear my thoughts. His intuition was strong, but it was surely the coupling around my arm allowing him a peek into my mind.

I took the coupling off and put it in my bag.

"Sorry," he said as he uncuffed his coupling, returning it to his bag. "Whenever you're ready, I'm all ears."

"Thanks," I said, returning to my thoughts.

Astrophel, Kamali, please tell me or show me what choices I need to make. Or what choices I will face. Give me a sign, please!

Begging my spirit guides, I made my thoughts as loud as I could. Looking around for a sign or answer of any sort, I was hopeful they would come through, but I saw, heard, and felt nothing. Perhaps they didn't hear my pleading thoughts. Or perhaps they would give me a sign when I least expected it.

I was so tired from lack of sleep, from trudging through the heavy sand, from lying and deceiving, and from wondering how much longer until I saw Darian again—if I would see Darian again.

I longed for my bed at the manor, for the time before Darian stepped into the grid. Or even lying in the manor's library with a good book, secretly wishing Darian would walk down the steps with each passing page.

We walked in silence along the white-sand beach for some time before Razz finally said, "Attica?"

"What?"

"Can you swim?" he asked with a glance.

"Yes. Why?"

"There's nothing to be ashamed of if you can't. I can teach you."

With growing irritation, I asked, "Why do you think I can't swim?"

"Because you almost drowned, twice."

"Twice?"

"Yeah. In the passageway at the manor and at the Kano Kingdom. Come to think of it, during the wielding game too."

I stopped him in his tracks, stepping in front of him when I said, "The passageway water that leaves you completely dry and stole Calder's scales? That enchanted, criminal liquid doesn't count. At the Kano Kingdom, I miscalculated how long I could hold my breath. And during the wielding game, I'm pretty sure Zella was trying to kill me."

It seemed Razz didn't hear a word I said as he looked past me with a still gaze, eyes widening. He slowly whispered, "Get behind me."

Instead, I turned around. My heart nearly came to a stop when two saber-tooth tigers—one white with black stripes, the other black with white stripes—trudged out from behind some bushes. They were both larger than any breed of tiger I had ever seen and were rather terrifying.

The moment they sighted us, their leisurely walk turned to a sprint in our direction.

"Get behind me!" Razz said again as he tried to force my arm.

But instead, my hands tied themselves to the molecules of the sea beside us, and as if by instinct, I cocooned us in a barrier of swirling seawater.

His chin dropped as my wielding shielded us from harm. Through the water, we carefully watched the figures of the saber-tooth tigers cautiously circling us, smelling the seawater blanketing Razz and me from head to toe.

Then a whistle sent the tigers running back to wherever they came from. I released my energetic grip on the water, allowing it to drop to our feet, splashing over the sand.

A man, nearly three times my age, dressed in an old tunic and shabby pants, lovingly petted the tigers before attaching each one to the front of his carriage. He then hopped on a seat behind the tigers and grabbed the reins.

As the tigers effortlessly pulled the carriage through the sand, Razz ran toward the man and shouted, "Hey!"

The carriage halted.

As I continued in their direction, I couldn't make out what Razz was saying to the man, but I noticed him digging in the red pouch filled with pentacles. The man nodded, and Razz dropped a couple of pentacles in his hand.

When I reached the carriage, Razz turned to me with a beaming smile as he said with a displaying hand, "Your chariot awaits."

I responded with raised brows.

"Carter is going to take us south," Razz said, taming his grin.

The man hardly looked my way when he said, "My girls are getting impatient."

Razz held out a hand to help me up into the carriage. Instead, I handed him my bag and helped myself up.

Inside, long cushioned maroon seats were in the front and back, facing each other a few feet apart. As I made myself comfortable, I held a helpful hand out of the carriage toward Razz. He chuckled as he handed my bag back to me and hopped in. Then we took off.

"I can get used to this," Razz said, sitting across from me with hands laced behind his neck, elbows resting against the curtained walls. "So, since when can you wield water so effortlessly?"

With a shrug, I said, "I wielded water before at the manor. But this time it was different."

I tried to make sense of it. To wield water used to be near impossible, as it always slipped through my fingers. But this time, it was like the molecules latched to my beckoning hands like glue.

Razz leaned forward when he said, "It's the relics."

"The relics?"

"Yes, the relics," he said in a playful mock. "You were the one who returned magic to the Kano Kingdom. Maybe some of that magic is within you now." He returned to his laid-back position. "Hell. You probably have magic from the Tera Kingdom too."

I considered his words, unsure if there was any truth to them. If I were being honest with myself, it didn't feel like I was harboring any magic since giving the two kingdoms their relics. I just felt a slightly deeper connection to the land and water.

I didn't respond to Razz's thoughts on the matter. Instead, as I looked out the carriage window, wondering for a fleeting moment how far the sea stretched, my thoughts journeyed back to Ridgewood Hollow. And then to Mama, Dad, James, Jasmine, and Jada.

How long had it been since Christmas? Were they all at home, together as a family? Had Jasmine and Jada already moved to New York to open their dance studio? What was James doing with his life now that he was back home? Why hadn't I asked him when I last saw him?

"Lost in your mind again?" Razz asked, pulling me out of my thoughts.

I broke my mindless gaze off the evening sky and turned to him. "Huh?"

"What are you thinking about?"

"Can't you figure it out with your intuition or your third eye, or whatever gift you possess?" I asked, not intending for my words to sound as sharp as they came out.

"If I tried hard enough, probably. But I'm trying to respect your private thoughts."

With a weak smile, I responded, "I was thinking about home—I mean, my family on Earth."

"Like what?" he asked, holding a firm hand against the carriage wall as we rolled over a bump.

"Mama always makes cinnamon rolls on Sunday mornings. So, I was wondering what day of the week it was there. And if it was by chance Sunday."

His brows raised. "Seriously? Earthlings have names for each day?"

"Well, yeah. Is that not how it works here?"

He let out a laugh so loud, it bounced off the carriage walls. "Wow. Calder was right."

"Right about what?"

"Earthlings take time way too seriously."

I straightened. "You judge, but life on Earth is different from life in Elloriya. There are jobs and schools and meetings and a million other things that require structured days and time."

"People in Elloriya have jobs, schools, and meetings too. And we do just fine without sunny days."

"Sundays," I corrected him.

"Whatever."

"This is the most ridiculous conversation I've ever had!" I sneered.

"I couldn't agree with you more!"

We broke our irritated stare, turning to the window. But the moment we turned back to each other, we laughed so hard, it was a struggle to catch our breath. It was at this moment I realized how sleep-deprived we were. And it was also at this moment that the last starlight arrived, as the sky turned dark, and the surrounding elements filled with a glowing light.

"So tell me about these cinnamon rolls. What are those?" Razz asked as he put his feet up on the edge of my seat.

I kindly scooched over, allowing his comfort, and reclined my feet on the edge of his seat before delving into the sweet and rich taste of perfectly buttered dough, cinnamon, and icing.

After learning about the food and sweets Razz and Darian favored as kids, the bumpiness of the carriage ride eventually lulled us to sleep.

It was early morning when we woke. The carriage had come to a stop long ago as Carter slept in a poorly pitched tent with his tigers.

When I stepped out of the carriage to stretch and catch a view of the rising sun, I searched around for a well-hidden place to relieve my bladder.

We were no longer by the beach, but rather in a dry and bare place with few trees. However, there was a nearby village with small market stands made of burlap and cloth. If I didn't know any better, I'd say we were somewhere in the desert.

It was behind a barrier of tumbleweeds that I decided was the best spot to squat and pee. As I nearly finished, I realized the black saber-tooth tiger was awake and watching me.

When I returned to the carriage, Razz was nowhere in sight.
Where did he go?

I scanned our mostly deserted surroundings to find Razz playing with some children in the nearby village. From the looks of it, they were playing tag. And for whatever reason, it swept a grin over my face. The moment Razz caught sight of me, he pulled me in to play.

Half a starlight later, Carter and his tigers were ready to go. As we returned to the carriage, Carter looked at me strangely, with a tilted head and squinted eyes. I awkwardly responded to his uncomfortable stare with a smile.

Once we settled ourselves in the carriage, we continued south. We spent the entire day in the carriage, most of the time throwing what looked like a hacky sack back and forth that the kids we played with had given us.

Our highest record of tossing it to each other without dropping it was eight hundred twenty-four. And if the carriage wheel hadn't rolled over a bump, it could have been higher.

It wasn't long after our breaking record of catch that we fell asleep again.

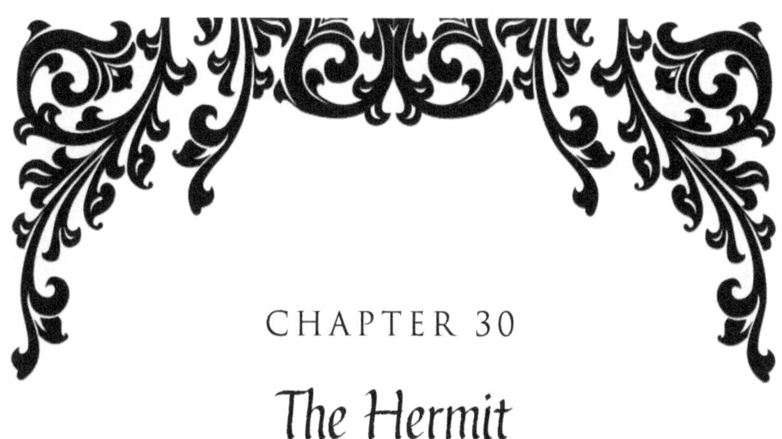

CHAPTER 30

The Hermit

Thud!

My head slammed the roof of the carriage so hard I plunged off my seat, ending up on Razz's lap. The carriage was suddenly lopsided.

Following a colorful array of cursing, Carter opened the door. "Get out and stretch your legs while I repair the carriage."

He was not the friendliest man. Nevertheless, I was grateful he made our travel south a little easier. Okay, a lot easier.

We climbed out to the darkest Elloriyan night I had ever seen.

Strange, I thought as I glanced at my surroundings. There was no glow of any element in any direction. The layered moons were our only light source in the dark, warm, sand-filled desert. At least until Carter twisted the head of a torch in a shabby miniature chest carrying black sand. When he lifted the torch out of the chest, it was lit with fire.

Carter tossed the lit torch on the sand beside the front of the carriage, where the metal was mangled and broken.

He unlatched the black saber-tooth tiger first, then the white one. "Go on, girls. Go play," he said with a pat on their butts. They ran in circles, chasing one another before rolling in the desert sand.

"Can I help?" Razz asked, stepping toward the mangled mess under the carriage.

Carter studied Razz for a moment before asking, "What do you know about shafts and axle clips?"

"Um, nothing."

"Then no."

"How long will this take?" Razz pestered.

Carter responded with a deadpan stare when he said, "However long it takes."

It wasn't much of an answer.

"Good to know Earthlings aren't the only ones who take time so seriously," I said smugly.

He chuckled. "Want to go for a walk?"

I scanned the sand that went on for miles in all directions. "To where? There are so many choices," I said playfully.

"That apple stand, over there," Razz pointed at the dark nothingness of the barren desert.

We walked a decent distance away from Carter and his under breath swears, always with a side of grunts. I was the first to lie on the sand and stare at the star-filled sky. Razz followed my lead and lay beside me.

"It's so beautiful. There has to be millions of stars up there."

"Billions," he corrected me. "It reminds me of home."

I looked over at him, and I could see the longing in his eyes. "How does it remind you of home?" I gently asked.

He half-smiled before he said, "I'm from the lunar node. The moons at my court feel so close. And the stars feel even closer. When I was a child, I used to look out my bedroom window and imagine what it would be like to jump from star to star. And somehow, I would always picture myself ending up on the highest moon, allowing me a view of all of Elloriya." A silent, almost unnoticeable tear rolled down the side of his face and onto the sand.

His eyes didn't part from the sky when I asked, "Do you remember the realm you came from before the wars started?"

"No. Not really. I was way too young. Still, I've tried to imagine what it was like. But my imagination never seemed to travel farther than the Elloriyan moons. Darian was always the one with the good memory. He was only a baby when we left, but I wouldn't be surprised if he somehow remembers more than me."

I ignored my rising heart rate at the sound of his name and instead asked, "How did everyone travel to this realm from the others?"

He pushed himself up onto his elbows, still gazing at the stars. "The same way people travel in this realm. Through the energy grid."

My mouth dropped half open at the thought of the grid expanding far outside of this realm. It only added to my fear of Darian being stuck in that very same energy grid.

"But not everyone has access to the grid, right?" I questioned.

"There are many ways to access the grid. Our friends can wield it open with the elements they possess. Some use spells, and others use rare crystals. My parents used the threshold. I'm sure there are many more magical ways I don't even know about."

I pushed myself up onto my elbows, like him, when I asked, "What's the threshold?"

"It's a special sort of door. My parents never allowed me anywhere near it. When they caught me sneaking around it once, they began locking the room it was in and only opened it when we would travel to some other part of Elloriya, like the solar node," he said with a playful nudge.

As I prepared to annoy Razz with more questions, the sight of a golf-ball size hermit crab crawling by suddenly distracted me. Razz didn't seem to notice it as his eyes continued to rest on the stars. I wondered what it was doing out in the desert when I was almost certain hermit crabs lived by the shore.

But then it got stranger. The soft breeze suddenly turned to strong wind, and a moment later, a golden glow appeared in the distance, quickly catching both mine and Razz's attention. He seemed to have been sparked by curiosity as he pushed himself off the sand and walked over toward the cryptic light. Curious myself, I followed.

Walking through the heavy sand was an effort, especially with the whistling air pushing against my every step.

When I was finally close enough to observe the mysterious light, utter shock stopped me in my tracks. Perhaps I thought it would be a firefly. What I didn't expect was an elderly man with a lengthy beard beneath a blue hooded cloak, holding out a lantern with one hand and a wooden staff in the other.

Razz immediately pestered him with questions. "Who are you? Where did you come from? Where are you headed? Do you need water?"

Not one question was answered.

My bones chilled when his heavy gaze narrowed on me. Then my breathing halted when he began trudging my way.

When he opened his dry mouth, a droopy voice spoke with great effort. "You have returned," he said.

Dragging out the space between each word, I asked, "Have we met?"

He inched even closer till we were face-to-face. "One choice will rise in difficulty upon all others. Your heart will lead you to the right decision. But your head will fight against it."

"Against what? What decision? What choice?" Desperation frayed from my tongue. Was he giving me the same warning the nixie had?

A whistle behind me turned my head. The tigers ran toward Carter, and he buckled them to the front of the carriage.

I turned back to the elderly man, but he was gone. Razz looked in every direction, just as confused as I was. There was no one and nothing but miles of sand all around. But then I looked down and saw the hermit crab was suddenly crawling away from the same spot the man had stood seconds ago.

"What the hell was that?" I asked Razz as if he knew any more than I did.

When I turned to him, his gaze was so far inward, I wondered if he even heard me. But then he spoke. "I think that was the man Gemma once told me about. He used to dwell near the Tera Kingdom at the top of some mountain, always alone. That man was exactly as she described him." He looked at me with a tilted head and said, "The hermit." When he saw my befuddled face, he clarified, "That's what people call him."

Goosebumps struck me hard. Immediately after telling him about the hermit crab I had seen, a sudden realization hit me.

My spirit guides responded to my plea through the hermit. And though I still didn't get much of an answer, I at least knew how to make the right choice whenever that unknown decision arose. All I had to do was listen to my heart. That's simple enough.

We spent another few days in the carriage and slept outside on a blanket over the sand each night. It was surprisingly comfortable, and the nights were perfectly warm.

We nearly ate and drank all our packed food and water. Carter and the tigers had already finished all their food and water too. So we shared the rest of what little we had with them. Thankfully, it was only a few starlights later when we arrived at our destination.

CHAPTER 31

The Azar Kingdom

It was a dark night when we arrived at the Azar Kingdom, somewhere far into the sandy desert. A rock-cut empire with a colossal step pyramid centering a tan stone city stood majestically before me.

Two men as imposing as Ignatius stood at the city's entrance. They wore leather torso armor and held long wooden rods beside burning torches hung on the sandstone walls.

Almost simultaneously, they lifted their rods and tapped them against the stone arch above the entrance. And in the blink of an eye, the step pyramid quickly had close to a hundred warriors holding fiery weapons.

The moment Razz took a step forward, ten rods of blazing fire flew toward us, each landing inches from our feet—a warning not to move another step.

A tall, stunning woman with silky skin as beautiful and dark as the night moved through the archway and toward us.

She was bedecked in glinting copper. But it was not jewelry on her skin. Perhaps it was copper ink decorating her forehead, neck, arms, and fingers. I couldn't imagine another wearing so much copper as gracefully as her.

Her walk was as mesmerizing and elegant as a dance. She looked and moved like a damn queen.

She strolled right up to us and said, "What took you so long?" in the same accent Ignatius had.

Razz looked at me, and I at him, both equally confused.

"I have two guest rooms prepared. Should I have another?" she asked, looking over our shoulders at Carter.

"I'm sorry, ma'am, but who were you expecting?" Razz carefully asked.

She glanced at him and then at me before she drawled, as if we couldn't understand her, "I am expecting the two who seek to bring my son home. So, I will ask one more time. Do I need to prepare another guest room for your friend?"

"Your majesty," Razz said with a bow.

I was so taken by how she knew of our arrival that I forgot to bow. But she didn't seem to care or notice my lack of respect. Understandably, she seemed solely focused on the safe return of her son, Ignatius.

But how did she know about our arrival? Had someone from the Tera or Kano Kingdoms warned someone from the Azar Kingdom of our journey?

Razz turned to talk to Carter. He pulled out another pentacle and placed it in his hand before turning back to her. "He will be staying and would like a room suitable for him and his pets. He said he didn't need much. Just a room big enough for the three of them."

"Fine," she said before calling one of her guards. "Ee taka to ko oohna," she said to him with a head tilt at Carter and his tigers.

"Ta ko," he responded with a nod, as he waved Carter over.

"Now follow me," she said.

So we did.

"May I ask how you knew of our visit?" Razz asked gently.

"By the visions of my mystic, Ziggy." She looked over her shoulder at me. "She requested to speak with you upon your arrival." And then she turned to Razz. "She is especially curious about you."

One guard trailed behind us as we followed the queen on a stone path. We passed copper bowls filled with lava rocks and swaying flames.

She led us through the entrance of the colossal three-sided step pyramid. The inside was more magnificent than I anticipated.

The interior walls had intricate engravings of symbols or, perhaps, writing I couldn't understand. There were many sets of stairs and even bridges on the higher levels.

Nearly every sight was of tan marble, with bits and pieces of polished copper in each rectangular block. The delicate details of copper sparkled in the firelight, reflecting its rich red-brown metal, contrasted elegantly against the sandy marble.

Dancing lights moved about at the pyramid ceiling, which was at least three hundred feet high, if not higher. And smack-dab in the center of the pyramid were two impressive marble thrones.

The thrones had the most beautiful copper-engraved steps leading up to them. And behind the thrones was an impressive open-winged phoenix statue made of glinting copper.

We followed the queen through vast marble halls. More fire-filled bowls graced us with their enchanted flames every fifty feet. It was a long stroll until, finally, we reached a set of high steps with a lit room at the top.

As we followed her up the steps, the sounds of chanting and drumming grew louder and louder until we finally reached the top—and then, silence. I looked around to find where the chanting and drumming had come from, but there was no one around. Razz must have been just as confused as he, too, was looking for the source of the sound.

We stepped into the fire-lit room, heavy with the smell of burning incense. A young, beautiful woman with long platinum-blonde dreadlocks, orange eyes, and tan skin turned to us. "So, you have finally arrived," the mystic said in a smoky voice.

"When you are done with my seer, my guard, Edan, will show you to your rooms," the queen said before turning to the mystic. "Ziggy, go easy on them."

"Queen Vesta," Edan said courteously, bowing as she exited.

Edan was tall, dark, and lean, with a shaved head and kind eyes. He waited outside the door in the stance of a guard.

"Sit, sit, my friends," the mystic said, orange eyes glinting upon us.

We sat on pillows alongside the firepit she sat cross-legged behind.

"So you're the mystic?" Razz asked hesitantly.

"You, of all people, should know the answer. You are a gifted seer among other gifts from the gods, yet you allow this gift to be clouded when it is convenient for you."

Something about her delicate, unwavering, smoky voice was unnerving.

"No disrespect," Razz said, seeming unsure as to if he should continue. "But through my spiritual experiences, I have only come to know one god—one creator."

"There can certainly be one creator with many gods. You have your god. I have mine. And mine are many. If you would like, you can try my ecstasy, and then you will discover your spiritual truth," she said, pushing a teacup filled with golden liquid toward him.

Razz looked almost tempted as he took in the sparkling sight and sweet scent of the tea. "That's kind. But I know my spiritual truth already, and that will not change."

"More for me," she simply said before taking a sip. "Now, let us see why you have really come here." She looked far into the yellow flames as if they held the answer.

"But you already know why we're here," I said, speaking up for the first time in her somewhat unsettling presence.

"I know what you are doing here, yes. But I do not yet know why you have come." She looked at me and then at Razz. "You are both emotionally invested in your reasons for being here. This much I know. But there are secrets behind your journey. Care to share them?"

Razz gave me a sideways glance. We both kept silent.

"As expected," the mystic said calmly. She blew a breath into the flames before her, somehow causing them to grow taller. "Spirits and gods, why have these two come to the Azar Kingdom? What are their true intentions?"

She started humming and swaying back and forth and side to side. Her eyes rolled around, and suddenly they turned misty gray. And then, as if by magic, there was chanting and drumming surrounding us, perhaps coming from the fire that had swiftly turned blue. As I gazed at the sapphire flames growing brighter, I could have sworn I saw a set of familiar eyes.

"Brother?" The sound of Darian's voice had Razz jumping to his feet. All the while, my heart jumped over several beats, skipping them entirely.

"Show me where you are!" Ziggy said, eyes fogged over, still in her swaying trance.

Silence took hold. But then, his voice—Darian's voice—finally spoke.

"No. Only them!" Darian said.

And then the flames vanished, and the chanting and drumming abruptly stopped.

"No more magic!" Razz pulled me up from the pillow I sat on beside the smoky pit. "Thank you, but we must go now," he said sharply, refusing to even look the mystic in her enchanted eyes.

I, on the other hand, felt the need to look back before exiting, perhaps hoping to hear Darian's voice again or glimpse some part of him in the flames. But instead, all I saw was the gray smoke of her eyes dissipating to reveal the orange behind them. Her eyes were without a doubt far stranger than mine.

CHAPTER 32

Wrestling with Fire

We followed Edan outside the colossal pyramid, passing many towering palm trees and arriving at a much smaller three-sided pyramid, one of many surrounding the city.

We stepped inside to find a single bed and a copper tub. Beside the bed was a long, winding torch, already lit. I had never seen a torch like it before.

There wasn't much else in the room. But it was a solid roof and a place to sleep. And I was grateful.

"This is for the lady," Edan said in the same accent as Ignatius.

"And where will I be staying?" Razz asked.

"Across the square."

"With all due respect, I request a room near Attica."

"But this is the female side of the city," Edan said carefully.

"Your people are separated by gender?" Razz asked in an almost judgmental tone. But before Edan could even respond, Razz said, "If you won't find me a room near her, then I will stay here!"

With a glance at the compact bed, I said to Razz, "I'll be fine. Go!"

He moved close to me. "We don't know these people. There are thousands of men here, and if any of them are half as 'passionate' as Ignatius, then I would feel responsible if anything happened."

"I will be fine!"

Edan tilted his head toward Razz when he said, "She is in the women's quarters. They will look after her."

"Fine," Razz said, before leaning in my ear to whisper, "Put your coupling on. If you need anything, just call me. I'll hear you through the connection."

"Okay, Razz. Thanks, bye!" I said, pushing him out so I could finally bathe, unworried about a word he had said.

After closing the heavy stone door and securing its lock, I set my bag on the bed, turned the bathwater on, and stripped down.

The water was the perfect temperature, warming my body as I thought back to Darian's voice in the mystic's room. I wanted to return and hear his voice again, but surely Razz would disapprove, considering the way he reacted when he heard his brother in the sapphire flames.

Why had he freaked out so much, anyway? Did magic scare him? And the mystic . . . how strong would her powers become once magic returned to the kingdom? Assuming we would even succeed in returning their magic.

I didn't even know where to begin in this place. Since the mystic already knew of our mission, perhaps she could help me locate where the relic belonged. Or would that go against Etiwa's rules? Did the mystic even know about the relics?

As my mind calmed, I thought back to the blue light I had seen the last time I bathed, the last time I wondered if Darian had any idea how I felt about him.

Though, I suppose my feelings for him were too complicated for even me to understand. He was so closed off, so difficult to read. And yet, I would still run through fire just to see him again. Or perhaps to feel his strong arms wrapped around me, his skin endlessly brushing against mine.

I had never been with a man—at least, not in *that* way. But the thought of being with Darian, no walls between us, nothing between us but bare skin, made my loins burn.

What would being with him feel like?

Would he be gentle or rough? Or perhaps the perfect combination of both. Would he look me in the eye, allowing his gaze to burn deep into mine? Would he savor every moment, every thrust? Did he yearn for me in the ways I yearned for him?

After a rather pleasurable bath, I hesitated to part from the water. But it was only a few starlights away from the first light of day. All I needed was a little shuteye so I could be well-rested enough to find where the relic belonged and move on to do it all over again in the last lower kingdom.

This journey was far more exhausting than I could have ever imagined—mentally, emotionally, and physically. Sleep was my only peaceful escape, though it was temporary. And if I were being honest, I didn't even feel worthy of sleeping at all. Not with Darian being lost in some asshole energy grid. But to finish this with any hope of success, I would need some rest.

Once I climbed into the beckoning bed, I blew out the torch, and the beige satin sheet cradled me into slumber.

When I awoke in the morning, I felt renewed and ready to take on the day.

Just as I finished dressing myself in a fitted tunic and cuffed pants, the door knocker sounded. I opened the door, sure that it would be Razz.

The sun's rays shone brightly behind a young woman, perhaps a few years older than me. She had dark skin, brown eyes, was quite tall, and looked like a warrior. Maybe it was the warriorlike way she dressed or even her high chin and straight back, but the strength she silently exuded beckoned my respect.

"Hello. You must be Attica. I am Enya—Edan's sister." Her accent was surprisingly heavier than her brother's. "I am to wake you, but I see you have already woken. Come with me for breakfast."

Was she ordering me to breakfast, or did I have a say in the matter? I was never a big morning eater since I hardly ever woke hungry. But I followed her anyway.

She led me to a sizable pyramid, though not nearly as giant as the main one with the thrones and the mystic's room of mystery and magic hidden in the back. The inside had several wooden tables filled with an array of attractive people.

They all looked like warriors with their brown leather armor and defined muscles. Many of them had patterned tattoos on their arms, hands, and even running down their chins—all the tattoos were made with copper ink, like Queen Vesta's.

There was a particularly rowdy table with a decent crowd surrounding two men arm wrestling. A short thick rope bolted to the table on both sides of the arm wrestlers, engulfed in red flames, burned inches from their elbows.

One of the arm wrestlers looked up from the table, landing his eyes on me. Enya must have noticed my interest in the game as she said with her head tilted at the opponent staring at me, "That is Titus. No one has beaten him yet. He is a powerful warrior."

He was a sizable man with tan, muscled skin, and pale green eyes. He was physically beautiful. His energy was powerful enough to make the fine hairs on my arms stand up. But something about his heavy gaze on me turned my stomach to knots.

I quickly broke his stare and turned to the pyramid entrance, where Razz and Edan were walking in.

"It is my time to guard the city. You can find Edan if you need anything," Enya said before exiting.

I made my way toward another wooden table full of food where Razz had already filled his plate with fruits and bread. I took a plum and sat beside Razz at an empty table near the exit.

"How'd you sleep?" Razz asked.

"Honestly, the best sleep I've had since leaving the manor. You?"

"Same, strangely. After seeing the mystic, I thought I wouldn't be able to sleep at all."

"Why?"

He sighed. "I'm not the biggest fan of magic," he said before biting into fruit.

"I gathered that. But why?"

He shrugged and didn't bother answering my question.

The sudden sound of cheering from the nearby table caught my attention. The crowded table suddenly grew louder as Titus had his opponent's arm pinned on the rope of scarlet fire until, finally, the flames burned out against charred skin. Titus stood up with a fist victoriously in the air and the other pounding his chest.

Though I'm sure the people of this kingdom could handle any fire thrown their way, the one who lost stood up with a noticeable burn on his forearm. It was at this moment I noticed how many men and women surrounding the table had burns on their forearms too, likely from playing that very game. The sight of it had me grabbing the part of my hand that was burned in the solar plexus portal when facing my wicked ego.

"Don't do that," Razz said, eyeing my fingers wrapped over my scarred hand. "Scars are important," he added.

"Why?"

He bit into a bread roll, and hardly finished chewing before responding, "Scars remind us of the challenges we faced and the lessons we learned. They remind us that pain heals, and that the strength we gain on our journey is from overcoming hard times."

I just stared at him with raised brows before finally saying, "You've been spending way too much time with Calder."

He laughed. "Yeah, I think I may have channeled his wisdom for a second there."

I took some bites of my plum before asking Razz, "So, if the Orpheus stole all the magic from the kingdoms, how can the mystic still do magic herself?"

"They can't take magic from people who harbor it," he said in a trance with eyes following a beautiful girl walking by.

When we both finished our food, Razz took my plate with his and discarded them in a corner piled with dirty dishes.

He grabbed an apple and put it in his pocket before heading toward the exit. I looked over my shoulder as I followed Razz out the door. Again, Titus was looking in my direction. Except, instead of staring at me, this time his heavy gaze fell on Razz.

CHAPTER 33

The Strife

I stood in the center of the busy market square, surrounded by palm trees, pyramids, and endless sand on the outskirts of the city. With the perfect view of the colossal step pyramid—the heart of the empire—I took in the curious copper writing and symbols framing each layer.

Where does the relic belong in this colossal city—in this massive kingdom?

There were so many people. Most resembled warriors. Even the children running around the market square, kicking around a leather ball, looked like warriors in the making.

Before I had a moment to think about where to begin with finding the relic's home, a heavy voice called out from somewhere nearby.

"Do you share blood with the nobles?" Titus shouted across the square with eyes pinned on Razz. Almost immediately, the onlookers cleared the space between Titus and Razz.

With squared shoulders and a chin held high, Razz said, "Yes." His stare did not waver from Titus as he took a deep bite of his apple.

I also came from the bloodline of a noble, from what I'd been told. Maybe more than one. All I knew was that my grandfather was a noble—the noble who killed Shakar's brother.

Titus sauntered toward Razz with a death-gripping glare, furrowed brows, and a tight jaw until he was face-to-face with him. Razz didn't waver or so much as flinch. On the contrary, he stood there unnervingly calm, taking another bite of his apple.

"We battle!" he said to Razz. Not a suggestion, not a question, but an order.

Titus turned to a beautiful warrior woman with his brawny arms raised at his sides. The young woman tightened the straps of his leather armor over his shoulders and stomach.

"Why?" Razz simply asked, with no hint of fear but rather curiosity.

Titus whirled around and pushed in on Razz. "Why? Why?" he shouted, his voice getting louder with each mocking question. "Because of your people. Because of the nobles!" He turned to the gathering crowd. "We were forced out of our realm as retribution for a war we did not start. We lost our men and women in battles we did not start. We fight not for peace but survival!" He switched his glare back on Razz. "We had to leave our homes behind because of your ancestors, and all their selfish, realm-robbing companions. We had to bury our young and our elders. And someone has to pay!"

Calder once told me that each kingdom agreed to the plan of sending the Orpheus to another realm, forcing them out of their homes to strip their world of precious resources. So this kingdom must have played some role, big or small. But Titus seemed like the type of guy who wouldn't, for a moment, listen to reason.

A couple of hundred people surrounded the square where Titus was cracking his neck, scorching his jade eyes onto Razz. Even the children had stopped playing and were watching.

"Ollo!" Titus shouted with an open hand held out. A warrior man, as stunning as the rest, grabbed a long wooden rod and tossed it to Titus. The moment it reached his hand, he sharply fired it at Razz's neck.

It was so forceful, it could have easily killed him if it hit just the right spot. But Razz was whip-smart and intuitive as hell. He saw it coming, and he caught it inches away from his throat, winning the right to use it. By the look of the widened eyes around the square, they surely expected a slower, less prepared, weaker-minded man.

Another rod was tossed to Titus. He turned to Razz and swung the rod at his feet in a flash. Razz jumped, and the moment his feet landed, he pulled the same move on Titus. But Titus—the great, undefeatable warrior—did not jump as Razz had, but instead tripped and fell to the ground.

Several seconds of murmuring and gasps later, the crowd went silent with mouths half-open.

Titus grunted, pushed himself off the dirt-covered ground, and ran toward a nearby wall. The people against the wall scattered.

Titus jumped in the air, kicked off the wall, and came down with his rod locked on Razz's chest. But again, Razz somehow saw it coming as he swiftly shifted to the side, missing Titus's rod. For a mere second, it felt as if time slowed because somehow, before Titus reached the ground, Razz lifted his rod with force into Titus's stomach.

His armor took the brunt of the hit. Razz, on the other hand, wore a black tunic without an inch of armor.

Why isn't Razz using his mind-bending abilities to his advantage? I wondered. He could have easily finished Titus by now if he had wanted to.

Suddenly, Titus pierced his rod into the ground as leverage to jump high as his feet launched into Razz's chest.

Razz fell to the ground with such force, his right cheekbone was quickly painted in scrapes and blood.

As the crowd cheered for Titus, Razz returned to his feet, puffing. Titus didn't give him so much as a second to catch his breath before swiftly spinning the rod around his fingers and whipping it on the side of Razz's neck.

Titus's rod danced around his fingers as he continued the wild spinning—too fast to know where on Razz it would strike next. He swung without hesitation, but Razz quickly shielded himself with his own rod, stopping the force of Titus's swing.

They were neck-to-neck with rods strenuously pressed against each other. Though Razz was already tall to begin with, Titus had an inch or two on him with a bigger build. Yet somehow, Razz and his modest muscles kept their strength firm against Titus's relentless force.

Titus released his rod from Razz's when he suddenly dipped himself down to Razz's feet, lifted him as if he were a sack of potatoes, and threw him over his shoulders. But instead of Razz flying across the square as seemingly planned, he latched onto Titus's back and wrapped his rod around his opponent's throat.

Titus quickly turned red as Razz pulled his rod against his throat even harder, until finally, Titus fell to the ground in defeat. He was still alive but was, without a doubt, knocked out.

Razz peered at the crowd panting, when he said, "For the record, I was a child when the raid of the Orpheus realm had been decided. I do not condone the choices made by my father or any of the nobles regarding their actions. Believe it or not, I too am paying the consequences for their choices, fighting for my life and my people." He looked at me before turning back to the crowd. "I am not your enemy." He dropped his rod and strolled off with a clenched jaw.

The crowd parted for Razz with what appeared to be respect.

I ran after him, following his trail into the main pyramid. By the time I caught up with him, his whipped neck had already begun bruising.

He stood in the deserted, flame-lit hall.

"You okay?" I asked.

He took a desperate breath before answering with a surprising smile. "Haven't had a thrill like that in a long time."

"Why didn't you use your mind-bending abilities on him?" I said, immediately regretting my question after what happened to Kai in the Kano Kingdom.

He tilted his head and genuinely asked, "Now, would that be a fair fight?"

And before I could answer, he continued down the hall with a pep in his step.

"Um, where are you going?"

"To find Queen Vesta," he said without turning back.

"Why?"

He stopped in his tracks and glanced at the empty halls before turning to me. "She already knows why we're here. Well, she knows some of it. And she's eager for us to succeed. So maybe she'll give me a hint to where the relic belongs."

"But Etiwa said—"

"I know what she said. I'll be cautious with my query." Then he continued down the hall and turned out of sight.

As for me . . . I decided it was time to return to the mystic.

CHAPTER 34

The Mystic

Dancing flames spread flickering light over the steps leading to the mystic's chamber. Burning incense had already begun to fill my lungs.

"I have been expecting your return," Ziggy said as I approached.

I took it as an invitation into her smoky room. Her hypnotic gray eyes shifted to bright orange as I stepped inside.

She stayed staring into the fire before her as she simply said, "Sit."

So I sat on a round pillow across from her firepit. I knew I wanted her help, but to form the right words to why I had returned seemed difficult. I opened my mouth, but nothing came out, so I closed it.

"Tea?" she asked, holding up a charred kettle.

"What kind of tea?"

"A simple herbal blend." Something about her monotone voice was unsettling.

"Will it make me . . . hallucinate?"

"No. But it will allow you to see truth."

"Truth?"

She set the kettle down. "If you fear the truth, then you are not ready for my tea. So let us get to why you have come."

I knew I should have asked about the relic and where it belonged. I knew I was being completely selfish for why I returned. But I needed to see him. I needed to know that he was okay!

"I have come to see . . . the man you heard in the flames when I first arrived."

"Yes, I know," she said, her gaze lost in the flames. "But there is another reason. Maybe more than just one. Is there not?"

I don't know why I was so surprised that she sensed it.

"Well, yes . . ."

"Let us address that frightful emotion, as it has already begun to tangle with your worrying thoughts in the back of that pretty head." She stared at the crown of my head as if she could see my thoughts. "I will give you the answers you seek. But first, you must give me something in return."

"I have some pentacles."

Her heavy eyes fell on mine. "That is not what I desire," she said flatly.

"Okay. What is it you want?"

"A taste of your blood." Ziggy didn't blink as her hypnotic gaze burned into my eyes.

I was silent at first, unsure how to respond to such an unsettling request. But if it meant I would see Darian again and maybe even get a hint as to where the relic might belong, then a taste of my blood was a small price to pay.

"Okay," I said somewhat reluctantly.

The light of the flames danced on her face as she feasted her eyes on my arm as if I were her next meal. Then, she took out a copper rod the size and shape of a pencil, with a very sharp tip. She spread it over the flames, and without warning, she grabbed my wrist and pierced the pointed tip between two veins running up my arm. I winced as blood spilled out of my broken skin.

With a look of ecstasy, she lifted my bleeding arm over her steaming tea, topping it off as if I were dripping honey. She then held the pointed tool over the flames for some time, and again, without warning, she pressed the scorching metal against my slit arm, sealing the wound. I bit my lip at the pain to stop from screaming.

My crimson blood mixed with her golden tea as she stirred the now glittering orange liquid with her finger. "Ask away," she finally said.

For a moment, I just stared at my blistering arm. A few blinks later, I realized I hadn't yet responded. I desperately wanted to say, "Show me Darian!" But instead, I said, "Um. Well, I was warned about something that hasn't happened yet. And I was told my choice may determine this realm's fate."

She appeared pleased as she sipped her tea with closed eyes and a swaying head. Had she even heard my question? Or was she too far gone in a world of hallucinations?

Her words suddenly rose and fell rhythmically. "There are choices only you can make that can save the fate of this realm. Your choices can also be the death of this realm and its dwellers. The first choice will have to be a sacrifice."

My stomach turned into knots.

"What kind of sacrifice?" I asked, my eyes following her sway behind the flames.

My heart leaped in fear when she suddenly opened her now gray eyes, landing them directly on me. And in her strange smoky voice, she said, "You are the sacrifice."

My stomach dropped. It was a struggle to speak. But I bit my nerves and asked, "Can you be more specific?"

She closed her eyes again. "You can always ask Astrophel or Kamali. But the gods will show me nothing more."

How did she know the names of my spirit guides? Had she seen them in the flames? Had they formally introduced themselves in her mind's eye? Frankly, her magic unhinged me.

I didn't care enough to ask. There were far more vital questions I needed answers to.

"You said I would have to make choices, as in more than one. What other ones will I have to make that have anything to do with the safety of this realm and its people?"

"Release your worries and fears, and the rest will reveal itself with time."

I wanted concrete answers. Instead, I got more riddles that only added to my list of questions.

"Fine!" I said, irritated. "Show me Darian." The words shot out as more of a command than a request. But my demanding voice didn't faze her in the least.

"How would you like to see him?" she asked sweetly.

"I have choices?"

"Of course."

"What are they?"

"You can view him in the flames or see him face-to-face."

The thought alone of seeing his perfect blue eyes again glitched my heart.

Nerves sprang through each syllable as I said, "Face-to-face."

"Very well." She poured a second cup of tea and pushed it toward me. "Drink up," she said with a slight thrill in her voice.

I took the warm cup in hand. My reflection peered back at me as I looked over the golden-yellow liquid. The steam alone was intoxicating, with its zest dancing through my senses, tugging my lips to its fragrance. I inched closer to the warm, steaming cup, my tongue eager to taste the pleasant aroma. Even if I wanted to back out now, I couldn't. My senses were in control, and they wanted nothing more than to taste every drop.

As my mouth folded over the rim, the mystic said, "You must say his name."

It tasted of cinnamon and spice, with a balmy caress of butter and sugar. With each sip, I became strangely more aware of my body and soul. They were very different, as only one truly belonged to me for eternity.

While realizing that my body was just a temporary home for my soul, I began to lose the sensation of my skin and muscles. Then my bones rattled, and suddenly my soul found the exit and opened the door. And just before it stepped out, my head swayed with the flames as I said, "Zaydarian Bader."

A single sip later—*whoosh.* I was no longer in the mystic's chamber.

CHAPTER 35

Phantom Body

My body stayed behind as my consciousness moved through space and time, which seemed to have suddenly stilled. As I magically traveled through a shimmering flame of stars, I realized I was not my body, and my body was not me. I was blind to it before, when I was trapped in a shell of flesh, once filled with insecurities and anxiety while facing the countless battles that come with simply existing. But here, stripped of my mortal costume, I felt the deepest and truest of me. This was my soul!

To see me was impossible, as I no longer had a body. I was just a soul of pure consciousness flickering toward a vast world of electric blue. The blue grew bigger and brighter until suddenly, it was as if I blinked. Blue light engulfed me in every endless corner.

I looked down to find that I again had feet, hands, and the same body I had left somewhere in the mystic's chamber. Perhaps that's why I didn't appear completely solid. But my soul—my consciousness—was in the grid in an apparition form of the body I was certain I left behind.

271

Now, where could I find Darian? I thought, scanning my infinite surroundings.

The grid responded to my wonderment as suddenly, a white brick path formed before my very eyes, growing longer and longer. As I followed the path, iridescent paint splashed from beneath my feet with each step. The moment I took my eyes off my splattering trail, glass trees formed alongside the pathway; each tree reflected the iridescent paint sprinkled beneath their branches.

I walked farther and farther into the blue light until finally, I arrived at a black gothic door, surrounded only by a beautifully carved dark stone trim—nothing else. I could have easily walked around it. Though somehow, I knew I shouldn't. My gut nearly succeeded in guiding my hand to the doorknob. But logic stopped me.

It wasn't until I looked back at the long trail of splattered iridescent footsteps lined by glass trees and again at the lonely grand door that I wondered, *Where the hell am I?*

Perhaps my mind was just burning a trail of hallucinogen ecstasy. Except, how could any of this be hallucinated when it felt more real than the air I breathed?

Without a moment to think it through, the finger-length size keyhole below the decorative doorknob released a swarm of stars. Instead of the stars passing by me, they moved in circles around me until they collapsed to the floor, shattering into stardust. Then, music started playing on the other side of the door. No longer able to contain my curiosity, I reached for the handle, turned it, and walked through.

If logic existed here, I would have just walked through to the other side of the door, continuing into the blue light as there were no walls or anything attached to the door that suggested I would step inside somewhere. Yet, here I was, in a grand castle with hundreds of milky paintings hung on the walls. Books upon books were flying with flapping covers, weaving their leathery wings and draping pages between every instrument I could ever imagine—each musical tool floating and playing in circles far above my head.

It was a symphony of beautiful absurdity. I felt as though I knew this silly sounding symphony long ago, perhaps in another life entirely. Something about the charming sounds of the piano, violin, and cello wildly playing their upbeat melody was nostalgic.

I caught sight of the self-playing piano toward the high ceiling. The thought of touching its enchanted keys had me yearning for it. And as if it felt the longing of my heart, it glided toward me, lower and lower, until it set itself down on the shimmering floor before me. The piano bench quickly followed as it settled behind my knees, welcoming me to sit. The moment I did, all the other instruments abruptly fell quiet.

The keyboard beckoned my fingers. Forgetting why I was even there, I began playing.

I had played the piano more times in my life than I could count. But never did it sound this rhythmically poised. It was as though my fingers had a mind of their own as they danced from key to key, creating a perfect melody.

I had completely lost myself to it, until a familiar voice shook my bones, speaking behind me.

"Are you real?" he asked.

I turned, and though I wasn't in my actual skeletal body, somehow, a beating in my hollow chest went utterly wild at the sight of Darian. I stood up, and instead of walking around the piano bench, it simply floated away.

For some reason, it took a great deal of effort, but I finally managed to say, "Yes, I'm real."

As he swept his gaze over my phantom body, confusion filled his heavy stare. He could see my legs and arms and every part of me as if I were actually in the grid, even if I didn't appear fully solid.

After a thorough scan, his eyes landed on mine, and he stayed there, staring in silence. I didn't mind it. In fact, I never wanted to leave this moment, locked in his gaze. The entire world sat in his eyes, and everything I ever needed was already there, just waiting to be explored.

He stepped closer. "Attica," he said. His voice caressed my name as he said a second time, even lower, "Attica."

I inched closer to him this time. "I'm here."

He reached out and brushed his thumb over my cheek. And when he did—*Boom.*

Every wall, every painting, every book, every instrument— everything shattered like glass. Bit by bit, the shards of our previous surroundings floated around us.

He reached his other hand up to my face, unfazed by the swirling shards circling us close and far. He was completely consumed by me and only me.

His hand caressed my cheek as if it were solid. And I could physically feel the tips of his fingers, except he felt more like pure energy against the skin of my soul.

Somehow, as he took me fully into his dreamy gaze, the glass pieces surrounding us reformed, except this time, they morphed into a galactic ocean with a star-filled sea, washing ashore beneath our feet. And as if from nowhere, holographic planets appeared just beyond the nonsensical starry ocean we stood beside in a world of blue.

"What is this place?" I asked, sweeping my sight in every direction, trying to make sense of the perplexing galaxy.

The rasp in his low voice cracked when he said, "I don't know anymore." His gaze drifted away for just a moment until he looked back at me. "Do you think about me?"

It was a question I didn't expect. Especially not from him—not from the person who so often consumed my thoughts. And not from the person who always had a wall up, keeping me at a careful distance.

He stayed, staring into what felt like my soul as he waited patiently for an answer. But I didn't know how to answer.

It was as if my mind had passed control to my voice when I said, "Zayd. I miss you."

I couldn't believe the words that had come out of my mouth. But then I quickly figured out it wasn't my mind or my voice in control. No. It was my soul speaking.

My soul didn't stop there. It practically grabbed my hand and guided it to Darian's cheek, mirroring him as his fingers still lingered by my chin.

He removed his hand from my jaw, and instead, placed it over mine—over the hand I rested on his cheek. The touch we shared was not solid, as it would be outside the grid. Instead, it was energetic. It was as though our cells were connecting to bridge our merging souls.

We stood there, beside an impossible diamond ocean, completely and utterly lost in our locked gaze and our shared touch.

We were becoming one. Or so it felt. Perhaps it was the reflection of the strange, beautiful planets surrounding us in a boundless blue gleam, but there was an entire universe in his eyes, and I was ready to jump in and surrender myself to it—to him.

But then, my breathing in the body I left behind in the mystic's room suddenly broke when everything began to wither away.

"What's happening?" I asked as I floated out of his reach while the curious galaxy vanished into the light.

I never received an answer, as the world I was in swiftly disappeared. The diamond sprinkled sea was gone. The many holographic planets were gone. But, worst of all, Darian was gone. And my heart felt like it had broken into a million pieces.

I didn't know how much time had passed. I didn't even know my eyes were closed until I opened them to find myself right back where I started . . . a million miles away from where I wanted to be.

"Welcome back," Ziggy said.

Tears streamed down my face. "I need to go back!" I pleaded.

"No, you cannot."

"Please!" I begged.

"If I send you back, you tempt the grid to keep your mind, never to return to your body."

It was terrible how tempting that sounded if it meant I'd be left with him for eternity. But suddenly, in the same second, logic abruptly returned to me. I couldn't help but judge my sanity.

For just a moment, I was considering leaving the real, physical world to be stuck in the grid with Darian—a man I hardly knew. Never mind the fact that I wouldn't physically be in the grid like him—just my consciousness, or soul, or whatever part of me had traveled to him. The thought of it was tempting, but completely and utterly absurd.

I hardly noticed how severely I was shaking, still in shock. Minutes went by with me sitting across from the mystic in complete silence, thinking back to every second spent in the grid.

Somehow, he created his own world there. And I had lost myself to it.

Finally, as my senses returned, I found the strength to push myself off the floor and utter, "Thank you," as I began to exit.

But then I remembered I hadn't asked the mystic where the relic belonged. I didn't even know if it was safe to mention the relic at all. Etiwa had warned me not to tell a soul.

"Did you forget something?" she asked as I stopped in my tracks.

I turned to her. "Yes, actually. If the Azar Kingdom had a place of generating magic, where might it be?"

"That is a peculiar question, considering these lands lost their magic long ago."

"Oh, I know. But still, it would be a place I'd want to visit to give my respects," I lied, wondering if she could see through my fib.

"You know, I too have spirit guides that have told me much about your being here. It is not just about bringing our heir home. It is about the young man in the grid too. Is it not?"

I didn't answer.

"But there is one element they will not show me. And I believe that is the reason you ask such a curious question. I cannot help you with something I cannot see in my mind's eye. All I can tell you is follow your instincts."

Just before I stepped out, she said, "One last thing."

I turned back around with a twinge of hesitance.

"The Orpheus know you have passed their barrier. And they will be looking for you."

My stomach dropped.

I swallowed and exited as my nerves unraveled.

CHAPTER 36

Tease to Escape

What now? I wondered, scanning the colossal pyramid I stood in. If I chose a place to generate the magic of this kingdom, it would be here, in this very pyramid.

I reached for the relic in my pocket, but my pocket lay flat and empty. I quickly remembered I had never put it in my pocket to begin with. How could I have remembered when my focus was sneaking back to the mystic to see Darian by whatever means necessary? As painful as it was to part from him, that wish had been more than fulfilled.

Before exiting, I took in the sight of copper-freckled marble gleaming off the flames in every corner of the pyramid. The many staircases along the walls and several bridges high above had me remembering my once terrible fear of heights.

As I passed the sunny square, nearly forgetting it was still daylight, I watched people pick fruit from what looked to be giant treelike pineapples a short distance away. There were ten of these generous fruit-bearing trees. Passersby helped themselves to the

279

fruit. Each tree had at least three spiles, supplying any who turned the knob with water.

When I noticed a young child jumping high, trying to reach one of the spiles, I went over and helped him. After he had his fill of water, I turned to find three more children waiting for a turn. After I helped each one and then had some water myself, I headed back toward my room to grab the relic that belonged to this kingdom, assuming I would know which one that might be.

Sun rays wrapped my arms in a gripping warmth with every corner I turned.

I caught sight of the two saber-tooth tigers chasing each other on the outskirts of the tan stone city, where miles and miles of desert lay. The black tiger had the white tiger pinned to the sandy ground just before the white tiger bit her sister's neck and sprinted off. Carter sat on a sandy hill watching with an amused expression.

After a ten-minute heat ridden walk, I finally made it back to the compact pyramid in the women's quarter of the city. All the women I passed were just friendly enough. Though none of them gave me a kind smile or introduced themselves, they at least glanced at me with a pleasant nod.

When I opened the door to the guest room, my stomach turned to knots at the sight of Titus sitting on my bed, examining the glass relics in his robust hand—a hand potentially strong enough to shatter them to pieces, if he wanted to.

He didn't so much as glance at me. He didn't even flinch his jade eyes at the sun now peering in on his handsome face.

"Wha-what are you doing?" I asked, words dry and clinging to my timid tongue.

Instead of answering my question, he stayed staring at the relics. "What are these?"

With a smooth accent, his three simple words practically purred over the relics. His energy had shifted from the last time I had seen him. It was calmer, but still, I tiptoed around his question.

"Oh, they're just something my mother gave me a long time ago," I lied, forcing a calmness over each word.

"They must do something," he said adamantly. He finally lifted his head, allowing his spectacular eyes to land on me.

"No. They're more for decoration," I said with a not-so-subtle squeak.

He dropped the relics carelessly onto the bed. All except one. He played with the pyramid-shaped relic in his hand—the relic I was nearly certain belonged to this kingdom . . . , the relic that should have been lit with flames since I had stepped into this city. But it stayed empty, as did the rest of them.

Did some part of him know that the pyramid relic he passed effortlessly between his fingers belonged here, to the Azar Kingdom?

I glanced at my arm in hopes of finding a coupling latched around it, as Razz had instructed me to do in case something was to happen. But I stupidly ignored him, leaving my arm bare of the silver band.

If I called out to him telepathically, would he hear my cry for help? Did I even need his help?

Titus stood up from the bed while scanning every inch of my body. His pupils dilated as his jade-rimmed eyes landed on my chest.

I didn't even care how far his sight and mind ventured over my body—though I certainly didn't like it. All I was focused on was the relic moving playfully between his fingers. But I did everything I could to keep my eyes off the relic, to not pique his curiosity any further.

Instead, I moved to the other side of the bed and said, "Why are you here?"

My palms began to sweat as he closed the door and locked the latch before turning back to me.

"We have not officially met," he said, inching closer toward me. "And I like to know everyone who enters my home. I even like to know their secrets if it means keeping my people safe."

I let out a chuckle and swept an innocent smile over my face. "I wish I had secrets. But, unfortunately, I'm far too boring."

His gaze rested on my lips. "You are too beautiful to be boring."

Some could say the same about him. But his rugged beauty could easily be overlooked by his dangerous energy, no matter how calm it was at the moment.

He moved in on me, every step pushing me farther into the corner until finally, he had me pinned between his muscled arms resting on the stone wall behind me.

His scent was heavy of smoldering mahogany. It reminded me of the first wake of autumn and was nearly intoxicating. My tongue deepened down my throat as my chest tightened.

I tried not to be obvious when I looked up at his hands, pressed against the tan stone above my head, as I searched for the relic he held. And there it was, nestled between a thumb and finger.

His voice lowered as he moved his breath to my ear and whispered, "Have you been with a man before?"

My mouth dried. I didn't know what the right move was. Was this a game I had to play to get the relic back? Was this a game I had to play to keep myself safe from his lusting eyes and tempted body?

I bit my bottom lip before ducking under his arm and turning back to him with a playful grin.

"Actually, I haven't." I leaned casually against the wall by the door, in case I needed a quick escape.

He followed my trail before pinning me a second time against the wall. It was at this moment, stuck between his sturdy arms once again, that I realized I had to treat this like a game if I were ever to escape untouched.

So I smoothly ran a finger over the copper tattoo wrapped around his forearm, dragging my hand toward the relic he held. "Tell me what it's like," I said sweetly.

His grin grew at my touch. And just as I gently gripped his hand—still wrapped around the relic—I pulled him to the bed, brushing the other relics on the sheet to the corner. And gently, so very gently, I opened his hand—keeping my other hand busy, combing my fingers through his chocolate hair. He didn't even notice when I secured the pyramid relic from his hand to mine.

Now, how do I break free?

His voice fell soft when he said, "I cannot tell you what it is like to be with a man, but I can show you."

His hands wrapped around my waist, each strong finger gripping the fabric of my clothes. His hand began to travel to an area he wasn't welcome, and I had no plan of how to escape it.

Razz! Can you hear me? Come! Come to my room! Now!

Unsure of how telepathy worked without the help of the couplings, I thought my thoughts as loud as I could, picturing Razz hearing every word.

Titus hardened as he pulled me onto him.

Razz! Please, come now! I begged inwardly.

Titus had already started untying my clothes, and instinctually, I grabbed his hand with force, stopping him.

"Is there a problem?" he asked, irritated.

"Um, yes. I have never—"

"Do not worry, darling. I will take care of you." He pulled me to his waist and flipped me onto my back. Straddling me, he peeled off his tunic and threw it to the floor. I tried squirming my way out from beneath him, but he was too strong.

"Please! I'm not ready to—"

"You do not need to be ready. I will take care of you," he said thickly, pulling the fabric off my shoulder with such force, the sound of it tearing had me clenching my teeth. His lips met my neck and quickly traveled south when—

"Attica!" a voice interrupted from outside. The doorknob rattled with force, and the heavy door shook. But the latch kept it shut.

Just as I was about to scream for Razz, Titus gripped my mouth.

I grabbed his hand and moved it with all my strength and then whispered, "Don't worry. I'll get rid of him." I removed his other hand from my waist and said toward the door, "Coming!"

With hesitance and an uncertain stare, Titus moved off me. I jumped off the bed, crossed the room as fast as I casually could, and unlatched the door. I opened it slightly to Razz on the other side with a wide-eyed expression of concern.

"Help," I mouthed.

He pushed the door open and saw Titus propped up on my bed, shirtless.

"Get out!" Razz commanded.

"No," Titus countered.

Razz's face turned to fury as his eyes drilled into Titus.

"Aghhh!" Titus roared in pain, clawing at his head.

"Get out!" Razz repeated, but still, Titus didn't move. Instead, he stayed sitting on the bed, clenching his jaw as thick veins surfaced on his forehead.

Whatever mind-bending Razz was doing had to have been far more severe than what he did to Kai, as Titus turned boiling red with his fingers pulling at his dark hair before falling off the bed to the floor in a fetal position. Razz stepped into the room and grabbed Titus by the neck before throwing him out on his ass, along with his shirt, and shutting the door.

"What the hell?" Razz said.

"He was in my room when I returned. He was holding the relics! What was I supposed to do?"

Razz scanned the room and then scanned me. His voice softened slightly. "Are you okay?"

"Yes," I said with a relieving breath.

"You have the relics?"

I darted to the bed, still holding the glass pyramid in my hand. One, two, three, four, five—including the one in my hand.

"Yes, they're all here!"

"Good. Let's find where it belongs and get the hell out of here!"

CHAPTER 37

The Firebird

Razz latched the coupling on my arm and stuck annoyingly close for the rest of the day. Not for a single moment did he let me out of his sight. And any man who so much as glanced at me began rapidly blinking and rubbing their eyes.

I took in the sight of the many palm trees and soft evening sky as we headed toward the colossal pyramid. Several more men continued to rub their eyes and harshly blinked any time they looked my way.

It happened so many times that I finally turned to Razz and asked, "Are you bending their minds or something?"

"Hardly," he uttered. "I'm just making you appear blurry whenever I catch a fervent creep looking at you."

"They're not all creeps. Plus, you're probably drawing more attention to me that way."

"I don't care. I don't want them to even think about what you look like! You don't want to know what thoughts go through a man's head at the sight of a beautiful woman," he said in a heated tone.

287

As we were nearing the main pyramid, three people ran directly into me. None of them apologized. In fact, they looked rather confused. It wasn't until a fourth person ran into me that I turned to Razz with clenched teeth.

"Have you made me invisible?"

"Maybe" was his only response, without giving me the decency to look in my direction.

"Stop it now! Or I will burn this damn coupling!" I said, more heated than I had ever been with him before.

He clenched his jaw. "Fine. But if anyone touches you or disrespects you again—"

"Then you are welcome to step in. But in the meantime, you have no right to bend anyone's mind or appearance without their consent."

It wasn't until we stepped foot into the colossal pyramid that he finally said with a struggle, "You're right. I'm sorry."

After I muttered a word of thanks, the tension quickly dissipated, and Razz began speaking casually, as if nothing had happened between us moments before.

"When I found Queen Vesta, I asked her where the magic was at its strongest before it was stripped from her kingdom. And as expected, it was here," Razz said as we stood in the center of the pyramid.

As I took in the powerful sight of the high thrones and the magnificent open-winged phoenix statue behind them, I turned to Razz and asked, "Where is Ignatius's father?" I had noticed a layer of dust on the king's throne.

His tone and energy shifted. "Ignatius once told me he gave his life to save several of his people during the wars."

My heart ached for Ignatius and his mother. My heart ached for this kingdom—for all the kingdoms who suffered through the wars.

We headed through the many beige marble halls, lit only by sizable bowls filled with lava rocks and flames every fifty feet. Razz held his swinging crystal pendulum as he pressed nearly all the stacked marble stones that appeared loose, as if they might be a secret button or easy to remove, revealing some hidden spot the relic belonged. But no stones budged.

After doing a thorough search on the bottom floor, we headed up a set of marble steps leading to a wooden bridge high above the thrones.

Though I had overcome my fear of heights not long ago in the root portal, still, the thought of being so high off the ground sparked nerves in my chest.

As we scanned the pyramid standing in the center of the bridge, a hundred feet or more above the floor, I swallowed my slight fear of heights and mustered enough courage to speak the words heavy on my mind aloud. "They know—the Orpheus."

"What exactly do they know?" Razz asked, with not even a slight tone of concern.

"That we crossed the barrier."

He turned to me with a raised brow. "How do you know they know?"

I kept my tone as casual as possible. "I stopped by to see the mystic." And as if I needed to defend myself before he reacted, I added, "I thought I could get some hints from her about where the relic belongs."

He squinted his eyes as if he could see right through me. "Okay. Is that all the Orpheus knows?"

Surprised he wasn't the least bit concerned, my voice dropped when I said, "I think so."

"Then we're still ahead of them." He crossed to the other side of the bridge.

I followed behind, my voice beckoning. "They're probably looking for us, Razz."

"Let them try," he said, without a care in the world.

We stepped foot into a dark room, lit only by a couple of torches hung on the wall. There were shelves of books and statues, big and small, many with jewel-filled eyes and copper coating. The sculptures were strange-looking animals—animals I had never seen before. But none compared in beauty or weight to the towering phoenix statue on the main floor.

Razz just about pulled and prodded at every book and statue while still holding that damn pendulum, even though it wasn't the least bit helpful. But nothing was out of the ordinary. And I had all five remaining relics with me this time, safe in the leather pouch strapped around my torso—none of which trembled or showed any sign of being close to where it belonged.

When we stepped out, we moved up another set of marble steps that took us to an even higher wooden bridge, at least fifty feet above the first one.

Razz had already walked across when he turned around to find me standing on the other side. "You coming?"

I swallowed. "Yes."

Don't look down. Don't look down. Don't look down.

The slight shaking of the bridge responding to my footsteps woke my nerves once more. It wasn't until I reached the other side that they finally settled, though not entirely.

The room before us now was even darker than the last one. But the moment we stepped inside, little lights flickered all around.

It took me a moment to realize the lights in this dark room were fireflies—unusually big fireflies—and it seemed this was the room they lived in as if they were domesticated pets. Of course, these were no ordinary fireflies. Not only were they the size of golf balls, but their bodies were covered in a brush of flames.

There was not much more than rough sandstone walls, almost appearing as the inside of a cave. They had nests made of tumbled rocks in pockets of the cavelike walls. And in the nests—my mouth dropped at the sight. These were no fireflies. Inside the nests were sleeping eagle-sized birds with red and orange feathers. And the fireflies fluttering around were not fireflies at all. Instead, they were baby birds just big enough to fly on their own.

Just as Razz began taking apart one of the empty nests, I stepped before him, placing a halting hand on his chest. "We are not destroying their home!" I commanded.

"You're choosing the birds' comfort over rescuing my brother?" he snapped as he stepped around me, removing slumbering birds from their nests. At least he seemed to show some consideration for the yellow-shelled eggs and the hatchlings.

"No!" I snapped back. "But if there were anything here, the relic would tell me." It was at this moment that I looked in my leather pouch to find the three-sided pyramid had finally lit with flames.

"Oh really?" he said in a patronizing tone, removing the largest bird with the longest feathers from the highest nest.

"Yes, really!" I said sharply, keeping the woken relic to my stubborn self.

Razz turned to me with his swinging pendulum in one hand and a smug smile before pressing a flattened rock inside the nest. And suddenly, the rocky wall behind us—a wall bare of nests—opened to a place so dark, it's as if we had been standing under the blazing sun in comparison. Without thinking twice, we entered.

CHAPTER 38

Underground

As the wall behind us began to close, Razz snatched a mighty bird from its nest, throwing it in the darkness with us. "Aghh!" he yelled as the bird lit its magnificent red-orange feathers with a coat of flames.

The wall closed, and there was nowhere to go but forward. The long-feathered firebird flew before us, allowing us a glimpse of our pitch-black surroundings.

We were in a tunnel with sandstone walls and stairs leading down. Kicked dirt and gravel sounded below our feet with each seemingly endless step. After about a few hundred descending steps, we caught sight of the bright burning bird again. We had finally reached the ground floor. Though I had a feeling we were underground.

Just as I prepared to step forward, Razz grabbed me by the arm. "Don't move," he ordered.

Hesitant to even speak, in fear that I might wake some wild beast he had glimpsed, I gently whispered, "Why?"

"You didn't see it?"

"See what?"

I could hear Razz sweeping the ground with his foot. A moment later, he threw a rock before us.

There was no thump or clunk or any landing sound. Instead, expanding light suddenly filled the darkness.

The walls and ground were rocky and covered in thin layers of dried dirt. Three bridges were before us, each about thirty feet across. And below the bridges was a pool of fire.

"Where—" My voice cracked. "Where are we?"

"Hell's child," he uttered while examining the furious flames under each bridge.

"Why are there three?" I asked, hoping Razz's intuition was strong enough to provide the answer, as he often surprised me with his intuitive accuracy.

Instead, he just looked at them, shaking his head with a faraway gaze, as if he were having some internal debate.

I moved toward him, sweeping my sight over the wooden bridges. "What are you thinking?"

"A trap, I think. Why else would there be three?" he said gravely.

Razz looked around and found a heavy rock. He threw it on the bridge to the right.

One, two, three, four, five.

Five seconds had gone by, and nothing happened. Then, just as Razz stepped a foot on it—*swish*—it fell to the flames below.

He grunted, looking around for something else to throw— anything. There was nothing but gravel and dirt.

I sighed. "What now?"

He didn't respond.

"Razz?"

"Shh! Let me think!" His words were sharp. Even his pacing between the two remaining bridges was sharp.

"Um, Razz!"

No response.

My veins filled with heat. "Razz! The flames!" I bellowed.

The fire below the bridges began rising.

"We need to run!" he said.

"Where?" I asked—heart rate rising.

"Across the bridges, as fast as we can!"

"Are you crazy?"

"We have no other choice. Let's go!"

And without so much as a blink, he darted to the middle bridge. It wobbled and swayed, and the moment he stepped to the other side, the ropes loosened, and the thirty-foot bridge fell into the pool of flames.

The wooden bridge, engulfed by the fire, seemed to have tamed the flames, slowing the rate at which they rose.

"You can do it, Attica!" Razz said, breathing heavy.

I pressed my feet farther into the ground. "I can't!"

"You have no choice."

My heart pounded so hard, I was sure Razz could hear it across the rising flames.

His voice was untamed when he shouted, "Now, Attica! As fast as you can!"

I chewed on my bottom lip harder than ever before as I chose Darian's life over my own and ran as fast as my ass could go to the remaining bridge on the left.

The wooden bridge didn't wobble as Razz's had. It didn't jolt at all as I sprinted like a damn cheetah after its prey. And just when I thought my heart would burst from its beating, I made it into Razz's arms, safely on the other side.

We both turned to the bridge, still there, unfazed by my intrusion. I felt pretty stupid. At least until the pool of fire suddenly vanished. What took its place was worse, and it swept me right back to the solar plexus portal.

Molten lava rose from the pool below the bridge at a much faster rate than the flames had. And this time, Razz didn't need to tell me to run.

With the firebird flying in circles before us, and the blanketing of volcanic blood behind us, we had enough light to see at least six to ten feet ahead. And what I saw in the short distance had me wondering which of us would die first.

"Get ready to climb!" Razz commanded as we headed toward nothing but a jagged wall—a dead end.

It would be me. I would, without a doubt, be the first to die!

Death had never scared me since a part of me always felt comforted at the thought of my soul roaming freely in the effervescent heaven above. Death, in some ways, appealed to me, as bleak as that may sound. But to die this way—to die engulfed by scorching, blistering lava—was the worst way I could have ever imagined my life ending.

But then we reached the dead end, and a glimpse of hope returned. The wall was certainly climbable.

The fiery gold lava was moving closer, maybe ten feet behind. We both had only one chance to climb to solid ground at the top, and it wasn't that high up. At least, that's what I told myself.

Razz was the first to begin climbing. I was only a couple of seconds behind. The first few feet were no problem. But the higher I got, the more difficult it was to scale. And just as I was a mere few feet away from the top, the rocky ledge below my right foot broke and fell to the climbing lava.

I looked up to find Razz pulling himself onto the terrace just a little over an arm's length above. He looked down to find me reaching for a ledge I couldn't quite grasp.

Razz swiftly threw a hand down. "Grab it!" he said, face turning red as he forced his arm lower than his chest allowed.

I tried to scale higher, but the wall on my side was not as generous as the side Razz had climbed. Just as the lava reached for my hanging foot, I shifted toward the part of the wall Razz had conquered—an area more willing to give me a generous lift. And with more stubbornness and pride than I should have had after balancing my chakras in the portals, I ignored Razz's gesture of saving my life and saved my own instead. I had finally made it to the top.

The lava continued to rise higher and higher until it reached the same level as the terrace and finally came to a stop.

Razz was smart enough to sweep every angle, ensuring no more danger was lurking in some hidden corner—at least for a long enough time that would allow our pumping chests to settle with what little oxygen we had.

We were safe, for now. And so was the firebird, perched on a serrated part of the rough stone wall. Its feathers of flames softened, with its sizable wings tucked on its sides.

As I stepped forward toward what looked like another dead end, my pocket shook, and relief fell over me. When I reached the wall—covered in some sort of sacred text—I took the trembling relic out of the leather pouch resting on my hip.

The moment I held the relic of fire, it practically led my hand to the center of the wall, where a little pyramid-shaped divot beckoned the glass tetrahedron from my fingers. It practically jumped in the divot itself, though I pressed it farther into the wall to secure it. And the moment I did, the sacred text lit brightly, and the torturous place we stood in shook. Swaying lava crept over the terrace as my skin suddenly filled with blood-boiling heat.

I screamed louder than ever before as the pain of my skin sweltered in what felt like a cocoon of flames. It was as though my insides had a raging wildfire spreading quickly, charring every organ and cell. But then, after several torturous seconds, my skin cooled. My insides felt a generous surge of relief. And above us fell a rope with several sturdy knots all the way to the top. My screams still softly echoed behind us.

Razz was too busy looking at me, wide-eyed, with hands lingering by his ears. His words were heavy when he said, "What in the fuck-filled cauldron was that?"

Instead of explaining my dramatic screech, I began to climb the rope, desperate to escape hell's spawn. Razz held the bottom, locking it in place, allowing me more ease in my climb.

When I reached the top, realizing there was no platform to climb onto and no door to go through, I was just about ready to climb back down in defeat. But then I noticed a part of the rocky wall with a thin, empty trim around it. And when I pressed its center, a stone door opened before Razz at the bottom of the rope. The bird flew through without hesitance.

As I cautiously climbed down, the door slowly began closing.

"Just let go. I'll catch you!" Razz bellowed, eyes rocking between me and the closing door. And for once, I listened to Razz without stubbornness and let go. As promised, he caught me, and we jumped past the door in the nick of time to find ourselves back in the colossal pyramid.

CHAPTER 39

The Ceremony

We stepped out of a hidden back wall behind the mystic's chamber.

All the sacred text and symbols in the pyramid were now filled with light, creating a deep yet uplifting enchantment of sounds. As the vibration of the music grew stronger, the shoulders of the thrones suddenly lit with sizable flames, then the massive phoenix statue behind the royal seats woke as its red-jeweled eyes lit brightly. Even stranger, the statue broke stillness as it turned its head and flapped its heavy copper wings. It soared in the pyramid for several minutes and then returned to its place behind the thrones.

As we exited, I turned back to the phoenix. Its scarlet eyes met mine, and to my surprise, it bowed as if it knew I was the one who had returned its magic—breaking the spell of its stillness. I responded with a smile.

Outside the pyramid, it was night, and many firebirds were circling above the city square.

Some people were on their knees, pressing their hands and foreheads into the ground, sobbing with what I hoped was joy. Most stood tall, pounding their chest with a single locked fist.

And suddenly, in the center of the square, appeared a spiral of violet fire, growing bigger and bigger, until finally, the flames vanished, and there stood Ignatius.

Everyone surrounded him, hugged him, and bumped arms, fists, and heads with him—all except Titus, who was looking curiously at me from across the square. And when his eyes widened, I knew he knew that I had played a part in returning their magic.

The crowd parted, allowing Queen Vesta to reunite with her son. It was a joyous sight, hard to walk away from.

Razz and I returned to our rooms to gather our belongings. We both took our time after the hell we had just endured.

I exited the room a starlight later, bathed and dressed with my stuff across my back and a straw-woven bag of food and water Enya had packed for Razz and me.

When I turned the corner, I took in the captivating sight of the kingdom's people. They were all circled with their rods beside them in an orderly fashion around Queen Vesta and Ignatius. The tip of every rod in each person's hand was lit with flames.

Pounding their rods to the ground with every syllable, they chanted in unison, "Oh va-ki, oh va-ki, oh va-ki."

Ziggy, the mystic, walked through the chanting crowd with a substantial stone bowl of heavy smoke. She set the bowl in the center of the circled people, and as everyone continued to pound their fiery rods to the ground, chanting louder and louder, a man turned up in the rising smoke; he stood tall and proud with a crown of fire around his head. It was, without a doubt, the king of Azar and the father to Ignatius.

Razz made his way toward me with a smile on his dapper face. "You made this happen, Attica," he said with a nudge on my arm.

"Well, I couldn't have done it without you," I responded.

"Oh, I know," he said as he wrapped an arm lazily over my shoulders.

We snuck out behind the ceremony, where a carriage led by saber-tooth tigers and Carter stood waiting for us. It seemed Enya had also given Carter and the tigers enough food and water for our travel ahead.

As we tucked our bags in the carriage, I turned to Razz. "We're not going to say bye to Ignatius?"

"We'll see him soon," he said, looking back at the kingdom and people of Azar with a broad grin before turning to me with a displaying hand. "Your chariot awaits."

CHAPTER 40

The Potion

The journey from south to north would be the longest yet. The thought of taking the journey without Carter and his carriage was unfathomable.

As I sat across from Razz on the wide maroon seat, his navy-blue eyes reflected the moons as he stared silently out the window at the sparkling night sky. For nearly an entire starlight, he had a slight smile on his face.

"You seem happy," I finally said.

His eyes stayed glued to the stars when he said, "We're so close. We're not only close to seeing my brother again, but to bringing Elloriya back from its death of magic." Razz ran a hand through his curls. "This is part of something much bigger than saving my brother. What you're doing with the relics is going to change the future of Elloriya."

"Etiwa and the alchemist are the ones who deserve the credit. If it weren't for the alchemist, there would be no vessel in the kingdoms for the relics, right? And if it weren't for Etiwa, there would be no relics. So, my gratitude goes to them. And to you," I added. He smiled. "What a wonderful coincidence that this mission to retrieve Darian from the grid also brings magic back to many kingdoms."

"There is no such thing as coincidences. It's all divine intervention," he said, looking out the window again.

"So you think all coincidences are magic?"

"Not magic!" he countered sharply. He then slowed his words when he said, "Divine intervention. There's a difference."

I didn't respond. Instead, we sat in silence for a while as the carriage shook from a sudden gust of wind. The silence continued until I remembered what Razz had said about the grid when we were stargazing in the desert.

"Didn't you say something about how some people have used magic to open the grid to travel between realms?"

He broke his gaze from the stars beyond the carriage window and looked to me with a raised brow. "Yes."

"Then why didn't we just buy bottled magic from the emporium to help free Darian? I saw some at the apothecary shop."

He let out an exasperated breath with no reply.

I was almost afraid to ask, "What?"

As if he were fighting against keeping his feelings to himself, he shot out, "It sickens me how much everyone relies on magic. Magic can't fix everything!"

Feeling attacked by his tone alone, I didn't tiptoe when I spat out, "What is your deal?"

It was the last thing I expected—to see tears suddenly run down his face. The light of the moons highlighted every single stream of sorrow as he rested his head on the carriage window, once again staring at the night sky.

"Razz, I'm—I'm sorry." I wanted to hug him and tell him that everything would be okay, even if I had no clue what troubled him so deeply.

He turned his face away from my sight and wiped his silent tears.

"Will you share with me?" When I got no response, I clarified, "Your pain."

He clenched his sharp jaw and sighed. He didn't bother to sit up or take his eyes off the stars. But he did speak.

"I was young when it happened, but old enough to know better. I was about ten . . ."

"What happened?"

He held his small braid behind his left ear with a faraway gaze, and his tears slowed. He almost smiled when he said, "My sister, Seren, was the most beautiful thing you'd ever see."

Sister? I thought it was always just Razz and Darian.

"She had just begun to talk in short sentences. Everyone was so proud of her." He settled himself in this moment for some time before he continued. "I was the oldest, so my mother put me in charge of watching her while she ran to help Darian, who had accidentally wielded a sword hanging on the wall onto himself. He was only three, maybe four—not yet able to control his wielding."

At first, I was confused about the age difference, since Razz only looked to be about a year or two older than Darian. He certainly did not look six or seven years older than him. But then I remembered Darian and I lived on Earth for a good portion of our lives. And time was different in the human world. We had more days; every three days on Earth was one day in Elloriya. So Darian grew up faster, shortening the age gap between him and his brother.

He continued. "My mother's lady's maid often helped with my brother and sister. But it was her birthday, so my mother gave her the day off." He buried his head in his hand. "At the time, magic intrigued me. Darian could wield at such a young age—though not very well—and I couldn't. I knew I could do things with my mind that others couldn't, but it wasn't fulfilling enough because I hardly knew how to put my abilities to use."

He lifted his head from his hand and sighed. "The alchemist and my father were close friends. He had given my father a potion. I didn't know what exactly for, but I knew it was made from magic. So when my sister was suddenly having a seizure on my watch, I couldn't find my mother or father, and I freaked out. So I ran to my father's chamber and took the potion. And then—" His sun-kissed face drained of color. "I poured the potion down her throat, thinking since it was magic, it would stop the seizure and make her better. But instead, it killed her almost instantly." More tears rolled down his face.

After a long moment of sitting in shock, I finally said, "Razz, you couldn't have known. You were just a child. And you did what you thought was the right thing to do in a very scary situation." I fell silent, wondering if I was making him feel better or worse. He was unresponsive. At least until I said, "But now I understand why you feel the way you do about magic."

It seemed to be a struggle for him to say, "I know not all magic is bad. I know it can do good. But I just—" He paused before forcing the words out, one syllable at a time. "I just don't love it."

"I know."

I wasn't sure if it was because my heart ached for him, as he sat once more staring out the window, or if it was just me wanting to be a good friend, but I moved to the other side of the carriage beside him and grabbed his hand. He didn't seem to mind. He actually embraced it, gripping my hand in response. So we sat in silence, hand in hand, until we fell asleep.

When I awoke the next morning, Razz wasn't beside me. And the carriage was still, no longer moving north.

I saw through the window that Razz, Carter, and the tigers were stretching their legs in a field of grass. So I stepped out to do the same, and the white-furred tiger immediately came to greet me. I ran a caressing hand over the black stripes on her head while taking in the overwhelming sight of her saber teeth—each tooth much longer and sharper up close. Both fangs were at least six inches long.

The black-furred tiger was chasing Razz, who had a sunny smile on his face as he turned to chase her back. The tiger I was petting turned to join the game of tag.

Carter stepped back onto the carriage in the driver's seat, and in my peripheral vision, I saw him staring at me. So I turned and asked how he was doing. But instead of responding, he tilted his head with lowered brows and said, "You have purple eyes."

"Yes, I do," I responded hesitantly.

He thought for a moment before he said, "The first life born in this realm also has purple eyes."

A pit in my stomach practically screamed for my attention. It suddenly dawned on me that we were relying on a stranger to transport us. He could easily take us straight to the Orpheus, and we wouldn't have a clue until it would be too late.

I played it cool when I said, "Oh, really?"

He thought to himself again before asking, "Where in this realm are you from?"

"A small village near the Tera Kingdom," I lied.

"Hmm. What was your name again?"

My heart pounded quicker. Why did he care what my name was? Why was he asking so many questions? Had he heard Razz call me by my name before? Had he overheard Queen Vesta when we arrived at her kingdom? Did he know what we were up to? He saw the Azar Kingdom using magic before we left. Since Razz's close call to death in the rainforest, I suddenly felt anxiety creep its way back to me again.

I took a breath and said as calmly as I could, "My name is Jada." It was the only false name I had used before, and the thought of using my sister's name—the sister that fears nothing—made me feel a little less anxious. "Well, thanks again for the ride."

Carter's eyes still lingered on me as I stepped back into the carriage.

When Razz jumped in and closed the door, I opened my bag and slipped on the coupling, giving Razz a gesture to do the same.

Curiosity filled his eyes as he latched the silver band around his arm. I tapped my coupling with his, feeling that same dizzying energetic tie lock between us.

I think he knows who I am, I thought. *Can he be trusted?*

Razz's eyes widened, and I felt him trying to tap into Carter's mind through the coupling. Perhaps he was even trying to alter it, if that was even something he could do. I didn't know the full scope of what a mind-bender was capable of.

Suddenly, Razz's voice filled my mind.

"He suspects and is questioning the reasons for our journey. The magic he saw at the Azar Kingdom frightened him. I can feel it."

I took a heavy breath. *What do we do?*

He sucked his teeth before telepathically responding, "We stay awake as long as we can. Maybe even take turns sleeping." He pulled out the compass. It lit upon his touch before the arrow spun wildly. When it came to a stop, it pointed north, and then the light of the compass vanished. "If this changes—if he veers off the path at all— then I will handle Carter."

Just when I thought we had nearly completed our quest, I questioned if I would truly ever see Darian again, as our lives were in the hands of a stranger we never thought of as a threat, until now.

CHAPTER 41

Intuition

The sun glared through the carriage windows. If the sun was up, the Orpheus was no threat, regardless of them knowing that Razz and I crossed through their kingdom. No one had ever seen an Orpheus out of their domain during daylight.

We had been going north for at least seven days with few breaks. Razz and I slept in the carriage each night, just in case Carter had plans to take off without us. But with the constant sitting and sleeping in the carriage in the last week, the thought of walking the rest of the way became more appealing, if only time allowed it.

Razz and I stayed silent most of the way in case Carter was listening. When we spoke, we whispered. Although, with the sounds of the moving carriage and birds twittering amongst the swaying tree leaves, Carter would have to have exceptionally good hearing to catch our whispers.

I finally broke a long silence when my curiosity got the best of me. "How does your intuition work?"

"Well, I've been gifted with the four primary psychic abilities."

"What are they?"

313

"Clairvoyance allows me to receive images in my mind—visions of the future or sometimes even warnings. Claircognizance is a simple knowing. For example, at times, I know what others are thinking, or days before a storm comes."

I suddenly remembered a childhood memory of me wearing a raincoat when my adoptive dad told me it would not rain, according to the forecast. But I just knew it would.

Razz must have picked up on my thoughts. "Yeah, I think you have the gift too. But I think you often confuse your claircognizance as your own thoughts."

"If it's a knowing, then how can I decipher if it comes from my thoughts?" I asked, trying to remember the advice my spirit guides once gave me in the third eye portal.

"Simple. If you think it up, then it's your thoughts. But if the knowledge or thought randomly appears in your mind, without you being the one to think it up, then it's your intuition—your claircognizance."

I noted his advice, and he continued.

"Clairsentience is a feeling—often a gut feeling. And before you say anything, yes, I think you have that ability too. In fact, I think many people have that ability."

Mama always told me to follow my gut. She must have had the gift of clairsentience too.

"And finally, there's clairaudience, which allows me to hear whispers, often from my spirit guides or angels. But as I've grown older, it has become my weakest gift. If I were being completely honest, I purposefully try to shut that ability down."

"Why?"

"Would you like to hear voices in your head?" he asked with a playful grin.

Instead of answering, my thoughts took me back to the day at the coliseum. "You saw them the day I died, didn't you?"

His brows lowered. "Saw who?"

"The angels."

He smiled. "If I remember correctly, there were seven angels that reunited your soul to your body."

"Yeah, there was. Why haven't you ever mentioned it?"

He shrugged. "I've seen a lot of angels in my life. So it's not a big deal to me."

"Do you see angels often?"

"I see them as a golden light, most often when someone is praying close by."

I continued to bombard him with questions since silence made this journey north feel seemingly endless. "You said you were gifted with the primary psychic abilities. Are there more abilities like them?"

He chuckled. "Much, much more."

Just then, we ran over a bump in the road, causing me to nearly hit my head on the carriage ceiling. When my rising heart rate settled, I asked, "Like what?"

He straightened. "Where do I begin? There are empaths who can pick up on other people's emotions. I have that ability too, as well as telepathy. There's astral projection, where one can have out-of-body experiences—something I used to do as a child. There's telekinesis, moving physical objects with your mind. Mediumship allows one to channel spirits. And the list goes on and on." He rested his hands behind his neck. "The thing about these abilities is most people have so many thoughts going on in their head at all times that they often miss whenever they receive a vision, a feeling, a knowing, or even a tiny voice in the back of their mind. And others who take notice of them often brush them off as coincidence. But there's—"

"There's no such thing as coincidence," I said mockingly, cutting him off.

He looked up with a slight smile. At that moment, I realized how often Razz smiled and how his brother never smiled. They were as different as day and night.

We sat back in silence, keeping a close eye on the compass pointing north. I couldn't help but think about Darian and the time I had spent with him in the grid.

What were the strange feelings I had every time I was in his presence? What was it about him that made my heart want to jump out of my chest? The way he looked at me in the grid was a look I could never forget; it felt as though he was looking into my soul. And at the same moment, he allowed me a glimpse into his.

My thoughts were so far gone as I sat in the sounds of nature, and for just a moment, I had forgotten Razz was sitting across from me. At least until he asked, "Are you in love with my brother?"

I gripped the coupling on my arm that strengthened my connection to Razz. I wanted to remove it so my thoughts wouldn't travel to him, but we agreed the safest choice was to continue to wear the couplings, at least until we finished our mission.

My chest tightened, and I was sure my ears turned red.

He sat there staring at me, waiting for a response.

I took half a breath before masking my face in surprise. "What would make you think that?"

The look on his face said it all. It was almost as though he was too embarrassed to say the words aloud—to say he could feel or hear my thoughts consumed by his brother. But he was kind enough to make it as comfortable as he could for the both of us when he responded, "I don't know. Just a feeling, I guess."

"Well, your feeling is wrong. I'm not in love with Darian," I countered, somewhat defensively.

But I could easily fall in love with Darian, if he only dropped his walls long enough to allow me to see the real him.

A hidden grin formed on Razz's face with a subtle shake of his head.

I no longer cared about our little agreement with the couplings. I immediately took the coupling off my arm and put it back in my bag. And to sweep the attention off me and my emotions, I put the attention on him and his feelings.

"So, what happened with you and Cece?"

He chuckled through a glimpse of heartache. "Obviously nothing."

"There's something between you two. Even if you don't want to admit it."

He let out a real laugh this time. "One to talk!"

I responded with a simple eye roll.

It surprised me when he continued. "When I first met Cece at the manor, we were about thirteen. I had a crush on her, but she and Ignatius had a flirtation. Whatever was between them ended quickly. I didn't want the same thing to happen between her and me. So I kept my feelings separate from our friendship. But as we got older and matured, it was harder not to flirt with her. I mean, she's kind, caring, thoughtful, and beautiful. But I had trained myself for so many years to keep my feelings for her buried. So, the exact thing I feared when I was thirteen ended up happening anyway. Only zeniths later. Whatever flirtation we had ended quicker than I thought it would."

"So you have never told her how you feel?"

"I didn't get the chance. She moved on to another guy on our first date. You saw for yourself at the gala."

I straightened on the cushioned seat. "Razz, you need to tell her!"

"No, I don't!"

"If she knew, things could be different."

To my surprise, he leaned his elbows onto his knees and narrowed his eyes on me. "Okay, fine. I'll tell her."

"Good! You can thank me later."

"But only if you tell Darian how you feel."

My mouth fell open, but no words came out. I tried to respond, but still, nothing.

He retracted his elbows from his knees and went back to staring out the window as he said, "Thought so."

We slid back into silence. Not much time had passed before the sound of rustling grass in the distance caught my attention.

Moments later, feathered wolves surrounded the carriage; they were without a doubt tikaanis. But they weren't the same tikaanis I had known on the edge. Instead, their feathers were primarily green, with accents of orange and yellow.

The carriage shook as the tigers roared, likely attempting to attack.

"Whoa, whoa, whoa, girls!" Carter said, pulling the reins.

Razz pointed to his coupling; a reminder to put mine back on. The moment I did, he tapped them together and our appearance instantly changed.

I didn't have a mirror, but I could see my hair now appeared gray, and my skin was dry and heavily wrinkled.

I hardly had a moment to digest my sudden change in appearance, that I almost hadn't noticed the child now sitting across from me. It was Razz, except he appeared to be around eight or nine.

The wolves turned to human form with long emerald feathers trailing down their heads and past their shoulders in place of hair. I counted four tikaanis, one of which was peeking into the carriage. When he moved the curtain over through the window, I couldn't help but notice how he was missing a finger. Even stranger, it looked like it had just been cut off days ago.

"What's this about?" Carter bellowed.

"We are looking for a couple of people. I'm wondering if you have seen them," said the one with the shortest feathers atop his head.

That very moment, Razz opened the carriage door, likely before the tikaani had a chance to describe Razz or me. Razz jumped out in a way a wild eight-year-old boy might.

"Hi!" Razz said, making himself sound as young as he appeared.

"What the—" Carter uttered, now looking at the child in place of Razz.

Razz immediately spoke over him. "That was so cool, how you turned from a wolf to a human!" he said enthusiastically. He looked back at the carriage. "Grandma! Grandma! Did you see what they could do?" He turned back to the tikaanis. "Can you teach me? Is it something I can even learn? Does it hurt to shapeshift? And can I pick my feather colors? My favorite color is red! I think I would pick red and black. Maybe even silver! How cool would that be? And how many feathers would I be able to have, anyway? How many feathers do each of you have?"

The tikaanis shook their heads in annoyance before taking a glance at me in the carriage. They didn't say a single word before shapeshifting back into feathered wolves and running off.

"Wow, you run fast!" Razz bellowed before climbing back into the carriage. "How you feeling, Grandma?" he said with a cunning grin before turning back to his usual appearance.

My skin went from dried and wrinkled to soft and smooth in just a breath. And my hair turned back to strands of dark golden blonde.

"That was—" I was at a loss for words. But I finally said, "That was brilliant!"

Just then, Carter opened the carriage door with a face of both bewilderment and fear. Razz handed him another pentacle.

"Thanks, Carter. Please continue north."

"But, but—how?" was all he could muster up.

Razz deepened his voice when he said, "I'm a mind-bender. My choices were to change my appearance or crush their minds to mush. Well, there is a third option. I could have tortured their minds into insanity. But I was feeling generous." Razz gave a smile before closing the carriage door. "Let's get a move on, shall we?"

And so, Carter returned to his seat at the front of the carriage with a face of utter terror.

With the couplings still on, I asked Razz through mind only: *Could you really do those things to them?*

He shrugged as his words effortlessly entered my mind. "I've never tried using my gift to torture. At least, not to its fullest extent."

Do you think those tikaanis also work for Shakar, like those on the edge?

"I'm sure of it." He must have read the hopeless exhaustion on my face. "Hey, we made it this far. Also, your telepathy is getting better." And with his reassuring smile, I had suddenly realized how truly lucky I was to be on this journey with Razz.

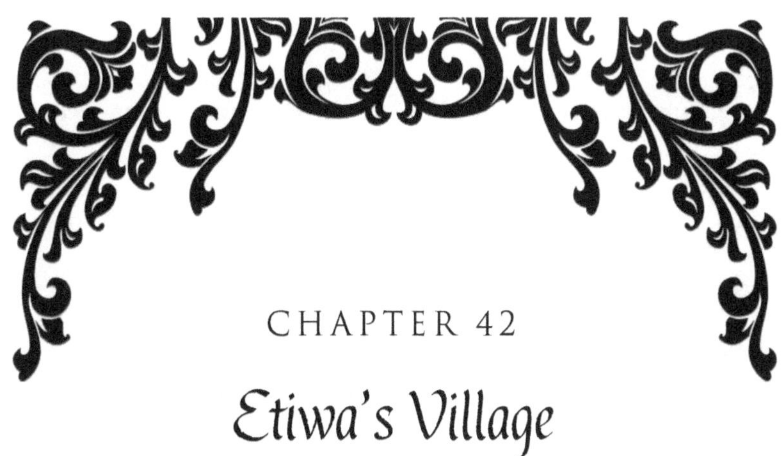

Etiwa's Village

Several more days went by, each night sleeping in the carriage on the cramped seats with growing neck and back pain. Since the carriage was so cramped for either of us to sleep comfortably, I refused to sleep another night on that damn maroon bench.

After riding the carriage several starlights into the night, Carter finally brought his tigers to a halt across a field near a village in the grasslands.

The people in the village had familiar ramlike horns. It was the same village Etiwa had come from. It was easy to recognize the older woman with only one horn, even from a distance. It was from Darian's memory of the day we were sent to Earth that I knew Shakar had ripped a horn from her head with his bone-chilling staff because she had refused to kill Gemma, Darian, and me.

A part of me wanted to talk to her. I'm not even sure what about. I just felt drawn to her. If I were to go to her, would she recognize me? Would she even want to talk to me? Or would she fear speaking to me at the thought of Shakar finding out?

Carter kept his tigers tied to the carriage but on a long tether, allowing them to roam a bit and sleep comfortably. Carter pitched a small tent for himself. He was snoring within minutes of closing his tent. He didn't so much as say goodnight to Razz or me. In fact, he had kept his distance from us after that mind-bending stunt Razz had pulled with the tikaanis days ago.

He feared Razz enough to put our minds slightly at ease that he wouldn't take us to the Orpheus. I mean, why else did he ask so many questions about who I was? He had to have known Shakar was looking for me. Unless—did he know me before I was sent to Earth?

"Voilà!" Razz said with a showcasing hand toward a blanket sprawled in the tall glowing grass with our bags atop it—both bags chained to the carriage.

I couldn't help but raise my brows at the sight. "What's with the chains?"

"We'll be sleeping with our bags on us, just in case Carter has plans to leave us behind. Unless he wants to leave his carriage too, he'll have to wait till we wake."

"Aren't these his chains from under the seats? Doesn't he have the keys?" I asked, my sight on the rusted chain locks.

Razz gave a hearty smile as he held Carter's keys in his hand before putting them in his vest pocket. Moments later, Razz lay with his bag on his stomach and the strap secured under his back. He then hugged his bag in his arms as he closed his eyes. A moment later, he glanced up at me. "Are you going to sleep?"

Though I refused to sleep another night in the carriage, I couldn't help but ask, "Is it even safe to sleep out here in the open? Won't the Orpheus be looking for us?"

"Probably. But do you know how big Elloriya is? The chances of them finding us in one night are unlikely."

I hesitated before saying, "I think I'll stay awake for a little while."

"Okay. Suit yourself," he said, eyes already closed.

Though I was tired, the thought of any Orpheus finding us would not allow my mind to rest long enough to journey into slumber. Plus, the warm night would keep me awake anyway. I never seemed to sleep well in the summer.

So instead, I chewed my bottom lip for some time before finally building up enough courage to enter Etiwa's old village. It didn't take long to reach it.

The moment I entered their territory, a man stepped out of the darkness. Before glimpsing his face, he had already snuck from behind, constricting me with merciless arms and a threatening tone. "What do you think you are doing in my village?"

I hadn't even tried to escape when replying, "I'm a friend of Etiwa's."

His arm loosened, but he kept a grip on me. "How do you know my wife?"

Wife? Etiwa is married?

"She is the one who sent me to Earth when I was a child. She also raised my friends in Elloriya's edge."

He finally released his grip and allowed me to turn and see him. He was middle-aged with dark green eyes, a strong-looking face, and impressive ramlike horns. He seemed to hesitate before saying, "How is she?"

"She's good, I think."

He studied me for a moment before asking, "What are you doing here?"

"I, um, well, I'm not sure. My friend and I are resting across the field for the night, and I thought I should introduce myself, considering how much Etiwa means to my friends."

"Come," he said, leading me to a vacant campfire. It was mostly silent, except for the sound of a crying baby in one of the wooden homes. "Sit," he suggested.

So I obliged. He offered me soup, and I happily accepted. It was a brothlike soup with herbs and leaves. And it was probably the best soup I had ever tasted.

"I am Bogo."

I almost shook his hand until I quickly remembered his hand had hooves—a small hoof on each finger.

"I'm Attica."

He kindly bowed his head.

"So you and Etiwa are married?" I asked, sitting across the fire from him.

The flames danced in his dark green eyes. "Well, we were supposed to marry. I still wear the loop," he said, gesturing to a brass band around his wrist.

At the sight of it, I immediately blurted out, "Oh, I've seen the same thing on her."

His eyes welled up. "Etiwa still wears it?"

"Yes," I answered honestly. A smile hit Bogo's lips. I set the empty bowl of soup down on a nearby log and turned back to him. "Why did she leave here, if you don't mind me asking?"

"You said you were one of the children she sent to Earth?"

"Yes."

"After that day—after sending three children away from their families—she wanted to bring the three of you back home, but without—" He lowered his voice. "Well, without the Orpheus finding out." He scooched closer to me, keeping his voice low as if talking about it would summon them. "When she heard there were more children the Orpheus had taken from their homes, she set out to find them. She sent me a courier, telling me she succeeded and had a secure home built for them. She spent all the gilds she had on making them as nice of a home as she could. She saved up quite a bit too. But it was not long before she stopped sending couriers. And she stopped answering mine."

Remembering what Razz had told Gemma's mother, I said, "She couldn't send you a courier. When Shakar stepped into full power, he created some magical barrier between the edge and the rest of Elloriya. Couriers cannot pass through unless a lot of magic is used, but even then, it is not guaranteed and is very risky."

Bogo blinked with a wistful smile. Before he had a chance to respond, a woman's voice sounded behind me.

"Who is your guest?" she asked Bogo.

He stood up. "Sifa! She is a friend of Etiwa's."

The woman moved into the firelight before me. And sure enough, it was the single-horned woman. Her gaze turned inquisitive at the sight of me. "Do I know you?" she asked.

For a moment, I considered telling her about the memory Darian had shown me. But instead, I stood up and said, "No, I don't believe so."

"But you know my daughter?"

"Etiwa?" I stupidly questioned.

She responded with a short nod.

"Oh. Yes. Etiwa's probably the reason my friends and I are still alive. She's been good to us."

Sifa sat beside the fire. I took it as a silent indication to retake my seat. But the moment I did, she looked at me with lowered brows, her gaze weaving between the lines of my face. She was suddenly studying me as if I were an equation she was figuring out. But then her brown eyes widened.

It sounded as though she was addressing herself when she uttered, "You have amethyst eyes."

Instinctually, for the first time in a long time, I shielded my face from the firelight with the strands of my hair.

Sifa sent Bogo away with a swish of her hand before turning back to me, inching closer to whisper, "I know who you are."

The strange, reluctant look on her face, along with her feeling the need to whisper, was unnerving.

I didn't care to lower my voice to her level when I responded, "Who do you think I am?"

"The first life born in the realm of Elloriya." When I didn't reply, she looked me over and said, "You do not remember who you are, do you?" Before I even had a chance to respond, she added, "All the magic in your soul lies dormant."

I cocked my head. "Magic? My magic? Do you mean wielding?"

"No."

"Then I don't think I have any magic," I said, correcting her.

"Everyone has magic, dear," she countered.

"Really? What magic is that?"

"The magic of thoughts and manifestation. You carry too many worries. You must let them go and think of only positive outcomes. After all, you attract what you think."

Sifa's sight fell on my necklace, brows lowering at the sight of the black and white stones lying on my chest. "Where did you get that?"

I wrapped my fingers around the stones. "The onyx is from my brother, and the moonstone is from—a friend." Her gaze was pinned so firmly on the stones that curiosity piqued my interest. "Why do you ask?"

"Do not part with it," she said, in place of an answer.

Again, my hand grasped at the stones. "I wasn't planning on it."

"Before I let you go, there is something you need to know." The seriousness in her voice tightened my chest. "Spirit is telling me, you must surrender yourself to aid Elloriya, for what is to come will be more than we can face alone."

I sighed, so sick of the damn riddles between the nixie, the hermit, the mystic, and now her. If the realm of Elloriya was trying so hard to deliver a message to me through those connected to the beyond, why not make the message clear so I could understand it?

I sucked in my bottom lip, trying hard not to let irritation get to me more than it already had. "What can't we face alone?" I asked in an impressively tame tone, considering my level of irritation.

Sifa's voice was cold and empty when she said, "A storm of enemies." Her gaze drifted to the night sky. And then a whisper of words turned my stomach inside out. "Peace can only last so long."

CHAPTER 43

The Unravel

To sleep under the night sky in the grasslands sounded far better than it felt. With my bag heavy on my stomach, chained to the back of the carriage as Razz had suggested, my sleep was rocky, to say the least. But thank goodness for his wild ideas and stellar intuition because the moment dawn broke, the jolt of the carriage attempting to move quickly woke us.

The sound of steps brushing through tall grass moved toward the back, where I sat up beside Razz, pulling stray grass from my hair. It was Carter, surprised at the sight of us chained to his beloved carriage.

Razz's voice playfully bounced off his tongue when he said, "Were you trying to run off and get us breakfast before we woke? That's sweet of you, but we're set, thanks."

He swept his hands over the pockets hiding under his ragged cloak. His gaunt eyes grew bigger, and his lips tightened.

Razz pulled the keys out of his vest with a smug grin, unlocking and unchaining our bags before tossing them to Carter.

Then he turned to me with a hand held out while opening the carriage door. "Your chariot, madam." When he stepped in after me, he popped his head out the door and said, "Continue north, kind sir." Razz's playful tone with Carter had me chuckling the entire time.

The carriage had just begun moving as I sat looking out the window with my eyes on the sunny village I had visited the night before, curious at the sight of ten children sitting in a circle. Most of their horns were about two or three inches long and had just begun curling. Someone seemed to be instructing them as they all simultaneously pressed their hands with the children beside them until their hooved fingers connected the entire circle.

The instructor nodded in approval and said something out of earshot. But what I heard was the children suddenly chanting with eyes closed, hands still connected to their neighbors beside them. And as if by magic, they all began levitating off the grass. The children stayed sitting cross-legged, eyes closed, with the continual chant. The instructor must have told them to release their connection from their neighbors, as they all dropped their hands simultaneously. And when they did, they fell back to the ground, laughing.

Razz must have been watching too, as he turned to me and said, "I told you we have schools in Elloriya. We all learn from our elders, no matter what kingdom or tribe. Our elders know best." After a moment, his gaze turned inward, and his subtle smile faded. "Well, not always," he added.

I knew he was thinking of both our elders—the nobles—who had led an army to raid the Orpheus realm; the very beginning of the war, with many battles that followed.

As the carriage trailed north at a steady pace, Razz's smile had yet to reappear. Perhaps it was my attempt to turn him chipper once more when I asked, "So, what's with the braid?" I pointed to the single braid tucked behind a black cuff on his left ear.

At first, it appeared he didn't hear me. That, or he was choosing not to respond. But then, he finally said with more effort than expected, "It's customary for my people to wear a braid for those we've loved and lost. It symbolizes that they're always with us, in spirit."

He didn't have to tell me that his braid symbolized the passing of his sister. But then a flash of Darian's hair came to mind. He had three thin braids trailing the back of his Viking hair. One was surely for his sister, but who were the other two for? I almost asked Razz, but the look on his face suggested he didn't want to talk about it. So again, I attempted to change the subject.

"What about the cuff on your ear? I've never seen you take it off."

He ran a finger over it. "Sometimes I forget it's even there."

"What's it for?"

"When I was a young boy, I was overwhelmed by the number of voices I was hearing in the back of my mind. They only stopped when I was alone. The moment someone was near me, I'd hear a voice again. It wasn't long before I realized I was picking up on other people's thoughts, even though they were always muffled." He paused, wistfully gazing inward. "And when I would get mad at my parents or Darian, I would accidentally bend their mind into headaches. Anyway, my father had this made to help tame my abilities so that I could develop and harness my gifts in peace."

He took it off and held it under the sunlight pouring through the carriage window. "It's mostly black titanium, but has pieces of hypersthene and ilvaite embedded throughout." The dark gemstones flickered the sun's rays brightly over the surrounding metal. He then put the cuff back on his left ear with a slight smile I was grateful to see.

He monitored the compass, still pointed north, while eating some fruit from the bag Enya had packed for us a couple of weeks ago. Perhaps it's because the remaining fruit had nearly gone rotten, but I wasn't hungry. So instead, I sipped water from my canteen and enjoyed staring out the window at the morning sky with the occasional flock of birds flying by.

Razz's eyes dropped to the wound on my wrist. When he finally asked about it, I cowardly confessed that I allowed the mystic to drink my blood in exchange for answers. I told him the truth while still leaving out the part about my visit with his brother in the grid. I saw no reason for him to know that part.

Not surprisingly, he showed some disappointment that I would allow someone to cut my skin as some magical invocation for answers. I didn't care, though. At least not to the level he did. He was quick to get over it anyway.

Two more nights had come and gone, one of which was filled with summer rain. While I slept in the carriage, rather uncomfortably with the rain splashing through the curtain windows, landing primarily on my face, Razz slept under the carriage with legs and arms easily sprawled wherever they pleased. I thought it was a stupid idea until the morning when I had a relentless kink in my neck accompanied by a sore back, while Razz stretched in an annoyingly chipper mood with a thin blanket in hand, mostly dried.

For some time during the bumpy carriage ride that morning, I mindlessly took in the sight of dewy grass as I thought of my family in Ridgewood Hollow before finally turning to Razz with a question I had wanted to ask him long ago. But perhaps I wasn't ready to ask before now.

My words were slow and spread far when I asked, "Can you tell me about my family?"

He seemed more eager than expected as he propped himself up and said, "Before the Orpheus raid in Elloriya, you and your mother were the light of the solar node. She's beautiful and kind, like you. Everyone adored you both."

For some reason, my heart felt heavy as I asked, "What's her name?"

"Aelia—Queen Aelia," he said. I played the sound of her name in my head repeatedly until Razz continued. "I remember my parents talking about how much your grandfather, Kiran, wanted a grandson. But when you came into this world, the love he felt for you seemed to exceed his expectations. Kiran showed you off to everyone he knew, no longer seeming to care about wanting a grandson. You were the only person to make him smile. And believe me, Kiran never smiled."

I knew my grandfather was the one who killed Shakar's brother, and I wasn't proud of that. As I searched my mind for what he looked like, my thoughts landed on the memory of Darian and me as children in the woods. "Was my grandfather the man with the wooden leg?" I asked.

He cocked his head. "Timaeus? No. That's my uncle—not by blood, but he was still family. You remember him?"

"No, not really. Only from a memory Darian showed me from when we were children. I guess Darian and I were traveling with him, trying to find you."

He looked out the window when he said, "Timaeus used to take my brother and me on adventures with him. His artificial leg hardly ever slowed him down. Man, I miss him."

Razz continued to tell me about my mother. At least, from what little he remembered of her. I wondered if I would recognize her. Or if she would recognize me. To come up with some image of my mother seemed impossible. My memories from this realm were too far gone, leaving me to wonder if I would ever get them back.

"And my father?" I asked, eager to hear more.

But the smile he had moments before vanished. Hesitance suddenly held his tongue. The unsettling look on his face reminded me of the time he said my mother was Queen of the Syrus Kingdom. He never mentioned my father or a king of any sort from the solar node.

What did he fear telling me? Had my father died in the war? Was he a terrible father?

Finally, Razz seemed to muster up enough courage to say, "I sort of only remember your mother." Then he turned his attention back out the window.

A part of me wanted to pester him for more, but on second thought, perhaps it was better to stay in the comfort of ignorant bliss.

When I imagined returning home after so long, I pictured both a mother and father embracing me in their arms. At least, I hoped.

Thankfully, I had fond memories of my dad in Ridgewood Hollow. He and Mama were the best parents a girl could ask for. So I truly had no right to be upset or complain about returning home to no father. I was lucky enough to have one as it is.

Just as my thoughts peacefully drifted with the wind pouring in and out of the curtain window, my heart nearly leaped with fear at the sudden appearance of a courier inside the carriage. The turquoise seahorse-shaped thing did not flutter in sweetly with its enchanting iridescent wings. Instead, it just appeared from thin air. And whispers upon whispers filled the swirled shell on its back, each carrying a glow so subtle, it was nearly impossible to see the many messages it held in the daylight.

An orange light escaped its shell, and out came a voice. But not just any voice. No. This voice was the last voice I ever thought I'd hear from a courier. This voice was like a ribbon of thorns, and it made my skin crawl.

CHAPTER 44

Time's Illusion

"You will be at the Node of Magic by the last starlight. If you do not show, your friends are mine."

It was none other than Shakar's bloodcurdling voice.

The courier fluttered in place for some time. Was it waiting for us to respond to the Orpheus king?

But then the courier released another light from its shell. Etiwa whispered, "Continue with the plan. Do not change course, or things will—"

"Etiwa!" a voice sounding an awful lot like Zella bellowed.

A scream was the last thing we heard before the courier vanished into nothingness.

"Cece!" Razz uttered with the face of a deer in headlights.

How could he know her scream? Perhaps this was just a trick of Shakar's to convince us he held Etiwa, Cece, and Zella, so we would show. But if he did hold their lives in his hand, then we had no choice.

"We have to go after them!" Razz said sharply.

"No! Did you hear Etiwa's message? She said to continue with the plan."

"I know what she said! But—"

I took a heavy breath and grabbed his hands. His eyes darted to mine. "We are going to finish our mission to get your brother back, and then our friends back too, all safe and alive! If we stray from the plan, we risk our lives and your brother's. You would likely never see him again. But if we stay on course, we could not only save all our friends but also bring magic back to all the lower kingdoms, strengthening their power against the Orpheus." His eyes flickered when I said, "Do not let fear cloud your judgment."

His tone softened. "How are we going to find where the relic belongs in the Zeru Kingdom in less than a day when we haven't even arrived yet?"

"We can use your pendulum, your intuition—we'll figure it out!"

"And how do you expect us to get to the Node of Magic by tonight?"

I sighed before saying, "Assuming we return magic to the Zeru Kingdom—which we will—the grid will unlock, right? So we'll ask someone to take us through the grid to the Node of Magic before the first dark starlight arrives."

At first, he just stared wide-eyed. Then he said, "You're seriously considering going through the energy grid after what happened to Darian?"

"If it's the only way, then yes! If you're not comfortable with it, then we'll find another way to get there on time!" I softened my voice when I said, "There's just one more kingdom left. We must return magic to the Zeru Kingdom before anything else. We are so close! Take your own advice and stop taking time so seriously. As Calder would say, 'Time is an illusion.'"

His eyes widened when he broke his gaze off me and uttered, "That's it!"

"What's it?"

"Time is an illusion." Razz threw his head out the window and said, "Carter! If you get us to the Zeru Kingdom by next starlight, you can have all my pentacles!"

The carriage suddenly moved twice as fast. Razz turned to open his bag and rummaged through it until he pulled out a small leather pocketbook that read *The Art of Mind-Bending*. He didn't say a single word to me before burying his face in it.

After a good ten minutes of silence, he set the book down and rummaged through his bag again—this time taking out a glass jar of dried purple petals he used every morning and evening to clean his teeth.

I didn't fully understand how they always made his teeth so clean and his breath so fresh. I, on the other hand, had been using a mixture of salt crystals and ground sage with a cloth to clean my teeth. I was still getting used to the ways of this world.

He stared at the glass jar for a moment before he opened the cork lid and dumped all the petals into his hand. He took a breath before throwing them in the air. They all fell straight to the carriage floor. He grunted and gathered them up before refocusing himself and throwing them in the air as before. They fell again. He did this at least twenty times until, finally, three of the petals stayed afloat while the rest fell to the carriage floor. He kept trying and trying until more and more petals stayed in midair, indeed controlled by his mind. But he couldn't seem to hold the gravity beneath all eleven petals. And frustration filled every part of his heated face.

I finally broke the silence. "May I make a suggestion?"

His eyes fiercely shot at me. "What?" he asked sharply.

"Remove your ear cuff."

With a slight tilt of his head and lowered brows, he seemed to seriously consider my suggestion before finally removing the black cuff from his ear, the very cuff that tamed his mind-bending abilities all these years. But he hesitated to throw the petals in the air again, as if he feared his power without the comfort of the cuff holding him back.

I leaned in and said, "You were just a child when you began wearing that cuff. It helped control your abilities all these years. Stop using it as a crutch. You have learned from it, and now you can mind-bend freely."

He swallowed, took a breath, and then threw the petals in the air. And as if it were child's play, he stopped every single one the moment he threw them before he turned to me in shock, allowing them to fall. He grinned and did it again and again until he finally said, "Want to see?"

"I already have seen. You're doing great," I said, unsure of what he was actually trying to accomplish. But then he grabbed his coupling and latched it onto his arm and ordered me to do the same. I followed instruction, and though I immediately became attuned with his energies, he still felt the need to tap our couplings, strengthening our shared frequency even more.

But this time differed from all the other times we had worn the couplings. His energy and frequency were much, much more powerful. It was so strong; the moment our cuffs tapped, a high-pitched noise pierced my ears, my chest became heavy, and breathing seemed difficult. It was a struggle to break out of his ripping energy.

Razz looked at the ear cuff in his hand and then handed it to me, suggesting I put it on. The weight of it was almost as heavy as a damn brick.

Before I secured it onto my ear, he had already thrown the petals back in the air. The heavy weight of the ear cuff vanished the moment I slipped it on. And as the black metal cuff rested comfortably over my cartilage, the piercing noise stopped, my chest lightened, and I could breathe with ease.

When my mind and body adjusted back to reality, I looked up from my lap and couldn't believe my eyes. Not only were the petals effortlessly moving in a swirling line, choreographed by Razz's mind, but the carriage suddenly moved at a snail's pace. I looked out the window to find a flock of birds in the sky were practically still, wings unmoved as they just stayed hovering a hundred feet off the ground.

"What's happening?" I asked, examining every aspect of the frozen life around us. At this point, the levitating petals had stilled themselves; Razz no longer controlled their movement.

"I'm slowing time," he said, practically beaming.

My mouth fell before I looked at the petals and said, "So then, you can wield?"

He looked back at the petals and again controlled where they moved without lifting a finger. "But—" His gaze turned inward as the petals slowly drifted to the carriage floor. He finally said, "But to wield, you're supposed to use your hands."

I smiled. "For others, perhaps. But for you . . . I guess all you need is your mind."

His gaze drifted so far, the carriage suddenly moved at lightning speed once more.

As Razz spent the rest of the carriage ride reading his book on mind-bending, I used the time trying to figure out how we could find where the relic belonged in less than a day.

Finally, we reached what appeared to be an endless bed of gray-stone mountains. Carter had taken us as far north as the carriage could go. Razz looked just as confused as me as he bobbed his eyes between the compass and the mountains—no kingdom in sight.

Nonetheless, Razz reached into the red velvet pouch of pentacles and gave Carter a small handful, which was surely enough to last him a long while.

Carter furrowed his brows. "You promised me all of your pentacles if I got you here by next starlight. And I did."

"Yes, you did. Thank you. And I held my promise. But the rest of the pentacles are hers," he said, petting the tigers, then handing the pouch to me while giving Carter a grateful bow of his head. Then Razz put an arm around me and pulled me toward the mountains.

"Ever been mountain hiking?" he asked, scanning the high rock wall before us.

"Not on mountains like this."

I scanned the gray rock surface, and to my satisfaction, a little, almost undetectable ledge caught my sight.

Heading in the direction of the ledge, I turned over my shoulder to Razz and said, "You coming?"

He seemed surprised, yet pleased, at me taking leadership for once. I climbed up on the ledge, allowing me leeway, and used all my strength to pull myself up to the mostly flat surface. The moment I did, I felt empowered. At least until I looked on the other side of the mountain and saw just how high off the ground we were; on the other side of the mountain was a deep valley, hardly allowing me a view with its heavy fog low to the ground.

Considering I once had a fear of heights, I stood as far to the left as possible, where I edged a grassy field that fell only about twenty feet to the ground.

The mountain went north for what looked like miles, blanketed by bone-chilling fog. Though the surrounding mountains were more pointed, the one we stood atop had a flat enough surface, allowing us to walk the distance with ease. According to the map, we were close, if not already there. But still, no kingdom in sight.

At this point, I wondered if we would make it in time to save Cece, Zella, and Etiwa. Would we even make it in time to save Darian? Or had we just screwed over all our friends? My stomach turned.

We walked nearly a mile before we finally heard distant voices. It sounded as though there were many people nearby. We scanned the mountains across the valley, but still, nothing.

To hear voices and see nothing could only mean one thing. "I think these mountains are haunted," I whispered to Razz, hoping not to announce our presence to any lurking spirits.

We had walked only a short distance farther before the voices grew louder. But what was spoken was still undetectable as the whistling sound of the wind passing between the valley below concealed every spoken word.

Razz glanced at me with pondering eyes. "Do you think the kingdom is hiding under the fog down there?" he asked with a pointed finger to the hidden valley, looking over the ledge with more ease than I ever could.

"If so, I don't see how we could make it all the way to the bottom without falling to our death," I said honestly.

Razz's face froze with fear for just a moment before giving a monotone response. "Your optimism is so helpful at times like this. Thank you."

The fog dissipated a short distance before us, revealing the end of the u-shaped valley. I prepared to continue the curving path to explore the mountains across the valley, but Razz grabbed me by the hand.

When I turned back to him, he held a finger to his mouth, keeping me silenced before pointing to a ladder carved into the rocky center of the mountain's bend. He silently made his way down the ladder, gesturing to me with his head to follow. He had already descended below the fog before I climbed down.

The farther down the ladder I went, the louder the voices became. It was a long way down before I reached the ground of the ladder-carved mountain. But we hadn't reached the bottom of the valley. It took me a moment to realize that Razz and I were now standing at the very top of the Zeru Kingdom.

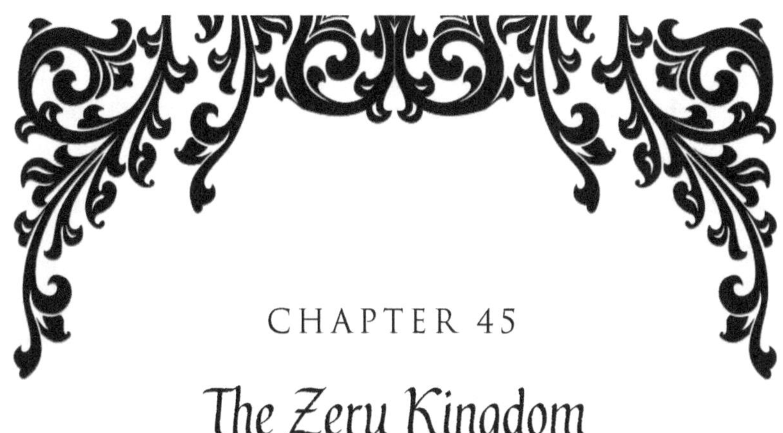

CHAPTER 45

The Zeru Kingdom

The kingdom we stood atop had eight stacked levels. Each descending level protruded farther out from the one above. Spiral towers framed every tier, made from the same gray stone of the surrounding mountains, sequined with dew.

The heavy fog settled itself over the massive kingdom. A marketplace and village were on the other end of the extensive field, nestled in the low valley between the towering mountains.

The fog hid us atop the peculiar castle. But we couldn't stay hidden forever, especially considering what little time we had.

We stood on the roof of the highest level behind the three tallest and widest towers. It was surely where the king and queen of the court lived—especially considering the many guards that stood before the skyscraping entrance.

The people of the court were all dressed similarly: black or brown boots, dark pants, dark green, gray, black, or tan tunics, with a leather vest that buckled in the front. Some carried a sword, while others carried a bow and arrows on their back. But nearly all of them had a dagger strapped on their side.

A whistling sound turned my attention to an arrow flying just past my ear. I wasn't sure if the air in my lungs deflated at the sight of the arrow hitting a ravenlike bird behind me or at the sudden realization that I had been seen by whoever shot the arrow.

"Don't move!" a heavy female voice said.

The fog parted between us, revealing a thick young woman holding a bow and arrow toward Razz and me. She had tattoos of swirling patterns mimicking the wind above her brows, dark hair, brown eyes, and was undeniably beautiful.

Suddenly, an eerie silence fell over the court, and everyone appeared to be moving at a snail's pace. And the girl before us had froze. Razz grabbed my hand and jumped down from the roof to the eighth and highest-level floor. I stupidly followed, thankful I didn't break a bone upon landing.

"Quick!" he said, running down the many stone steps centering the castle.

We passed others with similar swirly markings above their brows. Some had tattoos of three vertical lines below each eye. Others had both the markings but appeared older than the many around my age. I was never a fan of face tattoos, but these markings were flattering on each person. It seemed the only ones without tattoos were the children, which might explain Cece's lack of ink, considering she was taken from this kingdom when she was just a child.

Something else caught my eye as we hurried down the hundreds of steps, passing the castle's many levels while Razz bent time. There were small dragons, no bigger than house cats. And several of them were perched around the court. Some were white with silver eyes, and others were black chrome with ice-blue eyes.

We finally reached one of the few market stands on the first floor. Razz grabbed a pair of clothes for me and only a forest-green tunic for himself, since most of his attire already fit in. "Grab a pair of boots," he commanded. "Do you mind if we give her one of your pentacles?" He pointed with a thumb at the seller, still frozen in time.

He had generously spent all his pentacles on our transportation and clothing from the Kano Kingdom. I was happy to give the seller more than just one, considering how many I had left. But I wondered why he couldn't just bend the appearance of our clothing. Perhaps it was difficult to mind-bend while on the run.

Razz pulled us behind a spiral tower, where he quickly changed into a dark green shirt. Sound filled the kingdom once more when Razz said, "What are you waiting for?" He glanced at the clothes in my hand.

The weather was mild enough to layer the new clothes over my outfit, so I did before switching my worn-out boots to a new pair of black leather ones.

"What's the plan?" I asked, watching as the girl with the bow and arrow looked around, disgruntled on the highest level of the castle.

"We need to find a way inside," Razz said, scanning our surroundings.

"Can't you slow time again? Or turn us invisible?"

He turned to me with a sideways glance. "You make it sound so easy."

"You make it look so easy."

"Don't let me fool you. It's already given me a headache."

It was strange to view Razz without his black metal ear cuff. I had never seen him without it before today. And now that he knew how much it had hindered his abilities before, I didn't think he would ever put it back on. I had yet to take it off my ear since he suggested I wear it. It was the only way I could handle his heightened energy while bonded to him through the couplings.

"So, any ideas on how to get inside the castle?" I asked, peeking around the spiral tower we hid behind on the ground floor.

But before Razz could answer, the heavy fog above the court parted as a black chrome dragon flew down in the center of the grassy field with a young man holding reins on its back. When he hopped off, allowing me a decent view of his face, the beating of my heart came to a sudden stop.

James? No—it couldn't be James! Though he looked identical to him. But before I could get a closer look or even ask Razz if he saw James too, Razz had already tugged my hand as silence fell over the court once more, and everyone moved at a snail's pace, if not slower.

As Razz slowed time again, allowing us to move too quickly for any eye to catch, we ran up the many steps back to the highest level of the castle. I ignored the side cramp that formed halfway up the seemingly endless steps. When we finally reached the castle's top and most guarded level, it took all my remaining energy to catch my breath and not faint from exhaustion.

The guards didn't notice us as we passed them in their nearly frozen state. The moment we stepped foot into the castle, Razz released his grip on time.

Sounds filled the court once more. But they were distant— outside, mostly. Inside, however, it was quiet and appeared empty.

A medieval flair cast itself over the gray stone walls and gothic halls. In the center tower was a jaw-dropping chandelier, made entirely of swords. The same tower flaunted two sharply arched thrones of dark stone.

Knights with swords stood at the end of each hall—empty, just like the ones in the manor. But these knights appeared different. Their armor was the perfect blend of black and silver, permeating a polished chrome, and was heavily embossed with elegant swirls and twirls like wind and air around a dragon centering each knight's torso.

A double staircase framed the center tower. One staircase led to the tower on the left and the other to the tower on the right. Razz had already pulled out his pendulum, seeming to ask which staircase we should take.

"Should we split up?" I asked.

"No!" Razz said surely, walking up the left staircase.

When we reached the top, an older man carrying both a sword and dagger on his sides stood before us. The lined ink below his eyes was slightly more faded than the swirled tattoos above his brows.

He looked Razz and me up and down. With a side glance, I realized Razz suddenly had lined tattoos below his eyes. I was sure Razz had bent my appearance too, adding tattoos above my brows or perhaps below my eyes like his.

"What are you doing here? And why did the guards grant you entrance?" the man asked in a blade-sharp tone.

Air instantly deflated my lungs, and my chest tightened. There was no way out of this. We would undoubtedly be kicked out or perhaps have swords run through our necks.

Razz straightened. "I'm one of the court's dragon trainers."

The man lowered his heavy brows. "That doesn't answer my questions."

"A whelp flew in here, sir," Razz quickly countered.

"So? It'll leave on its own."

"Oh, of course. But this whelp has a broken wing, and I need to tend to it before it gets worse or" —Razz conjured up moist eyes— "it may not fly after today."

The man's eyes flew between Razz and me. "And the girl?"

"She's a healer, sir. I'm here to keep the whelp tamed while she tends to its wing."

I certainly couldn't lie as effortlessly as Razz. It seemed to come as easy as breathing to him.

"Make it quick!" the man commanded. "And I don't want to see either of you without your weapons again. You should know better."

"Yes, sir!" Razz said with a nod.

The moment the man was out of earshot, I leaned to Razz and asked, "What's a whelp?"

"A baby dragon," he responded, with eyes scanning every nook and cranny of the hall.

I kept the remaining four relics in my pocket-size leather pouch resting on my hip in case I felt one of them tremble.

Etiwa said we only needed to power the lower kingdoms with magic to unlock the grid. And since this was the last of the lower kingdoms, we were so close. So, so close.

We stepped into every open room—an impressive gallery, a library, several guest rooms, a weaponry room, and even the many balconies surrounding the swirled towers. But there was no sign of the relic belonging anywhere.

We even searched the tower on the right side, careful to avoid the guarded royal chambers. And as our miserable luck would have it, still, we found nothing. And time was greedy, stealing every valuable second from our search.

Any hope of saving our friends was quickly dwindling. And somehow, I felt responsible. I would be the reason we would never see our friends again.

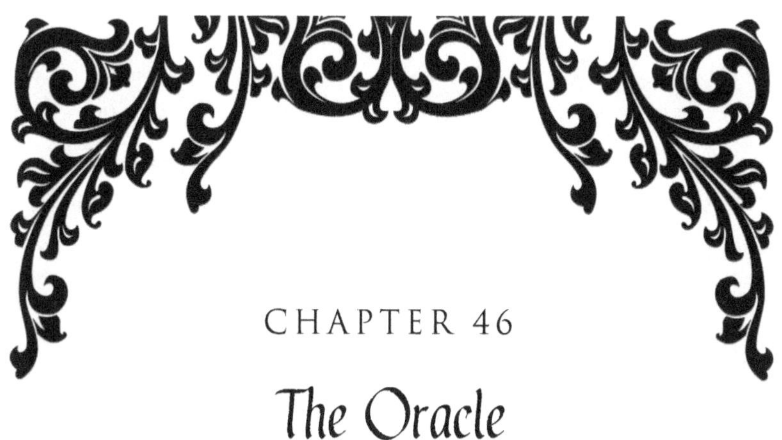

CHAPTER 46

The Oracle

We stood in the library, filled with leather books; some were black, some were dark green, and others were maroon.

"There's something here that can help us," Razz said, scanning the room agitated with his damn pendulum in hand, profusely swinging back and forth, confirming that we were where we needed to be.

"Let's try asking the compass," I suggested, even though Razz had tried it in the other kingdoms with no luck.

Razz pulled it out of his pocket and handed it to me for a change as he continued pulling at books.

Its brush of cold metal settled comfortably in my palm as if it wanted to be there—as if it wanted to show me where to go. So I asked, "Where does the relic belong? Show me where the relic belongs!"

The arrow didn't move. It had locked itself on "north" since we had arrived at the Zeru Kingdom.

"Point to something—anything—that can help us find where to return magic to this kingdom," I begged the compass.

As I paced by the wall of books, I felt a jolt in my hand—the same hand that held the compass. The arrow suddenly spun. At first, the spinning was slow, but then it grew faster and faster until it finally came to a halt. The moment it stopped, the face of the compass lit a golden light. The arrow pointed toward the bookshelf beside me.

I ran my fingers over the leathery spines, wondering which book it wanted me to pull out. When my hand reached the only dark green book on that shelf, the tips of my fingers tingled. I pulled it out and opened the book, and when I did, the pages rattled so hard it jumped out of my hands and fell to the floor.

Air rushed out of the book, written in a language I didn't recognize. The pages flapped wildly as the air grew stronger. A furious wind suddenly circled the room. The air became thick, and the circling quickly spread wider and wider, pulling me into its grasp. Razz grabbed my hand, trying to pull me out. But instead, it took him too.

It was as if the book pulled me into a dream, and not necessarily a good one. The sense of reality came to a halt. To keep my eyes open was a struggle as the wild wind thrashed into my face and every other part of my body. Razz pulled me close, wrapping me tightly in his protective arms until, finally, the wind turned to a gentle breeze, leaving me with a sudden headache.

I didn't know what to expect when I opened my eyes. But it certainly wasn't what I was now looking at.

There we stood at the top of a grassy mountain, so high up, all we could see were clouds blanketing our surroundings. But it got stranger. In the very center of the sky-scraping hill was a round glass table reflecting the supple curves of the many clouds. And floating above the table was an iridescent crystal orb.

"One of the many reasons I don't like magic," Razz said dreadfully as he rubbed his temples, seeming to share the same headache I had.

"What is this place?"

He glanced around. "Shit if I know."

As I wondered where in Elloriya we were, I turned to Razz, trying to make sense of our bizarre predicament. "I thought this kingdom was stripped of magic?"

"It was, but enchanted objects remained," he replied, still looking as though he were trying to solve some internal puzzle.

I moved closer to the table, both baffled and enthralled by the crystal orb. It was the most enchanting blend of blue, pink, and purple over a milky white surface. Just as I reached out to touch it, Razz grabbed my hand.

"Don't!"

I turned to him, realizing the tattoos on his face were now gone. "Why not?" I was tempted to ignore him as my fingers stayed lingering near the levitating orb.

With furrowed brows, he moved closer to it, narrowing his eyes. "I think it's an oracle."

"A what?"

But Razz didn't reply. Instead, he grabbed my hand that still held the compass. The arrow was pointing to the center of the glass table. Razz inched closer. "Can you tell us where the relic for the Zeru Kingdom belongs?" he asked the orb.

Its iridescent colors mixed and swirled, and when they settled, a gentle female voice responded. The voice sounded as if it were coming from everywhere. "With blades so sharp, a reflection will peer. You will know which one, as this one is clear."

Razz slammed his hands on the table. "No riddles!" he demanded. If anyone understood his irritation with riddles, it was me.

"Follow the voices," was all she said before the orb dropped to the glass table and shattered before turning into dust. A small diamond-shaped opal stone was among the pearly dust, gleaming the same iridescent colors as the orb had.

The moment I picked the opal stone up, the soft breeze grew stronger and stronger until a roaring wind gripped Razz and me. He was quick to pull me into his arms. My eyes couldn't handle the intensity of the wind. So I shut them tight.

When the wind settled, a familiar, unwelcoming voice said, "They're here!"

Before even opening my eyes, hands pulled me out of Razz's arms. I got a glance at my capturer's face, and sure enough, my heart came to a complete stop.

CHAPTER 47

Tower of Swords

It was him, holding my arms in place. It was James. Except, it wasn't.

He had James's towering height, his perfect caramel skin, and the same face apart from swirled tattoos above his brows. The only thing that differed was his eyes, which were not brown like James's, but sky blue. He was beautiful.

The thick girl hunting us the moment we arrived at the Zeru Kingdom forced Razz out of the room by the scruff of his neck. Razz surprisingly didn't seem worried that we had been caught. Instead, he shamelessly took in every curve of his capturer's body with lusting eyes as she dragged him down the hall.

When he looked over his shoulder, his eyes widened at the sight of my capturer. He surely noticed how much he looked like James as he kept turning his head back with baffled eyes on the young man pulling me along with a tight grip around my bicep.

The moment we stepped foot outside the castle's highest tier, we were dragged down the many steps as every set of eyes fell on us.

It was a discomfort beyond words. Each person's gaze was filled with either curiosity or judgment.

As they forced us to the grassy field before the castle, baby dragons—or rather, whelps—were squawking above our heads, only adding to the pressure in my chest.

She took Razz to the center of the field, where she tied him to an archery board. Several people of the court formed a line across the grass from Razz, holding in hand a dagger or a bow with an abundance of arrows on their back. My heart dropped at the sight.

James's doppelganger whispered in my ear, "You're next."

I didn't respond, but I turned over my shoulder, taking in every line on his face, trying to make sense of how he looked so much like my brother in Ridgewood Hollow. His baby blue gaze locked with mine, and as it did, I could have sworn his fingers loosened around my arms.

When I dropped my sight forward, the girl who forcibly escorted Razz to the archery board was first in line with a bow and arrow ready to launch across the field. My stomach turned as she pulled the arrow's tail farther into the sharply bent string with a narrowed aim on Razz. I forgot how to breathe when she released the arrow. It whistled as it flew straight to his chest. But before it reached him, all fell silent and still.

The arrow was moving incredibly slow now, just inches away from Razz's heart. He dropped his neck in a curvelike manner and caught the arrow in his mouth.

Everyone was so quiet and unmoving with shocked eyes and gaping mouths, I hardly realized Razz had stopped bending time. The same girl pulled out another arrow and quickly shot it again with tight lips. But this one was aimed directly at his head. He slowed time again and simply moved his head to the side. The arrow grazed the tip of the archery board before falling to the ground. She clenched her teeth and grunted as she moved out of line.

The next person up was a young man with muscles so defined, they practically screamed their strength. He pulled out a dagger and whipped it at Razz. It spun sharply through the air, breaking the thin layer of fog. And before it reached Razz, he had already thrown another dagger with his other arm. But time didn't slow. Instead, Razz must have bent his mind, as the young man looked puzzled at his terrible aim that had missed Razz by several feet.

Following in line was a short blonde girl covered in freckles. Her lip curled as she pulled an arrow from the quiver over her shoulder. She took her sweet time pulling the arrow back on her bow. Her aim was lower than the others. The moment she released her hand, all fell dead silent as the arrow moved slowly through the air.

Razz turned to me and shouted, "Go, now!"

While time was slow for only Razz and me, thanks to the couplings connecting us, I loosened my arm from my capturer's grip and ran up the many steps.

Just as I reached the top, panting like a dog, I heard Razz grunt so loud, it echoed through the air. I turned to find an arrow deep in his thigh. The sight of it stopped me from stepping into the castle.

Before Razz released his grip on time, he shouted, "Go!" in my direction.

I fought my hesitance and hurried back into the spiral castle. Holding the opal in hand, I asked, "Where to now?" as if it could answer.

To my surprise, a voice called to me. I couldn't hear what it was saying. All I knew was it came from the top of the left staircase.

As I ran up the stairs toward the left wing of the castle, another voice called to me, and then another. Or perhaps it was the same voice echoing off the stone walls.

All I could make out through the layered voices was a whisper that said, "This way," leading me up a hallway and down a corridor. The voices grew louder and louder until I reached the weaponry room.

When I stepped inside, all fell silent. I scanned the many swords, axes, daggers, and arrows.

With blades so sharp, a—shit! I tried to remember what the oracle had said, but I couldn't seem to conjure up the exact words.

I knew it said something about a reflection, so I eliminated the arrows from my search and focused only on the weapons with blades.

You will know which one, as this one is clear, I thought over and over as I passed many axes—all of which were sharp but scuffed. The daggers were too small to show much of a reflection. The swords—gleaming sharper than the other weapons—stole my focus.

At least twenty impressive swords were on the wall. Some were adorned with jewels, while others were embossed with decorative patterns.

I took in the sight of every single one until my gaze settled on a sword with more shine than all the others. I tried to remove it, but it didn't budge. I turned and pulled, but it stayed locked in place.

With a calming breath, I analyzed the sword. As I ran my finger over the decorative chrome handle, my nail—in desperate need of grooming—fell into a tiny nest, the same shape as one of the relics, except smaller . . . closer to the size of the gem from the oracle.

The gem! I opened my hand to find the little diamond-shaped opal sitting in my palm. I lifted it to the handle and placed it effortlessly in the metal nest.

Click.

The sound of something unlocking beckoned me to pull the sword's handle. And when I did, the stone wall behind the sword opened.

Swallowing my nerves, I stepped inside. I stood below about a hundred swords, all appearing to be floating horizontally as each dusty sword pierced the narrow gray walls of the lofty tower, all the way to the top.

Without thinking twice, without letting hesitance steal any more precious time, I dropped my backpack to the floor, grabbed the handle of the closest sword, tugged on it to ensure its blade was far enough in the stone wall to hold my weight, and began to climb.

The climb was relatively easy until the fifth sword handle I grabbed released its puncture in the wall, falling to the floor.

My lungs deflated until I forced a deep breath and continued. The next handle I grabbed was secure, and I pulled myself up higher. But the one after that fell to the floor as the other had.

Many swords surrounded me, some helping me higher up the spiral tower with blades acting as a ladder, while others tried to break my climb.

I was halfway up when the pouch resting on my hip trembled. It wasn't easy to ignore, but I tried not to break my concentration. My hands had gripped more sword handles than I could count. And my feet relied on the blades pinned into the stone wall to keep me afloat.

The higher I went, the narrower the tower became and the more my pouch shook. A relic was begging to reach the top. *I* was begging to reach the top.

Sweat broke through my forehead and ran down my temples as I continued climbing higher and higher until I pulled on another sword that fell to the floor, taking me with it.

There was nothing but air to catch my fall as I descended past many swords. But before I took the harrowing plunge to the floor, I grabbed a sword handle midair. Its puncture was strong, allowing me to pull myself up with the help of two swords below it.

I continued and tugged on every sword before relying on its handle to help me up. And this time, I reached the top of the tower. It was so narrow; I was grateful claustrophobia hadn't hindered me.

My leather pouch hanging from my waist shook so fiercely, it was a challenge to unlatch it. But as I kept one hand gripped on the highest horizontal sword, I finally opened the pouch with my other hand, moving my fingers through the sound of clinks and clanks as I felt for the glass relic that practically jumped in my hand.

It was a diamond-shaped relic filled with wispy clouds. At first, I didn't know where to place the glass octahedron, but I suddenly remembered how I got into this death tower and quickly took sight of the only vertical sword inches above me. And sure enough, in its handle was a diamond-shaped divot.

My hand shook so hard, I almost dropped the relic. I took another breath of air as I pushed through the tremble and placed the relic in the sword's handle.

Swoosh!

CHAPTER 48

The Flight

I was lost in the abyss once more. Darkness was quickly becoming a constant place of rest for my mind.

Something wet dripping on my forehead pulled me back to consciousness.

I woke in the hidden tower, lying atop several swords that had fallen, with a view of many still above. And the one at the very top with the relic embedded inside now had a gust of wind swirling around it.

Another drip from high above fell on my forehead. I brushed my fingers over the wetness. The tips of my fingers were scarlet from the liquid. It wasn't until I noticed a deep cut on my forearm that I realized it was my blood dripping on me from the sword that had sliced me during my plunge.

The last thing I remembered was putting the relic in the sword's handle and a rush of air sweeping below me. The energy must have been so vital, it sent my mind into a dark suspension, blindly dropping me, allowing only the emptiness of air and swords to catch my fall.

The plummet covered me with scrapes and cuts in more places than I could count, and the many blades that gave them to me pierced the spiral tower above my aching body. Perhaps even the swords I lay upon were responsible for a handful of my wounds. At the very least, I was sure they were the cause of bruises in the making. But I suppose I should be thankful that none of them had stabbed through me.

It wasn't long before Darian consumed my mind. And only then did I realize, I did it! The four lower kingdoms now had their magic again.

When would I see him now that magic had returned to the kingdoms? When would I see him now that the grid had reset and unlocked? Where was he now? Was he still stuck in the energy grid? Was he waiting just outside?

Wincing, I forced my pained body off the bed of swords, quick to notice a few tears in my outfit. My neck and back ached the most, although nearly every part of my body hurt to some extent.

I picked up my bag buried beneath the fallen swords and secured it on my back. The single leather strap over my torso had tattered so much since I had first left the manor a few lunars ago. Since I had worn my bag for most of the journey, I quickly became used to the added weight and nearly always forgot I was wearing it. But with the pain I carried in my back now, I felt every gut-wrenching pound.

As I stepped out of the weaponry room toward the castle stairs, a luster of renewed energy could be felt throughout the kingdom. The chandelier of swords stole my focus as sunbeams gently peering through the sharply arched windows bounced off each perfectly polished blade.

It wasn't until I peeked out the window overlooking the grassy valley with hopes of seeing Darian that I caught sight of Razz, still tied to the archery board with a combination of at least fifty arrows and daggers spread on the surrounding grass. His legs held three arrows and one dagger. Another two arrows had struck his shoulder.

I ran down the staircase and out the doors from the highest level. Outside, I hurried down the two hundred steps centering the exterior of the castle before I finally ran straight to Razz to untie him, quickly noticing the other daggers surrounding his body on the archery board.

The people of the court were so taken by the return of magic in the air, none of them seemed to notice I was untying Razz.

Some people were creating stairs made entirely of fog with just a swish of their hands. They even ran up each step, reaching at least twenty feet above the grass as if gravity didn't exist. Others who had artificial wings tied to their backs took off from the ground as if their weight was light as air as they now soared high above the field.

With magic returned to the Zeru Kingdom, these people defied the laws of gravity entirely. They created animals made of thick fog—creatures that ran and made sounds and played with other animals made of the same visible air. The people of this court were creating a foggy world of captivating art and imagination.

The moment I finished untying Razz, he pulled out every arrow from his body without a single wince or grunt. He stormed halfway up the stairs toward the top tier of the castle, stopping on the steps between the fourth and fifth level when he shouted, "King Aither!

Queen Aria! Help me save your daughter!" His voice was so loud, it echoed off the surrounding mountains.

Moments later, the king stepped out of the castle, and guards followed him down the stairs. His black silk robe dragged over each stone step. His eyes were ice blue, like his daughter's. He had a neatly groomed white beard with designs of swirls just below his cheeks and the same face tattoos the others had above his brows and below his eyes, but with ink that somehow glittered. His voice was calm when he said, "What do you know of my daughter?"

Before Razz could answer, Cece's mother—the Zeru queen—hurried down the steps, guards following close behind. She was by far the youngest queen I had met and utterly beautiful, just like her daughter. Her eyes were brown, her cheekbones high, and her hair was a golden blonde. She had three glittering lines of ink below each eye. Her belly was round, undoubtedly expecting to give birth before the end of the next lunar. She glanced around at the magic in the air and gasped with a hand over her mouth.

Razz addressed them both when he said, "I lived with Cece—" They lowered their brows. "I mean, Celestia. I lived with her on the edge, and now the Orpheus have her. If I don't meet Shakar at the Node of Magic by the last starlight, I don't know what he'll do to her."

"Boreas," the king called out behind Razz.

James's lookalike stepped forward. "Yes, sire?"

"Take him to the Node of Magic. Be on guard. He claims the Orpheus have my daughter. Strike a bargain if you must. Just bring her home safely!" he commanded.

"Yes, sire!" Boreas replied with a sharp nod. "Prepare my dragon!" he shouted behind him. Three others obeyed his command. When he turned back around, heading toward his dragon, he stopped beside me and looked me in the eye. "Will you be joining?"

I don't know why it was so hard to meet his gaze when I softly replied, "Yes."

Razz turned, heading back down the steps toward me.

"Young man," King Aither said.

Razz looked back. "Sire?"

"Did you return our magic?"

"No. She did." He threw a thumb at me.

King Aither moved down the steps until he stood before me. He was hesitant for a moment before gently grabbing my hand. "I am in your debt. If ever you need anything at all, you have the support of my kingdom."

"Thank you," I uttered.

"Your name?"

I almost didn't hear him as I watched a healer now tend to Razz's wounds by the queen's command.

"My name is Attica," I responded, drawing my attention back to the king.

"Just Attica?"

"Spark," I added. "Attica Spark."

His eyes widened. Queen Aria stepped forward and gently reached a hand up to my chin. "You look just like your mother," she said, taking in the details of my face. Then she released her hand from my chin. "Thank you for bringing our magic back. And say hello to your mother for me."

I didn't know what to say, considering I couldn't even remember my mother. So instead, I responded with a polite smile and nod.

She then kindly asked the healer to tend to me. And the healer did what Cece had once done for me at the coliseum, holding her hands over my wounds while muttering, "Cho Ku Rei." My scrapes and cuts healed as if weeks had passed, leaving only faint scars.

Everyone parted as we made our way toward the chrome dragon. Boreas stood holding the reins of the monstrous creature, waiting for Razz and me.

"You okay?" Razz asked. "You look like hell," he added before I had a chance to reply.

"One to talk! How are you not in more pain? There were arrows lodged in you."

At first, he didn't answer. It appeared he was trying to figure it out himself. Then he finally said, "I think when I slowed time, I also slowed the impact of the arrows hitting me. Not to mention, I had to bend most of their minds, forcing them to miss. I mean, they did hurt, and it still aches. But my energy is more focused on my brother, Cece, Zella, and Etiwa, and getting them all back safely. And for the record, I was only struck when more than one asshole took their shot simultaneously. I couldn't bend all their shit minds at once."

Without meaning to, I tuned Razz out as my eyes swept the vast valley, hoping I'd find Darian's face in the crowd of people. But he was nowhere.

"Where is he?" I asked Razz. I didn't even have to clarify who I was asking about.

"I don't know. Etiwa never told me how he would escape the grid once magic returned to the lower kingdoms." His eyes unfocused for just a moment. "She says Calder knows," he said in a trance, surely communicating with Etiwa telepathically.

When we reached Boreas, he hopped on the dragon's back with the help of the saddle and reins. He then put a hand out to me. "You'll be behind me," he said casually, as if he wasn't the one holding me against my will before I escaped to the weaponry room.

Perhaps it was his face that reminded me so much of my brother's that allowed me to move past the way he had treated me before. His held out hand didn't waver, even with how long I stood there deciding whether or not to take it. But I finally pushed past my stubbornness and placed my hand in his.

His hand was callused, but his touch was as soft as air brushing my skin. He pulled me up with ease. He didn't let go of my hand once I was straddled behind him. Instead, he reached his other hand back, grabbing my free hand. Then, with both my hands locked in his, he stretched my arms before me and wrapped them around his waist. "You're going to want to hold on tight," he said, before turning to Razz. "Waiting on you."

Razz looked around for a way to climb up the gargantuan dragon. But there was nothing for him to grab or step on to help him up. By the proud look on Boreas's face, he basked in the power of creating steps made of thick white air with just a couple of gestures with his pointed finger.

I saw only half of Boreas's face as he looked over his shoulder at Razz. A smile tugged his lips as he gazed at the steps he had created, as if he had longed to create such simple magic for so long.

Razz was hesitant at first but finally stepped up the short set of stairs helping him onto the dragon's back. He settled himself behind me. I ignored the discomfort of being sandwiched between Boreas and Razz and instead focused my thoughts on Darian.

"Hold on tight," Boreas commanded as silvery-black wings stretched out and flapped so furiously, it felt like I was in the center of a windstorm. It only added to my discomfort when the beast I sat atop let out a hefty breath of icy air before finally pushing off the ground. We lifted higher and higher, passing the layer of fog above as we rose over the valley and mountains, allowing us a view of the early evening sky.

Razz's hands tightened around my stomach, and mine tightened around Boreas's. Every time the dragon tilted and turned, Boreas freed a hand from the reins and grabbed my arms, ensuring my safety. It was something James would have done too.

CHAPTER 49

The Last Starlight

What should have taken us days in the carriage only took two starlights by flight to reach the Node of Magic in the grasslands. Dragons flew much faster than I expected.

We arrived early, just barely. The moment the dragon landed directly on the giant gilded star, Razz was the first to hop off. He hurried to the side of the tall grass and threw up.

He took his bag off his back and pulled out a canteen of water, gargling and spitting. He followed it by chewing one of his minty petals from the little glass jar he carried.

When Razz finally returned beside Boreas and me, Boreas turned to Razz and asked, "You okay?"

Razz's tone was far from friendly when he said, "Do you mean from flying or the arrow you shot in my shoulder earlier?"

Boreas dropped his head when he said, "Sorry about that. That's just how we deal with intruders."

Razz straightened with an arched brow. "There are far more civilized ways."

375

Boreas's face softened, as if he knew Razz was right. But before he had a chance to respond, a sudden whirl of water appeared feet away. It grew bigger and bigger until, finally, Calder emerged, stepping out of it.

"What are you doing here?" Razz asked.

Calder was so stunned by the sight of the dragon, I wasn't sure he even heard Razz. But then he said with his usual sarcasm, "Good to see you too, man! I take it Shakar invited you—" He cut himself off when his eyes landed on Boreas. "James?"

Boreas dropped his brows with a squint. "Who?"

"Shit!" Calder said, utterly dumbfounded. "You look just like—"

The sudden appearance of purple flames interrupted him. The flames unraveled, and Ignatius stepped out bearing gritted teeth. "Where is that shithole? I will kill him!" he said, not even slightly fazed by the monstrous dragon, James's doppelganger, or any of us. Instead, he was fuming with rage.

And then branches broke through the nothingness before us. Out stepped Gemma, though somewhat clumsily. "I hate the grid!" she signed with irritation before her eyes widened at the sight of the dragon.

"Did any of you see Darian?" Razz asked, his voice slightly cracked.

Calder glanced at both Ignatius and Gemma before he hesitantly responded, "I don't think so."

"But you know how to get him out, right?" Razz asked Calder.

"Yes. But we need Cece with us for it to work."

Razz started to pace.

We stood in the grasslands atop the gilded four-pointed star embedded in the grass, on guard as the pastel sky grew darker. As we waited in silence, somewhat paranoid, the plant life around us filled with light.

My heart began to pound the longer we stood waiting for Shakar's arrival.

How long until I would see Darian again? Was he okay, still trapped in the grid?

Where was Shakar? Were Cece and Zella okay? Was Etiwa okay? Were they safe, having been with the Orpheus this long?

After Calder pointed out the heightened energy from the full moon, I scanned all three at their varying phases. The largest of the moons was perfectly round. Somehow, gazing at it calmed my nerves.

Nearly an entire starlight passed before the sound of flapping wings pulled my attention to the dark sky. It was a white dragon I had seen once before.

The moment Shakar landed, Boreas's dragon stomped its feet. I wasn't sure if it was happy or disturbed at the sudden sight of another creature of its kind.

"Brisa?" Boreas uttered with narrowed eyes on the white dragon.

Shakar stepped off the gargantuan creature and opened a familiar cage on its back, allowing Cece and Zella to step out. Both their wrists were bound by slithering black snakes with gleaming yellow eyes.

Zella's mouth fell open at the sight of Boreas.

"Where's Etiwa?" Calder asked.

"She's fine!" Cece said. "She's still at—"

"Quiet!" Shakar commanded in a low but fierce voice.

The curved-back finger-length thorns on his head gleamed under the moonlight. He was the only Orpheus I had ever seen with thorns in place of hair. And he was alone. No other Orpheus was in sight.

His orange slit eyes scanned each one of us. His thorny head tilted at the sight of Boreas. "You are?"

"The son of the man who trained that dragon when she was just a whelp," he said with disdain, glancing between the white dragon and Shakar.

Shakar laughed menacingly. "Your father did a terrible job. I've had to whip her in shape."

Boreas responded with nothing but a glare.

Shakar scanned the rest of us. "Let's make a deal: I give you your friends, and you all return to the edge. No harm done."

No one responded. I stayed quiet, wondering what difference it made if we were on the edge or not.

Shakar pointed his staff on the gold star we all stood on. A black stone door suddenly appeared behind him out of thin air. When it opened, a blue light poured out. It was the energy grid. My heart sank as I waited for Darian to step out.

The sound of hissing snakes filled the silence as several yellow slit eyes appeared behind the door in the grid. They each walked out of the blue-filled light, one by one, until about fifty Orpheus warriors were standing behind Shakar. And then the door vanished.

Cece winced as the black snake binding her wrists slithered up her arm.

Red flames filled Ignatius's hands.

"Can we have a moment?" Calder asked Shakar.

He scanned us, and to my surprise, he said, "Have your moment."

Calder huddled me, Razz, Ignatius, and Gemma. Boreas stood out of the huddle with eyes glued to the pearly dragon as he stroked his own dragon's rough-scaled nose.

Calder whispered low enough for only us to hear. "He wants us back on the edge because it weakens the kingdoms. We are his pawns to maintain his power. He knows our parents wouldn't dare start a war with Shakar being the only one who can reach us on the edge. So whatever we decide, we cannot give in to his demand! At least not if we want to stay where we belong, with our families. Any ideas?"

I was the first to speak up. "Razz! Can't you bend time long enough for Cece and Zella to escape?" But before I allowed Razz time to answer, I turned to the group. "Most of you can escape through the grid!" And then the hope on my face faded. My gaze dropped to the grass when I said more so to myself, "But then, what about Darian?"

"Don't worry about Darian. Etiwa told me how to get him back. But if we were to escape, we would cause a war and put our people in danger," Calder said, with a look of still trying to think of a way out of this bargain.

"I don't have all night!" Shakar bellowed, stomping his staff on the ground. "My snakes are getting hungry. One bite of your friends, and they die. Unless they have a resistance to venom, which I doubt."

Suddenly, I remembered what the mystic had said about me having to make a choice—about me having to sacrifice myself. And then I remembered something I stupidly hadn't thought of until now: Sifa also told me I needed to surrender myself.

I turned to Calder. "Are you sure you know how to get Darian out?"

"Yes!"

Without allowing them a moment to talk me out of it, I turned to Shakar and said, "Take me."

"What?" Razz said, grabbing my arm.

I shook him off and moved closer to Shakar.

"Why would I take you when I can have you all?" The Orpheus behind him moved closer.

"Because just last year, you had people searching for me. I think there's a reason you wanted to find me that had nothing to do with what my grandfather did to your brother."

His face grew fiercer. He slowed his words when he said, "I want all of you back on the edge, or you will pay with your lives."

"No! You want me and only me because—" My heart suddenly sped faster as I knew what I had to say to keep my friends safe. And even worse, I knew it was a gamble of war or freedom. I swallowed my nerves before forcing the words out of my dry mouth. "I have returned magic to the kingdoms."

CHAPTER 50

The Bargain

Shakar's eyes widened in rage. "You what?" He clenched his jaw with such force, I wondered how his sharp teeth didn't shatter.

I overheard Calder say, "What the hell is she doing?"

I took another step forward. "Their magic is out of your reach. They will be more than ready to combine their forces and destroy every one of you," I said, scanning the Orpheus with my head held high, surely appearing stronger than I felt.

Shakar growled.

A familiar Orpheus woman that had caught me once before moved toward Shakar with hesitance and said, "She's lying. Don't listen to her! We can take them all!"

Shakar turned to her, baring his teeth. "I would know if she were lying, Nisha," he said with a glance at the smoke swirling at the head of his staff. "If you dare question my judgment, I will ban you from my force."

Nisha immediately lowered her head and stepped back.

I moved another foot forward. "You told me it was my grandfather who murdered your brother. Imagine how he would feel if he knew my life was in your hands." It was another gamble—unsure if my grandfather was still alive.

"Attica! Have you lost your damn mind?" Razz whispered behind me.

I ignored him, keeping my eyes steady on Shakar.

Shakar moved closer to me. "It's not enough," he said.

"If I could return their magic, then perhaps I can give your kingdom magic too. I can make you and your kingdom more powerful. It's your choice."

Shakar stood observing me in silence for an uncomfortable amount of time before finally saying, "You have a deal."

"Not yet. You need to agree to leave my friends, their kingdoms, and their people in peace. All of you," I clarified, looking at his army.

He stayed silent for a moment before finally saying, "Fine!" with a grunt.

"And you must remove whatever tracking you have on Darian's voice," I daringly added.

In the blink of an eye, Shakar zipped toward me and gripped my throat. "That better be your last bargain!"

I tried to respond, but I couldn't with his clawed hand cupped around my neck. So I nodded. He released me and pounded his staff to the ground. When he did so, a sky-blue light escaped the glass egg at the head of his staff and then vanished. "There. He is free to speak without a trace."

"Then, we have a deal!" I said, hoping he didn't feel my nerves screaming in my chest.

He moved so close, the thorns on his chin nearly pierced my forehead. "If you do not deliver the magic you promised, I will not only take your life, but the life of every single one of your friends too."

I swallowed my immediate regret.

"What about the magic protecting us?" I stupidly asked, knowing the protective magic likely expired years ago.

"I will sacrifice some of my people to kill every one of you, even if it costs them their life. Now, get in the cage!"

Since I had nothing left to lose, I dared to ask, "Can I just say goodbye to my friends, please?"

Shakar studied me for a moment before finally saying, "Get in the cage first."

Reluctantly, I grabbed the cold metal of the heavy bars and pulled myself in. Shakar looked me in the eye as he locked the cage before he turned and whistled.

The snakes bound around Zella's and Cece's wrists unraveled themselves, fell to the ground, and slithered toward Shakar. He picked them up and placed them in a large black pouch on the side of his armor before silently conversing with members of his army.

My friends looked at me as if I were already dead. Or perhaps as if it were the last time they would ever see me. Well, everyone except Boreas. He seemed more irritated at the sight of Shakar's dragon.

It was at this moment I realized I couldn't fulfill James's only wish: to give Zella a hug for him. My eyes didn't waiver from Boreas. He looked confused when I called him over to the cage I sat locked in. Shakar stood close enough to hear every word I said.

When Boreas stepped before the cage with raised brows and several cautious glances at Shakar, I told him how much he looked like my brother and about the soulful connection James and Zella shared. With a hand stretched uncomfortably through bars, I pointed Zella out. When his blue eyes landed on her tying her hair back while glaring at Shakar, his pupils spread dangerously close to the rim. She must have felt his eyes on her as she shifted her attention to him.

Zella didn't blush or bat her lashes at Boreas's lengthy gaze. Instead, she stood stiffly, analyzing him from a distance.

I told him about James's wish to hug her for him and asked if he would do it for me. He agreed without hesitance. The moment he walked away, my eyes met with Cece's.

Cece looked at me as if I were a ghost, sitting in the cage she had just sat in moments ago.

While Ignatius and Gemma checked on Cece and Zella, Calder and Razz came to me.

"Attica, what the hell were you thinking? I'm going to find a way to get you out!" Razz said.

"No! We made a deal you cannot break! All the kingdoms and people of Elloriya will be thrown into war if you do. So please, do not come after me."

His brows fell as he stayed staring at me with glossy eyes.

I turned to Calder, who was oddly silent, gazing at me with a look of defeat. "There is one thing you can do for me," I said to him.

"What is it?"

"Get Darian out of the grid, now, before I leave."

"In front of the Orpheus? What if they—"

"Please!" I begged.

Calder nodded before returning to the group.

My attention switched back to Boreas, just for a moment, waiting for him to hug Zella for me—for James. But Zella was talking with Ignatius and Gemma. So he stood to the side, likely waiting for the right moment.

Razz moved as close as the cage allowed him. "Attica, what can I do to help? You haven't even returned home yet, and now, you'll never see—" His words fell silent as he noticed the tears rolling down my face.

I quickly wiped them. "Thank you, Razz."

"For what?"

"For everything."

Suddenly, lights grew brightly behind Razz. In the distance were my friends opening the grid: Calder with light-filled water, Ignatius with violet flames, Cece with a twister of air, and Gemma with glowing moss-covered branches. But it wasn't until the water wrapped around the branches, and the air swirled the violet flames over the water that the doorway to the grid grew exceptionally large before them.

Blue light poured out of the doorway. One minute passed, and nothing happened. Two minutes passed, and still, no one stepped out.

"I can't hold it much longer," Calder said through gritted teeth. Cece, Ignatius, and Gemma seemed to struggle too. Gemma's face turned red as she fought to keep the grid open.

My heart fell silent, waiting for Darian to walk out. I could hardly breathe as the opening to the grid began shrinking.

No, no, no. Please, Darian, please! Where are you?

The Orpheus curiously watched as the opening to the grid continued narrowing. Gemma was the first to let go. It was not so much that she gave up, but rather that she couldn't hold her conjured branches any longer.

Calder's water dwindled the longer he held the grid open. And at the same time, Ignatius's purple flames were dwindling too.

I could hardly breathe at the sight. Darian was not coming out of the grid. It didn't work. All of this was for nothing!

Was Darian in the grid for too long now? Had he lost himself to the grid for eternity? Would I never see those deep blue eyes again?

Shakar laughed menacingly at the same time I broke into a downfall of tears. I would never be happy from this day forward. I had no right to be happy ever again! After all, it was my fault Darian stepped into that stupid energy grid to begin with.

Gemma tried to aid them in opening the grid larger, but her attempts were feeble. And the doorway to the grid was now the size of my foot. It was too small for any of us to get in or out.

For a moment, I wondered if I could break out of the cage and join Darian in the grid. Perhaps he and I could be lost in the grid together forever. Perhaps—

My tortured thoughts fell silent as Calder's water vanished, and Ignatius's flames became nothing more than the size of a match. Cece was the last to hold the grid open with a whirl of wild wind that fell tamer until her hands fell tiresome by her sides.

The Orpheus roared with laughter as the grid closed. Gemma, Calder, Ignatius, and Cece tried again, but they couldn't seem to conjure up their elements to wield open the grid. It was as though they had used up every ounce of their elemental powers.

Razz looked as though all life had been ripped from him before he turned to Zella and yelled, "Can't you do something? Can't you open the grid?"

She looked at Razz hopelessly with a shake of her head. "You know I don't have that ability," she responded.

To my surprise, Boreas stepped forward. He held up his hands, and a whirlwind of air powered out of his palms and circled before him. Blue light peered through the small opening. With a little more effort, he made the opening bigger until it matched his towering size.

As Boreas held the grid open with a slowly reddening face, Razz yelled, "Darian?"

There was no response. Calder shouted for him too. And then Ignatius and Zella. Cece seemed to be praying to the angels while everyone called out to Darian. Well, everyone but Gemma.

Instead, Gemma was busy crushing pollen from a nearby wildflower into her palms. She pressed her palms together, and when she pulled them apart, a wild ribbon of bright orange light filled the space between her hands. She threw the ribbon of light into the grid Boreas had held open for a couple of minutes now. But as the minutes passed with no response, Boreas's energy fell tiresome by the look of his body turning slowly limp.

It wasn't until the blue light from the grid was the size of a pin that I dropped my head in defeat at the realization that I would never see his eyes again. And I was sure I felt my heart break at that moment. At least until the pin of blue light Boreas tried all too hard to not let close suddenly sparked.

Gleaming yellow veins spread out around the pinhole. The veins and sparks grew longer around the minuscule opening to the grid. It took me a moment to realize the lengthening veins were bolts of lightning. And as the lightning spread through the tiny opening, the doorway to the grid grew bigger and bigger until, finally, a figure moved out of the light. And not just any figure. There stood the most beautiful man I had ever known. There stood Darian.

The Orpheus Kingdom

The moment Darian stepped out of the grid, he appeared dazed, as if he hadn't yet stepped foot into reality. Cece was the first to move toward him, but Razz pulled her back as if he knew his brother needed a moment to remember what reality looked like.

He scanned everyone, but it wasn't until he saw me in the cage a short distance away that his eyes widened. My heart nearly jumped through my chest when Darian ran toward me. The dragon didn't move at the stranger running its way. It was a very tame dragon I sat atop, caged. She acted nearly lifeless, as if she, too, were caged.

Shakar had just settled himself on the dragon's back, placing his staff securely in a holder attached to the saddle when Darian reached me in the cage behind the Orpheus leader.

"Where are you taking her?" he asked Shakar.

"To her new home with me," he said with a grave laugh.

"Take me instead!" Darian demanded.

Shakar watched Darian for a moment before finally asking, "What use would you be to me?"

"What use is she to you?" he countered.

"That's between her and me," Shakar said, grabbing the dragon's reins in his thorn-freckled hands.

"Then take me too. I can be of use. Whatever you need!" Darian pleaded with his fingers gripped to the cage.

Shakar only laughed before responding, "No."

He glanced at his warriors with a nod of finished business before kicking the dragon's stomach. It wasn't until the massive snowy wings stretched out and began flapping that Darian released his grip on the cage.

It was a struggle to break my gaze from him. But as I looked past him, I caught sight of Boreas talking to Zella, and a moment later, he pulled her in for a hug. I was sure she was thinking of James when her arms tightened around Boreas.

As we rose off the luminescent field and into the dark Elloriyan sky, Razz pulled Darian in for a somber hug, holding his little brother until I was so high up, I could no longer see them.

My heart clung so tightly to Darian, I wondered if he knew I would have also offered my life to save his. But why? Why would I offer my life for him when he kept me at a distance with his walls so high up? What sort of spell did he have me under?

I spent most of the flight thinking of how Darian seemed to care so deeply for my safety—for me—but never cared enough to let me in. But after some time of thinking back to every interaction we ever had, obsessing over every tiny detail, I suddenly realized that perhaps he had dropped his walls and let me in after all.

He showed me a memory of us as children together in the crystal cave where he gave me the moonstone I now wear around my neck. And after rescuing me from the dead passageway, he saved me a second time from Shakar after Queen Eloise Adaire's wretched gala and then took me to the same crystal cave and pulled me into his mind, showing me details of his past. Then he fought to save me a third time in the coliseum, offering his life ahead of mine.

After that terrible day when I had died before my soul returned to my body, it was Darian who carried me to my bed, whispering telepathic words when he pressed his forehead against mine. I'll never forget those words—his words—that had spilled into the core of my very being: "One day."

Though I had no idea what he meant by those two simple words, I finally realized he tried to let me in several times, in his own way—in the only way he could, considering the constraint on his voice.

How had I just now realized this? It was me who hadn't let him in this whole time. It was me who had built a wall between us. And now it was too late. It was too late to break down my wall and tell him how I felt. Or at the very least, to tell him how much I appreciated him and all he had risked for me, time after time.

The last time I saw Darian as a child was when I sat in this very cage with him. And now, I sat in this cage again—without Darian— thinking of the pained look on his face as his gaze had clung so tightly to mine before Shakar and I took to the sky. I thought of the tight grip of his fingers wrapped around one of the many bars separating him from me. I thought of how badly I wanted to wrap my arms around him. Then, for a second time in my life, I wondered the very same thing in the very same cage I now sat in: *Is this the last day I would ever see him?*

After a short flight, the dragon descended to an area beside the barrier, allowing me an aerial view of the Orpheus Kingdom. It was far bigger than I had calculated from the ground before trespassing with Razz in Orpheus disguise.

Upon a gentle landing, Shakar jumped off with the help of his staff and chained the dragon to the black tourmaline wall reflecting the glow of the moons. He pulled out what looked to be treats from a nearby burlap bag and fed them to her while petting her nose.

It was strange seeing him show affection for a living thing. But that affection quickly vanished as he opened the cage and pulled me out by my clothes, nearly choking me.

He pushed me through a stone door, into the Orpheus dwelling. Though it was dark, the black walls held tiny white crystals that created a wave of subtle light throughout the massive domain.

Young Orpheus children ran around, screaming and playing. Mothers disciplined, hugged, and looked after their kids as they played in the night. One woman cleaned a pile of clothes in a small pool of soapy water with a washing board while another hung them to dry. All the women and the few elderly Orpheus around greeted Shakar.

Besides Shakar, none of the Orpheus in sight had a shred of hate or even a presence of danger. It seemed Shakar and his warriors were the only ones I had to be cautious of. They were perhaps the only ones with pure and dreadful evil running through their veins.

To my surprise, the surrounding Orpheus backed away from me in fear, as if I were the one who threatened their lives. It was a feeling I despised.

Why did they seem to fear me when I had done nothing to them? I did my best to shrug it off and continued passing the women and children while at Shakar's mercy.

He led me up stone steps to the second level, where three doors were. He opened the middle one. On the other side of the door was a short set of stairs, taking me down to a room with nothing but a hammocklike nest for a bed. Again, the same moonlike glow filled the room, emanating from the tiny crystals embedded in the dark walls.

When I made my way down the stairs in silence, the sound of Shakar's heavy steps trailed behind. He sat on the bottom step, facing me as I stood near the hammock.

"What now?" I asked, unsure of his plan or why he was just sitting, staring at me.

His voice was calm when he said, "You tell me. . . . How did you return magic to the kingdoms?"

At first, I didn't answer because I feared he would steal their magic again if I told him. So instead, I tried to shift topics to avoid answering.

"Why were you searching for me last year? What would you have done if you captured me the night of the gala?"

The calm in his voice quickly shifted as he banged a fist against the wall, jolting my nerves. "Tell me how you returned magic to the kingdoms!"

My stomach turned every which way. "I—I don't know how to explain it."

His spiky nose flared. "I'll give you until the next full moon. If you don't fulfill your end of the bargain by then, you will watch your friends die. And then I'll make sure your grandfather gets a front-row seat to your death. Your twenty-two days begin now."

After he stood and headed up the steps, I bellowed, "I can't fulfill anything in this room!" He turned, glaring down at me from the top of the stairs. "I would need to explore this place," I said, knowing full well that there was no way in hell I'd be able to give his kingdom magic. But it would allow me to map out their dwelling and hopefully find an escape when the opportunity would arise.

Perhaps a lunar was enough time to escape, or maybe to conjure up another bargain in exchange for a kingdom of magic. Though coming up with such an appealing bargain seemed impossible.

Shakar didn't respond to my request to search his kingdom. Instead, he walked out in silence and shut the door. The hopeless sound of him locking it could be felt in my bones.

I might as well have dug my grave then and there.

With a heavy sigh and a deep feeling of regret for putting myself in this fucked predicament, my eyes landed on an empty metal bucket under the stairs. I didn't know whether to be put off by the sight or thankful that I had somewhere to relieve myself.

I had spent my dwindling time pacing, trying to find a way out of the bargain I knew was impossible to fulfill. I wondered what would happen if I escaped during the daytime, when the sun was too bright for any Orpheus to step outside. Maybe I would have enough time to warn the others. Or perhaps I would make everything worse for my friends and their kingdoms.

Stupid, stupid me! Why did I make a deal I couldn't fulfill? Had I twisted the mystic's riddle about sacrificing myself? Had I somehow made the right choice? Or had I made the biggest mistake of my life?

Because I sacrificed myself, Shakar released the trace he had on Darian's voice, and he let my friends go.

The grid finally released Darian. He was free to go home. All my friends could finally return to their kingdoms without the threat of Shakar or his warriors attacking.

So why was I so hard on myself? Perhaps because everything I had risked to save Darian and bring my friends back home was all about to crumble to shit, all because I made an impossible deal.

Etiwa's mother was right. Peace can only last so long.

CHAPTER 52

My Escort

I sat in the dark chamber, alone and in silence, cherishingly holding my Christmas stocking Mama had given me that had been neatly stuffed in the bottom of my bag. A couple of starlights had passed—most of the time spent trying to come up with some form of escape. If it wasn't that, then it was my battling thoughts if I had made the right decision to come here or not. My conclusion: not!

Another starlight passed. I spent the time calling upon my spirit guides, Astrophel and Kamali. I practically begged for some sign that would confirm I had made the right sacrifice by coming here. The response I received . . . ? None. Perhaps my mind was filled with too many worries and chaotic thoughts to receive any sort of clear answer.

As I nodded off on the stone floor in the corner of the warm room, the sound of a key turning in the lock tugged me awake. I sat up as the door opened. It was an Orpheus I had never seen before—certainly one of Shakar's warriors from the looks of his black metal armor.

397

As he walked down the steps resting a hand on the handle of his belted saber sword with such poised intimidation, I took in the sight of his elegant features and dark hazelnut hair, and I wondered if he was the most beautiful Orpheus in this entire wretched kingdom.

When he reached the bottom of the staircase, I stood up, brushing dinge and dust off my hands. I expected him to say something, but instead, he just stood there, dragging his yellow eyes over my body.

After he had his fill of scanning me, he finally spoke. "I've never met a human before. Only tikaanis."

Though something about his potent presence was frightening, I brushed my nerves to the side and asked, "Aren't they human?"

"Not entirely."

"Well, have I met your expectations?" I awkwardly asked.

His elegance magnified as he took a step closer. For a moment, he just looked at me through cold eyes as if he were reading my soul. "Too soon to tell." His analytic gaze broke when he demanded, "Let's go."

"Where are we going?"

He made it sound like a punishment when he said, "I'll oversee taking you through the kingdom."

"Oh. Okay. Do you have a name?"

His only reply was, "Yes."

He didn't seem like much of a talker, so I didn't ask any further.

As I followed him up the stairs, I wondered if one lunar would be enough time to gain his trust. If he would be the one to escort me for the next twenty-two days, then perhaps I could learn my way around this place and escape the moment he'd let his guard down before Shakar kills me for not fulfilling our deal.

When we reached the top of the stairs, he looked me dead in the eye and said in a low voice, "If you dare try anything, I will cut off your fingers and feed them to you."

Though my nerves unraveled, I didn't think his threat was genuine. At least until I noticed what looked to be a cigar cutter hanging on his belt. He didn't have to tell me what it was for. The dried blood on the blade revealed enough to make me feel sick.

As I passed him, his scent followed me. It was a rich musk of fresh pine, which told me he spent every free moment of his nights in the woods.

When he opened the heavy door, he grabbed me by the neck and pulled me out of the chamber toward the railing where countless warriors stood watching from the level below. He then pushed me forward with a face far fiercer than I had seen in the chamber.

He stayed a foot behind me as I turned a corner and walked the empty hall, running a hand over the rough wall. Curious, I brushed my fingers on the tiny crystals in the black tourmaline that shed a moonlit glow. It was like walls of a starry night sky surrounded me with every turn I took.

If I didn't fear this place or my self-doom here, I might enjoy its beauty, as it didn't appear as wretched in the night.

"Finding what you're looking for?" he asked in a gentle voice.

"No. Not yet," I said, prepared to take a mental note of any exit I found, which was none so far. "What's up there?" I asked, pointing up another set of stairs that led to a single door.

He studied me for a moment, as if trying to decide whether to take me up those stairs.

"That's enough for today," he said after only twenty minutes of escorting me outside the chamber. I didn't dare push him for more time. I needed him to trust that I could oblige his commands.

He took me back to the chamber without a single word. The moment I stepped inside, he locked the door and left me in the room for three days before allowing me out again.

The vicious female warrior, Nisha, was the one to deliver my food each day, though reluctantly. It was the same reptilian woman I had met near the manor right after Gemma and I saw the charzdaine for the first time, and the same woman that captured me the night of the gala. The first time she delivered my food, she threw it at me and said in a honeyed voice, "Enjoy, Jada."

Instead of ever walking down the steps to civilly hand the shit food to me, she always threw it down from the top of the stairs with a sneer. And it was almost always a near rotten piece of fruit and was never enough to fill me. Perhaps hitting me with rotten food each day was her revenge for when I lied about my name the first dreadful time our paths crossed.

When my escort returned three days later, he seemed to be in more of a foul mood than the last time I saw him. Just being near him turned my stomach to knots.

The more I saw of their dwelling, the more irritated he seemed to get. If I lingered too long in any room or hall, he would grunt.

He was either paranoid or following Shakar's instruction because he returned me to the chamber again after only a short time of searching for my escape. It's as if he knew I was lying to his leader about my side of the deal: to further power their kingdom with magic. Or perhaps he just knew I was looking for a way out. I wasn't entirely sure that he even knew about the bargain. What I did know was that the man hated me, and at the pace he allowed me to search, I would surely die in this shithole with no escape.

The third time he babysat me through their dark dwelling, he didn't say a single word the entire time. It seemed each time I left the chamber, the metal bucket under the stairs was replaced with a clean one. It was the only thing I had to be grateful for.

The next time he let me out, I tried making conversation with him. "So, what do you do for fun around here?" I kindly asked.

"None of your business," was his response.

Perhaps my unanswered question softened him a bit because he finally allowed me up the set of stairs on the highest floor.

When he reached for the door handle at the top of the staircase, I couldn't help but notice how his hand was so humanlike. The only difference was his razor-sharp nails and gray-scaled skin.

My heart pounded as he turned the handle, perhaps because he was hesitant to show me what was on the other side of the door when he first escorted me. But when he opened the stone door, I smiled for the first time in days.

CHAPTER 53

Venom

We stepped outside onto a balcony that seemed to wrap around the black mountainlike castle—or whatever the hell they lived in.

Though it was void of light, it was the most spectacular view of the Fatal Sea, separating the edge from the rest of Elloriya. I breathed in the smell of the salty ocean, grateful for the crisp air purring through each breath.

My Orpheus escort leaned against the stone railing, gazing at the night sky. His eyes rested on the three moons in the distance, each one painting the dark sea with a dreamy reflection. Their mighty glow stretched so far, they highlighted every handsome curve of his face.

Perhaps it was prejudiced of me, but I had never thought an Orpheus could be so utterly beautiful. I don't know if he felt my eyes on him, but he turned to me with a softer gaze than I had ever seen from him before. "Can you tell me what the sun is like?" he asked with a gleam in his eyes.

I was surprised at the question. And I wasn't sure if I could conjure up a suitable answer.

I turned to look at the abundance of stars in the black sky. "It's a deep golden yellow, like your eyes, and brighter than all the stars combined," I said, turning back to him.

He half-smiled.

I continued, "And it's very hot. But on a chilly day, its rays can be the most comforting feeling as they wrap around your body, warming you with its heat." My brows lowered when I asked, "Why don't you ever go outside during the day? Why don't you see it for yourself?"

The partial smile on his face quickly vanished. "The realm we come from has no sun. When we came here, we realized why."

He didn't answer my question. So I prodded. "Why?"

His eyes sat heavy on me with that considering look before glancing over his shoulder at the closed door. Then he said in a low voice, "If we step outside during daylight, our skin breaks out into a rash so painful that many of my people got very sick upon transition between realms. Some never recovered and died in agony over several miserable days."

It was a struggle to respond. But I managed to say, "I'm sorry."

He was staring out at the distant sea. I wasn't sure he heard me until he said, "Me too."

"No. I mean, I'm sorry for everything the nobles did to your realm and people." Now was my chance to hear their side of the story. Now would likely be my only chance at finding out what truly happened between the nobles and the Orpheus. So I dared ask, "How did it all start?"

He was silent at first. His eyes were unfocused, and his gaze turned inward.

"When the nobles had come with an offer, trying to make a trade of some sort, Shakar refused them, and then they left. We thought that would be the end of it. But then, one day, they appeared with armies. There were so many of them. Some used water to attack. Others used fire. There were twisters of air, and suddenly branches of trees appeared as if from nowhere, binding so many of us to the ground." He dropped his head. "I don't remember much after that. I was only a child when it happened. What I do remember is that" —he sighed— "that was the last day I saw my sister."

I was speechless. Just as I tried to say something, anything of comfort, he continued.

"There were so many of us before. Our realm was endless compared to this shit," he said with a sharp thumb pointing behind him. He shook his head, as if trying to rid the agonizing memories. His voice suddenly deepened when he said, "We should go back in."

Even though it wasn't me personally who had robbed the Orpheus of their realm and resources, my heart genuinely ached for him—for all the Orpheus.

He opened the door, waiting for me to go through. But before I did, I asked, "Will you ever tell me your name?"

He looked at me—that analytic gaze again. And finally, he said, "Pax."

"Nice to officially meet you, Pax," I said, just before crossing through the open door.

As I walked down the stairs overlooking their dwelling, I stumbled and fell back. Pax was quick to catch me and help me back up.

"Thanks," I uttered. But when I looked back over at the floor below, I caught sight of a familiar, heavily scarred warrior glaring at me.

Had the warrior seen Pax catch me? Though I hoped he hadn't, for Pax's sake, I was nearly sure he had. And from the look of his snarled lip, it displeased him.

When we reached the bottom of the stairs, we turned into the hall and went down another set of stairs, taking us to the main floor where many young Orpheus children were playing. Though they had slit yellow eyes, razor-sharp teeth, and gray-scaled skin, they had more similarities to humans than I had previously recognized.

Some were tall, and others were short. Some had tiny freckles on their noses or cheeks—though their freckles were thorns—while others were bare of freckles. There were those with light hair, dark hair, curly or straight.

But then I noticed how a few of the older children had orange slit eyes—the same eyes as Shakar. Were those children his? After all, he was the only adult Orpheus I had seen with orange eyes, while all the others had yellow.

The children had stopped playing tag to uncomfortably watch me. They almost appeared frightened by my presence. One little girl was brave enough to come near me. She looked up at me with her big eyes and blonde braided hair and asked in a little voice, "What are you?"

I knelt and said, "I'm sort of like you. Except I'm what you would call a human. But we're not that different, you and me." I smiled, but my smile instantly vanished as a stiff hand grabbed my neck from behind and threw me against the nearby wall.

When I saw the heavily scarred arm and deeply slashed face pinning me, I recognized the Orpheus as not only the one who had seen Pax help me on the stairs, but also as the one guarding the door when Razz and I had snuck through this place at the beginning of our journey.

His voice was heavy when he said, "How dare you use your human tongue to speak to my daughter! If you so much as look at her again, I will rip out your throat!"

I winced as he scratched my neck with his razor-sharp nails before grabbing his daughter's hand and pulling her away from me. The other children had scattered in fear.

Pax grabbed my arm and pulled me around a corner, bare of other Orpheus. I wanted to cry at the burning pain in my neck. My broken skin did not only sear but also felt as though pins and needles had woven around my wound.

"What did he do?" I asked through clenched teeth.

Pax's eyes widened at the cut. "Than used his venom. I'm afraid the pain will only get worse. If the venom travels far enough in your bloodstream, you could—" His face jumped from concerned to frightened. "I need to get you back to your room!" he said, leading me to my chamber door.

He closed the door behind him, and as I made my way down the stairs, it suddenly felt as though I had stepped directly into the scorching sun. I broke out in a sweat as I fell on the stone steps. Pax carried me down the rest of the stairs, and then gently placed me on the floor.

The pain intensified with each passing second, feeling as though scorching needles filled my neck. "Make it stop!" I begged, gripping Pax's arm. "Please, make the pain stop!"

His voice was gentle when he whispered, "I will. I'll make it stop. But the only way I know how to may be . . . inappropriate."

"I don't care. Just do it!" I begged louder, grasping his warm arm even tighter.

"Don't move," he whispered as he held my chin up and took his slit tongue out before pressing it against my neck. With each gentle lick of his tongue over my wound, the torturous sensation of pressing needles softened. His licks were soft and caressed my aches so much that I didn't want him to stop.

He was not just tending to the pain tearing up my neck, but the worrying of my mind and the pounding of my chest too. His licks, his scent, his presence were like my personal soothing drug.

The searing pain subsided after a few minutes. And when he finally released his fingers from my chin and his mouth from my neck, he picked me up from the dusty floor and laid me in the nestlike hammock.

"Feel better?" he asked, standing over me.

I didn't answer, but instead, I thought of Ignatius. "An Orpheus once scratched my friend on the face, and he was fine. Why didn't it cause him the same pain?"

"Well, whichever of my people scratched your friend may not have used their venom, which I doubt." He thought for a moment and then said, "I'm guessing your friend's bloodstream is filled with so much heat, the enzymes and proteins of the venom couldn't survive it, which would likely make your friend a fire wielder."

I partially smiled, impressed by the accuracy of his response.

He brushed a smudge of dirt off my arm. "You'll be okay."

Though I was now free of pain, I was suddenly drained of energy.

As I lay in the hammock looking up at him, I couldn't help but take in the soft yellow of his eyes. There was kindness—too much kindness to be a villain. He was not my enemy. Instead, he was someone that surprisingly cared about me, at least to some extent. He likely didn't feel the same, but I was beginning to see him as a friend.

CHAPTER 54

The Escape

With a slight shake of my waking head, I tried to recall what had happened before falling asleep. The last thing I remembered was looking up at Pax as I lay in the hammock, recovering from a pain-consuming venomous scratch. He was long gone when I awoke.

Instead, there was something new sitting beside the hammock. It was a towering pile of laundry with a note that read:

In case you need a break from boredom. I like them folded neatly.
-Pax

I rolled my eyes and didn't bother folding a single tunic or pants.

My stomach roared with hunger. I had lost several pounds since I first arrived. They were severely underfeeding me here, and I only received drinking water every other day. It was making it difficult to think straight.

I paced in circles, trying to come up with a plan of escape for what felt like the hundredth time. Finally, Pax was beginning to show his kindness. Would he help me? Even that teenager had

411

helped me before—what was his name? Ekon, I think. Ekon had helped me escape when Razz and I had passed through this very kingdom several lunars ago. But I hadn't seen him among the many Orpheus since returning.

The sound of birds chirping and whistling pulled me out of my thoughts. I ran toward the black wall and peeked through a crack shedding a slight ray of light. It was daytime, which meant most of the Orpheus—if not all—were asleep.

Now would be the perfect time to escape! But there was no way to escape while locked in this room. Unless, of course, I broke the wall.

So, I backed up and then ran into the part of the wall that already had a crack. I ran as hard as I could, ramming my shoulder into the dark stone. Immediately, I regretted my stupidity. My shoulder now ached as I continued to pace in circles.

There was no way out of this place. There was no way out of this deal. There was no way to save my friends or me for making a bargain I couldn't fulfill. What the hell had I done?

As I lay on the hammock, swinging back and forth, trying to think of a way out of the deal, I nearly fell to the floor when suddenly a little fluttering creature appeared beside me out of thin air.

A courier? How had I not thought of that before? A small orange light escaped from the spiral shell on its back.

"Attica, are you okay? I know you said for us not to come, but if you need us, say the word, and we'll be there!" It was, without a doubt, Razz's voice.

This time, a blue light escaped from its shell and silently floated before me. Was it waiting for me to respond? I waited for another message, but no sound came from it.

"I'm fine! Do not come here! I will find a way out on my own. Just be on guard." The light took in my message, changing color to orange as it returned to the whispering lights in its swirled shell. And then, *poof.* It was gone.

Razz's voice reminded me of the couplings. Was he wearing the other one? I reached into my bag and pulled out the silver cuff. I latched it over my arm and felt nothing. But after a moment of nothingness, the energy shifted, and my heartbeat shook.

After wearing the coupling for so long, connecting myself to Razz day after day, I knew his energy, probably better than I knew my own. And this connection I felt through the coupling was not Razz's.

This connection was different. It was enticing. I could easily melt into this energy. I wanted to melt into this energy with every fiber in me. Could the person wearing the other coupling possibly be . . . Darian?

My heartbeat glitched again, and I jumped off the hammock. I wrapped a hand over the coupling latched to my arm and held it over my chest as if it would magically bring me closer to this tempting energy.

But how could I be so strongly connected to the other coupling when it was so many miles away from me? How could I feel so connected to whoever this was when the couplings hadn't tapped each other, allowing our energies to fully sync together? Was my connection with this mystery person truly that strong?

If it was Darian wearing the other coupling, then I never wanted to take it off. Not if it bound me to him.

No man, no person, no one had ever made me feel the way Darian did. I wasn't even sure how he made me feel. It was too confusing to make sense of my feelings for him.

Was it love? No. I didn't know him well enough to love him. Maybe as a child—before Shakar had me sent to Earth—I knew him well enough. But those memories were wiped from my mind. Before I was sent to Earth, every memory—every moment—was practically nonexistent. Except maybe the ones Darian had shown me that time in the crystal cave. But those were his memories, not mine.

How many memories did he have of me? How often did we play together as children? What games did we play together? How deep did our friendship run?

Our friendship had to have meant something to him. After all, he painted a portrait of me as a child, hung beautifully in the manor's library. He remembered the lines and details of my face from when I was a kid better than I even had. For him to take the time to paint me from memory—that had to have meant something, right? And for the several times he risked his life for me . . . that definitely meant something. Could he have possibly loved me?

I was quick to shut off my thoughts when I realized I was still connected to him through the couplings. At least, I think it was him I was connected to. Whoever it was, I didn't want them to hear or feel my thoughts.

Or . . . maybe I did.

A part of me wanted him to know my feelings, no matter how confusing they were. He had, after all, let his guard down with me and allowed me into his mind, though I hadn't even realized it till recently. But he had tried. I had never tried the way he had. I had never let him into my mind.

So then, go ahead, Darian. If it is you I feel through this energetic tie, then hear my thoughts. If I survive this place, if I ever see you again, you'll know how I feel about you. One day, I'll look into those blue eyes again, and I'll let my walls down. I want to know you. And I want you to know me.

Suddenly, my skin broke out in a wave of chills before it warmed again, as if arms had wrapped themselves around me. But then, the feeling vanished as quickly as it had come on.

It was a struggle to pull my attention off Darian and focus on a way out of here. I scanned my surroundings. Black stone wall, black stone wall, nestlike hammock, black stone wall, stairs, black stone wall, black stone door.

My sight settled on the door. It was my only way out, unless Pax had locked me in here, as he always did.

I strapped my bag over me and stepped on the stairs.

Would Pax have locked me in here after letting his guard down on the balcony?

I took another step, eyes fixated on the door handle.

Pax was different. He was gentle.

I continued up the steps, convinced that Pax could have left it unlocked, at the very least by accident.

He cared about my well-being to some extent. He was kind beneath his usual grim exterior.

I reached the top of the stairs and stood before the door. It was either locked or unlocked. If it was locked, I would have absolutely no chance of escaping. But if it was unlocked, then I could find a way out and warn the others to prepare for war against the Orpheus.

I didn't know what the hell I was thinking, coming here in the first place. I had offered myself as a sacrifice on a whim—all because of what the mystic had said. Well, Ziggy and Sifa. Their voices in the back of my mind persuaded me to come here, convincing me it was a sacrifice I needed to make to help my friends—to help the realm of Elloriya and its people.

But I likely made everything worse for myself and everyone I cared for. So, my choices were: stay here and die, but not before I watch my friends die, or escape and warn them in hopes of coming up with a plan to stop the Orpheus from attacking.

My heart pounded as I reached for the door handle. It turned with ease. No way! There was no way in hell it was unlocked. But then, with a slight push, it opened.

CHAPTER 55

Repercussion

I looked over the second-floor railing to find the main floor was empty, which meant they must have been asleep in the chambers below, where all their nestlike hammocks were. After sneaking down to the main floor, I found the door that led to the outside where Shakar's dragon stayed. The door was surely locked with no key in sight.

I was stupid enough to sneak down to the underground floor, hoping to escape the same way Razz and I had escaped the first time, which meant I had to sneak past hundreds of sleeping Orpheus warriors.

My heart pounded as I stepped into the sleeping chamber. Shakar was in the highest and most kingly hammock nest, sharing it with two beautiful women. The only guard in sight was asleep in a chair by the exit, still in her armor.

This was my chance. I could either escape by going past the guarded door, hoping the guard wouldn't wake from my scent or the sound of my footsteps. Or I could exit on the top floor balcony, hoping to find a way down from the sky-scraping height of this place.

Just as I prepared to continue toward the guarded exit, I remembered Razz had used a key to open the door when we snuck through the first time. But I tried silently opening the stone door anyway. It was locked. Where Razz took the key from before, I did not know. The guard started sniffing the air in her sleep, so I twisted around and snuck back up the steps to the main floor.

I headed straight to the staircase that led up, passing two floors, continuing to the very top. My chest loosened as the door was miraculously unlocked. It took me to the same balcony I had stood on with Pax.

I hadn't explored the entire balcony—just a small corner of it. Perhaps it would take me to a set of stairs or a ladder that would send me down to my freedom.

The sun was bright, and the air was fresh, somehow fresh enough to mask the smell of the rotten bodies pinned to the front of this hellish domain—pinned to the barrier separating the edge of Elloriya from the rest of this realm.

As I walked the perimeter, my hand trailing the balcony railing, I looked everywhere for any way down to the ground. But there were no stairs or ladder or any safe way to escape.

I stood at least a hundred feet above the ground, if not higher. I couldn't jump down unless I wanted to break my neck.

I didn't lose hope. Instead, I continued to walk around the endless balcony until something stopped me.

Something was shaking. The balcony? Was it going to collapse? No. Not the balcony. It was me. It was the small pouch on the side of my pants.

No! No way! No way in hell!

There was no possible way that a relic belonged here, to this wretched kingdom.

I opened the pouch to find the faceted sphere with twelve faces—each face in the shape of a pentagon—trembling. The glass relic was longing for this kingdom. It was begging for me to pick it up and put it—

Where? Where did it want to be placed?

I scanned my black stone surroundings. And there, just a foot away, was a divot in the stone in the shape of a dodecahedron—the same shape of the relic.

I reluctantly wrapped my hand around the trembling relic, and when I pulled it out, it didn't fill with anything like the others had. Instead, it hummed with music so serene, it was an effort to break loose from its enchanting sound. But I did.

I froze, completely distracted from the quivering relic. I sure as hell would not give this kingdom any more magic. I needed to return to my friends before Shakar finds out about the relics; especially the one that somehow, against all logic, belonged to his kingdom.

Think Attica, think! How can I escape with no way down?

But then I remembered the pile of laundry Pax had given me to fold. I could make a rope by tying all the clothes together. It wouldn't be the most reliable rope, but it was my only chance. And it had to be now before the sun goes down and the Orpheus wake!

I returned the shaking relic to the pouch and ran back to the balcony door.

When I opened it, my breathing halted, and my stomach turned. A far too familiar unwelcoming face was on the other side.

It was the Orpheus who had scratched my neck, shooting his venom deep into my skin; it was Than.

He winced as sunlight poured in, highlighting the deep scars on his face. Before I could run, he grabbed my hair and pulled me inside. The door closed behind me.

Than grabbed my face, examining my neck. "Perhaps I didn't use enough venom the first time. But on second thought, you're not worth the effort." He moved his hand to my back and then pushed me down the stairs. My spine hit the edge of a stone step, then my head on another. My shoulder took the brunt upon landing at the bottom of the staircase.

I didn't even have enough time to register the heavy pain before Than hurried down the steps and lifted me with his heavily scarred arm, throwing me against the wall.

"What are you doing out of your chamber?" he asked with his sharp teeth on the tip of my nose.

"I—I—" My tongue tied, and my mind had locked, unwilling to allow me a moment to conjure up a worthy excuse.

"I think you need a punishment," he said, punching me in the stomach. Air escaped my lungs as his fist buried in my navel. "Try again!"

"I—" I tried so hard to say something—anything—but my tongue, my mind, had all shut down. All except the sensation of anger; raging anger and fear spread through me. But it wasn't my anger. And it wasn't entirely my fear that I felt either. The emotions that moved through me came from the coupling latched onto my arm. I was sure of it.

Just as Than grabbed me by the neck, a courier appeared out of thin air. The anger on his face only grew more furious as a light floated out from its swirled shell. But before it delivered the message, Than grabbed the courier in his fist and ripped off its shell.

The vivid turquoise of the courier turned gray as it fell to the floor, dead. All the whispers in its detached shell escaped at once. Words layered upon words made it impossible to make out a single message.

His voice was cold and raw. "Been sneaking messages, have you?" Than lifted his hand toward my face, and by instinct, I shielded myself. I cried out at the sensation of his razor-sharp nails digging into my palm as I protected my eyes.

Somehow, through the pain, I could hear thudding in the distance.

"Try again!" he said. He spoke slowly this time, as if I were too stupid to understand his question. "What are you doing out of your chamber?"

"Let her go!" a voice said behind him.

When Than turned to see who dared order him to do such a thing, I glimpsed familiar orange slit eyes. Than released me at Shakar's order.

At least half of the Orpheus were now awake, standing and watching us from the main floor. Pax ran up to the second floor, where we stood.

"Take her to her chamber," Shakar said to Pax before turning his attention to the dead courier beside Than's foot.

Pax gently wrapped his arm around my waist and my arm around his neck. The pain of his arm against my spine had me wincing the entire way there. He nearly had to drag me.

When we finally reached the chamber door, he lifted me with ease and carried me down the stairs. He kicked his pile of clothes to the side, placed me on the hammock, and then sat beside me.

He looked at my head and then at my palm. "Out of all my warriors you could have run into, it had to be him?"

"Your warriors?" I said through the pain throbbing in my palm.

"Yes. Shakar appointed me as his head warrior three seasons ago. They're mine to train and command outside the kingdom." He ran a thumb over my forehead. "It's already bumping and bruising." He then grabbed my hand. Even with his soft touch, I still winced. He took a sniff of my palm and then licked over Than's freshest scratch. "He didn't use venom this time. It should heal in a few days."

"Why are you being so nice to me?"

He let out a sigh before lifting his sunrise eyes from my palm. The black slits of his pupils narrowed on me.

"This world sees my people—all my people—as monsters. I can't blame them. Thanks to the previous head warrior training us so fiercely by Shakar's command, most of my fighters act like monsters. And the only way they will respect me and follow my commands is if they think I'm a monster too. But some of us are still the same people we were in our realm before the wars." His eyes fell to the floor as he released my hand. "Shakar may have turned most of his warriors into cruel, heartless things, but not all of us. Not me. No matter how much this world may think of us as monsters, I refuse to become one. I still have a heart. And I'm almost certain Shakar does too, no matter how hard he fights it."

I placed my hand over his, grabbing his attention. And when his eyes met mine, I said as deeply and as truly as I could, "I will never see you as a monster."

He tried to smile, but his effort failed. Still, nothing but beauty and kindness showed on his face.

Perhaps it was the silence between our gaze that caused him to finally pull his hand away from mine. He cleared his throat as he pushed himself off the hammock. "If your friend knew what Than did to you, he would probably try to kill him."

My ears perked up. "My friend?"

"Yeah. The one next door," he said all too casually, with a head tilt to my right.

I straightened, ignoring the pain in my palm, head, and spine. I no longer cared about the pain spreading heavily through my body. I just needed to know—

"Which one of my friends? Do you know their name?"

Confusion tugged his brows. He looked surprised that I didn't know I had a friend just one wall away. He opened his mouth at the very same moment Shakar walked in.

CHAPTER 56

The Realm of Keir

"Leave!" Shakar commanded Pax.

So he left without looking back or revealing which of my friends was just one wall away.

Shakar leisurely walked down the long staircase, eyes heavy on me, with the clanking sound of his staff on every descending step.

"Have you made progress?" he asked.

I didn't answer his question. Instead, I asked, "What are you going to do with the magic?"

He reached the bottom floor and studied me. "It depends on what kind of magic you provide my kingdom with. I may not get a say, as some magic acts of its own free will."

I certainly wasn't planning on giving his kingdom its relic. Despite that, there was one question that lingered in my mind. Even though Pax already told me, I needed to hear it from him.

So with a sigh, I asked, "Can you tell me how exactly the war started between your people and the nobles?"

To my surprise, he said, "I can show you."

425

My chest tightened as I asked, "How?" A part of me was unsure if I wanted to see it, because once you see something, there's no unseeing it.

He moved his bronze staff a mere inch away from me. "Your hand," he demanded.

I stood from the hammock and was hesitant, but I obeyed, wrapping my fingers around the warm metal. The dark smoke swirled in the glass egg atop his staff.

At first, the spinning was slow, but as it sped up, the smoke turned gray, and the staff shook so fiercely, it was difficult to hold on much longer. The swirling smoke broke through the egg and spread heavily around Shakar and me, so much so that my sight was completely engulfed.

The smoke dissipated as the trembling staff calmed, revealing an entirely different world. It was a dark realm with heat rising through the cracks of the blackened ground. There was no sun, but there were many soft light sources. Moonlit clouds scattered across the black sky. And between the illuminated clouds were stars so large, each one seemed nearly close enough to reach. They, too, provided a gentle, silvery light.

Growing out of the charred ground was an abundance of the most captivating crystals I had ever seen, each one radiating a subtle light. There were flower-shaped crystals of varying colors and towering emerald crystals in the shape of pointed cypress trees.

Blue crystals floated atop the water of a nearby sea—another light source. And along the sea were more homes than I could count. The many houses were made from colossal stones in wonderfully strange shapes.

This realm was an unusual mixture of darkness, heat, and a prism of glowing color; thankfully I couldn't feel the temperature, but I could see the many heat waves rising from the ground. It was a depressing realm, but beautiful as hell.

There were many Orpheus of all ages. Some were swimming in the sea near the shore, which seemed to hum an enchanting melody each time someone swam past the floating crystals. Others were climbing a mountain of red stone. Children were running on what looked like a pond covered in a sheet of ice a short distance away. The only time it glowed was beneath the footsteps of the dancing and running children. And as they stepped over it, the most eloquent music played, as if there was an incredible orchestra just beneath it. When the white sheet of crystal was bare of feet, the music stopped, and the glowing trail of footsteps faded.

"Welcome to the realm of Keir—my home," he said in a heartbreaking voice.

"It's enchanting," I said.

"It was," Shakar corrected.

In the distance, a scarlet mountain had a sizable door where an army of Orpheus walked out of all at once, as if a concert had just ended. It took me a while before I spotted Shakar in the center of the warrior group, looking much younger than he did now.

Just as the many warriors began to disperse, a violet beam of light pierced through thin air. And then an indigo beam beside it, followed by green, yellow, orange, and red.

As the beams grew taller and wider, revealing an expansive blue light centering each, I quickly realized I was glimpsing the energy grid. The grid openings continued to grow wider until, finally, an army slowly made their way through each one.

It was easy to tell the difference between the armies and which kingdom they belonged to. However, there were two armies I hadn't recognized. One of them wore dark holographic armor, with short braids tucked behind many of their ears, like Razz's. The other army dressed civilized for warriors, with ornate white iridescent metal armor. My chest filled with a strange mixture of joy and sadness at the sight of them.

The moment all the grids closed, and the beams vanished, an older man stepped forward. His silver hair matched his beard, and his violet eyes were possibly brighter than mine. He held a thin white-metal staff with a palm-size iridescent crystal on its head. "What did you decide, Shakar?"

An Orpheus resembling Shakar with matching orange eyes moved beside him; Shakar didn't have to tell me it was his brother.

The Shakar standing beside me seemed to struggle, watching this memory of himself.

"As I told you last time, I am not interested in making any deals," the younger Shakar said to the man.

I blinked. "Is that—"

"Kiran . . . your grandfather," he said.

My chest tightened at the sight of him.

"I told you what was going to happen if you couldn't agree to one of my deals," my grandfather said.

Younger Shakar scanned the six armies; each army had at least five hundred warriors. He surveyed the many warriors, with his own army gathering behind him. It was the first time I noticed the younger Shakar didn't have a staff. It was also easy to see that Shakar's army was extensive enough to match the number of warriors parallel to them. There were thousands of Orpheus warriors.

"Leave!" Shakar demanded.

"Not until you agree to a deal," Kiran said firmly.

"That will not happen," Shakar's brother said, stepping forward.

Kiran and Shakar's brother held eye contact for an uncomfortable amount of time before my grandfather held out his staff to Shakar's brother. A light shot out of the staff, striking Shakar's brother in the chest. He flew through the crowd of Orpheus warriors, hitting a crystal tree before plummeting to the ground, seemingly lifeless.

The Shakar standing beside me had turned away before it happened, refusing to relive it.

"Colburn!" younger Shakar bellowed, running to him.

But before he reached his brother, a group of Orpheus stopped him, and one of them said, "He's dead."

Younger Shakar pushed past them anyway and kneeled to his brother. He shook him as tears rolled down his face. And then he watched as his warriors carried lifeless Colburn away.

Shakar turned back to my grandfather in rage. He moved extraordinarily fast to Kiran before lifting him off the ground and throwing him toward the grid, over my grandfather's army.

"Leave!" Shakar bellowed so loudly that several warriors quivered at the echoing sound. Many more Orpheus in the distance stepped out of their homes, appearing frightened at what they were seeing.

My grandfather pushed himself back up and lifted his staff again, then pounded it on the ground. A light shot up to the sky, and all six armies began their attack on the Orpheus. The war between the Orpheus and the kingdoms had begun.

Gray smoke suddenly surrounded us once more as the ground trembled. When the smoke vanished, we stood back in the chamber.

CHAPTER 57

The Breakdown

Perhaps it was the exhausted, pained look on his face and my knowledge of how the nobles and kingdoms from the other realms destroyed their home, forcing them into a realm of ice and misery before they came here. Still, suddenly, unexpectedly, I broke into tears.

"What's wrong with you?" Shakar asked with his head pulling away from the sound of my sobs.

The tears kept rolling uncontrollably down my face. "I remember nothing of my past in this realm. And I know everything started before I was born. But—" I sniffled and tried to control the wobble in my voice. "I am so sorry, so deeply sorry for what happened to you and your people, and your brother, and your realm."

His reptilian eyes widened and dilated as he stiffened. Every sob and word only added to his face of discomfort. But I continued anyway.

"If I could give my life to make it all right, to bring your brother and your realm back, and the people you lost, I would." I inched

431

closer to him, catching my reflection in the watery gloss now glazed over his eyes. "I can't imagine what pain you have gone through. I can't imagine how strong you've had to be for your people. I wish I could make it all right."

A tear rolled down his face. He flung his cheek away, wiping it before I could glimpse his soft side. Too late. I saw it. I saw the gut-wrenching anguish in his eyes. And for the first time, he looked more human than reptilian.

The thorns on his face were nothing more than mere freckles. Nearly every part of his facial features were as ordinary as any human. Of course, his gray-scaled skin, orange slit eyes, and razor-sharp teeth were not quite as familiar to humans, but still, he was no monster.

I lowered my head. "If I ever get a chance to see the nobles or my grandfather again, even if I can't remember ever knowing him—" I shook my head as tears continued down my cheeks. I couldn't even finish my sentence, let alone my thoughts. Instead, I dropped my face into my unscathed hand and continued to bawl, loudly and wildly. A minute later, I finally took a deep breath and stopped wailing. When I surfaced my head from my palm, Shakar was gone.

I lay in a ball in the nested hammock, dazed in silence as tears dragged down my face. My thoughts were stale. My emotions were numb. I began to reconsider if I should give this kingdom the relic or not. But then, a droopy voice—a memory—sounded in my head: "One choice will rise in difficulty upon all others. Your heart will lead you to the right decision. But your head will fight against it." It was the hermit's voice.

I sat up, and with a deep sigh, I wiped my wet face. The hermit's message had to have been referring to the relic tied to this kingdom, right?

If I gave this kingdom the relic—whatever magic they lacked—they might use it against all my friends and family, and against all the other kingdoms. My choice could add to the destruction of the people I cared for most.

But if I withheld the relic from them—no. The thought of withholding it from the Orpheus felt wrong. It felt unsettling. The relic belonged here, to this kingdom, to these people. Yet, I didn't understand how or why, leaving me to wonder if it would be the ruin of Elloriya.

This single choice could determine the fate of this realm and the six kingdoms—seven kingdoms, including the one I sat in now.

It was, without a doubt, the most difficult decision I ever had to make. And once again, the thought of letting down my friends, my forgotten family, and all the kingdoms sent a wave of panic and pain through my chest.

Just when I thought I was emotionally dried, more tears rolled down my face. The thought of letting down Pax, Shakar, and all the Orpheus who had already been through hell made the decision a thousand times harder. I couldn't stop crying. I tried, but the tears kept rolling down.

"Attica?" a deep voice said in my mind. It wasn't Razz's voice. A slight rasp broke through when he said, "Attica? I'm here. I'm right here."

Only one voice caressed my soul; it was this voice—Darian's voice.

So then it was him wearing the other coupling. And with how clear his voice spoke in my mind, he had to be the friend Pax spoke of, just one wall away.

I sat close to the wall Pax had gestured to when he said, "If your friend knew what Than did to you, he would probably try to kill him."

Darian? I said in my mind, tracing the faint design etched in the silver coupling connecting us.

"I'm here, Attica. I feel your pain. You need to free it." His telepathic voice entered my mind effortlessly.

The soothing sound of his voice had already lightened the heaviness in my chest, but only slightly.

I tried not to sound as desperate as I felt when I asked, *How?*

"Close your eyes. Imagine your pain, worries, and fears as a ball of darkness."

I took his advice and imagined the ball of darkness. So much pain filled that darkness. So many worries and fears added to its size.

Now what?

"Take three deep breaths. With each inhale, imagine a bright sun shedding its healing rays into the darkness. And with each exhale, surrender your burdens to the light."

With closed eyes, I did as he suggested. The first exhale released a tranquil light. The second exhale freed pain, worries, and fears. The third exhale soothed me.

My tight chest loosened. My heart was no longer heavy. My mind cleared, and suddenly, I knew what I needed to do.

A logical voice in the back of my mind tried to fight it, but my heart justified it.

Thank you, I said to Darian through our telepathic connection, touching the rough, blackened wall between us as if it brought me closer to him.

"No, thank you," he responded.

For what? I asked in bewilderment.

"For saving me from the soul-sucking grid."

But it was my fault you entered the grid to begin with. My telepathic voice practically cried with each word.

"No! I chose to take your suggestion. It was worth trying. Don't blame yourself. Please. . . . Just accept my thanks."

Okay, I responded. A moment of silence passed before I thought, *Darian?*

"Yes?"

Why is my telepathic connection so much stronger with you than it ever was with Razz? When several seconds went by without a response, I added, *I mean, we never even tapped the couplings together, syncing our energy.*

A raspy chuckle stroked my mind. "I guess our connection is stronger."

I thought so.

I lay down beside the stone wall, eyes heavy and closing as I replayed his fleeting laugh in my head. I could have sworn I felt him lay down at the same time a few stony inches away.

I don't know how long I slept, but I awoke from the sound of the door opening. Shakar walked down the steps with a surprisingly fresh fruit in hand. His presence was no longer threatening.

"In case you're hungry," he said, tossing the mango-shaped fruit.

"Thanks," I uttered. "Can I ask you something?"

He sat on the stairs. "What?" He opened a sizable pouch on his belt. Two black snakes slithered out onto his hand.

I eyed the snakes as I carefully asked, "If I give your kingdom magic, will you use it against the other kingdoms?"

He heavily sighed. He opened his mouth to speak, but then closed it, and instead sat in silence for a long moment while petting his snakes until he finally said, "I'm tired. I just wish I were back in Keir, before they stripped it of life. This place is not life for us. I—" He hesitated. "I don't know how to give my people a life worth living. No matter how hard I try, no matter how much magic or power I gain, it's not enough. It will never be enough to give them the life we once had, a life free enough for them to step outside whenever they'd like."

He dropped his forehead into his empty palm and sighed again. "No. If you give my kingdom magic, I don't think I'll use it against the other kingdoms, unless they provoke me. They took my home from my people under my rule. No amount of revenge will heal the pain of that." As he stroked the snakes wrapped around his hand, I analyzed his gentleness and knew Pax was right: Shakar did have a heart.

Though I wasn't entirely sure I could trust Shakar, I had to tell him—warn him—of what I knew. "Shakar." He looked up at me. "Something—someone—invaders, I think, are coming to Elloriya.

I don't know exactly when or why. But I was told that when the moons align, the realm will open its doors, and invaders will reign death."

I was almost certain I glimpsed fear somewhere in his eyes.

"Who told you this?"

"A nixie."

He furrowed his brows. "What is a nixie?"

"Um, I'm not sure. A siren or mermaid, maybe."

"And who told the nixie about these invaders?" he asked skeptically.

"Uh." My cheeks flushed. "The water."

Any twinge of fear or concern had vanished from his face. Instead, a judgment of my sanity took its place. He must have thought I was crazy for believing a word the nixie had said because he pushed himself off the step and walked up the stairs, unfazed.

Before he reached the door, I begged, "I know it's a lot to ask. But when that day comes, will you fight with us—my friends and me, and whoever else will join?" Before I allowed him a second to respond or even look over his shoulder, I continued. "If you do—if your people help us defend Elloriya—I will spend the rest of my days trying to bring life back to your realm, back to Keir. I will find a way if it's the last thing I do!"

He whipped his head around and glared down at me from the top of the stairs. His face filled with hatred. "You're asking me to help defend this shit realm with those who robbed me of my realm? They destroyed my home! They killed my people! No matter how hard you try, there is no bringing life back to what we have lost. The realm of Keir is dead because of the nobles, and nearly every kingdom in this damned dimension supported them."

"I know I'm asking a lot, but innocent people may die."

"I don't care who of your people dies! I welcome death to take the lives of those who destroyed my home!" His hollering voice bounced off the chamber walls with such force, I flinched.

My mouth opened, but no words came out.

He turned back to the door and said through gritted teeth, "If you give my kingdom magic, then I will *think* about helping you defend Elloriya. At the very least, to keep my people safe."

"Thank you," I blurted, before he changed his mind. Then I grabbed my bag, strapped it to my back, and said, "I'm ready!"

He grabbed the door handle. "For what?"

"To give your kingdom magic."

CHAPTER 58

Cursed

Darian's tug on my mind didn't stop me from marching up the stairs with the relic. Before I exited through the door, his voice entered my thoughts through the couplings. "Whatever you do, just be sure."

For the first time since entering this kingdom, I was sure. I knew what I had to do, even if the world disagreed. My heart practically led the way, reminding me what had to happen. My head, however, told me otherwise.

My persuasive thoughts kept showing me pictures of the kingdoms destroyed by the Orpheus because of me. But I forced them out of my mind.

Shakar escorted me up the third-floor staircase to the balcony door as far as he could go. Though the sun's rays were soft, Shakar stopped from following me outside to the balcony, where it was still daylight. I'd guess late afternoon.

"Attica," Shakar said before the balcony door closed. He said my name with such gentleness.

I don't know how or why, but I suddenly wondered if he was playing me—playing with my head to get what he wanted.

"Thank you," he said with a struggle in his tone.

It only made me wonder more: *Am I somehow being manipulated into giving this kingdom a relic that would grant them some unknown magic?*

As I walked along the balcony toward the center of the dark mountainlike castle, my mind battled my heart to near-death—or so it felt. If I were to place the relic into the divot that bound its magic to every square inch of the Orpheus Kingdom, there would be no going back.

Whatever you do, just be sure. Darian's voice played in my head as the relic, still in the leather pouch, shook, squirming its way closer toward the divot.

I reluctantly opened my pouch.

My heart pushed, *Do it!*

My mind demanded, *Don't do it!*

I reached in and grabbed hold of the trembling relic.

My heart pleaded, *Yes!*

My mind barked, *No!*

The glass-faceted sphere, empty upon touch unlike the others, shook in my fingers, playing blissful music in my head—music I had heard before. A moment passed before I realized where I had heard it. It was the same music I heard in Shakar's memory, from the realm of Keir.

The closer I inched the relic toward the divot, beckoning desperately for it, the harder the relic shook and the louder the music became.

The second I released my grip on the relic, I could have sworn I heard Etiwa's voice somewhere distant in my mind, screaming, "Attica, no!" But it was too late. The singing relic now sat firmly embedded in the black tourmaline mountain.

A light shot out of the relic and pierced brightly over their entire dwelling. And then, the sound of distant screams had me running back to the balcony door and inside the dark castle. Except, when I opened the door, it was no longer dark.

A bright white light pierced through the walls and ceiling, wrapping around every Orpheus—each screaming in agony.

Logic suddenly hit me like a ton of bricks. Why would Magus—the alchemist—create a place for the relic to bless the Orpheus with more magic? It made no sense. This relic wasn't meant to give their kingdom magic; it was meant to curse them.

My chest pounded, perhaps harder than it ever had before. *What had I done?*

I knelt to Shakar, yelling on the floor so loudly that it felt as though my ears were bleeding. There was nothing I could do to help him. I didn't know how to stop the light or the pain.

The children! Will they survive this? I wondered while silently praying.

I ran down several sets of stairs to the main floor. No one was there. Everyone was still in their underground den, where they had woken from the light. Every single Orpheus was hollering through the torture. I felt sick at the sight of the children hysterically crying under the piercing brightness.

"No, no! This is not what was supposed to happen! How can I make it stop?" I cried over the chaos as the Orpheus desperately tried to shield themselves.

I saw the teenager who had helped me get through the barrier with Razz. Ekon was panic-struck and in pain as light shed over his skin.

Just as I was about to turn and run back to the relic to try removing it, I froze when my sight fell on Than. His teeth clenched, and his angry eyes grilled me. He moved so quickly in my direction that I hardly had a moment to digest that his hand was now tightly wrapped around my throat.

"You cursing witch!" Than bellowed.

He pulled me by the neck all the way to the guarded door in their underground den—an exit to Elloriya. He kicked the door open and threw me out like garbage. Though the sun was soft, more light shed into the castle, threatening the Orpheus and their health even more.

But then, that same teenager—no longer screaming in pain—brushed past Than toward the open door, and he held an arm out, under the sun's rays. No pain struck his expression, but rather, curiosity.

Than's mouth fell open as he watched the boy move closer toward the door—toward me knocked on my ass under the gentle sun. I had hardly noticed the loud cries had stopped. The Orpheus watched silently as Ekon stepped fully outside under the sun.

A smile spread over his face. At least until Shakar came from behind and yanked him back inside.

"Ekon! What were you thinking?" he screamed at the teen.

"I'm fine!" he snapped, holding his bare arm under Shakar's nose.

Shakar took hold of Ekon's arm, examining it with lowered brows.

"How?" Shakar asked.

"That light changed something inside us. Didn't you feel it?" Ekon responded.

I had brushed myself off and stood back up when Shakar's eyes landed on me. "What kind of magic is this? What did you do to us?" he asked through gritted teeth.

I moved closer to the open door of their dwelling. The light that hit them with pain had gone. And their home was once again dark.

"I don't know what kind of magic this is," I said, hoping it wasn't a curse. "I think the relic chooses what magic it gives."

"The relic?" Shakar questioned.

"Yes," I responded, wondering if I should have kept that part to myself, yet somewhat surprised he knew nothing of it. If Magus didn't create the vessel in their kingdom for the relic, then who did?

He stood silent, with a crowd behind him. Then, Nisha—the female warrior who irritably delivered my food for the last several weeks and despised me—moved toward Shakar.

"She can't be trusted. We should end her pathetic life! You felt the pain from the light. It did something to us. It may be killing us slowly because of this wicked bitch!" Nisha spouted, pointing at me.

Each heartbeat was like an explosion of fear that Shakar may take her word as truth and kill me. Or perhaps he would allow her to do the honors.

Nisha continued to whisper beside Shakar. "Kill her. Kill the girl! I'll kill her if you'd like." She glowered at me with a hiss.

To my utter surprise, Shakar grabbed his faithful warrior by her armor and threw her outside under the sun. The people inside gasped. At least those who could see past Shakar's massive stature.

"No!" Nisha screamed before turning to me with dagger eyes. "I'll kill you!" she hollered as she grabbed me by the hair.

"Your skin!" I bellowed. "Does it hurt?"

"What?" she barked, pulling my hair tighter.

"Is the sun hurting you?" I clarified, feeling strands of hair break from my head.

Her face went vacant. She released her grip on me and analyzed herself. Shakar and the other Orpheus watched from inside the open door.

Then Shakar stepped outside and slowly climbed the steps that took him to ground level. He looked up at the sun and laughed, almost menacingly, as he spread his arms out wide.

Pax pushed between the crowd at the door, his soft gaze traveling from Nisha to Shakar to me. I looked at him with a smile that served as an invitation to step outside. After some hesitation, he stepped out under the sun.

"Did you do this to us?" he asked me.

"I—I'm not sure. I gave your kingdom an enchanted relic. The relic decided what magic it would give, I suppose."

"And it gave us the freedom of light?" he questioned.

I looked up at the sun and then at him. "Do you feel pain?" I asked.

"None," he uttered with an unreadable face.

A grin tugged the corner of my lips. "You asked me what the sun was like. See for yourself."

He looked up at the golden ball of light and broke into a smile much bigger than mine.

More Orpheus slowly made their way outside, under the daylight. It wasn't long before smiles broke onto their faces as well.

Pax broke his gaze off the soft sunlight and looked at me with a fading smile. He pulled something out of his pocket and said, "Here," placing it into my hand.

I looked down at my palm as Pax strolled off. I was holding a black metal key. It took me a moment to realize what door it belonged to. But when it suddenly dawned on me, the sensation of butterflies filled my stomach.

I ran past the Orpheus standing beneath the early evening sun, back into the tourmaline castle, up two flights of stairs, and down a long hall until I reached the chamber door beside mine.

CHAPTER 59

The Answers

My hand trembled as I put the key in the lock and turned, waiting for my panting to ease before pushing the door open, desperate to see those damn blue eyes.

I had already unlocked the door. And the man that made me feel a hundred fanatic feelings in mind, body, and soul was on the other side.

Open the door, Attica. Just push it open!

My nerves had wildly unraveled and spread like a web tugging on every part of my body.

Stop shaking! I begged my hands and knees. *Just relax!*

"Deep breaths." Darian's voice filled my mind.

With all that had happened with the relic, the screams of torment, and the Orpheus stepping under the sun for the first time in their existence, it had slipped my mind that there was still a tether connecting Darian and me through the couplings we both wore.

I felt the flushing of my cheeks. He now knew just how much his presence affected me. After burying my head in my hands for

447

several long seconds, I wiped the humiliation off my face and took his advice.

As I took my first deep breath, I closed my eyes and felt my sporadic nerves. I directed my second deep breath to comfort those nerves with the new air filling my lungs. And with my third deep breath, I welcomed the image of a beaming light shining through the top of my head to the soil far below me, grounding my now calm body.

With forced confidence and a craving heart, I was ready to open my eyes and step through that door, but I felt a warm finger lift my chin before I could. I opened my eyes, swallowed, and ignored the fluttering feeling in my chest as I took in Darian's heart-shaped lips a short foot away. The fluttering grew wilder when my gaze landed on his entrancing sapphire eyes, unwavering from my stare.

He removed his gentle finger from my chin and then said, "Yes. At the very least, friends. And I absolutely do."

I tugged my attention off his hypnotic gaze long enough to say, "What?"

He stepped half a foot closer, a mere six inches from me. "Yes, I will let down my walls. I don't want you to think of us as anything less than friends, ever. And I do like you, more than anyone else in Elloriya, on Earth, and every world in between."

It took me a moment to realize what he was talking about; he was answering the questions I had asked him at the manor so many lunars ago.

"I'm sorry for the delayed response." He held his throat. "With Shakar's trace on my voice, I had to be careful not to speak, or he would have instantly known where I was—where the manor is. I didn't want to risk putting anyone in danger."

"You don't need to worry about that anymore."

He tilted his head. "And why is that?"

"Because the curse has lifted," I said, trying to contain my grin. "He's no longer tracking your voice," I clarified.

As a genuine smile began forming on his face—perhaps for the first time in his adult life—a far from friendly voice said, "You human filth are still here?" We turned to find Than with flared nostrils. He looked at the scratch on my neck and sneered. "I should have used all my venom on you!"

His slit pupils suddenly grew as Darian gripped Than's neck, pinning him against the wall.

"What did you say?" Darian asked. But his grip was too tight for Than to respond.

Faint bolts of lightning spread over Darian's hand. Than groaned as thin weblike bolts burned his neck. Finally, Darian whispered in his ear, "If you ever touch Attica with your shit venom again—if you ever look or speak to her again—I will hunt you down, pin you to a tree with a sword covered in my piss, and watch you die a slow and nasty death. Understand?"

The moment he released his grip, Than hissed his slit tongue and plunged for Darian. But before Than could get a solid grasp on him, Darian had already pushed him in the chamber, sending him in a tumble down the chamber's stairs. He closed the door, turned the key still sitting in the lock, and then gave me a quarter-smile as if he hadn't just locked an Orpheus warrior in his own kingdom's prison.

Darian didn't bother removing the key from the locked door. Instead, he turned back to me and ran a hand over my bruised forehead. He clenched his square jaw. "Are you okay?"

"Yes, I'm fine."

He stayed staring at the heavy bruising. "How did this happen?"

I didn't want any more trouble with the Orpheus. I just wanted peace. So I stayed truthful when I said, "I fell down the steps."

He dropped his eyes to meet my stare, perhaps sensing that Than had something to do with it. But he didn't push it any further.

I shook as a sudden bellow blared from inside the chamber, rattling the locked stone door.

Darian's eyes widened as he smoothly grabbed my hand and said, "That's our cue to leave."

He followed me through the castle that had suddenly filled with Orpheus women and children. Nearly all of them avoided being near us but still whispered among each other with many sets of yellow slit eyes in our direction.

Darian had a mask of shame when he glanced at me and said, "Now that I can speak freely, perhaps I should work on having a civil conversation before letting my temper get the best of me around scum like him."

I didn't disagree.

We passed through the enormous empty den with hundreds of nestlike hammocks, nearing the castle's exit, when an eerie silence took over.

I didn't know what to expect when we stepped outside. I certainly didn't expect Shakar and Pax to be standing at the end of a threatening aisle lined with warriors.

My heart pounded as every warrior reached for their saber sword. Darian protectively pulled me closer to him.

With nowhere to walk except between the long line of warriors, we slowly stepped forward, monitoring the many blades on both sides of us. Then, with a grunt from Shakar at the end of the lined army, Pax held out his black metal saber sword.

I immediately regretted giving the traitorous leader and head warrior my trust, and worst of all, magic that granted them the freedom to attack whoever they pleased during any starlight, day or night.

My stomach turned, and my regret made me feel sick until Pax dropped his saber. The sound of clanking metal around us stopped me in my cautious tracks. Every Orpheus warrior had dropped their sabers too.

A surprising number of them bowed their heads at us, Ekon being one of them, with an endearing smile on his boyish face and wearing black armor with the rest of the warriors. But there were still many who appeared displeased at the peace-offering, including Nisha, who gritted her teeth at me.

I finally reached Shakar at the end of the aisle, and before I had a chance to speak, he said, "You asked me why I was searching for you last year. A seer once told me you would take the darkness away from my people. Since we thrive only in the dark, I took it as a threat and thought my people would be safer if I imprisoned you or even killed you." He glanced up at the evening sun and beamed before looking back at me, still smiling. "Now I understand what the seer meant. You are no longer my enemy." His sunset eyes glanced between Darian and me, abruptly dropping his smile. "Now get the hell out of my kingdom." And then he walked past us, toward his dreary castle.

Pax hadn't left yet. Instead, he moved closer toward me, with Darian carefully watching. "You have far exceeded my expectations," he said with a much-too-serious face. Then, after a polite nod at Darian, he strolled off.

Darian looked over his shoulder, watching all the warriors pick up their sabers and return inside their dwelling before closing the door.

"Well, that was interesting," he said.

"And a little unnerving," I added.

He turned to face me. His deep blue eyes might as well have swallowed me whole.

I wondered if he was mad at me for the magic I had given the Orpheus Kingdom. But then he said, "You're amazing."

With a sigh of relief, I replied, "I have a feeling others might disagree. But thank you."

Darian held out his hand. "Ready?"

I placed my hand in his, prepared to go anywhere with him. Even so, I asked, "Ready for what?"

With a slight grin, he said, "To go home."

Did he mean the manor? Or—

"It's time we return to the higher kingdoms," he clarified, as if he were reading my mind.

His hand still held mine as I glanced at the coupling around his arm and then its twin metal around mine. He must have caught my traveling eyes as he said, "Razz gave it to me before I came here. If you don't mind, I'd like to keep mine on a little longer."

I half-smiled, trying not to show my bursting joy at just being beside him. "I don't mind," I said as casually as I could.

"Good. Do you have everything you need?"

When I felt my bag on my back and the single strap secured over my chest, I said, "Yep."

He took the hand he held of mine and spun me up into the air as if I were light as a feather. And when I landed, it was on a massive lionlike back—on the charzdaine.

My legs straddled his black mane as I reached for his horns. His spiraled horns were no longer sharp. Instead, they were rough and chipped.

I wrapped my hands around them and asked, "What happened?"

He stretched his mighty leathery wings out when his voice sounded in my mind. "I tried breaking through their walls when I first arrived until they threw me in a chamber. And then, when I felt you getting hurt, I tried breaking through the chamber door."

Before I could even think of a response, Darian telepathically said, "Let's go home," as he began to run in charzdaine form. His dragonlike wings stretched out even farther and flapped harder and louder until we lifted off the ground and into the sky.

For the first time in my life, I felt happy, free, and . . . satisfied. I had no regrets, bestowing a relic on their kingdom and giving the Orpheus the magic of daylight.

Now, I was ready to go home and see my mother for the first time in nineteen Earthly years, or rather, thirteen zeniths.

Darian's voice entered my mind. "Are you in a hurry?"

"No," I responded.

"Good. We'll take the scenic route!" His wings turned slightly, and off we went over an abundance of grass and trees and into the evening Elloriyan sky.